I0787993

I conceived this project in Boston during the summer of '92 while producing my first Shakespeare (Romeo & Juliet). It was staged at the Huntington Theatre Studio and sold out before we opened. That was when the notion of a prequel was born that would reveal how the famous families came to be at each other's throats, and how the associations between so many characters were first formed. The full story frame of Capulet (6 books) was written over 4 years writing 7 days a week 7 hours a day with just a few exceptions.

For the trivial record, my first experience with Shakespeare was as a punishment in my last year of high school. I was given a detention for fighting (a bully was harassing a friend and though I'm no hero I intervened). The English Mistress who caught us made me memorise the 'quality of mercy' monologue from *The Merchant of Venice*. It had to be word perfect to avoid another stay. She told me it wasn't word perfect. But she said I was 'good' and would let me off if I agreed to audition for the play. I did. Somehow I managed to get the lead.

That led me to a BA in Drama at the University of Queensland. UQ led me to a BFA in Acting at Cornish College in the USA. That led to specialised study at the National Shakespeare Conservatory in NY (closed after 9/11) and finally an MFA scholarship to study Directing at Boston University. Fast forward 25 years. I began this project in earnest during the last few months of the pandemic.

I hope their tale moves you.

I found it very moving to write.

Marcus Hogan

Capulet

a novel series by Marcus Hogan

*Inspired by the source material from 'Il Novellino' (33rd Section) by Masuccio Salernitano 1476
and all subsequent iterations thereafter until the play by William Shakespeare*

Book 1: Fate

Book 2: Verona

Book 3: Justice

Book 4: Ambition

Book 5: Retribution

Book 6: Folly

ISBN: 978-1-7638379-6-6 (Paperback)
ISBN: 978-1-7638379-7-3 (Hardcover)
ISBN: 978-1-7638379-5-9 (eBook)

Published by Poquelin Press
Copyright © Marcus Hogan 2025

Copyediting and proofreading completed by Katie Lowe
Typesetting and layout completed by Essential Self-Publishing
(www.essentialselfpub.com.au)

Capulet

Book 2: Verona

a novel by Marcus Hogan

the Ancient Grudge

Two unusual icons adorn the crest of Capulet, a cape and a hat. The first is proof that somewhere in their ancestral past, an artisan fashioned capes and cloaks to protect soft bodies from the harsh elements. Now consider if you will that cloaks and capes often have hoods attached to them. And so it's little surprise one of the Capulet ancestors also became a maker of hats.

Which came first, the making of hats or capes? I can't say for certain. What I can say is that one ancestor named Capulet was ordered to march into battle. Indeed he distinguished himself enough to add another icon, a sword of war. And so why, one may ask, did scarlet and black become the colours of their house? I can't answer that either. Never in my time among the Capulets did I investigate their origin.

One might expect scarlet to stand for the blood of war? Logical. However that's the colour of their hat and cape. Black sits behind the icons, the *field* they rest upon. The sword is silver of course. It sits horizontally to allow the pretty cloak to hang over it with the hat perched neatly above. But at some point after all those elements were combined, another portion was added that sits above all - three golden lilies on a field of blue.

I feel the lilies and blue add a splash of elan. Yet the Capulets added them as a gesture of loyalty to a higher power. Indeed, sweet friends it's very important to understand that a display of three lilies on blue represents their pledge of allegiance to a particular and powerful political faction.

That faction are known as the Guelphs and they support the power of his Holiness in Rome to the South. The Guelphs stand in opposition to another faction of course: the Ghibellines. Those cretins ... I mean to say the members of that faction, support the power of the emperor in the North. For many generations the struggle between his Holiness and the Emperor has waxed and waned, keeping the Guelphs and Ghibellines constantly at each other's throats.

Indeed, their ancient grudge had spread so widely, that few elite houses managed to avoid the need to declare for one or the other until ... ten years after Armand was born. For more than a decade after that time the lack of a crowned emperor saw their animosity settle significantly. Many on both sides hoped it had settled permanently. Some did not.

And though I've suggested the power of one faction lay to the north and the other to the south, since the trouble began, families loyal to each have lived side by side all over the Christian Empire. However, a small number of citadels sit more precariously near the dividing lines that separate the authority of the Emperor and his Holiness, acting as *gateways* between them. Life in those citadels was far more turbulent.

Finally, consider what might have happened in such a citadel when an event – such as the end of a great war or creation of a new Emperor or both – tipped the balance of power again? Forces were set in motion that encouraged the dormant ambitions of some faction members to stir again. Suddenly the lives of all became very fragile. Among the citadels fated to sit at such a gateway, the most fragile of all was fair Verona.

Chapter 1 rite of Succession

When the marriage celebrations were done, the feasting chamber nearly emptied, I began to stow my instruments. The proud parents of the groom, Olivier and Margot de Capulet, stood with the proud parents of the bride, Julien and Genevieve Marchand. The exhausted newlyweds, Armand and Ilaria, stood with them all as the Marchands announced it was time to depart. For the first time Ilaria would not be going with them. They were leaving her behind to spend her first night in Chateau de Capulet.

The Marchands planned to return in the morning of course, to see Ilaria depart on her marriage tour. And since Armand's orders to return to the war had been postponed, now the newlyweds expected to travel further than first planned, as far as Verona, perhaps Venice too. All at once our short tour close to Lyon had become a far-flung adventure.

Sieur Julien glanced at the women gathering together, exchanged a knowing look with Sieur Olivier, then wandered ahead to ensure his people had their conveyance ready. Seeing the tears welling in Genevieve's eyes and the sympathetic response from his own wife, Olivier suggested to Armand it would be more discreet to allow the women to exit together.

Now two Capulet Dames exited the grand salon, each on an arm of the tearful Dame Marchand. As they vanished, Armand sat with a sigh of relief. Perhaps in sympathy I too let out a sigh, then scanned the serving board for left over morsels and drink. With a tempting selection I sat quietly upon a window bench, to stare and drink and eat my fill.

I notice Sieur Olivier glancing about, as if to ensure he and Armand were alone. Oh yes, he saw me. Yet as always in such moments, the presence of a musician seemed to count for nothing. A server passed by with a tray of libations. She offered a cup to each as the patriarch sat adjacent to his son to draw him into conversation. I'm not sure why, nothing should have suggested it, yet the caution Sieur Olivier had taken to do so left me feeling unsettled.

'I'm glad you're finally wed.'

'Yes Father. So am I.'

'We've made you a wonderful match.'

'Mmm. I very much agree.'

'A wife like Ilaria can enrich your bond to our extended famille.'

'I'm sure they'll all love her as much as I do.'

'I hope so. For I must confess that some of our relations, whom you're both soon to meet, no longer respect my will as the premiere sieur.'

Armand frowned to hear him say so.

'I'm sure you misjudge their respect for you.' he said sincerely.

'Perhaps. But some harsh feelings don't just pass on, like water under a bridge. Sometimes Armand, no matter how hard one may try, a man can't help but make lasting enemies. Even among his own famille.'

'I'm sure you have no enemies among them.'

Armand sipped quietly. And though he appeared thoughtful I began to realise, those thoughts were elsewhere, so did his father.

'Well ...' Olivier looked at his son more intently. 'Let's just call them *rivals*. But for some, their bad will has a way of *accumulating* over time.'

'Oh?' Armand stifled a yawn.

Narrowing his eyes a little, Olivier continued.

'For a house like ours, rich with assets spread among a network of relations, lingering bad will is a threat to stability.'

'Sincerely Father, I didn't realise you sat at odds with *any* of our kin.'

'Sadly I do.' A frown creased his brow. 'And now a critical moment has arrived.'

'Has it?' Armand sighed, too obviously for his father's liking.

'It has. Their potential leader now has a wife like Ilaria at his side.'

Armand's brows lifted with recognition.

'Oh yes. I see.'

'And so now, any whose favour I may have lost will have a chance to gain a new first impression of their leaders-in-waiting.'

As I munched and listened, I considered how unlikely it would be for one such as myself to find themselves engaged in such a conversation. Cupid's Balls! What a chasm of difference separated our lives? I could see Sieur Olivier was scanning his son's responses carefully. Yet his son seemed to offer little care in return.

Armand replied casually. 'I promise you Father that during our travels, we'll take care to treat them *all* very well.'

'That will be needed Son. But it's more than just that.'

It seemed clear by that moment Olivier was attempting to prompt a more engaged response. Yet Armand continued to lack interest.

'The impact you and Ilaria can now have together Armand, may have a far-reaching effect on the willingness of our people to let you lead them.'

'Oh. Yes I see.' Armand said more thoughtfully but stifled another yawn, larger than the first.

'Do you?' Olivier offered more challengingly. 'They all know you are my *preferred* heir.'

Armand's brows wrinkled again. 'I suppose they do.'

'But they also know a *first* son is not always a *final* choice.'

'Yes Father, I understand that too.' he replied humbly.

Olivier leaned back as he stared. 'Then you should also understand that some of them consider themselves *more* worthy than you.'

Armand pouted in thought as he met his father's stare.

'Do they? Are they? Father I wouldn't know. Am I more worthy?'

Not expecting to hear such a response, Olivier blinked incredulously.

'Son what matters is that I think you are. And now you're married and a chevalier to boot.'

Finally Armand smiled. 'Happily on both accounts.'

He stretched his arms and legs in a ritual of preparation for rest. I felt sure he hoped to suggest it was time for the conference to adjourn. His father chose to ignore it.

'And so, having earned your spurs, and now after tonight, nothing's left to stop me from announcing you as premiere sieur of our faction.'

I blinked with surprise as I listened. Armand's eyes opened more widely, not so much with growing interest for the topic, yet because he finally realised, at such a late hour on his wedding night, where their conversation was leading.

'Father I'm flattered. I'm *very* flattered.'

'Don't be.' Olivier insisted. 'I think you've earned it.'

'Thank you. I don't know what to say. And when I return from our tour, we can discuss that possibility more deeply with Mother and Ilaria.'

'Oh I plan to discuss it. And I plan to *settle* it. Tonight.'

Armand's eye filled with more energy. 'Tonight?'

'Right now Armand and just between the two of us. Then before you leave in the morning, we'll sign a declaration of succession.'

My young master shifted in his seat as unsettled thoughts began to run. 'But so soon? Must we rush such an important decision before I leave?'

For Olivier, his son's tepid interest up until that moment had been one thing to bear. But now that he knew Armand clearly understood the issue at hand, his lack of want to engage was rankling the patriarch.

Olivier's eyes narrowed. 'Better now than later. We expected you to have time for a short tour and meet just a few. But now you leave in the morning to meet them all in one grand sweep.'

'Well yes we do. However –'

'This should be decided before. And to my mind, you're more ready to lead than I was at your age. So is Ilaria.'

That comment sparked a distant thought in Armand.

'Toulon said something similar to me in Carentan ... on the day he died.'

The mention of our fallen master, Olivier's great war companion, gave the patriarch pause for a moment.

'And he was right.' Olivier said drily. 'The sequel confirmed it.'

A grim pall of doubt was filling Armand's eyes.

'The sequel was that I *failed* to save his life.'

Sieur Olivier's eyes opened wide in disbelief. It was clear he had never imagined Armand would feel that way about that tragic event.

'You failed? Not at all Son. You showed those watching what you're really made of, that you're ready for more responsibility. And listen to me ... when you understand the *terms* for your succession –'

'Terms?' Armand echoed dimly.

'Yes of course. In fairness to all Son there are always strict terms to a rite of succession.'

'Oh.' Armand replied in a whisper. 'I suppose there must be.'

'So far you've never had to deal with such things. But now you're married, it's time to make a start.'

'Yes of course Father but –'

Hoping to stir momentum, Olivier ran on. 'There are rules and expectations. And it takes time to put such things into motion.'

From a short distance I sipped cool wine for my comfort. Gauging by Armand's reactions, it seemed until now, he had heard very little said on this subject. Yet I felt certain, the man Armand was just three weeks before, laid out in the abbey hospital after the Battle of Formigny, would have paid no attention to any of it at all.

But since escaping death at Carentan and Formigny and since bidding farewell to Eloise du Marche, an interest in his future had awoken. It provoked him to consider just how he might move towards it. Until that moment, the only solution he employed was to leave all to fate and the will of others. Oh yes, that sounds a comfortable way to manage one's future.

Yet it was becoming clear to Armand that some people, like his father and mother, didn't wait for fate to reveal a path or open doors for them. They imagined a path and opened doors for themselves. It's what had made them an effective premiere couple. But during the previous five years of Armand's life, everything had been decided for him; his assignment to Toulon, riding to war, even after returning to Lyon, all he had to do to accelerate his marriage, was to ask his parents to intercede for him.

All at once his father was suggesting, from that day forward, that youthful reliance on the guidance of others would no longer do. One more decision could be made for Armand, to pass the mantle on, but not in a year or three months or even three days. And though the hour to discuss it may have been chosen poorly, I felt that perhaps for the first time, Armand needed his father's guidance beyond muscular issues like hunting and war.

Yes Armand appeared reluctant. Yet I hoped his father would appreciate that was the result of Armand's humility and fatigue from the day's events. Though I felt sure my newlywed master was *also* distracted by one other matter. The groom still had one rather significant duty to perform after he and his bride retired above stairs to spend their first night together.

Cupid's Balls! Had I been Armand at that moment, my mind would have been filled with images of longing lips and eyes and every soft part of a woman's body that I'd soon be feeling under the press of my own. I wouldn't have been interested in discussing my *rite of succession*! Certainly not while my *rite of conjugation* awaited. Yet heedless of all potential for distraction, his father leaned forward and ran on.

'When we matched you at her birth, we couldn't have guessed what a rare prize Ilaria would become. But to see her now –'

'Father I don't think of her as a prize. But I agree, she's a rare person.'

'Oh yes Ilaria's pretty.' Olivier huffed. 'But she's much more than that. She has a way about her. People admire her greatly. Her qualities have a value that can't be taken for granted.'

Armand blinked with incredulity.

'She's in no danger of being taking for granted by me.'

Olivier frowned yet again.

'No Son. But I don't think you're following my point.'

'Then respectfully Father ... what *is* your point?'

The patriarch halted, then leaned a little more.

'I'm trying to discuss our *famille* and your future roles in it.'

'Yes?' Armand said politely.

For the first time, his eyes searched in the direction the women had departed. It seemed clear he hoped to hear or see them return. That also seemed clear to his father whose tone became more insistent.

'Starting tomorrow, Ilaria's influence over our people may prove the difference between your own ability to win or lose their loyalty.'

'Oh I see.' Armand said more thoughtfully.

'I hope you do. For that's a grave responsibility that's about to loom larger in both your lives.'

Realising his own distracted mind was falling behind his father's will to press on, Armand took a moment to consider his reply. I could see he was still caught between the topic in discussion and his interest in what should come next for him that night. His new bride would reappear at any moment, expecting him to quietly offer his parents good night, and lead her away.

'Father I've doted on Ilaria for as long as I can remember. I think I appreciate her worth far beyond the value of any *loveless* contract struck before she was even born.'

Olivier's expression grew darker. Armand didn't seem to realise how disparaging that remark may seem to one of the parents who negotiated that contract. I glanced and saw his father's eyes were bulging with indignation.

'Indeed?' Olivier spat with more heat to Armand's surprise.

'Why ... yes.' Armand stammered. 'It's simply not possible for me to take her for granted.' He smiled politely but his father's frustration was rising. As I sipped my last drop, I sensed if Armand's dismissive mood persisted, Olivier's patience for fond talk would soon reach its limit.

'Son I'm not speaking of *love* but of marriage and responsibility.'

Armand knit his brows. 'Doesn't the presence of love make the other things more compelling?'

Olivier's head drew back in amazement, then lowered to stare.

'Frankly no.' he insisted. 'It doesn't.' Armand narrowed his eyes as his father ran on. 'But if that's what you think, then before you depart tomorrow or ascend to the boudoir tonight, we better do some plain talking.'

Armand sighed again, seeming to accept he wouldn't be allowed to attend any other matter until this discussion was completed to his sire's satisfaction.

'Then by all means Father ... speak your mind.'

Olivier huffed indignantly then stared for support to the only other listener present ... myself! I gulped and gaped and shrugged my shoulders like an imbecile. He ignored me again!

'I will.' He ran on hotly. 'Not because *you* allow it. But because there's no other way for a man to speak.'

'If you say so.' Armand muttered under his breath.

The quip sparked instant resentment.

'If I say ... by Thunder!' he bellowed. 'You need to wake up Son.'

'Father.' hissed Armand. 'Please lower your voice.'

'Lower my ... I'll speak my *fucking* mind however it suits me! I'm still the master here *boy*!'

A hardening glance shot from Armand.

You already know he disliked crass language. Even the brutality of war hadn't altered his mind on that account. And you may recall that from the moment he became a squire to brave Toulon five years before, he was told never to allow any man to refer to him in a certain way. I was recalling it at that very moment. More than anything else said in their exchange until then, hearing himself dismissed as a *boy* pinched Armand's pride more than anything else. Yet what made me most anxious, not only had his father noted his reaction to that word, he now seemed encouraged to use the barb to goad his son further.

'You say you've always doted on her *boy*?'

Armand blanched again.

'Jupiter's Balls!' Olivier bellowed. 'Think! The only reason you *have* her now is because, while you were still young enough to wet yourself and she wasn't yet born, your mother and I drove a blunt bargain to secure your *loveless* contract!'

'Yes ...' Armand stammered 'of course. I know you did –'

Suddenly Olivier leapt to his feet, face red with anger, jabbing a finger in accusation. 'DO you!' he spat. 'For that's the only fucking reason you ever got the chance to dote on her at ALL!'

'Father!' Armand whispered in warning. 'Lower your voice.'

'Had we not done it, by now she'd be wed to a merchant's son with brats to tend already.'

'Father that's *enough!*'

'And tonight she'd be lying in a different bed, fucking someone else.'

Eyes lit with anger Armand leapt to his feet.

'I said that's ENOUGH! There's absolutely NO need –'

'No NEED! By the sound of your ignorance there's every need! Wake UP! Don't you see?'

'Sieur I see –'

'That's NOT a question you dolt!'

A finger jabbed Armand's broad chest. Olivier's tirade erupted like a volcano. I listened in shock to hear Armand allow any man to abuse himself so harshly, or speak so crassly about Ilaria. His lips pressed in anger as he glared in defiance but Olivier ran on.

'Life is long and fools fall in and out of love. But it's not all capturing banners to make women swoon! Not all drinking, eating and fucking *boy!*'

There it was again, spat with more venom to mock sense into his tepid son. Armand's blue eyes were blazing in anger.

'DON'T call me that again!'

'I'll call a fool whatever I want!' He shot an angry glance and finger at me. 'Your man can sing all he likes about heroics and codswallop!'

Armand's hands snapped by his side, fists clenching hard.

'Yes Father I understand!'

Armand was desperately holding himself back. I feared if the father didn't retreat his son would say something they'd dearly regret. But the old man stepped closer, his bellowing hushed to whispering contempt as he thrust a finger in accusation.

'I can see that despite having your first *little foray* into war, it's taught you too little.'

My own eyes leapt wide to hear that ignorant slur spill from such an overbearing braggart.

Olivier hissed through gritted teeth. 'Yet heed my words well *boy*.'

'I *warned* you.' Armand glared.

'Heed and you may lead our house onto something more than *oblivion*.' Armand began to turn. A large hand reached to wrench him back. 'Don't think I mean it less because I say it quietly. Speak softly and carry a rod, your grandfather used to say.'

'You've said *enough*!' Armand demanded.

'I shouldn't need to explain to you, that rod is your *reputation* boy!'

With no tolerance left, with the tenets of his hero, the great Charny, pricking at his conscience; that a true chevalier responds to a demon wherever it lurks, whatever form it takes, Armand clenched his fist. Then in a burst of passion, to the great surprise of his mother and bride re-entering, he lifted and launched and smashed his father's jaw.

Olivier sprawled back onto the polished parquetry. Two pairs of feminine eyes leapt wide in amazement as Armand, glaring with rage, stepped through and stood over his tormentor.

'Stay DOWN old man!'

'Armand!' cried Ilaria rushing to assist. 'Dear mercy Sieur Olivier!

Dame Margot stared soberly at her son who stared coldly at her husband who stared up at a finger pointed down at him.

'You will NOT refer to me as *boy*. I am an accoladed chevalier. Nor will I ever allow you to speak of my wife in that manner again.'

'Armand desist!' Ilaria scolded. 'You will show respect to your –'

'He *must* hear it!' Armand hissed.

'Ilaria let him have his say.' Olivier groaned. 'I *may* have asked for it.'

Ilaria stared up at Armand imploring him to regain his composure but his anger wasn't spent.

'*Sieur* ...' he mocked 'I'm grateful our lives are linked because of your effort to bind them when I was a child. But having just returned from a war let me warn you. If by now you mistake my quality as a man this much ... then must I assume you'll do so forever.'

The expression on Sieur Olivier's face softened. He glanced at Margot who stared down owlishly in disbelief.

'Armand' he said contritely 'I was only –'

'One thing I learned on my little foray, as you so disparagingly referred to it.' Dame Margot glared in disbelief as Armand glanced at Ilaria. 'Is that I ... *we* no longer require any assistance to make our way in the world.'

'Armand!' snapped his mother. 'What's this nonsense all about? Tell me at once.'

'Mother I apologise to you –'

'Tush darling. I knew this day would come.'

Margot laid an arm about Armand and kissed his cheek gently. She looked down at her husband with a tilt of her head.

'Imbecile.' She caught Ilaria's eyes. 'Oh yes I still love him. However ... I'm sure he *did* ask for it.' Margot turned to Armand. 'I'm just glad it was you darling and not *Tristan*.'

The comment made my brows lift in wonder. I still hadn't met their second son. But if Margot feared how much worse her husband may have fared to face him, suddenly I imagined Tristan de Capulet to be another Hercules. Margot extended her hand to Ilaria.

'Now lovely daughter-in-law, stand up and allow my embarrassing husband to rise of his own volition.' Margot arched a sceptical brow. 'Heaven forbid the mighty warrior needs a woman to help him to his feet.'

She rolled her eyes and sighed. Coming to her feet, Ilaria pressed a smile as they watched Olivier struggle to rise, nursing his jaw as he did so.

'Well is it broken?' Margot pouted in mock sympathy.

'By thunder Margot! I was a warrior once.'

I huffed to myself as I heard him say so. If Armand had reached the limit of endurance with his blunt father, then so had I. No it wasn't my place to think so. Yet lacking the ability to hold my tongue, I stepped forward.

'Sieur Capulet.' All eyes turned on me. 'Forgive me for saying so—'

'Ah!' he cut in. 'Now I've been knocked on my ass, even the musician thinks he can chide me.'

'As you know I served Chevalier Toulon. Now I serve your son.'

'And so?' He glared.

'And so ...' I gulped. 'I've seen both *men* fight in deadly earnest. If I had to say who was better, it would be hard for me to choose. But Sieur I can tell you plainly, that for every man, woman and child who stood on the walls of Carentan and saw him fight for them -'

'Marcel.' Armand glanced at Ilaria. Her eyes were on me. 'Enough.'

Sieur Olivier considered me for a moment then looked at Armand.

'He's loyal at least. You chose him well.'

Their bold blue eyes, an exact mimic, held each other for a moment. The old man's hand clapped my shoulder then offered the kind of smile only soldiers ever seem to do.

'Perhaps you're right skinny man. But Margot will tell you -'

'Be careful what you promise of me Olivier de Capulet.'

He continued. 'When I returned from the fight at his age, my head was stuck up my own ass with thoughts of how impressive I was.'

'Oh well yes.' Margot smiled at Ilaria. 'That's certainly true.'

Ilaria and Armand couldn't resist smiling in response. In an instant it felt as if the confrontational tone had vanished. Armand stepped closer.

'Father I can assure you, I'm not impressed with my own ... value.'

Olivier glanced at Margot, her expression still warning him to take care how he proceeded. Indeed it seemed clear no one else in their world could affect the stern patriarch the way Dame Capulet was able to.

'Yes son.' he said cautiously. 'I know you don't have that failing. And yes, I understand that you are not me. I'm grateful you're not.'

'Amen.' Margot whispered.

She squeezed Ilaria's hand with a smile as Olivier ran on.

'Now ... you wanted your wife and mother to join our discussion?'

Ilaria flushed with emotion. 'Did you say that?'

Armand pouted thoughtfully. 'I did.'

'Well ...' said Olivier 'here they are. So let's speak of it together.'

'Speak of *what?*' Margot asked cautiously.

'His succession my love.'

Margot drew Ilaria in protectively. 'You mean to say *their* succession.'

Olivier lifted his brows in acknowledgement.

'I do. You're a Capulet now Ilaria. Nothing can change it.'

She smiled at Armand. 'I wouldn't change it for the world.'

Olivier considered his new daughter-in-law for a moment, exchanging a glance with his still waiting wife. He stepped toward Margot then turned to Ilaria.

'Ilaria dear. It's sooner than we anticipated, but before you leave in the morning Margot and I had hoped to announce, to all in our faction, our choice of Armand as the premiere sieur.'

Ilaria's face lit with surprise. She turned to Armand. By his expression, she understood he already knew that much.

'As long as I ...' Margot's fingers touched Olivier's arm. 'As long as *we* can come to an agreement with him tonight.'

'With you *both.*' Margot corrected.

'Yes my love.' Olivier tilted his eyes to Heaven and smiled.

'I see.' Ilaria said thoughtfully. 'Yet Dame Capulet, perhaps we should take more time –'

Margot interrupted as Olivier and Armand shared a knowing smile.

'No darling take it from me, if you wait, anything may happen.'

'Yes I'm sure that's true yet –'

'Ilaria you're not the *only* couple our elders have considered. I agree with Olivier. While their ears are ringing with news of your marriage and Armand's accomplishments, the time will never be more right. If you delay now, a popular rival may rise and your best chance may be lost.'

'I certainly agree.' said Olivier.

'Oh.' Ilaria pouted in thought. 'Yet still. Shouldn't we –'

'No.' Margot took her hands. 'If I never get another chance to advise you of anything darling, be guided by me for this one moment.'

'Very well Madame.'

Margot looked thoughtfully at her son and returned to Ilaria.

'I know it's your first night together.' That brought a blush to Ilaria's cheeks. 'But this concern's your future. Let's settle it now.'

'Mother are you certain?' Armand put in.

'Hush Armand you've said quite enough. Sit down and behave.' Both women smirked as the muscular oaf rolled his eyes and complied. 'You see Ilaria, we wield the real power. He wouldn't dare clout me on the jaw. Now dear sit down with your husband.' Margot's eyes lit with pride. 'I've been waiting so long to be able to say that!' She smiled infectiously. 'Wine here!' Servers scurried. 'And you. Musician!'

'Yes Dame Capulet.' I sputtered in surprise.

'Less bold talk and more pleasant music.'

'Of course Madame.'

I was relieved to know for what was to come, she'd taken charge of both her men and checked their unruly behaviour. She glanced at her husband.

'Now ... *we* were about to negotiate the succession of *our* house?'

'Yes Margot.' He turned to the underlings. 'But we must start with an agreement from you both that we are not here to discuss *love.*'

Armand and Ilaria glanced at each other and smiled.

'Very well.' they bleated in unison, grinning like children.

Olivier massaged his jaw. 'We know that you love each other.'

'Father I'm sorry.'

'Armand don't be so naïve.' Margot cut in. 'Can't you see how proud he is? It was just what he wanted from you. As soon as you're both gone he'll brag about it to everyone.'

Olivier exchanged a knowing glance with Margot and ran on.

'This is about *wealth* and *power*. Making it. Growing it. Keeping it.'

'Yes.' Ilaria sparked with interest.

'Power and *survival*. Shrewd thinking, alliances, negotiating.'

'Smart play from both of you' Margot added 'to survive the bigger game, the *real* game of life in an elite world.'

A server stepped in to assess their comfort. Cups of mulled wine were offered to all. No, that didn't include myself!

'I see.' said Ilaria.

She glanced at Armand who was listening quietly.

Olivier took a moment to calculate his words.

'Armand you've just returned from a deadly fight' he said soberly 'and all petty arguments aside, I want you both to consider this, that the major reason people fight so savagely, is to *gain* power or to *hold* it.'

'Yes.' Margot agreed. 'To enjoy the security that comes from power.'

Innocent faces frowned at her assessment. Margot widened her eyes.

'Oh yes it sounds a little sad. But it's true none the less.'

Ilaria glanced at Armand. He smiled thinly and replied for both. 'We understand.'

'I'm not sure you understand it all?' said Olivier. 'Your mother mentioned *security*. Maintaining security means controlling *risk*. You risked your life to save Toulon.'

'I did.'

'Hmm.' he hesitated. 'Should you have done it?'

Armand stared soberly. That seemed an extraordinary question. 'I was sworn to –'

'I know you did your duty Son. But did Michele really do his? Or was he careless to make such a prize of himself? He promised me he wouldn't. And then he exposed your life into the bargain.'

Armand's eyes narrowed. 'Father I can't allow you to –'

'Son ... my intention is not to malign Michelle's character.'

Margot huffed as she took Olivier's arm and turned to Armand. 'Darling bear with him for a moment. Let's hope he comes to some kind of point.' Olivier smiled at Margot, lifted his brows and wagged his head.

As a silent watcher, such moments between them, made me wish I knew more about their lives together. He lifted her hand to kiss, then his eyes settled on Ilaria rather than Armand.

'I *will* come to my point. And here it is. I'm speaking of life Ilaria. Of deciding which risks to *take* and which to *avoid*.'

'Yes.' Ilaria replied soberly. She reached for Armand's hand.

It seemed clear she understood the gravity of this conversation and the potential it had to alter both their lives. Olivier looked at his son.

'The English wanted to take Toulon from you.'

'They did.' Armand stared stoically.

'In an effort to fetch his ransom, they were willing to *kill* you for it.'

'They were.'

Ilaria frowned and gripped his hand.

'Nothing more than greed and a bid for prestige lay behind it.'

'I agree.' Armand whispered almost to himself.

Olivier paused as he glanced from one to the other. 'Then before you depart on this tour, to meet a slew of ambitious people that you've never met before, I say this to you both. No matter if a man be common or noble, bandit or bishop –'

Margot cut in as their counsel became a duet. 'If you present a prize worth having to an ambitious man *or* woman who feels capable of taking it.'

'Then despite any notion of honour or friendship or even *famil-ial* ties' Olivier added 'many will behave like bastards –'

Margot glared. 'Or bitches.'

Olivier glared. 'Or thieves to take it from you. And they'll do so–'

'At *any* risk or cost and ...' Margot added coldly 'by *any* means.'

'Fair or foul.' Olivier concluded.

I blinked along with Ilaria and Armand to hear their elders speak so frankly, particularly Dame Capulet. She was finding it easier to do so on this topic than three weeks before when the issue of hastening the marriage was before them. And listening to her speak in tandem with Olivier made me realise how well matched they were, or at least how much the years had drawn their minds together on such matters.

Armand's mind seemed to hang in a haze for a moment. I knew that since that mention of Toulon, he had become lost in a faraway field, staring into a blue sky, waiting for Heaven to send him a sign. His eyes flickered. Silently he looked at Ilaria and back to his parents. I felt that even his father must finally be realising just how deeply the war had affected his son.

'Carentan taught me something of that.' he said quietly.

Margot laid her empty glass on an offered tray to draw another.

'If you both agree to share the burden of leading our house, you must expect to find treachery lurking about you. But ... you must not be looking for it only in the approach of strangers.'

'Not at all.' Olivier agreed. 'Once the wealth of our faction lies under your control, treacherous ambitions will start brewing in the minds of associates, neighbours, and the members of our wider *famille*.'

Margot brows lifted as she met Ilaria's eyes.

'And now that you're wed darling, you must expect to observe it even in some from the Marchand side.'

Ilaria's lips opened as if to respond but her thoughts held her for a moment. As she considered that possibility more deeply, considered some of those among her own *famille* and parents associates who were held in less esteem, she seemed to accept such a threat may become possible.

'Hard lessons from experience have taught us to be cautious.' said Olivier. 'Experience generates knowledge. Knowledge lends foresight. We exercised that when we made the match between you. Ilaria let me say –'

'Olivier.' Margot narrowed her eyes. 'Treat our new daughter-in-law with care and respect.'

His brows lifted. 'Let me say ... that you are a *rare* young woman.'

Margot smiled. 'Well that's a sensible start.'

Indeed we all smiled.

'A blind beggar can see how much you love our son.' Olivier added. 'And yes, the world seems to know he loves you.' Their hands came together. 'But you wouldn't be married now if Margot and I hadn't negotiated this match before you were even born.'

Ilaria blinked in surprise. 'That's certainly true.' she agreed.

'And ... that's what we were *discussing* before you both re-entered'

'Discussing?' Armand mocked. 'It was put more *colourfully* than that!'

Margot glared at Olivier who wore a guilty expression.

'Well Ilaria ... I *may* have suggested too bluntly –''

'Olivier.' Margot warned.

'That without our help, all those years ago, tonight you'd be keeping *intimate* company with another.'

Ilaria's eyes opened wide. Margot smacked her husband's shoulder.

'You insensitive clout!' she hissed. 'Did you say that to him on his wedding night?'

Armand winced to hear it confessed so openly. Behind them all I grinned to watch Dame Margot scold her bullish husband so openly.

'Margot I was merely attempting –'

'To be an indelicate buffoon! How could you make such a remark before they've even had a chance to –'

'But Dame Capulet it's true.' Ilaria interrupted. 'If we hadn't been matched, I would be with someone else by now.' She turned to Armand. 'And so would you my heart.'

I presumed that would be true. But listening quietly my own mind conjured an image from Normandy of just who that someone else might be.

'Darling' said Margot 'perhaps what my oafish husband's *trying* to explain, is that leading a faction is more than just having children and leaving the fortune of all in your care up to *fate.*'

That word was portentous. I knew that for Armand to hear her say so, his confession to me on that very subject in the abbey hospital at Formigny, would now be haunting him. His mother continued.

'Whether you find yourselves negotiating the merger of two young lives for the security of their future, or pursing the prudent conduct of daily business for the security of all.' Ilaria stared soberly, nodding agreement.

It seemed mother and daughter-in-law were striking a chord together. Ilaria glanced thoughtfully at Sieur Olivier.

'And so now, as we proceed together, Armand and I should take more care of which risks to *accept* as necessary and which to *avoid?*'

The patriarch was smirking. 'Well Margo that sounds wise.'

'Oh Olivier don't be so pleased with yourself. You ought to be –'

'Madame.' Ilaria interrupted softly. 'I think we understand.'

Margot smiled. 'Thankfully you are your parent's daughter.'

'I've grown up in trade. I know their gold didn't grow on a tree.'

Olivier huffed with amusement. 'By thunder Margot! There's hope for the future of Capulet.'

Margot arched a brow. 'Perhaps imbecile, you should have spared our son from the start and offered your great sermon to our new daughter.'

'I suggested as much.' Armand grumbled.

'He did.' said Olivier. 'But then I'd have no tale to tell tomorrow of how my eldest son finally –'

'Oh yes we know!' Margot rolled her eyes. 'Sweet mercy Ilaria. Men are so ... oh there's no word to describe it.'

Ilaria smiled. 'Countess de Viviers has one.' she replied.

'*Stupido!*' blurted Armand.

'Ilaria.' Olivier said solemnly. 'If I declare Armand to be my undisputed heir tomorrow morning, that will mean ...'

He turned to Margot who caught Ilaria's eye.

Margot's tone became potent.

'That you will be *my* undisputed heir.'

'I understand.' said Ilaria.

'It's not a small thing.' Margot warned. 'You'll both need to be ready to assume responsibilities far greater than you've experienced before.'

'And' Olivier added 'to ensure there's no doubt that you both understand, the agreement must be notarised and signed.'

Margot held Ilaria's gaze. 'The law only requires Armand to sign it darling. But for the safety of all, we will insist you both sign it.'

'I would ...' Ilaria halted to turn to Armand. 'that is, I believe that *we* would prefer it that way?'

'Of course angel.' he agreed quietly.

'Bravo.' said Margot. 'That's the first important decision you've made together. But be warned, if you sign the succession agreement tomorrow, once it's done, there can be no turning back.'

'Yes.' Ilaria said confidently.

'For that reason ...' Margot laid an arm across Olivier's broad shoulders as he drew her into him. Their eyes met as she leaned to kiss and I began to realise how long awaited this moment must have been for them. 'Once and for all, we must ask you both if you *truly* wish to bear such an burden together for the *rest* of your lives.'

'Or ...' Olivier paused for effect 'would you prefer that we offered that responsibility to another couple?"

Armand and Ilaria sat staring quietly. They still hadn't shared a bed together but were already sharing the burden of such a lifechanging decision. I understood little of haughty familial politics. But even a young musician could comprehend the gravity of such a moment. Just two weeks before, Ilaria's mother had warned her that deciding whether to marry Armand, sooner rather than later, may be the most important decision she'd ever make. If it was, and while present at that moment I believed it was, how quickly that pressing decision had led Ilaria to this.

Yet I felt the precipice she now teetered on with Armand was even more daunting. Before Ilaria lay a decision to accept or reject the power to wield control, for the rest of her life, over the mighty assets of the entire Capulet faction. The future of her role in the House of Capulet hung upon their answer. And with that answer, the world Armand and Ilaria would share for the rest of their lives would become very different. Cupid's Balls!

My own eyes widened as I held my breath. What would they say?

I still knew so little of Ilaria. Two weeks ago, during that weighty transaction to decide if she would marry, she hadn't appeared overwhelmed. And now in the moment they faced together, it was Armand who seemed more hesitant. Since his return from the war, while he was sure he'd be forced to return, he thought of little else but how to ensure their marriage was secured before he must depart. And since experiencing Toulon's death, his entanglement with Eloise du Marche, and the fatigue of the brutal fight at Formigny, that single goal, to wed Ilaria was enough to fill his mind.

Yet barely had that goal been accomplished before he felt forced to make a reverberating choice that would intimidate anyone. For one such as myself, it seemed gruelling. But now, despite my earlier feeling against his father's bullish tactics, I appreciated why he flared so hotly when Armand lacked the will to discuss it. With the premiere couple-in-waiting on the verge of meeting their extended famille for the first time; with so much at stake resting on the result of it; it did seem vital to answer this lifechanging question before the night was done.

My anxiety leapt as I watched and waited. Armand stared fixedly. I had seen that look before, felt sure he was questioning if he was *ready* or truly *worthy*. And though to my surprise, Ilaria showed no hint of misgiving, the challenge of it all seemed more difficult for Armand. In a fight, his actions were utterly instinctive, even cold and calculating. This was different.

In some very important ways Ilaria was already proving she could be stronger than Armand. Like myself at that moment however, I believe she was fearful of his instinctive humility. Yes we both cherished it as a hallmark of his character. Yet at that moment, Ilaria and I both suspected it may hold Armand back from taking that chance of their lifetime.

The silence extended. Margot and Olivier saw he was wavering and exchanged a stoic glance.

'Sincerely darlings ... we have no shortage of candidates.'

I had expected Margot's tone to be conciliatory but she was stern and foreboding. Even after all her husband's bluster, nothing until that moment had been said with such a sense of gravitas as the tail end of that comment. Perhaps Margot considered it a chance to teach her new daughter-in- law just what would be expected of a premiere Dame. Then she looked squarely at her son to offer another lesson.

'Darling' she said quietly 'if this is *not* for you, if you choose to put it by, the House of Capulet won't falter for the sake of that decision.'

It seemed telling she didn't suggest the same directly to Ilaria.

Sieur Olivier sat quietly. He understood hovering wouldn't help. Dame Margot followed suit, sitting on the arm of his chair, her arm still laid about his shoulders. Both held their words and their breath and waited.

For the time one may count twenty the young couple thought. Then Ilaria leaned and whispered to Armand. They murmured again and nodded. Finally Ilaria made her reply.

'Monsieur. Madame. For my part I feel very honoured by your offer and am entirely ready to accept it.'

Both parents smiled thinly. Their eyes fell on their son.

'Armand?' Olivier asked bluntly.

He pouted thoughtfully and lifted his eyes.

'More than anything I want you both and Ilaria to be proud of me.'

Ilaria squeezed his hand. Bright green eyes shined into blue.

'I am my heart.' she whispered. 'I will always be. No decision here can change that. Say only what you will. Speak your true mind.'

'Truly for me angel, if this is what *you* wish, I say it's what *we* wish.'

Olivier and Margot exchanged a look of relief then breathed a deep sigh of relief together.

'Darlings we certainly wish it for you both. Olivier?'

Margot's brows lifted in wait.

'Before you leave tomorrow, we'll sign the declaration together and send an announcement ahead of your tour to all. Are we agreed?'

Armand and Ilaria smiled and stood together.

'Sieur Capulet. Dame Capulet.' said Ilaria. 'We gratefully offer you our acceptance.'

Olivier and Margot rose to their feet, holding back their smiles.

'Sieur Capulet. Dame Capulet.' said Margot. 'We gratefully accept your acceptance.'

The sight of the heartfelt hugging and kissing that ensued among the quartet, completely belied the gravity of what went before. Yes, I felt left out. Oh yes boo hoo for me! Yet Armand did flash me a relieved smile and Ilaria glanced thoughtfully. That was more than enough.

Next morning a legal advocate arrived with a document to be signed by four signatories. Among the terms, a period of two seasons was stipulated to allow a smooth transition of power to occur. The terms also allowed, rather grimly, that should Sieur Olivier die before that time, control would immediately pass to Armand and Ilaria.

That final point was discussed only briefly, just before the newly-weds retired above to share their first bed together. No, I didn't attend that exploit! Next morning however, after they signed the declaration, I noted that for the first time since I met Ilaria, sobbing in the cathedral after her terrifying vision, and since Armand had survived the stampede of death in Carentan, now hand in hand as the premiere Sieur and Dame of Capulet, they finally seemed at peace together.

Yes, I feel sure you know what I'm going to say.

No, that feeling would not last long.

All too soon their peace, our peace, would be shattered.

Chapter 2 Cleopatra and Antony

The marriage tour was all but ready to depart. Our entourage was larger than the humble quartet that returned from Normandy. Coming with us was an inventory of destinations the newlyweds were expected to visit. On that formidable list were the many splendid chateaus and sumptuous apartments of relations and important associates who couldn't attend the marriage. Some were near at hand. Yet some, as we now understood, were so far flung they lay beyond the mountain passes which separated the French and Italian Kingdoms.

Since the Duke de Bourbon confirmed Armand would not be recalled that season, the furthest destination now sought would be the estate of Signor Sabatino and Signora Aurelie Cortellani (nee Capulet). It was lyrically named *Valle del Nocciolo* - Vale of the Hazelwood. I was told it lay nestled somewhere in the northern hills of Verona. Yes, Ilaria also hoped to visit the fabled port of Venice.

Whether or not that last could be managed would be decided after we reached the Cortellani estate. Much in that regard would depend on our timing. Once there we could stay and visit, but had to ensure our departure left enough time to ensure we re-entered the alpine path before it became inhospitable.

Of course we all hoped, that by that time, the new premiere Dame of Capulet would be bearing an extra bundle homeward. Yes sweet friends, Ilaria was now my mistress. Cupid's Balls! And so as I woke that morning I realised, never again would I address her as *demoiselle*. In truth it made me sad to think so, even though I was already used to addressing Armand as *chevalier*. It was one more adjustment to remind us all that our worlds were changing.

Ilaria was thrilled at the prospect that, after visiting those in closer proximity, we'd be passing through the alps and onto the Italian plains. Before she was born her parents had travelled great distances together in all directions. Once Ilaria arrived however, they never risked travelling far afield with her in their company. And so, longer routes were run alone by one parent or the other. Her mother usually travelled north in search of specialised labour and fabric. Her father took the longer routes south towards Marseille or east to Venice.

As we made ready to leave, Ilaria chatted excitedly that now, as a married woman, she could transit in safety and respectfully as far as she had a mind to travel. It would be an improvement on her ill-fated attempt to ride alone to Normandy! Now with Armand by her side, locations she had only dreamt of seeing were open for them to explore.

But no, my new mistress wasn't chatting excitedly about any of that to me, nor to her new husband. For among the trove of gifts the newlyweds received, one from Dame Marchand was the employment of a close server for her daughter. I marvelled at how elite people felt it was not unusual to be offered another person as a gift.

To me that sounded otherworldly. Or it did so until I considered, my own services were passed to Toulon by my first employer as the result of a drunken wager in a game of chance. But I digress. Where was I? Oh yes, Ilaria's new close server. Like myself, the young woman was older than Ilaria. Unlike myself, she was two years older than Armand.

Her name was Maxine Boileau. And let me state from the start of this new beginning that I thought she was fetching. Oh yes, settle down. Beyond that however, my glancing impression of Maxine before we left Lyon, was that in Ilaria's company she was talkative and appeared to amuse her. Yet I confess that when Maxine wasn't chatting, she seemed a little too *no-nonsense*.

Well bite my bare ass, yes she did!

I prefer a little nonsense in a woman.

I learnt that Ilaria's mother Dame Genevieve had secured Maxine's service from her elder sister, Lucille. Five years before, Ilaria's Aunt Lucille had retained Maxine as a wet nurse for her own daughter's first child, a boy. Like most wet nurses, Maxine had a child of her own at that time, also a beautiful boy. Sadly however, not only was the little saint born out of wedlock and his scurrilous father fled, but he didn't survive much beyond a year after his birth.

Even before we left Lyon, I'd learnt that much from scraps of gossip lurching about. As you may know, when a wet nurse raises a girl and serves well, she's often kept on until her charge is wed and sometimes beyond. But when a nurse tends to a boy, the tether of care is cut as soon as he's ushered into the company of men. That was Maxine's predicament at the time Ilaria's wedding date was advanced – the term of her service was due to expire in one week.

And though Aunt Lucille was loathe to lose Maxine, she was also too spendthrift to retain her without a genuine position needing to be filled. Then fate played a hand when the wedding caused Dame Genevieve to need to secure a server for Ilaria with very little notice. She had seen Maxine before of course and was impressed by her.

After learning from Lucille that Maxine was to be released so soon, Genevieve urged her to renew the service agreement before another employer could snatch her up. Ilaria's mother placed great value on a member of her own famille being able to vouch for the quality of someone's service. Oh yes, that certainly made sense to me. Four days after the new marriage date was announced, Maxine's agreement was renewed for five more years.

As soon as possible thereafter – at Dame Genevieve's expense and secretively for the sake of surprising her daughter – the agreement was transferred to Ilaria. However Maxine was offered as an *early* gift and so began immediately. All had been arranged in time enough for Maxine to learn many of the preferences of her new mistress before the wedding day.

Dame Genevieve's choice of Maxine would soon make it clear how well she understood her daughter. She knew the kind of companion Ilaria would be more likely to form a bond with and to heed counsel from. So when fate offered up the prospect of Maxine, the decision was easily made.

Oh yes, I heard Ilaria had been assigned a new server. Yet with so much to do myself to prepare for the nuptials, I paid little attention to that news. In truth I expected any minder that her mother may have enlisted would be a strict, ancient crone who would mumble and teeter about. Perhaps it would be whoever was once Ilaria's own nurse? Every thought had me imagining a mummified corpse, wrapped in linen shards.

What's more, the decision that a marriage tour would occur at all wasn't announced until two days before the great day. And the tour wasn't lengthened until after they heard the duke's news on the night itself. And so you see, at the time I learnt of Maxine's employment, the notion I may be travelling in close company with her for any length of time, didn't occur to me at all.

By the morning after the great event, the first few weeks Ilaria and Maxine had shared together saw them bond through the panic of preparing for a hasty marriage, and what they first thought, would be a *short* tour to follow. Then at the feast, and to their great surprise, they learned they'd be travelling not for several days but for several months! And no longer just within a few days ride of Lyon, but beyond the reach of the kingdom! And so yes, on that morning as we assembled to set forth, it's little wonder they were chattering so excitedly to each other.

That was how the company of two young women, hailing from the Marchand side of this match had been added to our entourage. Perhaps that sounds harmless enough. Yet until that time we had only toured in the company of soldierly men. Moreover as I noted before, the expansion of our ensemble didn't stop there.

From the Capulet side, courtesy of Sieur Olivier, the service of two men-at-arms was added to our number. However as a result of the news received at the feast, he realised his son was no longer embarking on a short jaunt that would not stray far from Lyon. Now with two young women in his care, Armand was bound for the far side of Italy.

In reaction to that knowledge, even before the *old man* went to bed that night, he dismissed the two younger men assigned to us, whose names are forgotten to history. They were promptly replaced by two hardened veterans, both Italian born and bred. Each had served Armand's father for more than ten years and I guessed ten years in age stood between them.

The elder was named Liberati. The younger was Boccolo. And despite their maturity both were fit, muscular warriors who presented themselves that morning well-armed, well-mounted and in liveries that displayed the Capulet crest. Armand assigned the warlike pair to trail as our rear guard. Our giant squire, Caspar von Ludolf, would of course lead our train aboard Loki, his painted monstrosity.

I call it a train, for we now had two wagons rather than one. Sadly Toulon's old wagon that saw us to Normandy and back was to be left behind us. Fabrizio continued as our page cum junior squire, now with the responsibility to drive the following wagon. With so many additions being made and extravagant gifts being offered, I did puzzle why a new page wasn't secured. Dame Margot had also suggested it to her son.

However Armand insisted that because a page is a *personal retainer*, anyone chosen should have the interest to follow on and become a squire. Deciding on a candidate suitable for that path should take more time. In truth, I thought Armand felt so pressed with all that was to do, the dizzy oaf simply considered it one thing too many.

No, I didn't say so to his face!

Yet I was glad Armand left that task aside because his health still concerned me. After all, he had promised the duke that granting his permission to return to Lyon would *benefit* his recovery. And he promised to treat the need to recuperate seriously. Despite that intention, by the day of his nuptials, he still hadn't fully recovered. Not at all.

And Cupid's Balls! After striking his father's jaw in an uncharacteristic moment of fury, he woke next morning to find the wound in his rib had reopened! Well yes, the rigours of intimacy with his bride may have also aggravated that injury. And every other injury! I hoped that once we were touring at their leisure, Armand and Ilaria would take more care to ensure he gained the rest that he needed.

They emerged from the chateau's grand portal after signing the succession agreement as our company and other servers bustled all about. He clutched his side and winced from more than one pinch of pain. She delicately stifled a yawn. It made me smile to recall what it was like to surrender my virginity and how little I held back thereafter.

'Ah!' I cried to gain maximum attention. 'Cleopatra and Antony emerge at last from their tomb into the sunshine.'

'How did fate determine you would be the first to greet us.' Armand winced.

'Are you hurt Chevalier?'

'Marcel.' he warned.

Ilaria stifled another yawn a little less discreetly.

'Are you awake Madame?'

'Marcel.' she warned.

'Were you set upon by bandits in your boudoir?'

Snickers rose all about us from the bustling servers.

'Rascal.' said Ilaria.

She had the blushing smile of one who is no longer a virgin.

'Did you manage to defend your honours bravely?' I enquired. 'Or yield them without a fight?'

Thanks to my audacity every busy ear and eye noted my taunts at their delicious expense. Their shared embarrassment was a priceless memory in the making.

Ilaria arched a perfect brow above a bleary green eye.

'Go see if Fabrizio requires assistance.' she demanded tiredly.

'Oh that's distressing *Madame*.' She smiled to hear that word. 'Is *that* your first official instruction to me?'

'It may be my last.' She puckered to kiss her husband.

'But this is an auspicious moment. I was hoping your first command would be more memorable? Marcel! Quickly man, fetch a surgeon! Marcel! Take this urgent message to the countess! Oh Marcel! My intimate garments appear to be tangled on my –'

'Buffoon!' she snapped. 'Desist at once or –'

'Or rogue I'll injure myself again to ensure your compliance.'

'Yes Chevalier.' I bowed with a ridiculous flourish. 'Yes Madame.' I did so again.

Muted snickers sounded from those flitting about.

'Good morning to you both.' I added. 'Oh yes and ... *congratulations* Monsieur and Madame Capulet.'

The remark set off a cascade of salutations from servers who, not wishing to appear idle, dipped or curtsied in passing. I was happy to see the newlyweds smirking. Now with two employers to please, I realised I must pay attention to striking a balance between poking and stroking. I did as I was told and went to seek Fabrizio out.

The lad was tethering the livestock. Seeing him there reminded me we had one other new addition to our entourage, a rather pretty beast that he disappeared into a stable to fetch. He had already hitched Victoire, Armand's mythical stallion, behind the lead wagon alongside the old gelding Dilettante. Since our time in Normandy they seemed to have grown used to each other. I had been instructed to use the gelding myself from now on. Yet I hoped to ride the more comfortable she-mule instead.

Fabrizio re-appeared leading the new beast to tether it behind the second wagon. This was Ilaria's new palfrey and her parting gift from Countess de Viviers. The elegant creature was dappled light grey with four dark stockings and a white mane and tail. In keeping with Countess Regine's custom, each departing swan chose their own beast but it was named by their mentor. Because they'd gone in search of the gift so soon after Ilaria's escapade into the wild storm, Regine felt inspired to call the mare *Tempest*.

Ilaria had smiled when her mentor signed the bill of sale.

'I hope' said Regine 'the future premiere Dame of Capulet will never forget her folly of that morning.'

'If I had such a formidable mount to make my escape on –'

'Ilaria?'

'No Madame, I won't forget.'

'Think more fully through an important decision next time.'

'Yes Madame.'

'Particularly if you're feeling impulsive.'

'I'll try.'

'Hopefully the presence of this pretty one will remind you.'

By mid-morning, our train was loaded and ready to depart.

Finally, we made our exit through the gates of Chateau de Capulet to strike south along the river road. For the sake of appearance, Armand decided to attempt one last physical feat and had ordered Fabrizio to saddle Victoire. Then with our giant ninny's assistance, he drew his gorgeous bride up to perch upon his lap.

She kissed him and beamed a smile. A splendid assembly of parents, grandparents, relations and servers waved and cheered farewell. Countess Regine was there with her excited gaggle. They watched in awe as their eldest swan departed, seated on the lap of her Adonis, riding towards her future on the back of that mythical beast.

Oh sweet friends I swear, on that lovely summer day it was a sight of farewell I'll never forget. And it was so different from our last. Not a single man had been required to lean and accept a favour for their arm, offered against a fretful wish for their safe return. We weren't riding to war on that beautiful morning. Or so we thought.

Defying my instructions I had mounted the she-mule and struck up a jaunty tune to play us on our way. I was trailing between the rear wagon and our two new veterans. Fortunately, as our auspicious parade made its exit, the she-devil under me had managed to control her bowels. Led on its tether at the rear of the wagon, Ilaria's elegant mare walked ahead of me. I admired it for a moment longer, then pushed forward with a mind to pester Fabrizio.

He was seated at the wagon's front end and as my jennet drew alongside was still settling into the task of driving without an overseer. Armand's fiery beast loomed ahead of us, following the rear of the fore wagon. I noted to our page cum junior squire, how Victoire and Tempest seemed to be so absurdly suited for each other.

'You should tether them together. They'd look so pretty.'

'You know little of the ways of fine horses Master Marcel.'

Somehow his youthful Italic accent always invited me to mischief. 'Fortunately, yes.'

'Even a stripling such as I knows that if you put them together, that stallion will spend all his time fumbling for access to that mare.'

'That seems appropriate. Why not give him some access?' His eyes widened. 'Well what's good for the goose and gander should be good for the stallion and mare.'

'Victoire's not a *goose* Master Marcel.'

'Of course he's not ninny! *She* is the goose.'

'Neither is a goose or –'

'But if you hitch them together we can enjoy watching –'

'Master Marcel!'

'Then soon after we'll see a little mimic of one or the other scampering all about.'

'Perhaps in time the master and mistress may allow it.'

'Well it hardly seems fair to make *them* wait if their riders have already started to –'

'It's *impolite* to discuss such things in relation to our betters.'

He lifted the postillion's whip from its holster and snapped it with surprising expertise.

'Impolite!' I pouted and squinted in mock indignation. 'What would you know? You can't even tell if you're a page or a squire.'

He huffed and rolled his eyes as I considered Victoire again.

Anyone could tell how beautiful the horses would look when they finally rode out together. The muscular dappled dark grey with his black mane and tail, the elegant light grey mare with her dark stockings, seemed a potent match. Moreover, what struck me as the real reason why they were so perfectly suited, was that like Ilaria and now Armand too, I was also becoming distracted by notions of *fate*.

Oh yes, perhaps I just had too much idle time on my hands. But since our experiences in Normandy, even I felt tempted to look all about us for tantalising *signs*. I turned in the saddle to glance back at Tempest. Suddenly I was mindful that, when Ilaria chose her, she didn't even know Victoire existed. Yet seeing them together, looking so complementary, it felt as if they were destined to be brought together. Yes, perhaps only a fool would have thought so. At that time I wasn't yet a professional fool, but most would have agreed I was a foolish professional musician.

Soon we were halfway to our first destination and it felt as if Lyon was left well behind us. Since we departed I had been hanging back, not wishing to venture forward too soon to engage the carriage wagon occupants. Given what I knew of Armand's need for rest, I planned to give them time to settle, wait for the right moment. I glanced rearward, tipping my forehead to the soldiers who followed. Having seen them for the first time that morning, I didn't know either one as yet. And having ceased my playing, I realised how quiet our progress had become.

Up ahead in the distance I noted we were approaching a bend. As I glanced up, Caspar on Loki was entering the curve. Perhaps a furlong separated him from the men behind me. The quiet scene reminded me, we were no longer an all-male quartet with a brash leader like Toulon bellowing orders like a Viking raider. We were a more formidable company of eight, which included two elegant women. We'd all have to become mindful of our behaviour in their sensitive company.

Yet even though that may be true, Fabrizio's reprimand to be more mindful of what I should or shouldn't discuss had rankled me. But it did reflect our new reality. So did the sight of the elegant Tempest following along. Perhaps what was making me feel insecure at that moment, was how little I still knew about the woman up ahead who had suddenly become our new mistress.

To that point in my life, I'd served a lecherous tavern master who kept a brothel above stairs. Then I moved onto a half-French, half-Irish chevalier who lived like an inveterate bachelor. Even when I signed on in Carentan to serve Armand, not only was he still unmarried, he was being passionately flirted at by a ward of the queen.

And for the love of folly, sharing our time with Eloise du Marche in the helter-skelter atmosphere of war had been tempestuous, yes, but also great fun. The thought of her perhaps becoming my mistress hadn't worried me at all. And I felt I grew to know Eloise in very quick time. Indeed, that adventurous demoiselle had felt like an open book to read.

Oh yes I liked Ilaria too, but she felt less easy to know. Yes, I had learnt more about her in the past few weeks. Yet I still felt I knew much too little. Moreover, I couldn't forget our first real encounter when she burst into the cathedral, breathless and sobbing after her unsettling vision. Soon after that we left for war and now had returned. I didn't want to curse our new relationship before it even began, by confessing I'd seen her dark vision come true in Carentan.

I wanted to put such memories behind us. Indeed, remembering that first meeting made me hope that now fate had thrown us closer together, she'd have no more visions of doom. As yet I knew nothing of her visit to the tea merchant with Douceline. That occurred before our first meeting. And since then her best friend had eloped with a musician! But their mystic encounter before left Ilaria with new warnings to ponder.

Not knowing that incident had occurred, I didn't appreciate how much the notion of fateful visions continued to fret my new mistress. Yes, there was still much for me to learn about her. And as of that morning, in addition to my teasing encounter when they emerged from the chateau, I'd only had four interactions with Ilaria since we returned from the war.

The first was our visit to Chateau de Viviers to offer condolences to the countess. But once there all our focus was given to that gracious woman. The second encounter was my attendance to Ilaria's intimidating conference with both matriarchs, pressing her to decide if she would marry later or sooner. I confess that was the first time her deportment impressed me, and more than just a little.

The third encounter – no I don't count my playing for them in the bathhouse the following day as an encounter! Cupid's Balls! I barely recall any of that fiasco beyond my own arrival. For the matriarchs allowed, indeed they insisted, that I drink with them as they chatted. And for the love of folly, when Dames Margot and Genevieve drink potent wine at their leisure, they drink it like water to a pilgrim lost in the desert.

Yes, I do remember appreciating the sight of their bodies being oiled, scraped and massaged before the feminine trio descended, still drinking and chatting, into the pool like watery sirens. Then I remember their eyes constantly glancing, making me feel as if I was about to become the victim of an ancient Roman conspiracy!

Finally, in the mist of my mind, I recalled their laughing insistence to come and sit on the edge as I played. I was still rather sober when I did so, until they insisted I taste each woman's wine to judge which was better. Cupid's Balls! They all drank the very same libation yet somehow I managed to declare the subtle *differences*!

And I certainly can't remember how I ended up naked in the pool thereafter, still playing my ... yet I digress. Where were we? Ah yes, the third encounter Ilaria and I had since my return, our next to last. That occurred before we departed, is easier to recall and was less harrowing. I was with Armand at Chateau de Capulet on the afternoon before the wedding. The day before it had been announced we would embark on a *short* wedding tour immediately after the event. Armand was told Ilaria had just arrived and sent me in search of her with a message.

I found the elusive young woman in the marshalling yard where her famille had delivered a pair of wagons fitted for the marriage tour. But these were no ordinary wagons, particularly the smaller conveyance which Ilaria was inspecting with care. For her generous mother, along with securing a close server for her daughter, also ensured Ilaria would travel in comfort.

And so this pair of fine wagons had been added to the assortment of gifts with two healthy teams of horseflesh to draw them. Of course, a merchant empire such as theirs was bristling with such equipage. But these were not hand-me-downs. Both were shining and new. They were also built to allow the stout coverings of leather, wood and canvas, all elegantly decorated with the Capulet crest, to be entirely retractable.

The larger wagon was fitted out for goods and baggage. The smaller wagon was customised for personal carriage. For comfort, its stout leather coverlets could be lifted in sections to allow in light and air. When the wagon was commissioned, Dame Genevieve took care to ensure that, in the event of travel misfortune it was ever required for sleeping at night, the floor was long and wide enough to lay Ilaria and her future husband down together without cramping their forms.

No, Dame Genevieve hadn't anticipated a need to convey that future husband for a longer journey while he was still convalescing. So, with that need in mind, Ilaria's her new close server was arranging stowage casings to raise the floor and create an improvised daybed. Above it, they placed a layering of quilted linens to lie upon and an assortment of cushioning to prop up a head or torso or two. Then to ensure the comfort of any other who may repose with the invalid, a slather of sumptuous furs was laid on top. I understood it was Dame Genevieve's idea to create the elevated boudoir. One look left little doubt what result, beyond Armand's recuperation, she hoped to achieve with it. The result looked fit to lounge or make love upon.

Finally you must understand, the improvised boudoir was raised so much that with the coverlets all drawn back, any passenger who lay on it was lifted enough to enjoy the view in any direction. The result gave the impression it wasn't a wagon at all, but a reincarnation of Cleopatra's barge for travelling the high road.

Having been told I would find Ilaria inspecting the new wagons, I rounded the chateau's western corner, toting my message and stopped to stare in amazement. There she was with her new close server. They were not just inspecting their work but giggling like a pair of mischievous children as they tested it together for comfort.

By all the Saints that pray and every sweet Angel that sings in Heaven sweet friends, that was the first moment I ever saw Maxine. I was startled to realise she was such a young woman. And I was instantly captivated by her mischievous eyes, friendly smile and long dark hair. For some, such a moment of captivation would leave them speechless. Not for me.

'Ah! It's Cleopatra and her handmaiden.' I cried. 'Have either of you seen Demoiselle Marchand? I have a message from her fiancé.'

'I'm listening. Speak your message.' said Ilaria so playfully it completely surprised me.

'Oh! There you are Demoiselle.' I made a ridiculous bow. 'I'm sad to see you're to travel in such *discomfort*.'

'It's for the comfort of my husband-to-be, to ensure that he rests, not for myself.'

'Interesting. Yet you seem quite prepared to enjoy it yourself.'

'I hear much chattering, yet very little of my message.'

Next to Ilaria, the pout of unvarnished lips supressing a smile drew my attention.

'Oh yes.' I droned. 'A messenger sent from your mother to communicate with you came to your fiancé who called for me…'

'Get on with it fellow!' Ilaria spat with mock heat.

But my antics managed to draw a smile from her handmaiden.

'The messenger sent by your exalted mother has departed.'

'And so?' Ilaria's brows arched in punctuation.

'His message on behalf of your parents, begged that you depart post-haste for the citadel.'

'For what reason?' she huffed with a sigh of frustration.

'That much is unclear. Perhaps Cleopatra and her beautiful handmaiden are summoned to the temple to make a human sacrifice.'

A burst of muted laughter sounded from Maxine.

Ilaria tutted her into silence.

'If I *was* Cleopatra you rascal, I'd have you whipped for bothering my handmaiden.'

'Oh he's no bother Madame.'

'Maxine! Don't encourage that imbecile. Slave be gone!' she said imperiously with a sweeping gesture. It made me want to smile.

'Yes high priestess.'

Instead of bowing, I lay flat like an ancient servile. I heard giggling. I dared not look but knew it was Maxine.

That had occurred two days previously. Ilaria told Maxine not to encourage me. But her own quip to call me her *slave* was encouragement from herself for my antics. I took heart from that encounter on account of both women. Hence my quip that morning when I had hailed the newlyweds as Cleopatra and Antony.

My last meaningful encounter with Ilaria before we departed was at the wedding feast after all were gone. You know I witnessed her behaviour in that foreboding conference with her new parents. Yes, she also impressed me then. More importantly, it revealed how she and Armand might face the weight of difficult challenges together.

With each encounter, I saw more evidence of why Armand was so drawn to the Angel of Lyon and why so many spoke so well of her. However, we had one more interaction of a much more personal nature on their wedding night. Just after their *negotiation* ended, before she and Armand retired together, he left Ilaria alone for a moment.

She came to me quietly as I was stowing my instruments.

'Thank you for coming to Armand's defence.' she said shyly.

'Not at all Demois ... I mean *Madame*.'

'You know he speaks highly of you.'

'Does he? Perhaps in time he'll gain a more *lowly* impression.'

'You can't fool me Marcel. I'll never forget what you did.'

'What did I do?'

'When you played for the countess. That was very ... moving. She loves you for it.'

'Well I confess ... secretly I love her too. Please don't tell.'

'And then when we met that day in the cathedral ... you distracted me, calmed my anxiety.'

'Oh well that was just an accident.' I lied. 'I meant to mock you for my entertainment. Inadvertently I mended your spirits.'

Her gaze was unwavering and began to disarm me.

'I asked you then if you ever took anything seriously?'

'Yes, I recall it. No, I don't think so.'

'Really? Armand says that in Normandy you counselled him in his troubled moments, more than once, made his experience much more bearable.'

'Well I admit, when I met you in the cathedral, doting on him so fretfully, I still thought he was just a shallow muscular oaf –'

'And now?'

My mind drew back. The memory urged me to lower my guard. 'Since Carentan ... since the death of Toulon and more –'

'What more?' Her green eyes implored me.

'More ... for *him* to tell you, not me. And not 'til after you share your first night together.'

'Rascal. I'd like to know what else happened in Carentan. Won't you tell me?'

'Hmm?' I searched her troubled face. 'Let me tell you this.'

'Yes.' she whispered in anticipation.

'He'd never tell a lie if asked a question directly.'

'Of course.'

'But for the moment, your new husband is less in need of questions and more in need of ...'

'Care and patience?'

'Ah. You're not as dull as I've been led to believe.'

'Oh you're incorrigible.' She huffed and rolled her eyes.

'And there goes your high opinion of me. How fleeting it was. Now I'd bid you good *night* and good *rest* however, I feel certain that for what's left of this evening, there'll be little of the latter for *you*.'

'No.' she spat with insistence.

'No you expect *no* rest tonight? Or no you don't plan to be *intimate* tonight?'

'No I won't let you mock your way into my low opinion.'

Just as she did at the end of our encounter in the cathedral, Ilaria was smiling when I departed. Taken in all, my gathering opinion of her was that she seemed passionate, intelligent, strong-willed and somewhat ambitious. And though I'd twice seen Ilaria wearing a brave face when the burden of a difficult decision tried to shake her, under it all, I still had the impression she was kind-hearted. My new mistress was also revealing a lively streak of good humour. That was heartening. Oh yes, she was pretty and elegant and engaging, but any dullard could tell that much at a glance.

Finally of course, in certain moments, I couldn't help but compare her to Eloise du Marche. Perhaps that was unfair of me. Yet I think you understand that I just couldn't help it. I thought of Eloise as an adventurous spirit, a kind of warrioress attempting to live her life in the image of the Maid of Orléans. I didn't think of Ilaria that way, at least not yet. I didn't expect our elegant new Dame Capulet to sully her hands in a crisis by fending off danger herself.

Yes, I understood she had attempted to run away on horseback. Yet, not being there when it happened, it sounded more like a romantic notion than a perilous reality. We still knew nothing of the ruse to abduct her or how she had reacted. Yes, in hindsight, I underestimated Ilaria's sense of adventure and her potential to respond to danger.

Unfairly to her, I thought of Eloise as Armand's mimic in feminine form, perhaps even his perfect match who may have slipped from his grasp. Time would reveal to me however, that Ilaria was more of a match for him, and in many more ways, than I could have imagined. Not the least of which would be because, Ilaria and Armand were not such mimics of each other.

But at that moment, with our journey just begun, I felt Ilaria's personality hadn't been tutored by the same harsh lessons Armand, Eloise, Fabrizio, myself and Caspar, had already endured. Indeed, while I considered the quality of both women who now graced our company, I guessed Ilaria's new server would be more capable of handling dark trouble in a difficult moment.

Which brings me back to the question of Maxine coming among us. And to our departure from Lyon as I rode alongside Fabrizio, distracted by the sight of Caspar far ahead of us. Less far ahead, indeed just in the next wagon, was this new stranger who would have a far-reaching impact upon all our lives, yet mine in particular.

From the moment I saw Maxine I wanted to know more. Before we departed I had only seen her twice. Once was in the marshalling yard, as you now know, and then again during the wedding feast. Despite those encounters I still hadn't spoken directly to Cleopatra's captivating handmaiden. At the feast we were too busy to gain a chance to introduce ourselves. As I played and sang Maxine hovered about her new mistress. I saw her being held in fragments of conversation with Armand and speaking to Fabrizio as he hovered about his new master.

By then I was pleased to know she was joining our company. Not just because I found Maxine attractive and she was close to my age. As a musician, I've always preferred the company of women. Particularly when sober, women have always proven to be more appreciative of my talent and ability to chatter about almost anything.

And so, after we'd been on the road for perhaps two hours with my tolerance for Fabrizio's company all but spent, it was time to venture forward. It was time to discover more of this young woman. As fate would have it, my life was about to change forever.

Chapter 3 the Handmaiden's Touch

Maxine was showing the diversity of her skills by driving the wagon ahead of us. That was intriguing, for up until the day before we left, I had been assigned that duty. An hour before our departure however, Maxine approached Armand and asked permission to be assigned the task. He looked at her patiently, yet doubtfully.

'Can you drive a wagon?'

'Oh many types, Monsieur. Whether they be led by horses or mules or even oxen.'

I immediately thought that was more than I could claim to do.

'How did you come by that capability?'

'My father is the ostler to a livestock merchant. I have six brothers Monsieur, who all worked with beasts of burden. One's an ostler, two are farriers, one is a smith, one is now a squire and the youngest is a medicus.'

'A medicus?'

'Yes Monsieur. Our maman finally had her way.'

'I suppose they all taught their little sister a thing or two?'

'I rather think their big sister taught them a thing or two.'

'I see.' Armand glanced at the smaller wagon. 'Well, let me see you unhitch and re-hitch the lead horse in that team, then drive it about the circuit. Be careful on the bend, even at a trot that may be difficult'

Maxine did as she was bidden. Armand watched on stoically. She extracted the lead horse with dexterity, walked a short circuit and returned him to reset his tack. At one moment, the cheeky devil thought to offer her some nonsense, but she quickly imposed her will. She set herself on the postillions seat, extracted the whip from its holster and drew the wagon away with care. Then all at once she let loose the whip and careered about at such a breakneck speed, I thought her the reincarnation of an ancient charioteer.

She climbed down with a grin. 'Will that suffice Monsieur?'

'Until we're set upon by bandits.' Armand said soberly.

'Pardon Monsieur?'

'Then I'll expect you to drive that fast, ring the alarm and fend off intruders with the whip. Are you ready for that?'

'I'll fend with two whips if Madame tends the bell Monsieur.'

I smiled. Armand glanced to warn the smile off my face and then looked back at Maxine.

'Yes, that's amusing Maxine. But if we meet such a moment in earnest, I expect all in this company, yourself and *even* my musician to lay down their life to protect the most important person.'

'Madame Capulet?'

'Before any other. Are you ready for that?'

By the sober glint in his big blue eyes, there was no doubt of the question's sincerity.

Maxine frowned, realising her new master would brook no murkiness in her reply.

'In truth Monsieur ... I don't know. I've never had to do so. I hope that I can.'

He pressed a thoughtful smile. 'Good enough. You can drive the wagon Maxi ... What do your brothers call you?'

'Cat when they love me. Max when they don't care. Cunt when they hate me.'

His eyes narrowed as he frowned. 'Well you'll never hear the latter from me. Don't ever let me hear you say it again.'

Her expression was fretful. She feared she had miscalculated. 'No Monsieur. Please pardon my mouth. I just meant to –'

'I know. But vulgar talk doesn't impress me. Does it Marcel?'

'No Chevalier.' I tilted my eyes to Heaven.

'However, daughter of an ostler, handling that team like the sister of Judah Ben Hur did impress me.'

'The big sister. Thank you Monsieur.'

'And so, *Max*.' She smiled to hear it. 'Tell madame you asked permission to drive and I have agreed. But don't discuss the latter part of our conversation. Is that understood?'

She hesitated for a moment. Armand watched her carefully. 'I won't *offer* that information Monsieur. But if madame asks directly, I must be honest.'

'Of course Maxine. And well said. Now you're dismissed.'

She curtsied and turned to go.

'Oh and Max?'

'Yes Monsieur.'

'If we were attacked and you needed that whip ... cracking it well above the backs of a team is *not* what you need to practise.'

'Set me a task Monsieur. I'll get it done.'

'To become accurate, practise splitting leaves on shrubs.'

I widened my eyes in mock disbelief.

'Will bandits come at us armed with branches Chevalier?'

Maxine repressed her smile. Armand shook his head dismissively.

'However they come armed, you rogue, that whip gives my wife's closest guardian the reach on them.'

'Yes Chevalier.'

'Max, you don't have to hit right on the mark. But if you aim for the face of rider or horse –'

'Oh!' I spat, blinking in mock-horror. 'That sounds violent.'

'I hope the bandits think so.' Armand replied. 'When you practice Max, nominate your targets and vary the distance. Smaller and smaller leaves 'til you can split one the size of a thumbnail.'

'I'll practise Monsieur.'

Armand's heavy hand settled on my shoulder.

'I may enlist this buffoon to hold the branches while you do.'

That conference occurred just before we left the safety of Lyon. It was clear the former wetnurse had hidden talents. Yes, Maxine may have been less educated than her younger mistress, but she seemed more practical in the troubling ways of the world. And so there I was on the she-mule, about to learn more for myself.

I spurred the jennet on to draw alongside yet remained out of sight for a moment. The nearside coverlets were lowered. I assumed Armand lay resting within, perhaps asleep. In anticipation of making a good show, I lifted my left foot up and over to cross my knees in the saddle, turning my hips toward the wagon. Dropping the rein over my knee, I swung my lute from my back to play.

Then, like a nervous groom before the bedchamber, I changed my mind, slung it back, swung to sit rearward and decided to hum instead. Cupid's Balls! I simply intended to offer warning of my approach, appear more engaging and set a pleasant mood. I even considered myself practised at setting the perfect tone for flirtatious encounters. In truth, however, I was more used to setting it for others. So far in my own romantic encounters, most approaches had been made to me rather than by me, usually after a fond doter watched me sing and play. And so in such cases, the tone had already been set without much consideration. This time, not only did I have to do it for myself and with forethought, I found I couldn't decide what to do! Perhaps that was because, for the first time in my life, I hoped to affect a woman who may represent more than a fleeting interest to me.

I knew Maxine wouldn't be alone. Armand and Ilaria were settled in the wagon too. Yes, they had ridden out together when we departed. Yes, that was romantic. But as soon as we fell from view of the chateau, they halted. Caspar wheeled and dismounted, drew the lovely bride down, then assisted her handsome invalid from the saddle. I noticed Ilaria frowned affectionately as he did so, moved by the giant warrior's care.

Once aboard, coaxed by Ilaria, Armand agreed to lie on the sumptuous day bed. From her pleased reaction to make him comply, I suspected it was the first command of that nature Ilaria had managed to impose on her new husband. With the wagon's coverlets open, I saw it all happen from a distance until Maxine scampered through to puff pillows and draw the coverlets down.

As the last coverlet shut, while Ilaria helped Armand recline in comfort, the look of happiness they shared made me envious. Moreover sweet friends I confess, so did its promise of permanence. I began to feel that I wanted that kind of permanence in my own life. And so I began to hum, not sing, as I urged the jennet forward.

I hoped to discover Maxine seated alone. Given Armand and

Ilaria had exhausted each other the night before, I assumed after he lay down to rest she would have fallen straight into his arms and still be sleeping beside him. My hope rose as I breasted the front of the wagon and I caught sight of Maxine from the corner of my eye. Then nudging further ... I saw our new mistress seated beside her! And to my great surprise, Ilaria was driving!

Sometime after Armand retired, Ilaria had quietly re-emerged to join Maxine. She had also insisted, against a case of urgent future need, that Maxine instruct her how to drive a team. By the time I made my entrance, she was settled into the task.

Instead of driving, Maxine fussed at the side of Ilaria's regal new headpiece with rolls of fine fabric intertwined over braids. The Angel of Lyon was a married woman now. Unless it was by accident, we'd no longer see her hair worn loose or heavily exposed like an unmarried demoiselle. Yes, that made me a little sad.

Yet I swear by every sweet angel that sings in Heaven, the change suited her. Suddenly she looked more mature and imposing. Oh yes, she still looked elegant. But it reminded me of the day I first saw Armand after his ascension, clad in his suit of bright steel – no longer a follower but a man to follow. Ilaria was emerging with that same quality.

My humming caught their attention as I emerged. Ilaria leaned forward, glancing in my direction

'If you're hoping to linger –' she began.

'Thank you for the invitation Madame.'

'You know full well I was going to tell you to –'

'Play something festive? Very well Madame. What would you like to hear?'

'Hush your tone. Armand is sleeping.'

'Then' I hushed loudly 'I'll play something restive?'

'Hmm. Perhaps something soothing may keep him settled.'

'I have a hypnotic repertoire that will ensure it.'

'Oh very well.' Then suddenly she started and her whisper became a hiss. 'Rascal! What are you doing?'

I had lifted the jennet's reins to tether them and was reaching to climb aboard.

'Soft music calls for my harp Madame. Too delicate to play aboard this bumpy beast.'

'Delicate?' she mocked. 'You?'

My eyes met Maxine's. She pressed her lips to resist a smile.

'Maxine don't you *dare* smile.' Ilaria hissed in a mock-whisper.

'No Madame.'

Ilaria glared at me again. 'Oh yes, very well. Just make no sudden sound that might –'

With no warning at all the she-devil farted loudly! No, not Ilaria, the blasted she-mule!

'Dear mercy that's unpleasant!' Ilaria whispered with heat.

'Give her a moment Madame, she's fond of the harp. It has a way of settling her ...'

'Yes, yes you rascal, just play.'

I tethered the beast and climbed aboard, settling with a smile. Ilaria rolled her eyes, but just as she did so the lead horse skittered and drew her attention. I snuck a smile at Maxine. For the love of folly she smiled back at me!

'I heard that beast.' groaned a sleepy voice behind us.

Ilaria pouted and glared, damning me for a troublemaker.

'Fortunately you can't *smell* her Chevalier.' I said.

'Armand my heart, you must rest.' She glared again. 'Oh rascal I knew you were trouble the moment –'

'It's alright angel. I'm well rested. Let him stay and play. However I do feel a little –'

'A little what my love?'

'Well ... a little *thirsty*. And a little *sore* here and there from laying on this ... ahhh!'

Ilaria's eyes filled with alarm. She began to lift.

'Don't trouble yourself Madame.' urged Maxine. 'I can attend to the master.'

Maxine turned briskly to whip the coverlets apart. I sat mesmerised. It was only the second time I'd heard her speak and her voice was as sweet as warm honey. Her tone was deeper than Ilaria's, with a working woman's breathy husk to it. Armand lifted to peek through the opening.

'Oh angel that's impressive. I didn't know you could drive.'

'Maxine's my tutor. Lay back and relax my heart. She'll take very good care of you. Now's our chance to let her make a start.'

As Maxine began to fuss behind us, she promised to offer some drink forward to us. That sounded wonderful to me, at first. Our wait for it however became extended as Maxine became distracted by her need to tend to her handsome new master.

Then it began.

First there was a great deal fluffing of pillows and rearrangement of cushioning. Such things require much fluffing and rearranging of course. Then he let out another groan of discomfort, as he lifted to offer her more access to the soft furnishings under him. Maxine, as former wet nurses do, then demonstrated her great skill in soothing every manner of hurt that might ail an infant, child or childlike adult. In just moments, from a secretive little hide-safe in her skirts, she produced a balm for muscular pain, proudly announcing it was her *own* concoction.

Then she produced a vial of exotic oil. Yet before she set to applying it, Maxine leaned between Ilaria and myself, offering it to our noses to sample.

'An elder nurse put me on to this oil Madame. It's from Cairo.'

'Dear mercy Maxine what a gorgeous aroma. That's Heavenly.'

'Infants can be pungent. And their teeth can be brutal.'

With my hands occupied with plucking and strumming, she held it under my nose.

'Mmm.' I muttered sharing another glance. 'Enticing.'

She offered it to Ilaria again. 'It's very expensive. But your aunt took one sniff and agreed to purchase a generous quantity. I used it every day to soothe my nipples.'

'That's a shame you had to go to such expense.' I said.

'Oh I felt it was well worth it.' said Maxine.

'For no cost at all I'd have gladly soothed your nipples every –'

Behind us Armand burst into a fit of laughter then groaned.

'Marcel for pity's sake don't make me laugh!' he cried.

'Imbecile!' spat Ilaria glaring yet again. 'Mind your music!'

Amid the confusion, Maxine flashed me another flit of a smile.

'Yes Madame.' I said soberly yet repressing the want to laugh.

Oh sweet friends, that was the first moment of fun the four of us ever shared. I'll never forget it for as long as I hope to live. Dear Heaven, why can't life just be full of such moments? And I was well pleased with the result of my first flit of conversation with Maxine. I made her smile again. Perhaps she had some nonsense in her after all.

Moments later, I became far less certain of my progress and wondered how much of an impact I had made. Maxine had turned to respond to Armand's discomfort, of course. A moment later still, with only a crack between the shielding coverlets for Ilaria and I to spy through, behind us we heard the start of an alarming sequel.

'Oh no Monsieur!' cried the voice I liked so well. 'Show me where that hurt you.'

It sounded a little too nurturing for my liking. Ilaria's brows lifted, ears pricking at the ginger tone, as if Maxine cooed to a child. One moment later and her new close server quietly insisted, not that *he* remove, but that her new master sit up and be still while *she* removed his upper garments! I saw Ilaria's eyes widen.

Then we heard Maxine declare that she must, upon the *surgeon's orders* no less, help him lie back so she could rub her concoction onto his wounds. All at once I wished I had a brace of injuries too.

'First … I'll apply my special balm to your rib and chest.'

'Hmm.' his drowsy voice murmured. 'What are you doing?'

'Just warming my hands master. Just lay still and relax. There now you see … we're ready.'

'Ah that's better.' Armand *groaned*. 'Sweet suffering Max, your hands *are* warm. Mmm that feels nice.'

Beside me a frown was creasing Ilaria's brow as a pout pushed forward on her lips.

'Now Monsieur…' she said hypnotically 'before I massage the muscles I'll dose them with my sweet smelling oil.'

'That sounds pleasant.' Armand sighed.

Ilaria glanced at me, tilting her eyes to Heaven. Despite my own pangs of jealousy, I found hers too entertaining not to smile at.

Then from behind the coverlets, it began in earnest!

Manly groans and sighs of content began to rise, initially in quick spurts, then more elongated. I attempted to hum and play as if nothing out of the ordinary was occurring. Yet the sound of deepening comfort that continued behind us caused Ilaria to knit her brows more and more and ever more firmly.

I glanced and glanced again. With every sound Ilaria became more vexed by her awkward predicament. Then to add to her chagrin, as if tempting an infant to sleep, Maxine began to shush and cluck and coo at her mistress's pliable husband. It blended so harmoniously with his sighs and moans. Cupid's Balls! I hadn't heard anything like it since I worked at the cat house!

Ilaria glanced at me ever more frequently with growing impatience. Groans of content continued behind us. Finally, I raised my brows to suggest I also felt far *too* much comfort was being indulged behind the coverlets. However, the next exchange between healer and patient brought our young mistress to the limit of her patience.

'Now Monsieur I've done your chest, your rib ... yet the Surgeon said you had another hurt. Where is that?'

Green eyes beside me leapt open wide. I pressed my lips hard to hold back a desperate want to burst into laughter. We both knew exactly where that hurt was!

'It's on my thigh Max. But be gentle there. It's still very –'

'Maxine!' Ilaria blurted in panic.

'Yes Madame?' Maxine's muted voice said so innocently.

'I think that I've had enough driving for today.'

'Oh? Yes Madame. As soon as I apply some balm and oil to –'

'Perhaps Maxine, as with the driving I should learn to perform that task myself.'

'Yes Madame. If Master Marcel can tend to the driving while I demonstrate –'

'That won't be necessary. I'm sure I can manage alone. Just leave your potions. Come forward please and take the reins.'

Unwilling to await her compliance, the flighty Ilaria ran the stout reins under my thigh and over. She turned in haste and ushered her close server out. I glanced inside as one went back and the other came forward. Although there was ample room to lay side by side, Ilaria drew close and up onto her side, draping an arm over Armand.

It didn't appear as if she intended to continue Maxine's treatment. Yet a look of contentment came over them both. I had to admit, it made me envious again. Moments later, Cleopatra summoned her handmaiden one last time to help draw the coverlets for *shade*.

As the handmaiden scrambled back to comply, she offered me the reins again. With that task complete, the high priestess expelled her from the inner sanctum. Looking a trifle vexed, Maxine settled on the wooden seat, regathering the reins as I glanced back inside. The rearmost coverlet was lowering discreetly, reducing, then blocking our view of the rearguard in the distance. I turned to glance at Maxine and looked ahead.

Suddenly Ilaria's head appeared between us.

'Until further notice Maxine, I'll attend to my husband's recuperation in person.'

'Yes Madame.' she replied a little testily.

'And Maxine.'

'Yes Madame?'

'After I shut this coverlet, no matter what sounds emerge from within you will *both* keep your eyes forward.'

'Oh High Priestess of Healing.' I said. 'We'll be far too busy *listening* to watch!' My impertinence distracted Maxine's poor mood.

'You rascal, shall be too busy playing loudly to mask whatever may be listened to.'

'Yes Madame.' I muttered.

To my very great relief, both women smiled.

Ilaria's head disappeared and the coverlet snapped shut. I thought in silence for a moment. All-in-all I felt that so far, on the first day of our first journey together, our extended ensemble was off to a rather wonderful start. Maxine and I exchanged a knowing look.

Taking Ilaria's parting quip as my cue, I decided it was time to transform back into a musician. Cheekily cocking one brow, I handed Maxine the reins. Then in one practised movement, I drew my lute from my back and slid across the board to offer her more space to command the beasts. For punctuation, I cocked my hat.

Maxine smiled, snapping the long leather lightly against a pair of shining black rumps. Ilaria had named them Velvet and Silk. The thought made me smile as I watched their gait settle under her firm hand. I leaned against the coverage frame for comfort and set to work. Tuning for a moment, plucking each string, I hummed a pitch melody.

Then, with an air of concentration, I began to strum and sing a languid tune. My companion watched on with a sheepish smile but appeared more thoughtful. I glanced back intermittently to ensure the smile remained and catch glimpses of her pretty face and pleasing form. It was enough to make her blush a little as she watched the road.

All at once I realised, life was better at that moment than I had known for some time, perhaps better than ever. How it had all happened seemed to be a blur. Then a hazy thought rose in my mind.

If this was where fate wanted to take me?
For now at least it was welcome to do so.

That was to prove a fated thought. For all too soon, some of us would feel much less welcome than others.

Chapter 4 Pure Ambition

We expected to arrive at our destination well before sunset. There we would meet the first of many Capulet relations and watch the newlyweds attempt to charm them. Most on the visitation list would reside on our side of the alps of course. Thereafter, we would cross the alpine trail to the Italian plains and be bound for Verona. But as I said at our start together, the story of my time among the Capulets is also a tale of fate.

Fate's most defining tool of course is *timing*. I know sweet friends, many times you'll have felt its impact on the path of your own lives. And so as fate would have it, on the very same day we left Lyon and began adjusting to our new lives together, another mighty famille were gathering in Lyon with very great haste.

And though the roots of this famille began elsewhere, first in the north, then the far south, they had shifted the seat of their power to Lyon two years earlier in anticipation of a bold new future. As a result, though fabulously wealthy and influential, their faction and the House of Capulet had no shared history at that time.

In the lull after the battle of Formigny, every member of that faction was summoned to this soiree. Yes, Armand knew he wouldn't be recalled until the next season. But some in that other famille were not so fortunate. To ensure the war was seen to its very end, there was still some dangerous work to be done. And for those hungry powerbrokers, the advantage to be gained by being conspicuous at its end, was considered an opportunity not to be missed.

Therefore, for some in attendance, it would still be a feast of farewell before duty returned them to danger. But three in attendance, including their charismatic leader, were destined to depart in a *different* direction. War and the confusion that follows in its wake, can cause the most experienced leaders to lose their heads and flounder on the path to their future. Yet the leader of their mighty faction was keeping her head, which was why she had called the unexpected assembly.

Despite her youth, fear of her power was the reason every invitee – no matter how senior they stood in the famille or how far away they resided – ensured prompt attendance. For this wasn't a call to arms for the mighty House of Paris, it was a call to affluence. And if their new premiere dame had her way, that gathering would ensure that despite any cost the war may inflict, their futures would not only remain secure, but would grow beyond all imagining.

The elegant cavalcade arrived in grand style at *Hôtel Nobel* upon the Rue Juiverie to embrace and kiss and chatter in anticipation. No, this particular establishment in Lyon – situated on the Jewish way close enough to the livestock market to be assailed by its odour – wasn't the typical locale an elite Christian faction would gather at. But their host was a merchant of exceptional influence.

His name was Auguste Malakai Nobel and he was a Rhadanite Jew and longtime rival to Ilaria's own famille. The earlier call to arms against England had spurred an urgency in Sieur Nobel to parley with the leaders of that faction, who had so recently shifted to Lyon. He sent a discreet message simply stating he wished to discuss a *proposal*.

Having matured his negotiations with their upper echelon, this lull presented an opportunity to parley with their entire flock before many were scattered again. A new plan had been conceived that would alter their future. Yet before it was set in motion, Nobel and their new leader had to ensure every player understood the nature of the plan and pledged support to it.

Finally, the faction members had arrived and were ranged before him in the eye-catching circular reception chamber of his vast home. To Auguste Nobel, the House of Paris represented the personification of French prestige and power. A glance in any direction over their assembly was met with a display of opulent couture, stylish coiffure and dazzling adornments.

Silk, damask, brocade, velvet, fur and leather were on decadent display in hues of scarlet, amber, blue and emerald. All were shimmering with gold or shining with silver accents. Buckles and brooches were set off with diamonds, rubies, onyx and sapphires. It was as if the stores of every merchant from several citadels had been emptied in a breathtaking effort to adorn each member of the glamorous flock before him.

All that was missing were ermine and purple. Yet even those present – as glamorous and ambitious as they were – knew better than to flout the apparel laws that prohibited wearing that rare fur and tint, which were restricted for use only by anointed nobility. Oh yes, the Italian elite were rumoured to flout such rules with abandon in almost every citadel. The elite of France were not yet so flagrant.

And yes, I hear you ask, '*How could a musical ninny such as you know any of the details from that auspicious and secretive gathering?*' Let me confirm, I was *not* in attendance. At that time I was busy flirting with Cleopatra's handmaiden. Over the years, however, intimate details were offered in pieces to me by two of the most important attendees who the Capulets came to know.

One was the leader herself. The other was her little brother, Astor. Yet before you meet them I must offer a stern warning. There could not be a more stark difference between the moral fabric of those who led the House of Paris and the newlywed Capulets.

At that time, little brother Astor was just twelve years old. Six months before, he began service as junior squire to a Scottish Knight. Indeed when we arrived in Saint-Lô before the great battle, Astor was there with his master who rode in the Breton Cavalry with Armand. As far as I know, the pair never met. Yet I'm sure they must have seen each other. Nor did Astor's master survive that vicious battle.

And so, Squire Astor de Paris needed a new mentor. For safety, he was assigned to serve his big sister's new husband Reynard. You may recall that if possible, a squire shouldn't be mentored by his kin, so that arrangement was intended to be temporary. Temporary or not however, when their soiree was done, Astor would be returning to the fight under the command of his recently acquired, and much elder, brother-in-law.

Four days before this gathering, Astor's big sister was in Loches, attending to urgent business with a woman she hoped would become a sponsor to her ambitions, her Majesty Queen Marie. The young leader revealed the tantalising plan she devised with Nobel to radically alter her people's path towards a new source of wealth.

If successful, it also promised to generate a flow of riches to France that the King and Queen wouldn't wish to be excluded from. And so, her Majesty listened with interest to every detail. She understood, of course, that whether one was a monarch considering support for an enterprise that may grow a kingdom's wealth, or an elite investor seeking to enrich themselves, the real wager was laid upon the people who intend to lead the venture.

Such leaders must be the kind who have the capacity and will to see ambitious plans through, not just be dreamers excited by vision itself. In that case, Queen Marie felt she knew the potential to be worth the risk. After revealing the scope and scale of her vision, the young woman also revealed where she planned to travel to begin its implementation.

But those two extraordinary women weren't alone during their secret conference. Listening distractedly was a third party who, due to recent disappointments experienced during the war, and knowing the main flurry of it was done, felt at a loose end. And so for the most part they paid little attention. But when travel was discussed, particularly when the first destination was revealed, she listened more closely.

That topic had ignited a sudden expression of interest. The listener revealed her hope to travel in that direction, even to escape the boundaries of France altogether, at least for a time. It was the first spark of interest her Majesty had seen in this person for some weeks. Therefore, as a personal favour, Queen Marie asked the young matriarch to consider taking them along.

'You're close in age Yolanthe.' said the Queen to the Duchess. 'I'm sure you'd make wonderful companions.'

'I'm happy to agree your Majesty. But you do understand, I leave at once for Lyon.'

'Of course. Time and war wait for no man.'

'Or woman.' said the Duchess.

'Amen. I'm sure this one needs no time to prepare.'

The Duchess glanced at the young woman in question.

'I'm glad to hear it. I have no time to waste.'

The bluntness of that reply drew a royal look of consternation. 'God speed you then Duchess. I wish you the greatest fortune in your endeavours.'

'Now *our* endeavours Highness.'

'Indeed.' said the Queen considering her suitor.

'Though I hope to convince our people, luck will have little to do with our success.'

'Dear, you remind me of myself at your age.'

'Then I'm greatly flattered.'

'Don't be. At the very beginning I was a naive imbecile.'

The Queen stared soberly. The Duchess frowned in thought.

'Then perhaps your Highness, given I'll not have a chance to return 'til the end of the season, may I ask if you have any parting advice for a budding matriarch.'

'Budding? Well, since you're bold enough to ask. Yes I do.'

'Any scrap would profit me.'

'You're driven and blunt Yolanthe. Bravo. So was I at your age, *when* it was needed.'

'You think me too bold and too blunt?'

'Be nothing less, my dear. But here at your start, be careful how much you show it, and when, and to whom. Those who know you already are one thing. But from this moment on, to enlist more support from the quality of allies your venture will require, in the field you aspire to, in the sophisticated territory you intend to penetrate?'

'It does sound ambitious.'

'It is ambitious. That's what I like about it and yourself. But to many potent suitors, particularly potent *male* suitors, if you can't present a more *convivial* demeanour to them, you may fail to even draw their attention let alone their interest.'

'I see.' Yolanthe said hesitantly.

'I know you don't *yet* think so. But most of your important dealings so far have been confined to those within your own faction.'

'That's very true.'

'And I know you understand that information is power.'

'Of course.'

'For this enterprise to succeed, you'll need to gather a great deal more information from sources well beyond your faction dear. And in my experience, people offer far more vital information to those they don't suspect are very capable of using it.'

Yolanthe blinked in surprise for a moment as she digested her grave mentor's full meaning.

'You suggest I cultivate a façade of *less* capability?'

The hint of a smile played on her Majesty's lips. Her brows lifted as she drew a blossom from an arrangement of early hollyhocks.

'Or disinterest. Whichever suits the occasion.'

'To *disguise* my capability.'

'Overt conviviality suggests overt *social* interest rather than alert *political* interest.' The eyes of her pupil widened in comprehension. 'Use the mask when it's needed until the tactic's worn out its use. After I became queen, too many knew me too well. Its value was spent. However when I first began, I was a stranger to most, sifting among new acquaintances, deciding whom to align with or disregard.'

'That sounds familiar.'

'Like yourself at the start, I was candid and blunt by nature. Upon similar advisement however, I practised being convivial, amusing, even flirtatious. I even began to flit my lashes and call everyone darling. The more I did so, the more who approached, came with their guard lowered.'

'That was the first victory, putting them at ease.'

'Whenever I hoped to draw information on a well-guarded subject of importance, I pleaded deep ignorance.'

'While under it all, you soaked up information like a sponge?'

'And sifted it carefully. One counsellor taught me a clever trick of investigation.'

'I'd love to know it.'

'And so, you shall. Rather than ask a direct question about an issue you wish to know, declare a *misguided* statement about it.'

'To what purpose?

'Many will feel instantly compelled to correct your error and reveal what you sought to discover.'

'Is that true?'

'Oh yes. Direct questions cause most to be more guarded. Yet misguided statements trigger that instinct in almost everyone.'

'Why that's ... extraordinary.'

'Isn't it? Behind a convivial façade I still cultivated my strength and resolve. I didn't hesitate to wield either if needed. However, back then, I had to wield my power more discreetly.'

'None would celebrate discretion as a strength of mine.'

'Not yet perhaps. But for one such as yourself, who assumes power at a young age, its natural in the face of elder peers to feel the need to compensate with blunt shows of strength.'

Her Majesty stared to suggest how undeniably the description fit her protégé.

'That does sound like me. Recently, I've resorted to hard language to put some in their place. Men do it so often with instant results. I've found that tactic very satisfying.'

'I understand that impulse Yolanthe. But if left unchecked, all such behaviour can form poor habits that become *predictable*.'

'To me predictability feels like armour I can depend on.'

'I understand that too. But *unbending* predictability denies the use of more potent tools that require more subtlety, yes, but enhance the element of surprise.'

'Subtlety and surprise.' she echoed, as if considering apparel she felt sure wouldn't fit or flatter.

'Two potent tools an elite woman should have at her disposal.'

'Til now I've relied on being seen as a bold blunt instrument.'

'Who asks bold blunt questions.' The queen considered her. 'I knew another bold blunt woman once. She learned to strike a potent balance. When approached by new people, she had a way of being devilishly hard to predict. She approached all with a signature style of what I can only describe as *confronting conviviality*.'

'That sounds eccentric.'

'It combined a provocative sense of humour with a blunt sense of social confrontation and rather bald flirtatiousness.'

'That sounds erratic.'

'And that's how she appeared. Not to me of course. I knew Esmeralda was playing her part. But she used them all in a kind of swirling flurry. It kept new approaches, male and female, quite off balance, until she felt settled in her dealings with them.'

'That sounds dangerous. Did she survive her volatile efforts?'

'She did. And enjoyed spectacular success. Esmeralda is Portuguese, but now lives in Italy now as prima donna to one of their most powerful factions.'

'She sounds exciting.'

'Back then, I thought she was very exciting. For myself as a princess, I couldn't emulate such extreme behaviour, nor did I wish to. Over time, her method cultivated a reputation of her being so volatile, very few felt it worth the risk to earn her displeasure.'

'I like the sound of that.'

'I thought you might. And now she's matured, whenever her very intimidating husband is absent, that reputation still keeps her safe from unsolicited approaches.'

'Ah, and so you suggest that, here at my beginning, I should consider my ending?'

The queen raised questioning brows to suggest confirmation.

'Finally dear, remember there's a difference between *deception* and *dissembling*. I rarely needed to lie. But if I felt I must, for the genuine safety of our kingdom or my famille, then I did so. But I confessed to God immediately thereafter and did hard penance for it.'

'I understand. I'll take it all under advisement your Majesty.'

'Dear, call me Marie.'

Yolanthe's expression betrayed her surprise. Their onlooker arched a brow to hear the queen offer such a concession.

'Only if you –' the young duchess stuttered. 'If you insist. '

'I do dear. Say it now, then it won't be a lie when you reveal to others that you enjoy the privilege to do so.'

'Thank you ... *Marie*. I'm greatly honoured.'

'Tush, not at all. I'm extending that privilege to use as a tool. One of your stature must be able to boast of her intimacy with more potent people. Sometimes to impress and sometimes to reassure. Sometimes to warn or threaten.'

'I have your permission to take it that far?'

'If you must but exercise discretion or I'll revoke the privilege.'

'I will your ... Marie. Yes of course.'

'I want the women I sponsor abroad to be a stunning success. They must be given the means to achieve that success.'

'I'm heartened to feel I have your support.'

'You do. Now, take this one and go. Return when you've enlarged both our fortunes.'

'Thank you, Marie. I won't let you down.'

'Oh yes and darling? Give my fondest regards to your very handsome husband.'

Yolanthe's eyes flitted in a wince of frustration at both the comment and its heartfelt tone. She hoped that wasn't visible to her sponsor and tried to dissemble it as she curtsied deeply, pressing her lips in obedience to the offered hand.

'Oh no, darling.'

The genuflecting duchess blinked in confusion.

'Your Maj ... Marie?'

'I gave you permission to use my name.'

'Yes. And I'm very –'

'When you pay homage, that also gives you permission to look your Queen in the eye. Show that you understand, Duchess de Paris. Look up at me.'

Never being one who required encouragement to activate for her own benefit, her blue eyes lifted, blazing with the fire of pure ambition.

'That's better dear. From this moment on, unless your knee bends for an emperor or empress, king, queen or his Holiness himself, then lower your eyes for no one.'

'I won't Marie. Thank you for your guidance.'

'Thank me by returning with news of your success. Now go bold woman, you're dismissed. Take your new companion along and show the world who we are.'

Yolanthe lifted and turned with the grace of a swan then stalked on like a prowling lioness. Her new guest followed quietly in her wake and they left the Royal Chateau together.

That was four days before the duet joined the gathering of Yolanthe's faction at the home of Sieur Auguste Nobel in Lyon. Her younger brother Astor was there, but would be returning back to the discomfort of war. However, the duchess and Auguste Nobel were set to depart the next morning with her new companion, planning to travel far from the war and in opulent luxury.

Before that the Duchess and Nobel would reveal their ambitious plan to her faction.

As Yolanthe stood at the head of their glittering assembly, she reached for the arm of her husband, Duke Reynard. They had been married for a year. They chatted to Nobel and introduced him to any who dared to approach. Yolanthe wanted to ensure that all in her flock understood the merchant was held in high esteem and enjoyed her great favour. She had also decided to use the occasion to practise offering a more convivial façade.

Yes, her effusive display felt awkward and lacked a sense of balance at that early stage. Yet she was determined to master the use of all the tools her royal mentor suggested. Her Majesty had also said, that those who already knew her were a different story. So despite that effort the duchess was taking to practise new behaviours, her flock were about to be treated to a serving of the bold blunt instrument they'd already learned to fear. Indeed, that soiree was perhaps the last time that version of Yolanthe de Paris was publicly displayed before she transformed into the incarnation we encountered thereafter.

She had been chosen to lead just two years before, after the retirement of her Uncle Alain. He had led the faction after her grandmother, who received control from their founding couple. Yolanthe was nineteen and unmarried when chosen as premiere dame, the youngest to date. On the eve of her great enterprise, she had recently turned twenty-one.

And though young and unwed when chosen, to judge by the impact she'd had so far, the new leader's capability appeared to validate the wisdom of what all referred to as their *House Rules*. Often simply referred to as *the Rules*, they formed the legal framework created by their founders, Viscount Bertrand and Viscountess Hilda de Paris.

Bertrand was a young crusader who had returned from the holy war to marry a barefoot, flame-haired shepherdess. Hilda lived independently on the first estate he gained in return for his war service. A quiet crusader and a barefoot shepherdess may seem an unlikely match. But the familial empire they forged over just three generations, appeared to be lasting and expanding. And thanks to their foresight with the creation of their House Rules, it was becoming infinitely stronger.

For among its important tenets of guidance, the Rules clearly stipulated the manner in which a new leader may be chosen. They allowed for the ascension of any blood male or female, married or not, aged from seventeen. They also stipulated, any leader who lived to forty years *must* retire. That ensured a wise elder counsel accumulated around each new leader. So far, strict adherence to the Rules had ensured only the cream of their famille rose to lead them. When I heard more of the dark sordid history behind the turbulent rise of Bertrand, Hilda and the House of Paris, I confess I found it shocking. As tantalising as that deeper history is however, we have scant time to offer more here. Yet for any who would dare to know more of that hedonistic tale of power, passion, betrayal and revenge, I created a special work to satisfy them:

The Untold Morsels of the History of Capulet and de Paris.

For safety however, I suggest you read these morsels alone and by candlelight! Yet I digress. We were discussing their current leader. And I must draw you a clear picture of this impacting woman.

I know Yolanthe de Paris was born under the sign of Sagittarius. In time, you'll agree that's hardly surprising. The young duchess was tall but not towering. At a glance, she cut a commanding physical figure: lankish, buxom and with a head of lustrous carotene hair. Any who saw the rare sight of her hair worn free, might report that she appeared like a lioness who had plucked her lover's mane to wear as a trophy.

At the time of the gathering in Lyon, many would have described her face, not yet so heavily prepared with powder, rouge or gloss, as a little plain-featured. The exception, as always, were her striking blue eyes that contrasted so starkly against that fiery frame of hair. Among her faction, both traits were admired as hallmarks of her descent from the wild shepherdess.

She had previously cultivated the more blunt aspects of her demeanour, yes. But she also supported them with a less sophisticated approach to her appearance. That all began to change, but at the start of her reign, Yolanthe had felt that simplicity was a source of strength, and revelled in the thought that many among her flock of preening relations, considered her to be rather plain.

Those meeting her for the first time often whispered that she appeared more like a potential monastic than a potent matriarch. Even a smattering of girlish freckles were still visible on her face and shoulders. However, after that meeting, the arts of enhancement began to lend an alabaster appearance to every visible inch. Once her brows were plucked to perfection and lashes adorned, her already striking eyes appeared even more distinct and engaging.

And no matter how the young duchess might have appeared at that time, her charisma, and much there was to it, instantly affected all those who met her. I feel it sprang primarily from her ability to speak with a mixture of fearless candour and sharp intelligence whenever the need arose. That combination led her on with utter confidence. And even at rest, her eyes appeared alert, constantly suggesting the presence of calculation and a lively intellect.

But when Yolanthe's eyes lit up with real passion, they shone with a driven sense of purpose. Something of the fanatic rose in her at such moments. It would be easy to imagine a befuddled executioner attempting to burn Yolanthe at the stake, only to scratch his head at her ability to survive without a mark. I can see her there, casually dismissing her bonds, emerging through flame as if self-belief were all she needed to defeat condemnation.

Alright, enough. Yet let me add one final thing before we allow Duchess de Pravity to meddle in our lives. For one such as I, who have stood witness when Yolanthe de Paris was confronted by threats or danger, in all sincerity I say this – *Heaven help the dull bastard that may seek to harm that woman or any she holds dear.* For when Yolanthe is risen to unbridled anger, she's a force majeure, possessed of the ability to rail like a goddess spitting venom from the height of Mount Olympus.

Standing before the assembly she leaned to kiss her husband who was perhaps twenty years her senior. At that moment Duke Reynard appeared to be her extreme opposite, a handsome, pampered, profligate. Yes, he was a hardened soldier, but he also enjoyed luxury. By that time however, he lacked ambition and was considered a charming sycophant.

Reynard was carefully chosen for Yoli, as her intimates called her, by the powerbrokers of her house. He held an exalted title, but had also surrendered its value completely. The duke was recruited to accept his wife as the power broker, to lend her his title and, as some Italians do, take up *her* name. Finally, while shows of equality between them were tolerated in the public forum, in familial matters of any import, Reynard was expected to remain silent and keep his place.

And though I say at that moment, Yolanthe and Reynard appeared to be opposites, they were alike in one significant respect. They shared an insatiable appetite for one another. Perhaps knowing he controlled nothing in her life made it easier for her to surrender to him in that way. However it came about, like many women, the young duchess found her elder husband to be irresistible.

Oh, I can vouch that Reynard was attractive. If I were a woman, I'd say he had a sensual, smouldering quality. Whenever he was at hand, and they could find time to be together, Yolanthe lusted after him. When he wasn't at hand however, her needs became nomadic. So did his. For they also shared, for the sake of practicality, consent to stray.

However, they were standing together, her lips upon his cheek. Nobel had wandered apart to give directions to his servers. As Yolanthe drew her lips away and Reynard surveyed the assembly, her eyes ran over his handsome profile.

He smiled mischievously.

'That was nice.' he whispered conspiratorially without averting his eyes. 'Are we flirting in front of your people now?'

'Are we?' she whispered, signalling her want to conspire.

'Oh ho. You're in a mood. Are you wet little minx?'

Her eyes widened. The hint of a smile lifted the corner of her lips. 'That's a blunt question.'

'You prefer it that way. And don't answer me now, your flock appears restless.'

She scanned her gathered famille as he turned to enjoy her profile. 'Yes they do. Perhaps we've created enough anticipation.'

'Between ourselves or them?'

'Darling please ask Auguste –'

'Darling?' Their eyes met. 'That's different too. Yoli ... what's come over you tonight?'

'Darling.' She offered a smile. 'Ask Auguste if he's ready.'

'Yes of course *darling*.' He stepped to go, then spun a pirouette and stepped back. 'Oh by the way darling.'

'Yes darling.' She was enjoying the effect her attitudinal adjustments were having on him.

'Since I arrived we've barely had a moment yet ... I must know. What did Marie say?'

His insistence and use of the Queen's fore name so casually made Yoli suspect that *Ren*, as she called him, expected *Marie* to mention him.

'Marie ... told me to address her as *Marie*.'

'At last. Make sure everyone knows it ... darling.'

'And I was instructed to look her in the eye.'

'Tits of Venus!' he hissed excitedly. 'Even better.'

'Hush Ren. Behave!'

'Oh yes, very well. But that's wonderful progress. I knew she'd support you.'

'Did you? She also suggested I be more *convivial*.'

'To me?' He smirked. 'She's a wise and beautiful woman.'

Though Yolanthe rolled her eyes, he sensed something he said had tilted her.

'She also cautioned me not to *lie*.' He smirked again. 'But she sanctioned it in cases of dire urgency, as long as I seek contrition immediately and do hard penance thereafter.'

He muted a spurt of uncontrollable laughter. 'Oh Yoli that's hilarious! Does she understand nothing of the Paris pedigree?'

'I know you do my love.' She stepped closer, leaning her chest against him, grazing her nails along his arm. 'The fact that I control you utterly is testament to it.'

'I'm happy to be under your control. You know I am.' His brows lifted. 'Which makes me mindful to ask little minx, if I'll have the pleasure of your company later?'

'We're leaving tomorrow Ren ... in opposite directions.'

'Yes.' He nipped softly at her cheek.

'We'll not see each other for months.'

Her fingertip reached for his palm.

'Yes.' He nipped again.

'When I drive out with Nobel in the morning –'

'That doesn't sound pleasant.'

'I hope to be struggling to remain awake.'

'That sounds promising.'

'Or to stand without discomfort.'

'Very promising. What about your guest?' He sensed another flit of annoyance.

'Hands off her Ren. She's important and not ready for that.'

'That sounds dull. And what happened to *darling*?'

'I'm sure she'll be ready by the time we return ... darling.'

'That sounds better. Meanwhile you can immerse her more

gently into the world of untethered license.'

'How do you manage to make the sordid sound sensual? I wish you were coming. You know I prefer not to play alone with strangers.'

'We do what we must.'

'Do we?'

'Besides, you enjoy me ravishing you after we've been apart.'

'Until now it's never been more than a week or two.'

'Yes I know.'

'Ren, just promise me ...'

'Anything delicious woman.'

'Promise while I'm away, you won't become *too* attached –'

'Yoli.' he scoffed gently. 'At *my* age I'm far more concerned a wandering wife of *your* age is more vulnerable to forming attach-ments.'

She turned to face him and leaned in a little. She loved the smell of him. They were lost in each other's eyes for a moment as she held a wicked smile in check.

'We do what we must darling. Oh ... and I *must* introduce our new travelling companion to Auguste.'

'You've not introduced them? You arrived before noon.'

'The moment we entered Lyon she requested an escort to go in search of something.'

'What something?'

'She wouldn't say. She tried to appear composed. Yet I knew she was very unsettled. Since she returned she's been pensive and dull.'

'There you see? It's the perfect moment to invite her to –'

'Ren.' she hissed. 'Desist!'

'Yes Yoli.' he said with mock contrition.

Her stern look softened. 'Tonight I'm in the mood to keep you to myself. I'll be far more than you can handle.'

'We'll see.' He searched her face and his expression became sober. 'Yoli, during this absence while we're *both* doing what we must.'

'Yes my love.'

'I hope you don't enjoy doing it too *greatly*.'

Her brows lifted in surprise as she turned. It was the first time she'd heard him sound as if his sexual confidence was shaken.

'Ren what's the matter?'

'I'm not sure. There's something about you tonight. I feel ...'

'Off balance? I hope so. I'm tired of being the jealous one.'

'Have you been jealous? Of whom? I didn't think we got jealous of our distractions. I don't get jealous. And when we're together, we share them on occasion. So how on Earth –'

'I don't like it when a queen sends her *fond* regards to my *very* handsome husband.'

'Oh. I see.'

'Royal bitch. I could have scratched her pretty eyes out.'

'Ah, there's the Yoli we all fear and worship.'

'Now I want to look more closely at her fourteen brats to see if any of them have your –'

'Oh just a *few*.' He pressed a smile. 'Not more than half.'

She shot a hot glance and locked on him fiercely.

'Ren don't tease me when I'm angry. I'll make you pay for it.'

He knew she meant it. It certainly bothered him.

'I don't want that.' He stuttered a nervous laugh. 'I do want to know you'll return from your travels to give yourself back to *me*.'

Yoli pouted girlishly. 'Ren I'll be surrounded by foreigners with no connection to the home I love –'

'Or me!' he quipped.

'Yes.' She frowned. 'No matter how desirable any man I encounter may be –'

He gripped her hand. 'Now I must know if you're wet?'

'Hush. If they choose to stay behind when I leave them, how could my interest be any more than fleeting?'

'Well I'm calmed by that logic. However I won't be calm if I hear you announce from afar you've decided to be absent for *longer*.

'Oh Ren don't be absurd.'

'I've learnt that life has a devilish way of becoming absurd.'

'Now enough. I think Auguste is ready.'

'Yes little minx, here he comes.'

'And yes, darling.'

'Yes, what?'

She leaned close, putting her lips at his ear to whisper, 'I am wet. But before I permit you access to –'

'The gates of Heaven.'

'I must think of a way to hurt you for making me so angry.'

He knew she never made idle threats. He didn't fear she may deny him later as punishment. He did fear what she may do before to right her sense of balance. His little minx was rarely angry at him. Yet when she was, his vanity was the preferred target of her retribution.

Sieur Nobel drew towards them with a smile of anticipation. Astor came along at his side, looking boyish, gorgeous and spoilt. He had his grandfather's deep brown curling hair. And by the features of his face, anyone could tell he was well named for the image of a *hawk*. In just one decade, Astor de Paris would grow into an imposing, muscular young man with an insatiable taste for martial conquest. He would rise to become Count Astor de Paris and stand beside his all-powerful sister to negotiate his betrothal to a daughter of Capulet. That evening however he was still the babe of their famille.

'Astor stay near. I don't want you to miss anything.'

'Yoli what's everyone here for?'

'You'll see little soldier. And when you return to Normandy you must stay close to Ren. He's a very experienced chevalier. Pay him close attention. Obey all his commands.'

'If you say so.'

She glared in mock demand. 'I do.'

Nobel signalled his readiness to begin. Yoli ruffled Astor's thick hair and drove him away with a fond kiss. As she watched him go, her uncharacteristic smile surprised many. Even with that gesture, she was testing the effect of the Queen's counsel. By the looks on faces as she turned and the effect on Reynard so far, her façade of conviviality and spurts of impulsivity were generating an impact.

In the grand circular hall, the chattering died to a sudden whisper. Nobel ascended the dais to stand by the duchess's side. Then came the duke to complete the picture. Profligate or no, Reynard certainly looked his part. And when cued to his role, he filled it with grace and a deep sensual voice to charm them all. Yolanthe's eyes began to gleam.

All stood ready to hear.

What urgent news would their young matriarch announce?

Chapter 5 Dark Secrets

The coverlets were still shut behind us. As I strummed and sang and Maxine drove with her eyes fixed ahead, I had my first chance to consider her more closely. With more than a little knowledge, she had wrapped the rein leathers loosely about her wrists, separated her feet and slipped them from her clogs. As she leaned back to feel the pressure, just as any farm wench might do, the sight of her body filling her grey velvet bodice distracted me.

Her garment was a recently offered hand-me-down from Ilaria, whose travelling cases were all brimming with elegant new couture. The folds of Maxine's scarlet linen skirt were drawn up and draped revealing the shape of her thighs. Yes, she was an appealing young woman. Yet I began to sense that she may know she was.

As distracting as my view of Maxine was however, the sounds we were warned to ignore behind us began to distract us both. In that closeted recess, and despite the surgeon's orders, our warlike master was being roused from his rest. For Maxine, compelled to drive and listen to it as I played, it appeared to be more than a distraction.

Oh yes, at first she attempted to ignore it, keeping her mouth firm and eyes fixed ahead. Soon enough, a smile turned the corner of her lips. Then her glances to me became more frequent. I did my best to remain aloof. Yet every now and again, I flashed her a knowing or antic look. Every time I did so, I felt close to drawing out a grin or giggle. Finally however, any attempt to withhold our amusement was simply too much.

She snickered once. So did I. Her snickering increased. Fearful her reaction would draw unwanted attention from behind, I added voice to my song. That attempt was not just to suffocate Maxine's laughter, but the swelling chorus of smothered sighs and groans which sounded from within the touring boudoir.

Our predicament seemed a preposterous irony. Here was my first chance to sit with Maxine and get to know her better. Instead we were compelled to sit without discussion and get to know the sound of our new mistress reaching her crescendo. Cupid's Balls! And we quickly learned Ilaria's rise to pleasure had a unique signature to it.

From my time in the cat house in Paris, I had heard my fair share of feminine eruptions. In that environment I quickly discovered that most were for show. Yet by that time, I felt able to tell the difference between the feminine sound of pure theatre and pure joy. May all the Saints mock me for a fool but I felt certain that eruption was authentic. And I swear, in my experience to that moment, I'd never heard the like of it before.

Nor, it seemed by her reaction, had Maxine.

Ilaria's rise began in a kind of singing refrain that lifted in short spurts, rising in pitch as it went to be crowned by an elongated howl of pleasure. I barely had the volume to mask her crescendo and felt absurd attempting it. Maxine found my efforts too much, alternating between spitting out bursts of laughter and holding them in! The sight of us before the coverlets and sounds from behind suggested utter mayhem.

It seemed that for two lovers who were novices the night before, that result defied all the logic of intimacy. I wondered if Cicero had a quote to make sense of it. I also wondered how large the instrument of pleasure was. Oh, bite my bare ass yes I did! I'm a man after all. I'd seen him limp of course. No, I'd not seen him otherwise! He was certainly not small though I wouldn't describe him as huge. Yet despite that description just offered, as we listened to the result he was generating, I was no longer certain of what I thought I knew.

And Cupid's Balls on fire! Watching Maxine's eyes respond was as memorable as hearing the eruption itself, which was followed by bursts of muted and shuddering groans. Maxine clapped a hand to her mouth as we heard the aftermath begin, trying to hold in her laughter. It made me want to do the same. We were trapped together in our own silent ecstasy of riotous humour.

Oh yes, my telling of the saucy incident is coming to a close. And perhaps I should reveal, there's an ulterior reason behind offering so much intimate detail of their antics. I promise that will become clear before too much longer. When the shuddering groans began to run down in pitch to the other direction, we felt sure the end was nigh. Despite that hope, Ilaria's decrescendo lingered for more than a minute while the gaps between each fading burst grew longer.

Yes, I know that seems like too much to reveal. Yet I confess, hearing Ilaria made me wonder what sounds Maxine would make in such a moment. Well bite my bare ass on the other side, yes it did! What else would I think at such a moment? Though never before had I harboured such a venal thought so quickly in new company.

And even more truth be told, it made me wonder what Maxine may think of the sounds I might make? For Armand's part, we certainly heard grunts of effort and groans of pleasure, though more muted. Maxine flinched and glanced every time he sounded one or the other, then pressed hard to stifle her smiles.

Yet of all the details I feel shy to confess, I also noticed that despite Ilaria's memorable performance, we heard no sound to suggest Armand had reached a crescendo himself. At least it validated the notion they were still novices, albeit noisy novices. Perhaps injury, fatigue, abashment or even a focus on pleasing his new bride had affected him.

No, I never asked him to explain it! I knew from my own intimate experiences, it could take several encounters before a lover and I may be able to comfortably navigate the currents of our passion. Perhaps that was all that was needed – practice.

Out on the board, as we sat and listened, I was no longer singing but humming. It seemed the eruption of Mount Capulet was over. We anticipated one or the other would begin to snore at any moment. Except for my humming and strumming, the roll of wheels, clip of hooves and summer bird song, all was quiet. Having survived the passionate incident, I decided to cease my humming too but continued to strum.

Truly we had done well to restrain our want to laugh beyond all control. Yet more than just the humour of it had affected us. For I tell you in all honesty, I was shamefully thankful my lute remain perched on my lap! Well? I was young. And in fairness to me, if Maxine hadn't become wet by then too I would have been surprised. No, I've never asked her if she was! What do you take me for? Yet I've often thought how much easier it is for a woman to hide such things. Oh yes, boo hoo for me!

Our silence continued.

Then to my surprise, unable to resist the effect of it, Maxine began to flirt more provocatively. I could see the interest in her eyes. She could see it in mine. Not wishing to disturb our betters, who we thought may be sleeping, we began a conspiratorial conversation. In an effort to make a start, she pretended to struggle to recall my name.

'Marcel?' she whispered.

'Maxine?' I whispered.

Cat-like grins broke across our faces.

'Liar.' she whispered.

'Liar.' I whispered.

We grinned again then faltered for a moment, yet only for the sake of our want to explore each other's eyes in the silence. She noticed the scar on my forehead. No, I've never told you about it. Some things are more personal. But I was pleased to see her lift a fingertip to run it along slowly.

'Tell me.' was all she needed to say.

I told her the truth. It was from a belting I took in my youth, one of many but it was the worst. As the child of a refugee with no father or brothers, I was an easy target to some in the poor outskirts of Paris. Her brows knit, lips pouted. She kissed her fingertip and touched my scar. Of all the women I had attempted to be close to, none had ever done that.

I whispered. 'When a skinny boy lacks the muscularity or wit to diffuse the kind of trouble my tongue kept making for me –'

Her brows lifted. 'No. I *can't* imagine it.'

My heart warmed at the way her eyes lit to mock me so gently. 'I'm sure that you can. And so, lacking brawn, for safety I learnt to be fleet of foot.'

'I can imagine you running amok to escape oafish bullies.

'Frequently. Are you attracted to slender cowards who say more than they should?'

'Mmm.' She held me with her gorgeous eyes. 'I must confess … you lack the brawn I'm *usually* attracted to.'

'I'm glad you're willing to confess it, yet devastated to hear it.'

'However …'

'*However* is a wonderful word.' I interjected.

'You're handsome all the same. And so far you have a winning way about you.'

'*So far* is not a wonderful phrase.'

'However sweet man … beyond doubt you're amusing.'

'Beyond doubt so are you sweet woman.'

She tilted her pretty eyes to Heaven. 'Bless the Angels, you don't lack for confidence.'

'I have been told so.' I couldn't help smiling.

'When you smile you appear naive.'

'Perhaps I am.'

'I doubt that greatly. Your smile has charm to it. However …'

'That word again!'

She snapped the reins. 'However you seem to *know* it!'

I pouted and raised my brows in question.

'Hmm. Is that so bad? I'll confess to wishing I had thicker hair!'

'Oh but I like your hair, the way it frames your face. It has a soft, intelligent look.'

Suddenly, like a buffoon, I ruffled my hands through my hair to entangle it. She tried to remain sober-faced.

'Yes, that looks *less* intelligent.' A smile burst open. 'But when you're being clever, you look mischievous.'

'Do I?'

'But now enough of *you*, tell me of *myself*.'

She took me by surprise with that. I love surprises of course.

'With alacrity sweet woman. There's *so* much to tell. I know you're chatty, confident, practical –'

'Practical?'

'Beautiful besides.' She tried not to smile. 'Mischievous too?'

'Oh Master Minstrel, that's my middle name.'

I discovered she meant that somewhat literally. For when Maxine was a girl her pet name was *Little Mischief* until one of her many brothers began to call her *Cat*.

'Cats can be mischievous.' I said thoughtfully.

We stared for a long moment. Then our whispering confessions continued. Maxine felt her mischievousness was one part of her nature that encouraged employers to retain her. Ironically for me, she also confessed that, between her senses of humour and mischief, she considered herself to be a kind of entertainer to them.

Maxine felt the presence of those qualities not only caused women to want her by their side, but encouraged them to take her into their confidence. I confessed I had discovered the same. Leaning closer, even more quietly, she further confessed that, in the short time they'd spent together, Ilaria had already begun to share intimate confidences.

'Interesting. Tell me something juicy.'

She glanced sidelong and back to the road.

'Perhaps in time. When I know I can trust you.'

'Bravo pretty cat. At least you're no gossip?'

'Not at all sweet man. Are you?'

'Sometimes, for the sake of my profession, I appear to be.'

'But you're not?'

'Oh for everyone's amusement I spout all kinds of nonsense. And yes, I love to do it. But I'd never willingly reveal a secret that had any power to hurt a friend.'

She considered me with care for a moment, as if contemplating something more important than flirtation. 'I hope so Marcel. If we're to work together, closely together –'

'That sounds inviting Maxine.'

'Now that they're wed, for the safety of both, it would help if we could trust each other.'

'Agreed. Of course, real trust takes time to develop.'

'Agreed. And so, perhaps we could make a start by ... sharing some secrets of our own.

That suggestion did more than just take me by surprise.

'Interesting? Light and innocent secrets or dark and sinister?'

She hung in a moment of indecision. I opened my mouth to speak, but she suddenly burst out a whispered confession.

'I had a son Marcel. He was born out of wedlock.'

'I – yes I did hear tell of it.'

'Oh.' Her brows knit. 'I tell most people he died of an illness.'

Suddenly I held my breath.

'But ... he didn't?'

'No. One evening when I couldn't stop his crying, his father was drinking and fell into a rage, bellowing at me. I tried to keep him off but he pushed me away and –'

'Oh. Oh no Maxine. By every Saint that prays in Heaven I'm so very sorry to hear that. That must have been –'

'No Marcel, please. Oh I don't want to dwell on it. Not right now. Now it's your turn.'

'Very well. Hmm. Then perhaps ...'

'I'm sorry. That was very secret and dark. If you're not ready to tell such a ... well mercy I hope you have nothing that's so grim to tell.'

'No, it's alright Maxine. As fate would have it there is ...'

'Oh no.'

'Yes there is something. Something quite difficult ...'

'Dear me.' Her eyes hung on the verge of tears, the potency of her own secret still heavy in her mind. 'I promise Marcel, any secret you tell is safe with me.'

'I believe you. Well ... I was five when my father died in Calais.'

'Yes.'

'I tell people I don't remember him. But I do.'

'Oh.' She hesitated. 'Why ... why do you say you don't?'

'Because after he died, I lied to my *maman*.'

'I don't understand.'

'I was born in Calais. Papa was a fisherman. He was killed during an English attack.'

'Oh no. No, I'm so sorry.'

'After it was done, I pretended to come back into our hut and discover Maman there with him. But the truth is, I was inside our hut when they – I saw them murder him.'

'Your mother –'

'She was down at the shore with my grandam. Papa heard the soldiers coming and glanced through the crack of the door. He pushed me up the ladder to hide me in the loft.'

Maxine's eyes lit with anxiety.

'Oh dear Marcel, no!'

'I drew the ladder up just before they stormed in. Peeking through the cracks I saw them attack him. Papa knocked one down but the other one stabbed him and ...' I faltered.

'Oh no. Oh I'm so sorry.'

'After he fell ... they moved on quickly. Moments later Maman rushed in to warn him. She found him there of course.'

'It must have destroyed her.'

'A moment later Grandam arrived, urging her to leave – to find me and flee – but Maman didn't want to leave him. Grandam said she had to be strong, that the soldiers would return and I feared she was right. So, I climbed out the loading hatch. When I came through the door I pretended to know nothing, said I was hiding up a tree. I just couldn't let her know ...'

'Yes. Oh Marcel I'm so very sorry. Mercy, what have I done? We were doing so well.'

'Please don't fret. I'm glad we told each other. I never told Maman ... or another soul. Not even in confession.'

'No. Nor have I.'

We blinked at each other and drove on in silence.

After a time of deep contemplation, slowly and sleepily at first, another distracting preamble behind our backs led to the rise of another performance! Maxine and I glanced and rolled our eyes. Then for a second time during our first real encounter we shared the experience of hearing our new mistress sing, sigh and shudder again in such a particular manner that it made me wonder how many women might do the same.

I leaned to whisper. 'She sounds very *musical*.'

Maxine smirked again, trying to control her want to laugh aloud. In truth, I felt we were both glad their passion had reignited to drive away the dark mood we shared. That sweet flirtatious look had returned to Maxine eyes. Suddenly I couldn't help being more scandalous, it's in my blood of course.

'Do *you* sound like that?'

She fell silent, gazing ahead with a pout. Suddenly I feared I had taken a terrible misstep. Then just as suddenly, a smile broke on her lips and she leaned to whisper.

'Wouldn't you like to know?'

'Well since you ask, yes I would!'

We burst into a fit of muted laughter. I realised that, quite by accident, our strange situation had generated more closeness more quickly than I would ever have anticipated from a first meeting. Then to add to our enjoyment, the early summer sun burst through the clouds and poured its warmth onto our skin. It was intoxicating. Maxine turned her face to it and closed her eyes for a moment.

Just as I began to consider sliding a little closer to my paramour Mount Capulet erupted again. Maxine's eyes opened. Her head turned. We grinned and stared at each other.

'Cupids Balls!' I gulped. 'Is this what marriage is like?'

'Oh I hope so!' she squealed.

Chapter 6 the Path of Silk

Sieur Auguste Nobel scanned the readiness of his servers in the grand circular chamber and finally his maître d'. The last offered a sober nod. Nobel reached to touch Yolanthe's forearm. Their eyes met and the duchess scanned the faces of her flock before them, still mingling and distracted. Many who were destined to travel back to the war had questioned why they were summoned at all, let alone so unexpectedly. And why had they gathered in a premise situated on the Jewish road, hosted by a merchant of whom they knew so little?

Still linked by their arms, Yolanthe leaned into her husband.

'Ren, are you ready?'

'I'm always ready minx.' His handsome face smiled as she stared soberly. 'Oh. You mean the – yes Yoli. Unleash your power.'

'Imbecile. You're meant to be my mature counsellor.'

'Am I?'

'Yes. *Unleash my power?*'

'Well minx, that's what you do.'

'It is. Yet be careful what you ask for. I'm still angry at you.'

Yolanthe caught Nobel's eye again, nodding her consent to begin. He glanced to his maître d'. An instant later the spacious round chamber ominously began to empty of serving attendants. They vanished through seven hefty doors that were all closed quietly behind them. A delicate glazed bell was lifted by the maître d'. It's tinkling chime called for the glamorous flock to hush and pay attention.

'Honoured guests!' Nobel cried. 'I bid you welcome to the House of Nobel.' He held for a murmur of reaction. 'I humbly request you offer attendance to his Grace, Duke de Paris.'

Raising a beaker of his favoured alpine ale, Reynard strode forward and scanned the watching faces.

'Good evening. Heavens Yoli!' He smiled at her. 'What a fair assembly stands before us. I know you all of course. Yet as a result of short acquaintance, some far too little. Before I return to Normandy in the morning with my new junior squire ...' His hand swept to Astor. 'it's my sincere hope we'll have a chance to remedy that tonight.'

'Yes old fox!' bellowed a young chevalier. 'And when we do I'll drink you under the table!'

The challenge burst the tension apart. Reynard grinned as a wave of hearty laughter rippled through the assembly.

'I look forward to joining you under it!' he replied.

Yolanthe and Nobel exchanged smiling glances. Something about this evening was unleashing a tide in her. Suddenly Reynard's hand swept towards their enigmatic young leader.

'You all know Yoli, of course, my duchess, my love, my star.'

She beamed with a smile, lifted both hands and blew him a smiling kiss over stretching fingertips. That show of affection raised brows and drew gasps. Even Reynard blinked in surprise at how willing Yoli was to shed prior reluctance to display her emotions.

'She'll speak to your business in a moment. I suggest we all listen closely.' He waggled a warning finger. 'In my experience, whenever my wife speaks –' A brow lifted in punctuation. '– woe betide those who fail to pay her close attention!'

A nervous ripple of laughter followed. Their anxiety was rising again. Yet to hear Reynard speak of her that way, Yolanthe's eyes lit like a burst of sparks in a crackling fire. She knew he hoped to diffuse her anger, hoped to reduce the severity of his punishment or encourage her to forgive him entirely. He usually managed to charm her to do so. But Reynard didn't understand that his minx was not just in a *mood* that evening. Since her visit to the queen, a new incarnation of Yolanthe de Paris was emerging.

'You all know matters of trade are beyond my ability to speak on convincingly.' Giggles and guffaws rewarded his humility. 'And Yoli will make the purpose of our host known to you on such matters.'

Reynard's hand swept out to Nobel as he laid a palm on his shoulder. He knew the gesture would gain Yoli's approval and he desperately wanted to placate her.

'For my contribution, let me say this. On behalf of Yoli and myself I bid you all welcome. And on behalf of my fearsome new squire and myself' He winked at Astor. 'on the eve of our return to the fight ... let me raise my interest to you all.' He lifted his beaker of ale.

A sea of hands lifted in support, holding vessels of the finest craftsmanship. Reynard's eyes turned on them soberly.

'I offer you death to the English! Long life King Charles and Queen Marie!' A chorus responded with gusto.

Around the chamber, the delicate white vintage Nobel had imported for all to sample, was tossed back with a flourish. A volley of excited whispers ran through them. The duke's head turned and his hand extended. Yolanthe stepped forward, drawing him into a soft embrace to kiss his cheeks.

Her eyes held him for a moment. It reminded Yoli how easily she could be drawn to him, made her consider her own vulnerability for an instant. Then, a thin smile spread on her glistening lips. She lifted the fingertips of one hand to her lips, kissed them softly and turned them to lay upon his cheek. The time to be effuse was done.

She drew away, reminding herself that Duchess Yolanthe de Paris was the better of their match and he saw the change lift in her eyes. She turned to face her formidable famille. It was time for her to remind them why she and no one else stood before them. A flit of her eyes signalled the maître d' to sound his delicate bell again.

To the left of the dais, a door pushed open. All eyes glanced. A page boy appeared, clutching two important totems as he marched forward reverently. Following him, as if it were a ritual of the ancients, came the eleven elders of their Inner Circle. When they halted, the man at their head – her Uncle Alain the former patriarch – drew the totems from the page. He handed them to his successor. Yolanthe adorned herself with one and held the other.

'Welcome brothers and sisters. I wear the crown that bears the crusader's cross. I hold the crook of the shepherdess. You recognise both. You know they declare that this is not a social gathering to renew our acquaintance. Nor do we gather in grief and indulgence to send our men back to the folly of war.'

Not a murmur rose to disrupt her.

'Sadly, some of our men who responded to this call to arms are already gone forever –'

'*Vive de Paris!*' shouted the young chevalier from before.

The assembly erupted to echo his passionate sentiment. The circular chamber amplified every word, the tumult expanded until a pair of delicate hands lifted. The young matriarch scanned her animated flock. Quiet descended. Yolanthe's eyes met the young man.

'Yes. *Vive de Paris*. And God keep all their brave souls. But despite that wish, we know some here now, returning to the fight may also never return.'

Her lingering glance rested on Astor in the front rank. He stood looking up at his enigmatic big sister. Perhaps only he could tell that the hint of a tear threatened to moisten her eyes. She dared not turn to face Reynard. Despite her ability to display masterful control, something about that moment made her feel that if she did so, she'd relinquish it all.

Something about that moment, indeed the entire night and occasion, seemed utterly fateful.

'We all know how fickle life can appear to be. Wars loom, unleash their chaos, then in time, desist. Yet in spite of all cost, time marches on. God grant the lingering cost of this fight will not prove too high for the House of Paris.'

A chorus of agreement sounded.

'But before we allow the wind of this war to scatter us again, I've summoned you here to consider our future *beyond* it.' She took a demi-step forward. 'I have a vision for that future. I see it waiting for us. My vision required consent. That consent demanded planning. And the effort that followed has created an important result. For now we have a new Master Plan.'

A ripple of muttered surprise raced through the gathering. This was indeed unexpected news.

'For some time, our Inner Circle has been privy to that vision. The Outer Circle was then consulted. Now all have approved the plan and this very evening ... we shall initiate it.'

Another murmur rippled about.

'You're not here to judge our new plan.' she continued. 'You've been summoned to learn of its nature and what parts you'll be called to play to ensure its success.'

The volume of response was rising.

'Our legal advocates are in attendance with their secretaire. They'll record our intent and directives to you all. They'll also record all of your responses.'

Suddenly, it was clear to all that lasting decisions for futures were about to be made.

Smack! Smack! Smack!

The butt end of her crook sounded on the dais.

Every lip sat still. Every eye watched. Every heart beat faster.

'I remind you of our *House Rules*. This new master plan is *long-reaching* but your efforts to assist me must begin at once. The work to lay its foundation will take a decade or more to bring to fruition.'

Eyes glanced. Heads inclined. Another murmur rose and fell.

'Under this plan the business of our house will begin to *transform*. We're drawing away from traditional efforts, the kind whose results are too much affected by war and the factionalism that follows. From this day, we begin to focus our energy on a new style of enterprise, the kind that thrives over time despite the obstacles wars can unleash.'

She held to give them time to consider. Yolanthe knew she was ushering in the greatest change for their house since it's inception.

'For a time, as this new course emerges, we will continue to use our skill to play the game as we've always done. However ...' She breathed against the confinement of her corset, arched her back and stretched her gorgeous neck to release a pinch of tension.

'Mmm.' she purred, as if responding to an invisible masseur. 'That's better.'

She turned at the waist, extending a hand to Reynard to take his beaker. She sipped for a moment, then returned it, before turning again to narrow her eyes on them all. The lioness was in her element, relishing the power to make them all wait on her comfort. Every moment of silence was a tantalising moment of compliance.

'From this evening, one patient step after another, we'll apply our considerable means to reach for a *new* goal upon a new *path*. This path will have hurdles in it, yes. But no matter how great they appear to be, I will not waver at the sight of them. Nor will any of you.'

Her eyes began to glow. The familiar feeling of youthful confrontation was rising in her again. She remembered the queen's counsel to resist it and forced herself to halt and breathe until she could push the impulse down.

'In a moment, Sieur Nobel will explain the details with more clarity. But let me assure you –' Her volume was rising. '– our House *will* travel this new path and reach this destination. And by the time we arrive, you'll all agree our journey to it ran as smoothly as the touch of fine *silk!*'

The word was a cue. Every door about the circular chamber flung open dramatically. A marching line of liveried servers strode in together as one. They halted, turning into the walls to grasp and draw down thin leather strips that hung above their heads. As they did so, a cascade of fluttering silk ribbons with tassels at their ends descended beside each one. The assembly gasped in surprise, then smiled in appreciation. Yoli suppressed her smile, knowing more was to come.

Behind her, in an attempt to mask his thoughts, Reynard inspected his fingertips. To him, despite their unquestionable power, it was droll to see how easily impressed so many in her flock could be. But that muted show of disinterest was as much as he dared display of his jealousy of the faction's power and his wife's power over them.

So far, his greatest consolation had been the power he exerted over her in their intimate life. When they were naked together, he could make Yolanthe respond in ways that suggested a want to surrender to *his* power, even to show an urgent need for him above all others. But as he listened, and from the way the event was unfolding, he began to wonder if even that would last.

He glanced at her as she swept a hand towards their host.

'I present to you all, our great new ally, Sieur Auguste Nobel.'

All eyes followed her hand. Nobel stepped forward with a bow, smiling through his full and greying beard.

'Auguste is a vital player in our plan.' she ran on. 'He controls a substantial merchant empire. Indeed, his interests are now so closely aligned with our house that today we've drawn the interest of both our factions into a legal partnership.'

Even Reynard blinked in surprise. He had no notion the association with Nobel was intended to be so far reaching. Yes, he knew they were going to conduct business. Suddenly the thought of his young wife traveling on the road for months with Nobel was more foreboding.

'Before Auguste speaks to you, let me say this.' Her eyes lit with that spark of intense fire so many feared to see. She took a second to glance at Reynard and spied him inspecting his nails with disinterest. 'In the past, we've grown wealth by the acquisition of land and securing the social titles required to control it.'

Reynard furrowed his brows. He was one such who had surrendered his title to them.

'Candidly I say here among our famille, we've expanded subtly through marriage alliances or bluntly by brute conquest to gain estates, counties ... even duchies.'

Hearing that last, Reynard felt uneasy but refused to look up.

'The trick of course is that once an asset is gained it must be *held*. War and the way it affects politics can make that hard – even impossible at times. In just a single generation, much of what any faction may gain by such methods can be lost in a blink of time's eye.'

Reynard was glad he had averted his eyes before this part of her sermon began. He guessed by now many would be glancing at him.

'Darlings –' she let the new word hang coquettishly on her lips. 'We've been good at that game so far ...*very* good.'

Silence descended. Reynard knew something was wrong.

His eyes lifted. A shock of lewd awareness smacked him in the face. Suddenly he realised as Yolanthe had spoken she turned to stare directly at him. His blood froze. His mind was suffocating. He wanted to cower from that ribald accusation, made before all, what a social cuckold he had made of himself to serve her interest, their interest.

Never before had Yolanthe launched such a scathing attack. Her cold blue eyes pierced his heart as she continued to stare mercilessly. Every ounce of endearment his charm had earned from his opening remarks had vanished in an instant, incinerated by her mockery of him.

'Our holdings have grown.' she purred. 'Our reach has grown. Our power grows.'

Abashed by the brutality of her candour, Reynard stood paralysed for a moment. His fingers itched. He wanted to snatch Yolanthe by the throat with one hand and smack retribution into her cruel face with the other until she begged him for forgiveness. Instead, he dipped his head in a pretence of returning to his fingertips, pretending it all meant nothing.

With that, he had made her wet from the thrill of manipulating him so easily and inflicting her retribution to such devastating effect.

She pouted to supress a smile in reaction to the sight of his submission, then turned to face her flock.

'But that pattern of enrichment has limits, imposed by the outcomes of war such as this current episode may inflict. We've learnt that to our cost far too often, but no longer.'

An excited murmur rose at the notion of revealing a safer path to further expansion.

'And so my famille, rather than continue to suffer *avoidable* restrictions to our security and appetite, to move forward from here, we've adjusted our thinking.' Her eyes glowed with the fire of her vision. 'Fortunes more vast and more lasting are rising all about us, more quickly through *trade* than we could manage through the use of our *traditional* methods.'

Yolanthe caught a glimpse of the youngest of her four sisters standing by Astor. Astrid was his twin. Knowing he was returning to the fight, tears welled in her eyes as she stood gazing at her brother.

'Yes darling I know. I've said a great deal about business while some here shall return to the war tomorrow. Our time is precious.'

Astrid reached a hand to Astor. He frowned, yet took it gently.

'Therefore in conclusion let me state this bluntly. Auguste Nobel is a Jew. Unlike some he's *not* a convert. Yet the elders and I respect his strength, while living in a Christian world, to remain unwavering in his faith. This is business. This is familial business.'

She took a moment to breathe. Then she narrowed her eyes as they filled with venom.

'From today the House of Nobel is our *partner*. Auguste is *my* partner. *Any* slight to him or his followers from *any* of our famille or associates will draw a swift and considerable response from myself.'

She scanned the eyes of those she knew to be weaker links or rebels. They understood why she did so. 'This evening I urge you all to think very carefully. As we have a new master plan, each of you will be asked to *resubmit* your affidavit of loyalty to our house.'

To say the room fell quiet would be a gross understatement.

'It's only fitting you all declare your wish to continue, to serve within this new frame. If you cannot, truly I shall understand. Therefore tonight, only tonight, any who wish to may withdraw their support and separate from our faction without penalty.'

A murmur rippled about the room.

'To do so however, will be to do so *forever* but ... before you decide, I urge you all to listen to Auguste.'

Her constant use of Nobel's forename and the fond kiss she bestowed on his cheek as he came forward, were calculated to convince. The sooner her famille accepted he was her very close ally, the better. She would lead by example. She would love by example. Yolanthe turned and smiled at Reynard. It confused him utterly for a moment, then left him seething. Suddenly he felt he had no way of knowing how she felt at all. Suddenly he wondered if the consolation of control he thought he wielded in their intimate life had been a mere convenience, waiting on an occasion such as this, to allow her to incinerate it before his eyes.

Perhaps their sequel in the boudoir later may tell the tale of it? Perhaps no sequel would be offered at all?

For Yolanthe's flock however, the effect of her words was mesmerising. They held their breaths or chatted wildly as the convivial Nobel attempted to restore calm.

'Honoured members of the House of Paris, welcome again to the House of Nobel! You are my very special guests. And as you've heard, any who wish to will also become my partner.'

He smiled heartily. Auguste Nobel has an affable, casual way about him that was infectious. It's very hard not to like him. And he spoke to a group or individual alike, as if a beloved tutor who hoped to engage far more in a pupil than just their attention.

'Because our plan is particular I can be brief. As her Grace has revealed, yes we have *trade* on our mind. For this exciting partnership however, we have a singular target in our sights. It's a target of great *value*. A target of great *prestige*.'

Nobel glanced at his maître d' who tinkled the gorgeous bell again. Quietly in the moment before, when the word *value* was uttered, each server grasped the tassel at the end of their ribbon. At the sound of the bell, they drew them down and then as if by magic, a breathtaking cascade descended as silk of every description unfurled in a shimmering waterfall. To keep the fabric hidden until the moment of unveiling, each roll had been concealed at height under a brown hessian cover, coloured to blend with the wall panelling.

'*Silk* is our goal my friends! Not just to sell it in volume, oh no. A campaign to capture the dominant interest all the way along the Silk Road from Lyon to Venice!'

Two servers marched to new positions. Each gripped a tassel disguised in brown then tugged in unison to release another surprise. A gasp of astonishment echoed through the circular chamber. Like the mainsail of a Viking raider, a veritable wall of fabric descended with a flutter to cover the space behind the dais spanning the wide length from one door to another. The ponderous surface displayed an extraordinary piece of work marked in vibrant colours. It was a map. The largest map any had ever seen.

All eyes stared in wonder at the marvel designed by the eminent cartographer, Friar Mauro of Venice. Any could see it transcended craftsmanship, escalating its creation to be an indisputable work of art.

'A master plan of such scope deserves a map of such scale!'

Yolanthe beamed a smile and pressed her hands together in triumph. Reynard had forgotten his fingertips! Astor and Astrid gazed in childish wonder at the scale of the hanging.

Nobel once confided to me that "to be a great merchant one must learn to sell anything." He was certainly a great merchant. And he understood how unadulterated enthusiasm, wrapped in a mantle of charm could fixate attention. Moreover he understood that a flair for the dramatic could excite more interest in an item he intended to sell. The item to sell that night was a bold *notion*.

'Oh my wonderful friends! Note for yourselves that two hundred leagues stand between us here in Lyon and my recent acquisition, a large emporium in the Rialto in Venice.'

A rod of light cane, double the height of an ordinary man in length, was handed to the master merchant as he spoke. With sweeping gestures and snapping punctuations of its tip, he indicated upon the stout fabric to dramatic effect.

'By ship beyond this point lay the sea lanes to Greece.' SNAP went the tip! 'The Black Sea.' SNAP! 'Slavic ports.' SNAP! 'The Caspian Sea.' SNAP! 'The mighty port of Constantinople.' SNAP! 'Dual gateway to the exotic markets of Cathay to the Far East.' SLIDE-SNAP! 'Or Egypt to the south.' SLIDE-SNAP!' His dramatic use of the tip had eyes following and minds devouring. 'At the far eastern end of the Silk Road lies ...' He stepped to trail the tip along, lowering to a loud whisper. 'the fabled citadel of Eternal Peace where the creation of silk began.'

Sighs and murmurs punctuated the revelation.

'My friends, all silk worth buying or selling is drawn along these routes to Venice, Genoa or Marseilles, yes?' Nods and mumbles agreed. 'There it transits north through Verona or Milan or Lyon to be traded up into the vast upper reaches of your Christian world.'

By the expressions of interest upon the faces massed before him, clearly Nobel understood, if one intends to offer a partnership based on *specialty* knowledge, then from the very outset, one must leave no doubt they possess such knowledge.

'Now please pay *very* close attention.' ! 'For this stretch of territory between Vicenza and Verona is of very particular interest.' He encircled it with the point. 'This region is where the most northerly silk-worm farms are now producing.'

A mutter of understanding ran among his captivated audience.

'Our knowledge of this makes Verona a destination of *double* interest. It's the gateway to the central and eastern Germanic trade routes.' CIRCLE. CIRCLE. 'While just to the east, it offers fast access to those important raw materials. CIRCLE. CIRCLE. CIRCLE.'

He offered a moment for the flock to digest.

'Verona is *essential*.' SNAP! 'Like Venice however, it's value is *well* established. And so it shall take some time to lay foundations there that are firm enough to disrupt local competition and assert control.'

He stepped forward a little to adjust his position.

'As a result, in the chain of citadels along the silk road that command our interest, Verona is our most *urgent* target.' SNAP!

The master merchant paused for effect and took a moment to glance and wink cheekily at his happy new partner. Reynard scowled.

'Now although Verona is paramount, remember the ancient Roman road stretches from Venice to Lyon.' CIRCLE. SNAP! 'So please understand, we intend to dominate *every* strategic centre that lies between the two!' In a rapid flurry the smacking tip asserted its authority on each citadel in turn. 'And so Yoli!' His use of her pet name deepened the frown on Reynard's face. 'We have much to do.'

Nobel's pointer tip swept off with a flourish as he stepped from the hanging to gain more intimacy with his now excited audience.

'Not only shall we need to establish trading emporiums in each citadel, in some we must secure outlying holdings of much greater size. These will be particularly needed on the outskirts of Verona and Vincenzia where silkworms are already being grown.'

Yolanthe came towards him with sober expression.

'Auguste ... what would we use such holdings for?'

'Outlying estates are vital for storage and innovation.'

'And dominance in silk ... may then lead us on to trade in other products?'

'Yes indeed. Velvet for example is of very great interest to me.'

'Yoli?' said a young voice from the front rank. 'May I speak?'

Utter silence fell. Yolanthe glanced and held back a smile.

'I yield to a question from Squire Astor de Paris.'

'Well ... I feel the need to confess. I'm *not* fond of silk.'

Anxious murmurs and mutters rippled about him.

'No?' she frowned in mock challenge to be met with a mimic on his boyish face.

'No. But I like *velvet*.'

An avalanche of laughter broke the silence. Suddenly, Yolanthe was laughing too and wiping tears of joy. Her hands lifted for attention. She glanced at Nobel who smiled.

'Then by all means my brave little soldier, we shall have velvet!'

Astor beamed a smile as Astrid's embrace smothered him. Pats on his back and shoulders landed from every direction. Yolanthe rested a palm on Nobel's shoulder. Breathing a sigh of relief, he signalled for the bell to ring as he fixed his eyes on Astor.

'I acknowledge the valuable contribution of my newest ally, Squire Astor de Paris. Velvet it is, young master! But before velvet, my friends, before all ...' Nobel stepped over to lift the shining silken ribbon that hung nearest to him. 'This is our supreme target!'

He resigned his pointing staff to a server as he approached Yolanthe but kept his lively eyes on their audience.

'My friends if we follow our plan, if all play their roles diligently, then in just ten years, no patron from any Christian territory will be able to admire the shimmer of silk without considering ... how the partnership of Paris and Nobel delivered it to their world!'

It was an extraordinary final statement to sum up their interest. For the briefest instant, the gathering stood in pregnant silence. Nobel knew just what to do to release the tension. Like a consummate entertainer he bowed with a flourish, causing an excited bubble of commentary to burst wide open.

The young matriarch scanned the room, her eyes were ablaze with the fervour of conquest. Now the image of Verona, a citadel she had never seen was rising in her mind. Her scanning halted on the image of her quiet guest, hovering alone at the rear of the throng. Yolanthe caught her eye and curled a beckoning finger.

She noticed her new travelling companion had remained apart, sipping and listening with a distant look in her eye. Yolanthe extended a hand as she approached, drawing her on to Nobel.

'Auguste. I must introduce the travelling companion who shall be joining us on our tour.'

'Ah, the mystery guest.' He smiled. 'I've heard only whispers.'

'She is one of her Majesty's favourite wards, so you must treat her with very special care.'

Nobel's eyes opened wider. Clearly that had remained a secret.

'So that's the mystery. Then her every need will be my priority.'

'Unless my *own* precedes it darling.'

'Yoli that goes without saying.'

'But it warrants repeating. Now allow me to formally present Demoiselle Eloise du Marche.'

'Enchanted Demoiselle. Are you excited by the prospect of Milan, Verona and Venice?'

'I was excited to come to Lyon Monsieur.'

'Lyon? Yet you hail from Paris?'

'As her Majesty's ward, I hail from every court citadel.'

'Well I understand Lyon may have a certain charm for some –

'I had hoped to find the charm in it.'

'But you didn't?'

'Alas by the time we arrived, it was gone.'

Nobel and Yolanthe exchanged a quizzical glance.

'Eloise, are you going to speak in riddles all the way to Venice?'

'By the time we're so far away ... life may seem less of a riddle.'

The mention of travel tweaked Yoli's mind. While Nobel engaged Eloise in chatter, she scanned the chamber for the injured

Reynard. She wanted to find him and make amends. She knew that despite the pain she had inflicted, he'd never forego a chance to spend a passionate evening together. Perversely now, she felt more fuelled for him than ever before.

Even more wickedly, after such a damaging assault on his pride, Yolanthe wanted to know just what it would take to soothe his hurt and restore his interest. To accomplish it, she felt ready to submit to his cruellest will and so wandered in search of him. But her smouldering duke was nowhere to be seen. Then she realised Astor was missing too.

With an anxious frown she beckoned the maître d'.

'Yes your Grace. His Grace and the squire have departed.'

That plunged her into thought. Ren had never left an event without her before. Yet despite that thought she remained confident. And so the confident young matriarch took her time to draw Eloise away and follow them back to their newly purchased chateau.

Yoli knew Ren would be waiting there for his little minx, perhaps in their bedchamber, perhaps engulfed with another woman just to spite her. As she neared the chateau, she decided. No matter what state she found him in, or with whom, she wouldn't waste another moment of their final night together.

When Yolanthe arrived with Eloise, she was shocked to discover that Reynard and his entire entourage were gone. Her pair of flustered close servers described how he arrived in a violent passion, ordering all in his train to depart at once for Normandy. He had never deserted her in such a way before. Suddenly she fretted the cost of miscalculation, unsure of whether the only person in her life so far who seemed to understand her, would want to remain in her life.

More grimly now, if the war took Reynard before she could return to France and know that answer for herself, Yolanthe may feel cursed by the memory of how wilfully she had hurt him.

Eloise stood confounded as her host settled in the grand salon on a large, sumptuous, lonely settee and began to cry. She laid an arm around her shoulders and ushered Yolanthe up to her bed chamber.

Next morning Eloise awoke in Yolanthe's arms. Misery loves company they say and the Duchess de Paris loves whoever she pleases.

By the time they departed for Venice with Nobel, the two new companions felt they shared more in common than either had expected. Yet despite having been seduced already by her new mentor, Eloise remained distracted by her thoughts of another.

Unlike Eloise du Marche however Yolanthe de Paris had a greater capacity to rebound from romantic folly ... or any kind of folly. She knew she couldn't stay to repair the damage she'd inflicted. It reminded Yoli of a favourite adage her grandmaman used to repeat:

Tut little lioness. Don't fret what you can't fix.

When time allowed, she could return to Lyon and the task of repairing her rift with Reynard. At that moment however, she wasn't certain if she cared to fix it at all. Indeed the young duchess was beginning to wonder what her future may be like without reliance on his love. And now to distract her, Yoli had a bold new plan, two new travelling companions and a bright new path to follow without him.

Most of all the young duchess had a burning desire to complete her transformation. She wanted to unleash its result on the world ahead of them. And so now, with no notion at all that the Capulets or I existed, or any notion of our own that the Duchess existed, fate was placing the leaders of both familles on the high road together, making for the very same destination. One premiere dame was happily married. The other was not. And one brought the burning passion of another woman along with her, in an unwitting effort to help Eloise forget the man her heart had broken for.

In hindsight sweet friends I can see, fate was no longer simply playing a hand. It was scheming with wicked intent.

Chapter 7 Threshold

After a week of touring we stayed overnight in Valence. I was up to greet the dawn, yet before any in our entourage broke their fast, we were summoned to the Capulets bedchamber. Having travelled together for that long, their intimacy in our presence was becoming less discreet. Perhaps that was due to the way *the barge*, as we now called it, served their amorous needs while we were in transit. Or perhaps it was simply because they were newlyweds sharing a great adventure.

As a result, the experience of our ensemble being called to their intimate chamber to attend a hasty conference, didn't feel as uncomfortable as it would have done before our departure. Well, not for the close servers. At a glance, the two veterans in the chamber, particularly the elder, Liberati, looked abashed by his proximity to the barely covered form of our mistress.

Our giant squire Caspar however, who had to duck his head to enter, didn't seem to care one way or another. I expected this kind of informality wouldn't last of course. Once Armand and Ilaria were settled into a glamourous home in Lyon, perhaps a wing of Chateau de Capulet, I felt sure stricter codes of decorum would be imposed.

'Pardon the informality.' Armand said in salutation.

He was standing naked at the wash basin. His muscular back, ass and thighs flexed as he leaned, splashed and wiped with wet hands. Maxine stood nearby and struggled to avert her eyes, though his yawning young wife - still seated in the expansive bed - did not. Ilaria stared thoughtfully, knees lifted under the coverlet, a sheet of finest Egyptian linen drawn up to her chest and tucked under her arms.

Fabrizio stood on the other side of Armand and refilled the basin. Maxine attempted to hold his undershirt ready in one hand and a drying linen in the other. He beckoned for assistance. She tilted her eyes to Heaven and reached out sheepishly to offer the linen.

Armand continued. 'But our hosts have laid out a dizzy itinerary for us today, going until late this evening. And so this will be the only opportune moment.'

Suddenly he turned and there they were. No, not his endowments! Well yes, they were there for all to see of course. Well yes, more substantial than my own if you must know. No, I won't describe my own! At least not now. What I refer to were the three livid marks left to show where he was shot, lanced and stabbed so violently.

Ilaria frowned as soon as they became visible until the undershirt lifted above his head and dropped to cover them. Caspar, who was present when each wound was inflicted, didn't bat an eyelash at them. Liberati and Boccolo however, seeing them for the first time, exchanged a stoic glance of respect. Despite their master's youth, he was no novice.

Armand smiled and continued his briefing. 'Dame Capulet has *finally* agreed on a path for our eastward journey.'

'Armand' she chastised 'I make decisions quickly.'

'At times impulsively.'

Ilaria's brows lifted. 'Oh that's not fair at all.'

'You're right angel.' He glanced at our company. 'And now listen closely, Dame Capulet has the floor, or bed, as the case may be.'

Maxine pressed a smile. Every playful exchange between Armand and Ilaria seemed to amuse her.

'Thank you Sieur Capulet.' Brows lifted. 'Maxine the map.'

'Yes Madame.'

I rather enjoyed watching Maxine rummage for a moment.

'Here it is!' she announced, spreading a worn merchant's map across the gorgeous brocade.

The map showed the span from Paris to Venice and passages north, through alpine passes to Germanic territories above.

'Please gather round.' she said soberly, as if our setting was perfectly routine for such a conference. Her eyes tilted to glance at our giant. 'Caspar can you see from up there? Perhaps you should kneel.'

The giant ninny pouted in consternation, yet he knelt without complaint. Even after he did so, the top of his head still reached the tip of Maxine's shoulder beside him.

'Oh Maxine.' Ilaria smiled. 'Now you look so tall.'

Armand drew over to sit and lean, smiling at the sight. Maxine smirked, daring to pat the giant's broad head. It made me spurt with laughter, yet his scowl shut me up. I hadn't forgotten the threat he'd offered at Formigny to teach me a lesson if I failed to amuse him.

'Tomorrow we divert northeast to Grenoble to enter the alps.'

'We're travelling the Silk Road Madame?' asked Caspar.

Armand answered him. 'The merchant's daughter will have it no other way.'

Ilaria sighed and tilted her eyes to Heaven. Yes, Maxine smiled.

'Pardon Chevalier.' said the elder soldier.

'Yes Liberati.'

'I feel Madame's choice is prudent. I know all the main routes east. The old Roman road is wide and direct, much safer than the winding coastal route from Marseilles to Genoa.'

Ilaria's eyes lit with satisfaction. 'Thank you Liberati. I'm gratified someone appreciates the value of my pedigree.'

Her smile was enough to bring a thin smile to the grizzled face.

'Angel?' Armand pleaded playfully. 'You know I support –'

'Once ...' she interrupted to chastise him. 'we leave the French side ... until we reach Armand's sister –'

'Your sister now too, angel.'

'Yes my heart. Until then, for me, for *us*, my parents –'

'And now *mine*.'

'Yes dear Mercy! *All* our parents want me – want *us* to –'

Maxine giggled at her frustration. That set a ripple of guffaws and smiles in motion.

'Oh dear Heaven I must sound like an addle-head.'

'But it's a lovely addled head.' He leaned to kiss her temple.

'Look!' I pointed to the window. 'The sun's going down!'

As the one who was usually chastised for wasting time, I felt it only fair to tease them for the same.

'Musician!' growled Caspar. 'Don't be disrespectful.'

'No, no Caspar. He's right.' said Ilaria. 'There's so much to do. I must be more brief.'

I knew if I smiled in triumph I may regret it. So I drained the elation from my face.

Ilaria continued. 'And so, as we go along that path, we'd like to observe as much of the merchant world's doings as possible and nurture local connections.'

'Passing onto the Italian side, our first halt will be in Turin.'

'Pardon Chevalier.' said the younger veteran.

'Yes Boccolo.'

'If it please you Madame, I have a cousin in Turin who runs a very reputable post-house.'

'Ah, that's wonderful!' Ilaria's brows leapt high with enthusiasm as her hands lifted in exclamation and completely released the covering that shielded her chest. Every male eye before her averted discreetly. Except my own of course.

'Oops, pardon me.' She snatched the sheet back up. 'Yes Boccolo, that's *exactly* the kind of useful connection we need.'

Her unintended display sparked me with mischief. 'Well your mishap reminds me that my old master from Paris has a bordello there too! It's run by his ugly sister.'

'And that ...' scowled Fabrizio 'is the kind of connection Madame does *not* need!'

'Dunderhead!' I spat with mock disdain. 'How would you know? You couldn't tell a bordello from a bathhouse!'

'Aren't they the same?' he protested.

'Of course not imbecile! Well, not all the time! Well, sometimes they are, yet –'

'Pardon me Madame' Caspar butted in 'while I toss a musician out your window.'

He grabbed me by the belt and scruff of my neck, lifting me from my feet. At such a rare moment I couldn't resist thrashing for ludicrous effect. Suddenly Maxine burst into laughter and Armand was grinning at his young wife, struggling to restrain our antics.

'Caspar!' cried Ilaria making him halt. 'Thank you Caspar but please put him down. Dear me, we must be the most impromptu rabble to ever plan a conquest of the merchant world.'

'I have faith you can do it Madame.' said Fabrizio.

She stared in complete surprise. 'Oh. Oh bless you Fabrizio.'

'So do I Madame.' said Maxine with a grin.

'As do I angel.' He leaned to kiss her again. 'And yes, they may be a bit of a rabble. But they're our rabble.'

I looked about me. Cupid's Balls! Every eye wore a twinkle of pride. Every mouth pressed a stoic smile of support. Right before us, over us and through our minds, the Angel of Lyon was weaving her spell, unwittingly of course, which simply made it more potent.

'Armand I must prepare. Tell the rest while Maxine assists me.'

He cast a dubious glance at Ilaria. 'Hmm. How do you intend to manage that?'

Before she could answer, Maxine clapped her hands briskly. 'All you men! Turn your backs. *Allez!*'

Every male except Armand and myself complied. Maxine stared at me defiantly.

'I'm not a man! I'm a musician.'

'Oh Maxine' muttered Ilaria 'Marcel and Fabrizio don't matter. Marcel played for us in the bathhouse for hours. He's already seen more of me naked than Armand has.'

With no more explanation and behaving as if Fabrizio and I didn't exist at all, Ilaria slipped away from Armand to the further side of the bed, standing and drawing up the linen that had covered her.

'They can assist us by holding a screen.'

She walked the circuit around to the basin, reaching fingertips to Armand as she went. I hadn't noticed until that moment, but her sashay was the mimic of my secret love, her mentor, Countess de Viviers. Given Armand was once her page, I wondered if he had noticed. Despite what Ilaria had said, Fabrizio still averted his eyes. No, I didn't.

Well bite my bare ass, no I didn't! I spent two years working in a cat house, followed by four years serenading every intimate rendezvous of Chevalier Toulon. The sight of a naked woman was no revelation for me. Yet, having said so, I do confess that seeing her rise before us at that moment to walk like a naked goddess still took me by surprise. It was rather mesmerising.

Ilaria held my eyes as she passed, shaking her head with a sigh. It was the disapproval of a mother who caught an errant child revealing a bad habit she knew may be difficult to curb. Oh yes, I'm a man. Perhaps you think the sight of any naked woman would still affect me. Perhaps you're right. But Ilarja's body was ... well I won't say it was perfection. Everyone has their own idea of what that may be. I will say, if there was something about her body that wasn't pleasing to see, I couldn't see it.

Nor could her young husband. His eyes followed, devouring every motion and accent of every curve as her golden mane draped beyond her knees. I watched him watching her. It made me wonder if I'd ever have the chance to enjoy the sight of Maxine that way. Ilaria halted and glanced at the page.

'Fabrizio, lend a hand.' She offered him the linen she trailed. 'Marcel take this corner. Hold it up. Higher. Just here.'

I smiled and turned to be confronted by Maxine's glare.

'Dolt!' she snapped. 'Face the *other* direction.'

I spun about and held my corner with my other hand as Maxine began to attend her.

'Armand?' said Ilaria. 'We should hurry.'

'Oh yes. Let me see.' He sat up and leaned over the map. 'So men ... and women. From the gateway of Turin we'll make our way to Novara, Milan, Bergamo and Brescia, then finally reach Verona.'

'Venice?' asked Ilaria glancing over Maxine's shoulder.

'If time allows for it angel. And so I declare our path to be set. Consider it well. And if anything useful comes to mind let me know.' Ilaria glanced at him with a frown. 'Let *us* know.'

She smiled. 'And don't forget my heart. We have three *natives* among us.'

'Quite right. Knowledge is power. Particularly local knowledge. So, you three men –'

'Two men and an *urchin*.' I drawled.

Armand ignored me. 'As we go, if something important occurs to you about our plan, don't fear to speak your minds.'

'I like to speak my mind!' I said.

'Blitherer!' said Maxine. 'Speak it silently to *yourself*.'

Armand glanced at her.

'Pardon Monsieur.'

'Not at all Max, bravo. And Maxine?'

'Yes Monsieur.'

'If you two are going to *continue* to flirt together ...'

Maxine's mock surprise met Armand's mocking frown.

'Despite the *folly* of it!' cried Ilaria, glancing over the screen.

Maxine and I stared at each other like culprits.

'Then in future Max' Armand continued 'I'll leave all my scolding of that rogue to you.'

Her pretty eyes held me. A pout supressed a mischievous smile. 'Oh with pleasure Monsieur. I'll temper his deportment.'

'But I'm a musician!' I pleaded. 'I have no deportment?'

'You do now rascal.' purred Ilaria, busy behind her screen.

Everyone else smiled or snickered. Yes, I loved the attention.

'Squire von Ludolf.' said Armand. 'Final thoughts?'

The giant crossed his massive arms and held his massive chin in his massive fingers as he pouted thoughtfully with massive lips.

'Travelling anywhere comes with risk Chevalier.'

'Amen.' muttered Liberati. He twisted his greying moustache.

'Even more so in foreign domains.' Caspar continued. 'I've done a good deal of it coming from my home to England and France. When we do cross the border, I urge us all to be more vigilant.'

'Wise counsel Caspar. Angel, anything before we conclude?'

Ilaria turned on her heel to pay attention. Comically Maxine swirled as she went to attend to gathering the thick golden hair.

'Oh I agree with Caspar of course. We must all remain vigilant. However my heart, let me just say that neither myself nor Maxine have ventured this far beyond home.'

'Ah. Yes and so?'

'And so as we continue, yes, we must remain safe. But I want us to be able to enjoy our travels too.'

'We'll keep a close watch to offer you the freedom to do so.'

'And you. This is *our* marriage tour. It's once in a lifetime.'

'Amen my love.'

With her kiss our casual conference was concluded.

No, we didn't all receive a kiss!

Next morning we left for Grenoble, gateway to the alpine path. One final visit within French domains was to be made there. For the first time however, we wouldn't be hosted by the Capulet family. An associate of Ilaria's famille were receiving us. Grenoble is of course the centre of the glove-making trade. Therefore to the Marchands, it was a market citadel of very great importance.

Until that day, at each new destination, we'd been hosted in the lap of Capulet luxury. To me, it all seemed luxuriant and glamorous. But the luxury we were about to experience hosted by merchant associates of the Marchand famille, was even more decadent and far more modern.

Until that destination, the charismatic couple's arrival at every stop had resulted in the same outcome. Ilaria wove her spell of enchantment around all she met. Having put her fears for the delay of their marriage and Armand's return to the war behind her, Ilaria's mind had settled. We watched as she entered each new household on his arm as a stranger, only to exit days later, smothered by insistences to stop on their return and stay longer.

It's true that the fond invitations were for *both* Capulets. But Ilaria in particular, won the devotion of every new relation she met, old or young, male or female. I wasn't surprised of course. Nor were any who had the chance to meet her for more than a fleeting moment. And all in our entourage marvelled at how effortlessly she seemed to manage it all, without attempting to fawn or ever needing to feign for a single moment.

Yes, our young premiere dame was beautiful in her way. But our hosts didn't meet a smouldering siren who oozed sensuality with every glance. They met a young woman with an immutable quality of grace and loveliness, the soul of interest and care. And, almost as if she were a saint, in very short time Ilaria seemed to engender the trust of all she met.

Oh yes, yes they liked Armand too. Particularly the women. The word *handsome* was used so often I wondered if it should be added as a device on the Capulet crest. He proved to be very popular. Yet worryingly, I began to notice, he was also proving to be the kind of man that some men felt instantly jealous of. And for some, the presence of a wife like Ilaria by his side seemed to magnify their envy.

Yes, little wonder perhaps.

And despite how amicable and humble I knew Armand to be, to those meeting him for the first time, particularly among his famille, a reputation had been circulating ahead of our arrival. Before we reached any destination, his exploits in Normandy were already on their lips. He was becoming known to all, at least among his faction, as a warrior hero.

Everywhere we halted of course, I literally sang his praises for those heroics. But until I began to notice the effect for myself, I didn't understand there may be a cost to carrying such a reputation. Before Normandy, I sang about heroes I'd never met. Now I sang about the man I saw every day. Nor did I understand how much his growing reputation might act as a double-edged sword. Yes, pun intended.

For you see, any who acknowledged his martial achievements, must also acknowledge that the man now entering their house, handsome or not, humble or not, even if his wife Ilaria appeared to be a living saint, was now a celebrated *killer*. Armand was a hero, yes, but only because he was also a killer.

And so as they arrived and were greeted warmly together and entered, I started to realise that fear and caution also began to colour how people reacted to him. You know I saw him kill for the very first time in Carentan. I knew Armand before he killed and after he killed. I was one of few who understood that the look he now carried in his eyes, wasn't the same as before. Yes, Ilaria understood that too.

His innocence of before had an unmistakable look to it.

Now the look of the loss of that innocence, had taken its place.

Watching those colours of reaction to him, including the flits of jealousy I saw rising in some, made me wonder. As I observed their startling progress, first among his famille, now with associates from the Marchand side who were veritable strangers to both, I wondered if the stern advice of his parents was still ringing in their ears. Sieur Olivier and Dame Margot had cautioned them both to be wary, even among famille and associates. I remembered it well.

Yet it seemed to me that, despite that animated warning, taken so seriously by both at the time, the longer Armand and Ilaria mingled *en tour*, the less mindful they became of any need to keep watch for perilous people. Almost every night I was called on to play as they caroused among new faces. And as I played each night, after much wine had been consumed, I detected veiled, sour looks passing between some and particularly in Grenoble. Yet I felt sure Armand and Ilaria didn't notice.

Maxine however, had noticed it too. At every stop there was at least one, often two or three, hovering pretenders who seemed to be masking discontent. Sometimes they were in the party of the host, others were lurking among the many guests who arrived to meet the potent young visitors. Most were looks of envy, perhaps understandable, perhaps unavoidable, hopefully fleeting.

I felt sure, however, that a select few harboured deeper resentment, perhaps even more treacherous thoughts. Even among the elite, Armand and Ilaria were not an ordinary couple. Since their marriage they had become a premiere couple with more to lose, which meant they had more for others to take. Oh yes, I kept wondering if it was just my imagination ... until that night in Grenoble.

Over the previous week, I had felt such looks began appearing more frequently. More dangerously, over the previous few days, I feared some who masked themselves, were beginning to combine their interests. As we moved from one destination to another, one malcontent in particular reappeared to hover and whisper to newly met malcontents.

I pointed him out at first sight to Maxine. Then she saw him reappear. We grew more anxious that our betters didn't seem to sense the duplicity in such masqueraders. By the time we reached Grenoble and he appeared again, we were both convinced. Though Armand and Ilaria were intelligent, they were also young and distracted, and had become far too trusting of too many in our close proximity.

That night we spent in Grenoble before entering the alps next day, our newlyweds were carousing in the decadent grand salon as if they cared little or nought for vigilance. They danced together, laughing and smiling in a swirling throng of merchant associates. Yet just one day before, all in that chamber had been complete strangers. All save one. Ilaria reported having never met the man, but she vaguely recalled his name from the casual mention of her parents.

When the feast had ended, Armand and Ilaria began drinking and revelling. I played and sang their favourite dance, a slow pavane. It set a mood. They rose and danced like sorcery together. Every eye devoured every movement. They were elegant and tantalising, smouldering with desire, eyes transfixed and pouring their love into each other.

All about them I saw conviviality, heard mirth and sensed the pulse of charm and sensuality being delivered through every touch. Yet for the life of me, all that day and evening, I couldn't sense a sliver of caution from the Capulets. Even though that morning I had heard a troubled whisper among the local servers.

One among the guests attending that night had been a belated suitor of Madame Capulet. I was shocked to hear it said. As far as I knew, there had been no others. Their talk suggested that when the war had postponed Ilaria's marriage, this suitor approached her parents and sought to break her betrothal and commit her future to him instead. Until that morning, I had never heard anything of the kind.

I knew there was a moment before their courtship was approved when Armand feared the same notion. At that time his fear proved to be misplaced. I felt certain Armand knew nothing of this more recent matter. But I had no notion of whether Ilaria knew or not, or how much she might know. I felt sure that if she knew, it would not have been a proposal she would have condoned, nor one she would have initiated. Then just before the feast that evening Maxine discovered the man's identity.

All at once I realised how much a man like that might gain by plotting the removal of a rival, even a married rival. And it wasn't just the fortune that would come with Ilaria that attracted them. Any rival who saw her for himself would imagine the added incentive of taking her into his bed, and be tempted to stop at nothing in the hope of having her too.

Suddenly Maxine and I were babbling like frightened children.

'Am I being too suspicious?' I muttered as she brought fresh wine on a pretence to conspire with me.

'No.' she hissed. 'I don't like the way he looks at her!'

'Or at the master! Should we say something?'

She frowned and pinched her pout, wracked with indecision.

'I want to.' she hissed. 'Yet we must be careful not to speak out of turn. Before it was *his* famille but these are *her* important associates.'

'Perhaps you're right. We leave for the alps tomorrow. Perhaps for now we should wait.'

'Yes. For now let's keep it to ourselves. But before we return here and risk meeting him again, we must tell them what we've heard.'

'As soon as we leave. I fear they've become far too trusting.'

I felt Maxine's soft hand squeeze my forearm. Our eyes met.

'Hmm. What was that for?' I asked.

'A sign of *my* trust handsome man.'

'A welcome sign, pretty woman. But I must confess to you ...

'Another confession?'

Yes. I feel certain if we're given the chance to spend more than half an hour alone ...'

'Yes?'

'You won't be able to trust me at all.'

'I could say ... I feel the same.'

'Do you?'

'We'll see.'

'Will we?'

'Yes.' She held my hand and turned it over, grazing her fingertip across my palm. I'd never felt so impassioned by such a simple gesture.

'If they call you into their chamber to play again tonight –'

'It's become their habit.'

'When you exit their chamber I'll come to you in the hall.'

'Perfection. Where shall we go?'

'Silly. I intend to *remain* in the hall.'

'Oh. Shall I make love to you in the hall?'

'Until the sun rises you and I ...' she whispered and stared.

'Yes.' I gulped in anticipation.

'Will keep watch by the door to ensure their safety.'

'Oh.'

'I won't rest easy 'til we're quit of this place.'

'Agreed.' I said a little forlornly.

'Don't be so glum handsome. We won't want to wake them.'

'No.'

'That is to say ... I don't intend us to bide our time with *talking*.'

Our eyes held each other so fixedly that every other thought vanished from my mind. We had discovered we shared our fears. We also discovered we wanted to share more.

Then as Maxine skittered away to gather refreshment for the Capulets, I discovered something more disturbing. Ilaria had taken her leave of Armand and was retiring alone down a darkened passage. Without Maxine at her side for a moment, I assumed she intended to attend to ablutions. Yet the sight made me instantly mindful of the cretin Maxine and I had discovered. I scanned the chamber feverishly to discover his whereabouts.

I spied him hovering at the edge of the throng with a few other malcontents. He was glancing about cautiously. Suddenly he cast his eyes in Ilaria's direction, broke from his clique and followed her! My heart leapt into my mouth. I looked for Armand but had lost sight of him. A thought lit my mind and I searched for the giant form of Caspar, normally so easy to see. Yes, there he was!

But I instantly cursed my luck when he ducked and disappeared through the main entry doors as Liberati and Boccolo passed by to replace him. I glanced with wide eyes in their direction. I saw Liberati scanning, looking everywhere but at me! I glanced back to Ilaria to find her gone! More grimly her fixated follower was vanishing too!

I reached for my lute, gripping it like a hammer. Then for a fleeting instant, just as I determined to go, Liberati scanned and caught my eye. I widened them in horror and pointed ridiculously in Ilaria's direction with my lute. Yet the dunderhead just smiled, convinced I was playing the buffoon as usual, so I scuttled away in a terrified panic.

Cupid's Balls on fire! This was not an antic performance!

I rushed through the throng, dodging and weaving, apologising, smiling and grimacing all at once. Surely I did look like a clowning buffoon. As I rounded the corner into a long hall Ilaria disappeared through a door. I felt sure her pursuer, not five yards behind, had gone completely unnoticed by her.

From a distance he seemed tallish, widish and muscular. Up close he looked even more so. With my heart in my mouth I walked up behind him to announce my presence.

'Pardon Monsieur.'

He turned without so much as a start and frowned darkly. That reaction worried me more.

'Who are you? Oh, the musician.' His expression relaxed. 'Well done man. I noticed Ilaria seems to like your playing.'

'Does she?' I blithered. 'Ah yes, she does.'

'I'll ask her to have you play at our wedding.'

'You mean... *your* wedding Monsieur.'

'What?'

'She's already married, perhaps you noticed.'

'Yes of course. Well now. Go your way.'

'Yes Monsieur.'

Then like an imbecile, too accustomed to being ordered by my betters, and with no greater plan, I bowed, passed by and disappeared around the next fucking corner! The instant I did so however, I leapt against the wall, holding my breath and my lute at the ready.

I heard a door open.

'Monsieur Soulier?'

'Ilaria. Please call me Claude.'

'Of course Claude. Are you rejoining the feast or departing?'

I dared to peek. Oblivious to me, he faced her before the door.

'I'd love to return and dance with you.'

'Oh. Oh well yes. I'm sure –'

'I'd love to know that you'd only *ever* dance with me.'

'I –' Her brows knit in a frown. 'That's a little confusing.'

'You know who I am?'

'Well yes. Yes I do.'

'You know that your parents signed an –'

'Alternate betrothal? Yes the told me. In case anything happened to Armand after the war delayed our marriage. However –'

'However sweet Ilaria, your parents seemed more disposed to *me* as the better match for *you.*'

He stepped closer.

She withdrew against the door.

He began to move again.

'If they were so Monsieur, they never said it to me. Now please allow me to pass.'

'Oh no lovely dame. Your father in particular made it clear I was his preference for you.'

He leaned against the lintel. I clutched my lute firmly.

'Don't you agree Ilaria, that you'd be better off with a man whose life will always remain untouched by war.'

'You won't remain untouched for long.' said a growling voice.

I held my breath! I knew that voice.

'Back away slowly Monsieur.' said Liberati.

'This is none of your business old man.'

'You're very lucky I found you.'

'I warn you ...'

'Had Chevalier Capulet found you in this darkened hall, hanging in such close proximity to his wife, he'd feel obliged – like the gentleman he is – to challenge you to a duel. And when he killed you thereafter, your famille would be left to deal with the stain of disgrace.'

'Do you know who I am?'

Liberati looked at Ilaria calmly. 'By your leave premiere Dame?'

Her anxiety was transforming into a surge of stony confidence. 'By all means Liberati.'

Liberati closed the distance between them. 'I know who I am Monsieur. I'm not Chevalier Capulet. I'm his father's most trusted *old* man, the one he assigns to do what no one else can. I'm the man who will kill you so quickly and quietly in this hall that none will hear you die or see you die. Nor will I leave a trace of it.'

'How dare you –'

'Then before any understand that you're missing, I'll dispose of your body even more quietly.'

'You like to talk old man.' Soulier's hand lowered to his waist.

'Want to reach for that rondel boy? I can see you do. Go on. I'll let you draw first.'

The cretin hung in thought for an instant, then drew the shining dagger as fast as he could! Ilaria gasped. So did I. For as if by sorcery, in the blink of an eye and before Soulier could even point his rondel, the blade spun back against his thumb and leapt into Liberati's hand. Suddenly the point was levelled at the craven's pounding heart.

Cupid's Balls! I wish you could have seen the look on his pallid face! His eyes flitted back and forth between them.

'Perhaps ...' he muttered 'I should return.'

'Or perhaps you should vanish without a trace, become a mystery?' Liberati reached for a flower bowl on the sideboard. 'They'll still be searching for you tomorrow as we cross the border and stop to buy trinkets or a bouquet of flowers.' He drew a chrysanthemum from the arrangement. 'Do you like chrysanthemums Madame?'

'Oh yes Liberati. I like them *very* much.'

The blithering Soulier stared at the white flower of death.

'I really should return –'

Liberati stared at him coldly. 'After you apologise to our premiere Dame for your gross indiscretion.' He offered the flower.

Soulier took it. Shaking in his hand, he extended it to Ilaria. 'Ilaria. Please accept my deepest apology –'

'Enough little toad.' said Liberati. 'I'm sure every moment of your continuing presence is a torment for Dame Capulet.'

'Yes Liberati.' Ilaria glared. 'It certainly is.'

'Now get out of her sight before I ask permission to exact a different solution.'

Soulier moved to go.

'And Monsieur.' Liberati's hand gripped the cretin's neck. 'Any tricks, plans or schemes to make good against this little incident and I warn you ... I'm old because I'm hard to kill. Long before your people manage to kill me, I'll kill you first. And even if I failed to do so, the chevalier's father would never rest 'til he made you pay for your insult to our House.' The grip released.

The brave Monsieur Soulier left without further ado.

'Come out.' said Liberati. 'He's gone.'

Ilaria's eyes widened in surprise. I appeared sheepishly clutching my lute like an axe.

'Marcel.' Ilaria frowned in confusion. 'Were you there?'

'He alerted me to your predicament.' said Liberati. 'And went after you alone, armed with nothing but a ... lute.'

'Cupid's Balls! I feared you misread my panic. Thought I was being a buffoon.'

'I did at first. Then I realised Maxine was present with the chevalier but madame was not. That made me wonder ... yet all's well that ends well. You're unhurt Madame?'

'Thanks to you Liberati. Thanks to you both.'

'Not at all. I've seen his kind many times before. There'll be no sequel. Please dismiss the incident from your mind Madame.'

'If you say so dear Liberati.'

'I do. Now I told Boccolo to keep watch in the salon. Let's rejoin him. Strength in numbers, yes?'

'Yes.' Ilaria glanced at me. 'But ... please give me a moment.'

'I'll wait at the end of the hall.'

As Liberati turned, I bowed and began to move away.

'Rascal where are you going?'

'To wait at the end of the hall.'

'How much did you hear?'

'Oh I heard... too much.'

'What do you think you know?'

'Well I know ... too much.'

'I fear that's true.'

'However fretful dame, I also know you played no one false.'

'Nor did my parents rascal. That alternate agreement was severed when our new date was set, after I agreed to be betrothed to another Capulet if anything ... well, you know the rest.'

'Yes.'

'And I knew nothing of the alternate 'til *after* it was rescinded.'

'Oh. I see.'

'Do you believe me?'

'Of course fretful one. And rest assured that I won't tell tales that amount to nothing but may hurt you to no end.'

'Thank you Marcel.'

'Do you trust me?' I asked.

'Not at all.' She held coy for a moment, then smiled.

I rolled my eyes but her antic moment had impressed me.

'Oh yes, humour will settle your fluttering heart. But so will more wine and dancing.'

'It *was* fluttering.'

'Not as much as mine! Cupid's Balls!' She smiled. 'And not as much as Monsieur Sourface!' Her green eyes glinted 'Truly Madame, you handled yourself bravely.'

'Thank you.' She turned to go as did I. 'And Marcel, in good time I will tell Armand everything. I promise you.'

'Oh, take your time. He doesn't need to hear that kind of nonsense tonight. And now, since I *didn't* have to destroy my only lute, I want to see you dance the pavane again.'

'You know it's our favourite.'

'Ninny! Why do you think I play it so often?'

We returned and attempted to behave as if nothing had happened. Yet despite Liberati's grave warning to Soulier and that he seemed to have vanished before we returned, after the Capulets retired Maxine and I still kept watch in the hall. Seated upon the floor in the lamplit hall, we leaned against the wall and each other.

Yes, we were tired. But more than our hands began to touch. Then the depth of her eyes, the taste of her lips, the sweet smell of her skin and hair made me forget all else. Not until just before the sun rose, did we leave. A few hours later, I stifled a yawn as I watched the Capulets offering a fond farewell to our host.

In spite of my tiredness, I was happy we had taken that extra care for their safety. I wasn't raised among the elite, nor was Maxine. I grew in the poor outskirts of Paris and survived on my wits. My skill as an entertainer had drawn me away from squalor and vice into elite company. Now it seemed clear that just as much trouble lurked in this elevated world, though the troublemakers were harder to see.

As I glanced around our company, the Capulets rose into their saddles on Victoire and Tempest side-by-side. It was the first time we'd seen them that way. Ilaria adjusted in her side-saddle while Maxine fluttered about to ensure the hem of her dazzling gown of emerald and silver silk damask was draped to perfection.

Armand was becoming a picture of health again. He needed to be to ride Victoire. Dear Heaven sweet friends I tell you, they looked so perfect together. And I was convinced once and for all that Victoire was also madly in love with Tempest. With Caspar leading at the fore, and Boccolo and Liberati guarding at the rear, we drew away.

Yet even with the presence of such warriors to watch over them, I felt that the more the Capulets continued to glide among strangers, weaving webs of new acquaintance, the more Maxine and I needed to act as guardians too. Yes, by all the Saints that pray and all the Angels that sing so sweetly in Heaven, I had become very fond of them. I think by that morning we were all entranced by their spell.

They were intoxicating to be around. I was intoxicated by the thought of sharing more of my life with them. Oh yes, very well, I was also intoxicated by the thought of sharing more time with Maxine. I wanted her to sashay around the bed like a siren in the morning light, just as Ilaria had done, hopefully straight into my arms.

Well bite my bare ass, yes I did!

However, for the first time in my itinerant life, I wanted more than just that. I wanted to be married, to have a family and hear a child call me papa. Oh yes, who was I to dream of such things? And now, also for the first time, I was leaving the borders of our kingdom. Mercy dear friends, all at once, anything seemed possible.

Considering my own future caused me to consider how the future between Armand and Ilaria may progress. As we travelled eastward, the connections from her side would become more important to our travels. Until we reached Verona, wherever we stopped along the silk road we would be entertained more lavishly by Marchand associates than we had been by Capulet famille. After our stop in Grenoble I had realised something. The Marchand's trading network was not just extensive, it was breathtaking.

Years later, I also learned from Ilaria, that after the long marriage tour was announced, indeed on the morning of our departure, she was summoned to an impromptu counsel with her parents, alone. That meeting was what gave Maxine time to approach Armand about driving the wagon. Perhaps it was telling that the Marchands didn't request Armand's presence. And the counsel Ilaria received was quite different to that which she and Armand had received from his parents.

Sieur Julien and Dame Genevieve Marchand had built a merchant empire together. They both agreed that, for it to flourish, their trade in fabric, dyes and couture required the guidance of feminine instincts. They built it all together, yes. But in their world Ilaria's *maman* was no shrinking violet, indeed she was considered by all to be the driving force of their enterprise. At that conference Dame Genevieve left Ilaria with no illusions. She expected the tour to be productive and wasn't referring to children.

'If fate decrees, you may be pregnant upon your return Ilaria. Your father and I hope so. But we also expect you to present us with a list of aged associations that have been *reinvigorated*. Moreover we expect to receive a list of *new* associations to exploit in the future.'

After Ilaria shared that with me, it seemed little wonder in hindsight that she hadn't flinched during the late-night consultation with Armand's parents just hours before. As we left Grenoble, a citadel that meant more to her *famille* than Armand's, I sensed she was beginning to relish the thought of playing a more meaningful part in her parent's lives and the expansion of their interests.

Looking back I realise, from that visit onward, Ilaria began to see her role in their future looming more potently. No, I didn't understand that quite so precisely at the time. Yet I felt that something important was shifting. And though much of Ilaria's behaviour as a newlywed was still timid, even so soon, I felt her deportment as a premiere dame was becoming more confident.

Perhaps the incident in the dark hall with Soulier and Liberati made her feel more protected. Whatever it was, after Grenoble our young premiere dame appeared to be reaching for the life ahead of her with both hands, relishing her chance to become the kind of woman who could rule as the matriarch of that formidable House.

With such able mentors as Dame Marchand, Countess de Viviers and Dame Capulet to guide Ilaria, I felt her result may be a *fait accompli*, except for one thing. As we headed into the alps bound for Italy, while watching them ride ahead together like a vision of matched perfection, a troubling thought entered my mind. I could see now how eminently suited to an expanding life in trade a Merchant Princess like Ilaria may be. Yet I was beginning to wonder, just how well suited to that style of life a young warrior like Armand could be?

With France disappearing behind us, every fated footfall of Victoire and Tempest together, every roll of the wheels of our train, drew us closer to a foreboding answer to that question. And despite that first sign of trouble we left behind in Grenoble, how could we know it was barely a hint of what lay ahead of us? How could we know?

Chapter 8 Madame Capulet's Fool

We departed Grenoble with a flourish and entered the French side of the alpine path. Ahead lay the border of Italy's northern domains. Our journey east to visit Armand's sister Aurelie had begun in earnest. In Verona she was the prima donna of the House of Cortellani, living with Don Sabatino on their estate in the northern hills. Just the sound of their titles gave me the impression they lived an enchanted life together in that citadel fabled for its beauty.

Once on the alpine path, Ilaria and Maxine became excited by the vista of steep rising foothills swathed in green and strewn with wildflowers. I had to agree it was an enthralling sight. Mountains loomed all about us, like sentinels of Heaven on a glorious summer path, drawing us on towards the border crossing and Turin beyond it.

Caspar was leading of course. The barge followed him, Maxine driving it at an idle pace. I ambled beside her on the back of the jennet, tuning my lute and chattering away. For a time Armand and Ilaria rode ahead on Victoire and Tempest. They had been riding between Caspar and myself until, wheeling together, they disappeared behind.

A glance revealed they'd fallen all the way back to ride in conference with Liberati and Boccolo. Both veterans knew the pathways to Italy well. I guessed their wisdom was sought as we made ready to enter a kingdom foreign to us but was the place of their birth. All in all, our company were falling into a rhythm of familiarity. And since our bedside conference before we left Grenoble, and Caspar's grim warning, we had become more vigilant.

Yet what of Fabrizio you may ask? Or did you forget him?

Oh yes, he was there, driving the baggage wagon behind us. Or so I had thought until, disrupting my chattering to Maxine, an urgent hail at my offside announced his arrival.

'Master Marcel! Master Marcel!'

I cocked a brow to glance. There he was afoot beside me.

He *had* been driving the wagon behind. Yet Armand sent Boccolo to relieve him with orders to come forward and seek my release of the she-mule. Maxine and I looked down at the lad as he huffed and puffed. Despite his thinning physique, it was still hard for me to imagine how he would survive service as a junior squire, let alone become a senior one.

'Yes little knave I see you. Now go away.'

'Chevalier Capulet instructed me to deliver a message to Squire von Ludolf.'

'You mean Caspar.'

'A junior squire –'

'Is that what you are?'

'May not refer to his senior squire with such familiarity. And I *must* have the ass.'

'You have enough ass for two junior squires.'

The back of a feminine hand slapped my shoulder.

'Marcel stop taunting Fabio! And –'

'Fabio? That sounds a little too familiar.'

'Don't change the subject. Give up that smelly beast.'

'Sweetheart be careful what you say. She's very sensitive. She can't help it if she's fragrant.'

'Fragrant! Marcel get off that ass.' she demanded. 'Come sit up here with me.'

'Well sweet woman, when you put it that way ...'

I'm not a horseman of great skill of course. Indeed I have no skill at all. But despite being tall and lankish, I am an acrobat of some skill. And since I'd begun to ride the mule more frequently, I'd practised a trick to stand in the saddle and revolve about.

The incentive to join Maxine seemed to provide an opportune moment to display my skill. In a moment I was up, teetering with a satisfied grin, then I leapt to the wagon and settled in beside her.

'Show off.' She tilted her eyes to Heaven and nodded.

Fabrizio attempted to halt the jennet to climb board her. 'Whoa Fleur! Whoa Fleur!' he blurted.

'That's not her name!' I insisted, like a tutor chiding a pupil.

'Master Marcel? Whoa Fleur!'

'Use the new name I've given her ninny. She's used to it now.'

'Master Marcel! Whoa Fleur!

'Or else vault aboard like a bold chevalier.'

'I'm not a chevalier yet.'

'The master can vault into his saddle in full armour.'

'Yes I know.'

'Then surely his junior squire can vault onto the back of that lowly she-devil.'

Fabrizio was a timid youth yet I suspected that challenge would irk him. And since being mentored by Armand, he was becoming more game. Then I saw an adventurous look spark in his eye.

'Oh sweetheart watch this.' I whispered mischievously.

I also knew the jennet had a very particular reaction whenever I tried to vault onto her back. Gripping a chunk of mane in nervous hands, Fabrizio attempted to rise to the challenge. His tongue stuck from the side of his mouth as he concentrated in preparation. Up he launched, driving himself over her flank. Then the instant he hefted onto her back, a fulsome fart exploded.

'Mercy!' squealed Maxine. 'At least he's aboard.'

I laughed aloud then squealed. 'And with a fanfare!'

'Bravo Fabrizio!' said Maxine.

'Oh sweet woman, don't encourage him. Encourage me.'

Yes, Armand had assigned the she-mule to Fabrizio and the ancient gelding, Dilettante, to me. But that beast was a hand-me-down from our old master and devilish to sit upon. Dilettante had been the mount of every senior squire for seven years. And as you know, creatures with no consistent master become cantankerous.

Moreover, I was a musician! I needed a placid beast that allowed me to drop the reins as I rode to play, not a pig rooter that constantly turned its head to snap at my knees! All the way back from Saint-Lô I attempted to convince Fabrizio we must share the mule. Yes, he agreed. But after arriving in Lyon, I hoped to dissuade him from any further use of it himself and devised a plan to do it.

First, I rechristened the beast and began teaching it to respond to the new name. I chose a name I felt sure Fabrizio would detest, hoping the inconvenience of both tricks would convince him to leave her to me. To pave the way more gently, I even agreed that while he grew used to the gelding, we'd still share the ass for a time but not for much longer.

That morning as we left Grenoble, I declared that time had come, insisting any future use would be considered a loan that would require some form of payment! I thought it a very clever trick to lend a creature for payment that didn't belong to me! But you know what my grandam used to say about those who think themselves clever?

The only truly clever man is the man who knows he's nothing.

'Consternation!' Fabrizio blurted. 'Why doesn't she respond!'
'Use her proper name!'
'I will not!' he cried. 'And it's *not* her name.'
'Then flail and flap and flabbergast little knave.'
'Oh Master Marcel! Mistress Maxine!'
'Speak her name.' I cried.
'Oh very well! Whoa *Scorregiatore!*' he cried.
Instantly the beast began to settle, though Maxine had to stifle a laugh for the new name I gave the she-beast was Italian for "farter."
'Remember little knave, that creature belongs to me now.'
'But Master Marcel ...'
'And now I've renamed her you *must* use that name. Otherwise she'll learn bad habits!'
I glanced at him beside us. He sighed with relief as the jennet appeared to settle, or so he thought. For when the reins were drawn tight and the rear of another beast hovered in front, it was also her habit to try to outpace any rival ahead. All at once she began to surge!
'Whoa Scorregiatore!' he squeaked.
'Be assertive boy!'
'Whoa Scorregiatore!' he cried in high toned frustration.
'Deep voice Squire Cavoli!'

Another backhand slapped my shoulder smartly.

'Marcel desist!' Maxine protested.

'Whoa!' Fabrizio bellowed ridiculously. 'Scorregiatore!'

Despite her reprimand Maxine smirked to hear that word spat with such passion.

'Master Marcel! Mistress Maxine!' he pleaded. 'This is not amusing! My own beast won't respond to my call!

'*Your* beast?'

'And why must you abuse my mother tongue to misname her?'

'Dunderhead, what's ails you about her name?'

'Honestly Mistress Maxine, who names a working animal so?'

'Smelling as she does' I cried 'what ninny called her *Fleur?*'

'Perhaps.' he conceded. 'But what sort of name is *Farter?*'

'She's an ass? What else does that body part do?'

'Master Marcel you must rename her. It's a deep humiliation to say such a word in the company of our Master and Mistress. Madame Capulet's a refined lady. I feel so greatly ashamed!'

'Marcel?' purred Maxine in a warning tone.

'Oh very well.' I glanced at her. 'But the name must be *fitting.*'

'Well she's full of mischief.' said Maxine. 'Why not *Cupid?*'

'That does have a charm to it, yes. But for that *smelly* beast?'

'She's cantankerous.' said Fabrizio. 'Call her *Brontolone.*'

'Oh Fabio, what does that mean?' Maxine queried.

'Grouch, Mistress Maxine.'

'Oh yes. That suits her.'

'Yes not bad.' I sniffed. 'But I'm a poet. A sensitive man of learning and culture.'

'If you do say so yourself!' Maxine snapped the reins.

'When I renamed her before I adopted a *theme.*'

'Crass body functions!' railed Fabrizio.

I feigned contemplation. Maxine's elbow dug my rib firmly.

'Ah! I have it. If not Farter, then true to our theme, henceforth the she-beast shall be called ... *Shitter!*'

'Oh yes!' Fabrizio spat in disgust. 'Sensitive man of culture!'

'Marcel?' Maxine warned more intently.

'Shame on you!' snarled Fabrizio. 'Let's see how long you retain employment entertaining our dame in fine company with wit themed upon crass language!'

His anger was priceless but Maxine's amusement was spent.

'Oh Master Troubadour what a broad vocabulary you possess for vulgarity! Why in Italy only the basest fool would ever ...'

'Fool!' said an interrupting feminine voice from behind us.

I glanced with a gulp. Suddenly the Capulets were there. And given I'd not heard the approach of their beasts, I feared they had been stalking us and listening for some time.

'Yes, Fabrizio.' said Ilaria thoughtfully from the back of her mystical mare. 'That's a *very* good word to use as a *name* for someone. And Fool is a very poetic word too.' she added slyly turning to Armand. 'Don't you think so, my heart?'

'Mmm. Yes angel I do.'

'Ah! It's Madame Capulet.' I smiled. 'And Chevalier Capulet. I trust you're both well, enjoying the alpine atmosphere.'

'Rogue you're as cheeky as an ass.'

'Touché Chevalier! Pun intended of course.'

'Humour has its place.' added Armand.

'Even base humour from time to time.' added Ilaria.

'Yes angel. But my junior squire, who's been gravely distracted from his duty, is quite correct.'

'I'm sorry Chevalier.' Fabrizio bleated. 'I tried to –'

'Yes Squire Cavoli, no matter. But next time I give you an order and someone –' He stared at me soberly. '– attempts to divert you. I'll expect you to deal with them.'

'Yes Chevalier. Yet ... he's bigger than me.'

'He is. However Squire, that's what weapons are for.'

My eyes leapt wide. 'Cupid's Balls!' I cried in protest.

'Marcel!' hissed Maxine, glancing at Ilaria.

'Pardon Madame. But surely Chevalier? To give that dolt any manner of weapon –'

'Would befit his rank as my junior squire. Indeed I had my first rondel at his age.'

'Oh my heart, that sounds like an important token.' She spurred to one side of Fabrizio's mount.

'Yes angel, very important.' Armand spurred too, and laid a hand on Fabrizio's shoulder as the lad puffed with pride.

'Well then ...' Ilaria began. 'oh what did you call him, Maxine?'

Suddenly, I realised they'd heard much more than I hoped.

'*Fabio* mistress.'

'Oh yes, I like that.' She smiled. 'Then Fabio, we must find you something special in Turin.'

'But for now Squire Cavoli ...' said Armand 'a mule crop will suffice to silence your detractors.'

Armand drew the tool from its holster on the she-beast and handed it to Fabrizio.

'Yes Chevalier.' He glared at me with a warning frown.

'Keep it with you. And don't hesitate to use it if necessary.'

'Yes Chevalier.'

Oh I know, Fabrizio was young to call a *man*. But it was our old master's way to use that term for every squire, no matter their age. I must confess, it stirred me too to hear Armand say it. And for the love of folly, it made the urchin grin from ear to ear.

'Max!' cried Armand. 'Halt the wagon.'

'Shall I ring the bell to recall the men Monsieur?'

'Not yet. I want to see how long it takes them to respond.'

'And Marcel, while we wait?' said Ilaria.

'Yes Madame.'

'We heard your little exchange. *All* of it.'

'Well then I'm sure you understand it was all said in good –'

Armand interrupted me. 'Rogue, as Squire Cavoli pointed out to you so passionately, we no longer keep exclusive company with hard military men. Do we, my dear *wife?*'

'No, my darling *husband*, we do not.'

Both had a gleam in their eyes. It's seen only in newlyweds when they hear those enchanted words, *husband* and *wife*, while they still have a new flavour to them. Her fingers drew the tendril of a gauze sail away from her cheek that had blown from the heart-shaped escoffion on her head. Its pale azure and pearl tones accented her hair perfectly of course.

Ilaria continued. 'And as we travel Marcel, I intend to enlarge our social circuit extensively. Therefore as our *Fool* –'

My brows leapt high in genuine dismay.

'But Madame I protest! I'm much more than a –'

'As our *Fool* … if we need to call upon you this evening to entertain us in mixed company, I will expect much *better*.'

I opened my mouth to retort but Armand glared in warning.

'Oh yes Madame … of course.' I grumbled.

The clatter of new arrivals drew our glances. Caspar came from one direction, Liberati and Boccolo from the other.

'Or else …' said Ilaria glancing at Armand.

'There is an *or else* Madame?' I groaned.

'There is. Or else by Maxine's report, I understand Fabio not only speaks …' she glanced for support.

'Five!' Maxine twittered.

'Five languages but he also *sings* pleasantly.'

My eyes leapt with disbelief.

'And Madame' said Maxine 'Fabio's skilled with the piccolo.'

'I love the piccolo.' Ilaria twittered

'I hate the piccolo!'

'Hush rascal!' snapped Ilaria. 'Moreover I'm told Fabrizio dances gracefully too!'

That was the final straw of course! And so, I launched into a mockery of protest.

'Sing in my stead! That impish hobgoblin? Huff and puff on the piccolo! And dance! Perish the thought Madame Capriciousness!'

Ilaria's brows leapt in shock. But she instantly supressed a smile. Even Armand smiled to hear me rail with such inventiveness.

'And you!' I spat to Maxine in mock disgust. 'Demoiselle of the Bedpan! Cease your ill-informed interjections too!'

By now, to my relief, all were smiling except our giant ninny. I stood with a pirouette, holding the lute behind me with one hand and doffing my hat to my heart with the other.

'Rest assured, my demanding dame! This evening I'll attend with cleverness and sensitivity to all the tastes required by yourself and your esteemed husband.' I bowed deeply.

'You're an incorrigible rogue.' said Armand.

Victoire tossed his mighty head apparently in agreement.

'I thank you for the compliment Chevalier.'

'And Marcel, I'll thank you to ensure that before we cross into Squire Cavoli's homeland, you return to calling that mule by its given name and no other.'

'Fleur?' My mouth dropped open.

'Rogue! You know it's ill luck to rename a beast!'

'Very back luck.' spat the giant without warning.

'Aye.' added Liberati.

'Indeed.' agreed Boccolo.

My head spun on a pivot to the source of each comment, and I glared at each ridiculously.

'Oh, oh, oh ... as you wish Chevalier.'

Ilaria intervened again. 'Moreover you charlatan, I'll no longer allow you to speak of that mule as a *loan* to Fabri - to dear Fabio!'

'*Dear* Fabio? Oh but Madame -'

'By my reckoning of its history -' She glanced at Armand. '- correct me if I err, it was purchased in Carentan by my thoughtful husband for the use of his new page?'

'I do recall assigning the little beast to the little man.'

'Whilst you, prince of fools, were assigned to the gelding no longer required by Caspar.'

'Oh yes, but Madame ...'

'And so, clever fool, since you've ridden it constantly against Fabio's want -'

'But Madame Capulet -'

'Oh no, clever fool. I'm Madame *Capriciousness!* And so if you hope to retain the use of *any* beast at all, or perhaps my heart ...' she turned to Armand 'he may prefer to follow afoot for a day or two?'

'Afoot!' I cried. 'No Madame. I would NOT prefer that at all!'

Armand lifted her hand and kissed it with a smile. 'Ah rogue, see what comes of marrying a merchant's daughter?'

'Yes Chevalier.' I frowned. 'It's clear I am indeed Madame Capulet's Fool.'

'Not just *my* fool rascal. Now you're fortune's fool because you're the first unfortunate in our entourage I feel obliged to assign *punishment* to.'

She looked soberly at Armand as if pleading she had no choice.

'Yes dear wife, it only seems fitting.'

'Punishment?' I blurted. 'Fitting? A punishment *for?*'

'Taking unfair advantage of ... another in in our employ.'

'Precisely angel. And perhaps also –' He glanced at Fabrizio whose stupid face was filled with delight. '– for the excessive use of *vulgar* humour?'

'Just so, my heart. Those are his crimes.'

'My crimes?'

'I'm glad you agree. Now for a penance to match them.'

'But Madame I protest!'

'As you will. But from this moment I declare that the title of *Fool* shall be the only manner of address allowed throughout our company, for *any* who wish to hail your attention.'

'Cupid's Balls! How long must I endure that indignity?'

'Until?' she raised her gorgeous brows and glanced to her husband for guidance.

'Until my very appealing wife proclaims it may be otherwise?'

'Oh handsome husband you took the words out of my ....'

With a kiss before she could finish, one that was far too loving for my liking, the fond couple sealed my fate. Never have I witnessed a more putrid display of affection or insidious abuse of power.

'Now Fool!' snapped Armand playfully. 'Get down off that wagon and drive the baggage cart. Angel, I believe it's time for my convalescent massage.'

'It is my heart.'

'Convalescent massage!' I cried in spite. 'Is that what you call your ribald antics?' The look on their staring faces caused me to reconsider my outburst. 'At once Chevalier.' I bleated. 'I will shut my mouth and go at once.'

For now I was done with foolery and felt crestfallen as I went. I climbed aboard the baggage cart, miserable that even Maxine would be forced to address me as *Fool*. I ask you, how much ardour could her lips hold for me after hearing that on the lips of all in our company?

Ilaria declared that when we arrived in Turin, she'd boast to all new acquaintances that they employed a dedicated fool! Yes, I knew in exalted circles that was considered an even greater luxury than a dedicated musician. And yes, I knew the punishment was meant to be temporary. Yet by the look on her face as she said so, I feared her hope to make the title permanent. Yes, yes, yes I know that now I claim myself to be a professional fool. At that moment however, it was not my ambition.

By the end of that day the last milestone sighted put our location halfway to Turin and so we halted to stay the night in a high mountain village. The rustic post-house had an intimate drinking room and a very large fire. Our people gathered together in the fore chamber to enter and dine. Yet before Ilaria entered I pleaded my case again.

'Please Madame I beg you. I consider myself a musician who toys with fooling, not a fool who toys with musicality.'

'We'll see *Fool*. Take your penance with patience and we'll see.'

'I can see you're enjoying my ...'

'One more word *Fool* and you'll trot tomorrow too.'

Maxine threw me a glance of mock concern.

'Yes Madame.' I bleated sourly and tilted my eyes to Heaven.

That night I performed before our entourage; a small audience of rustics, a travelling merchant couple and an elite elder couple who, like ourselves had underestimated how long it would take on the alpine path to reach the next citadel. I also decided I was in the mood to exact some revenge for my discomfort. If I must suffer the rare punishment of being anointed a fool, then I must offer my punishers a rare dose of fooling.

After much intoxicating liquid was drained by all and I'd sung and played a little, I began to chatter. I teased the Capulets, gently at first. Then I began to recall the first day of our travels and Maxine's attempt to attend to her new master's hurt with her potions and skill. Oh yes, eyes began to open. Ears began to lean.

In rather quick time, my tale reached the point where Ilaria spurned Maxine from the improvised boudoir, declaring she must attend to her husband's needs personally! Merry glances and tittering rose through the intimate chamber. Despite the bashful looks growing on the Capulet's faces, and goaded by my want for sweet revenge and the smirks and smiles rising on every other face, I threw all caution to the wind.

Running on fast, I recounted how the newlyweds became so passionately engulfed behind the coverlets while Maxine and I sat upon the other side, listening and imagining! Then in a ribald rendition of his voice and hers, I began to mimic the passionate sounds of their love play!

A burst of laughter erupted as the chamber sprang to life.

Sitting nearby, completely unwound by the effect of her wine, Maxine was squirming with delight. All at once, I was panting and huffing and sighing and groaning in mimic and mockery of the Capulet's noisy amour. Then to my utter surprise, Maxine rose and rushed to my side to take up Ilaria's part herself!

Oh for the love of folly! It was utter delight! We rose together in a lustful cacophony until suddenly Maxine lost all control. In a ridiculous mimic of what she imagined they may look like, Maxine leaned and reached and groped at my body. Fingers clutched and pulled my hair. I couldn't resist following her lead of course and matched her wild efforts with reckless abandon!

At first Armand and Ilaria squirmed and winced, their awkwardness adding to the hilarity. Yet to give them their due, having drunk just as deeply the rest of us, before very long they both began to smirk and titter. Soon they were laughing outright! Finally they fell into cackling fits of enjoyment, taking it all with a very good grace.

In a moment of rare sport, encouraged the sight of Ilaria now laughing for all she was worth, Maxine shoved me down, clambered on top and shunted her hips wildly. Then to the amusement of those from our own ensemble – who had heard her more than once already – Maxine captured that singular manner in which Ilaria sang, sighed and stuttered her way up to delirium and then came shuddering down the other side.

I did my best to replicate Armand's hefty grunts and groans. I even added the spice of nonsensical noises! He later confided that portion had caused him to laugh until he hurt again. And finally, to borrow the panting phrase of Maxine, when we were spent and catching our breath together, the result was *unforgettable*. I confess that our duet was much better than my solo effort which had started it all.

I swear to you all sweet friends, having Maxine join the cast of my revenge comedy was the most magnificent mischief I've ever experienced, simply enthralling. Even the abashed Fabrizio – after protesting strenuously at the start before Ilaria hushed him herself – finally found our devilish antics entertaining. I think seeing his glamorous mistress laugh so heartily at her own mimic, and his warlike master smiling and hugging his young wife to see her enjoyment, finally calmed our sensitive junior squire.

Fabrizio was beginning to understand. There was more to being a premiere sieur or dame than simply being resplendent or holding aloof for every moment of every day. I must confess that after that evening, Fabrizio, Maxine and I began to keep more convivial company together. Strangely, with each passing day thereafter, we found ourselves wanting to remain in closer company.

And that very night, to my surprise, Fabrizio was first to cease calling me *Fool* even though Ilaria hadn't yet declared my time as served. Wilt all the guests retired from the drinking chamber, we were leaning against the wide sill of an open window casement, gazing into the star studded night sky with the chill of brisk alpine air on our faces.

'Don't want to enjoy twisting the knife while there's still time?'

'I don't gain any joy from the discomfort of others.' he said.

'That sounds noble. What about when Maxine and I mimicked

our betters in such an ... intimate way?'

He glanced sideways, pouted in thought, then stared ahead.

'I thought it was hurting them. When I realised it wasn't ... Besides, I remember ...' He faltered and fell silent.

'What do you remember?' I asked quietly and glanced.

Fabrizio gazed into the middle distance. I recognised the look.

'I remember that on the worst day of my life, when our brave chevalier died ... a person who kept my spirits up.' He glanced again. 'When I couldn't close my eyes he played me to sleep and watched over me until Chevalier Capulet offered us service together.'

'Is that what he did?' said Ilaria emerging like a phantom.

She drew closer behind and between us but leaned to Fabrizio.

'Oh Madame Eavesdropper!' I spat mockingly. 'Cupid's Balls! You should be a *spy* not a merchant.'

'Madame he does that on –'

'Purpose?' Ilaria whispered. 'Yes Fabio I know.' She leaned to lay an arm around his shoulders. 'He did it to me. Pay him a compliment, tell him you know he cares about someone? Oh, he becomes so greatly offended.' She tilted her eyes to the Heavens. 'It's very perverse.'

'What is perverse Madame ...'

'Don't say it rascal. Now we *all* know you're a complete fraud.'

'A complete fool you mean.'

'Oh I think you're a much too *sensitive* a fellow to be made to suffer that title any longer.'

'You mean...?'

'As of this moment you're no longer my fool but my musician.'

'Hmm.' I pouted, grimacing.

She huffed in mock consternation.

'Oh well now what's the matter?'

'I must confess. I was growing rather fond of being Madame Capulet's Fool.'

She tilted her head to the junior squire. 'Fabio why did I suspect that may be his response.'

They smiled together. Watching her intimacy with him it suddenly occurred to me. Ilaria had come to realise she was more to Fabrizio than just his new employer. She understood Armand had become the father figure he'd lost in Toulon. She knew she must become more to him too. In my mind however it begged a question: what was Ilaria to me?

I was older than herself yet younger than Armand. She was not my new *mother*. My long-suffering maman, bless her beautiful heart, was still alive in Paris. But yes, Ilaria was becoming something more than just my employer. Indeed, all in our entourage were beginning to feel more like famille. And the relaxed esprit we were discovering in each other's company was making time pass more quickly.

As we left early for Turin the next morning, with more smiles showing on more faces than usual at such an hour, all seemed enlivened by the fun being experienced through our companionship.

All but one.

Leading us forward, one still appeared to pass his time more quietly, with less sense of belonging. Mounted alone each day at the fore, Caspar's solitary form began to make me consider his isolation.

With Fabrizio driving the baggage wagon again, I tethered the mule and sat up with Maxine in the carriage wagon to share my thoughts.

'That's ... considerate of you.' she replied.

'Well don't sound so surprised. I can be considerate.'

'I know you can. As for Caspar? Some souls prefer isolation.'

'Do you think that's what *he* prefers?'

'Hmm. Best leave him to himself for now. See how he adjusts.'

'He's far from his home and famille. No chance of returning for a very long time.'

'Yes. And he went through that battle with the master too.'

'At Formigny, yes. Not at Carentan.'

'You said at Carentan he was sided with the English.'

'He was. And they tried to kill each other. Fate is perverse.' I looked far ahead to see him on his painted stallion. 'The giant ninny entered that war on one side and exited on the other.'

'How very strange.' Maxine snapped the reins a little. 'Heaven knows what they experienced in that final nightmare together.'

'The master said Caspar saved him more than once at Formigny. And that night after the battle, before he slept, Caspar said the master rode into the fight like he expected to die.'

'Dear mercy.' Maxine shook her head confoundedly.

'Since then however ... he's said no more of it.'

'Caspar's used to the company of rough, martial men. It must be difficult for such a foreboding man from another kingdom to warm to a mixed company of foreigners.'

'Hmm. Perhaps.' I gazed and mused.

'Unlike Boccolo and Liberati. They seem like amiable fellows.'

Maxine smiled, yet her compliment of them drew my interest.

'They are. But they're disciplined too. The master's sire said he picked them for their ability to *respond in a dire situation*.'

'They're Italian. Surely that played into their selection.'

'I believe Boccolo hails from Milan.'

'And Liberati told me he was born very near to Verona.'

'Oh did he chatty woman? Anything else to know?'

'As a matter of factum, yes. He said their service had been contracted with a period of *probation*.'

It took me a moment to process that. Then it made me start.

'Oh? That seems odd for veteran soldiers.'

'It's because this service is more a gift to them than the master.'

'Yet how so?'

'His sire offered this chance to return home to Italy and see if they may gain employment there before –'

'Before the end of probation finalises the new agreement?'

'And compel, whoever stays on with us, to return to France.'

'And so by the time we return, one or both may have left us.'

'I believe the notion of it is, if the master loses one or both by then, he'll recruit men of France working in Italy that wish to return.'

'That would be a crying shame! I'm just getting used to them.'

'Yes. I feel safer in their company. So does the mistress.'

'I can understand that after the incident in Grenoble. I wonder how they feel? Each has served the Capulets for over ten years.'

'I think they're growing fond of us. But they're going home Marcel. They must have famille to return to who miss them.'

'*Famiglia* is the Italian term. But yes, that may be.'

'Oh *famiglia* or *famille*! I don't want to lose either of them.'

'Nor do I sweetheart. I do hope they stay. At least for a while.'

At that, Maxine fell quiet.

Yet given what she had explained, one way or another, we would know that answer quite soon. For in less than half an hour a pilgrim we passed informed us that we had already crossed into Italy. Maxine and I stared at each other. The kingdom of our birth lay behind us. Neither of us had ever ventured beyond its border.

Nor did we realise our safety was about to be tested again.

Chapter 9 the Loss of my Head

Turin drew into sight, little more than a speck in the distance. Yet our first Italian citadel loomed larger with every passing moment. Ilaria and Maxine were tantalised by the sight, chatting excitedly. Somehow the antic episode the night before of Maxine mimicking Ilaria had seemed to secure their bond even further. The range of experiences they began to share were expanding. Countess de Viviers once told Ilaria, bonds of shared experience often proved more potent than ties of blood. It felt like this may be the start of just such a bond between our two most important women. Oh yes, our only two women.

The development of such a bond between mistress and server was not always a foregone conclusion. If Ilaria's mother hadn't chosen so wisely, it may well have been otherwise? Then what a torment it may have been if neither cared for the company of the other. I've seen poor matches made between close servers supplied for young mistresses by parents. That can prove volatile.

It's more important, of course, that a mistress cares for the company of her server rather than the reverse. A server who develops disdain is more likely to sustain a pretence of affability for the sake of retaining employment. A confident young mistress is far less likely to reciprocate. However, in the case of our most important women, I can safely report, despite my own favour for Maxine at that time, much like Ilaria, Maxine was considered by all she met to be very easy to like.

And it was also clear from the start, that Maxine liked her new mistress. Despite the six years between them, she admired Ilaria greatly. She also loved the prospect of serving a mistress with a merchant's interest in the craft of couture. Maxine envied Ilaria's refined taste and sense of style. What's more, she seemed determined to make herself a more sophisticated companion to match Ilaria.

Now upon the road together, becoming more and more like a

pair of fond cousins – one very refined and one a little rustic – they began to complement each other's company. And as we had travelled on, the soundness of their match began to matter more greatly to Armand. For that spark of awareness for our safety, which I feared had become so lacking by the time we reached Grenoble, had finally resurfaced in him.

No doubt Liberati's report of the *Hallway Incident* stirred him from his stupor. Or perhaps it was triggered by the sight of Turin, our first real foreign destination. Knowing it was right there ahead of us meant we had certainly left the safety of France behind us. And so, I was sitting on my gelding – yes, yes, yes *my* gelding – as the sight of the citadel drew closer. In front of me was the rearmost wagon, and at a distance behind me were Liberati and Boccolo.

I was distracted with constructing a melody, humming a refrain back and forth, when I spied our giant man mountain. It wasn't hard for Caspar to attract attention. He was well to the fore on his painted beast, Loki. He only fell into view as he drew along a wide turn on the path up ahead. Yet he seemed to notice a signal from behind me and wheeled, coming about and spurring to a canter. And so yes, he was coming my way, but I was engrossed and planned to pay him scant attention.

Then a moment later, Liberati cantered past from behind me. He offered me a stoic glance going forward, as I now assumed, to take Caspar's place at the fore. Had I not been distracted by my music, I would have considered that change of their posts to be unusual. While I gazed forward at the oncoming monolith, Armand approached from behind on Victoire. He drew alongside me, the black mane and tail of his dappled grey stallion dancing in the breeze.

I blinked in wonder at the mythical beast that always drew fond glances. What's more I stared in daft surprise, wondering what Armand could require of me. Then as Caspar reached us, though I expected him to pass and fill the vacancy at the rear, to my further surprise he wheeled his brown and white monstrosity to fall in upon the other side of us.

The giant ninny stared ahead as if I didn't exist.

Armand frowned in thought.

'Marcel?'

'Yes Chevalier?' I asked warily.

Though in less formal moments I had begun to address Ilaria more casually as "mistress" just as Maxine did, I hadn't yet taken to calling Armand "master." Something about watching him kill five vicious men in Carentan still held my tongue at a formal distance. Moreover I felt that, as our new premiere sieur, that title may continue to remind him more soberly of his new responsibilities.

Oh yes, if I was vexed, or in a grave hurry, the term *master* might escape my lips. In the case of our former employer, Toulon, I was certainly used to saying it. At that moment however, with my lute on my lap, I felt neither vexed nor hurried. That was about to change.

'Once in Turin and then as we travel onward ...'

'Yes Chevalier.'

'If for any reason, even for a *moment* I'm forced to leave sight of our company, I expect you to draw close to Ilaria and keep watch.'

'You want me to stay close and watch your very beautiful wife? Of course Chevalier.'

The giant ninny rolled his giant eyes. I rather expected his creature to do it too.

'Watch *about* my beautiful wife you rogue. For signs of *trouble*.'

'Oh, yes of course. However, if we were put upon by brutish trouble makers? I fear I'd be of little assistance.'

'On the contrary. Caspar and I agree that you're uniquely suited to the task.'

I stared soberly at Armand then glanced at Caspar.

'While I see how a witless giant may misjudge such a thing ...' I lifted a brow as he glared. 'as a man of intelligence Chevalier, how did *you* manage to agree to that absurdity?'

'When fire breaks or an enemy looms at the citadel gate, what's the first thing that must occur?'

I considered his riddle for a moment. 'Well ... I suppose some noisy blitherer must sound an alarm.'

'Just so!' spat Caspar with an uncharacteristic smile.

'Then you agree the first mechanism of defence is?' Armand riddled me again.

'A noise maker!' I smiled with satisfaction.

'You make more noise than anyone I've ever met.' said Caspar.

'Therefore rogue ...' Armand added 'at the first sign of trouble, raise the alert as *loudly* as you can and help will come.'

'Help will come?' I echoed sceptically.

'Yes. In a dangerous moment, that service from you will amount to far more than nothing at all.'

'Ah!' My eyes lit up. 'Then I'll be gratified to be of *more* help to your beautiful wife than *no* help at all.'

Almost in tandem, both warriors tilted their eyes to Heaven.

'At least with you hovering in my absence, she won't want for amusement.' said Armand with a smile.

'So *you* say Chevalier. I'll do my best to fulfill your command, but our premiere dame is not always patient in my company. What say she orders me *out* of her company?'

'Rogue. Don't give her reason to. If she enters a private closet to see to her ablutions? Well then of course –'

'I have permission to *follow*?'

'Stay *out*. In every other circumstance, stay *close*.'

'Fool!' snapped Caspar losing patience. 'Even if you're entertaining madame, keep a close watch.'

'Easy for you to say lummox! You're not entertaining at all!'

'Marcel.' Armand reached to draw my reign and halt us. 'All I require is that if you *ever* feel her guardians have missed something –'

'Yes Chevalier. I'll raise the alarm. *Very* loudly.'

He clicked his tongue and every beast started again.

'And Marcel?'

'Yes Chevalier?'

He reached an arm behind him. 'Take this.'

It was a stout mace, rather like a sceptre, yet evil-looking.

'But it's *ugly*. I'd look more threatening with a shiny dagger?'

'At least with that mace' blurted the monster 'you don't have to be very *accurate!*'

'And' Armand added 'it will pack more clout than a *lute.*'

My eyes widened with comprehension.

'Oh. You heard about that?'

'Never mind what I heard, pay attention.'

'Yes Chevalier.'

'You'll need to fashion a hanger for that mace. From now on, rogue, I want you to keep it on your hip at all times.'

'And...' spat the giant 'you must practise drawing it quickly with a good firm grip.'

I raised my brows. 'Are we still talking about the *weapon?*'

'Marcel!' I recognised the same stoic look Armand had the day Maxine was asked if she was up to *the task.* 'If anyone reaches an uninvited hand toward Ilaria –'

'Smash that into their head.' growled Caspar. 'Hard and fast!'

'Precisely.' said Armand.

'More than once if you have the presence of mind for it.'

The Giant spat to punctuate the offering.

'Yes.' Armand agreed. 'If you don't knock them senseless while you have the chance –'

'Yes, yes, yes I know.' I pleaded. 'They'll knock *me* senseless!'

'Better *you* take a beating than Madame.' snapped Caspar.

'Agreed.' said Armand, much too decisively.

'Well, I'm not so sure of that!' Both glared at me. 'Oh very well. But I won't agree to *enjoy* being beaten senseless.'

'By the time any can *try* Caspar or I should have their measure.'

'Should?'

A crooked smile creased the lummox's face. 'Well ... I may take some time to intervene.'

'Master do I have permission to clout that ninny as well?'

'Marcel.'

'Yes Chevalier?'

'You're welcome to try.'

'No Chevalier.'

A moment later they were riding forward together to leave me holding the ugly war mallet in my delicate musical hand. Cupid's Balls!

We entered Turin soon after. And from the moment we did that conference made me suspicious of every moving thing! As instructed, I sought a hanger for the gruesome instrument. Near to our lodging, I discovered a leatherworker who fashioned one nicely. Then, also as bidden, I began to practise drawing the club and swinging at the imaginary heads of imaginary bandits. Yes, my aggressive rehearsals drew supercilious looks from all who observed them!

I still considered the metal club far too ugly for a friendly entertainer to tote as an accessory. Then, to my joy, I happened upon a marionette maker's workshop which gave me a clever idea. Hanging in his window was a larger marionette, fashioned in the image of a fool! Yes, I purchased it. Yet I asked him to detach the head. He hollowed it to allow me to place it over the ugly head of my mace.

The inspiration to do it was partly for show, partly for my own amusement. Yet I soon realised, all who now saw the weapon considered it an object of mirth, cloaking its true nature. I felt sure if called to use it, that deception might afford me the element of surprise. When Armand and Ilaria saw it, they congratulated my effort. By then he had apprised her of his expectation for me to linger whenever he was drawn away.

Despite my misgivings, she didn't seem to mind the notion too greatly. She did sternly warn me however, if I earned her displeasure at such moments, I'd regret any sequel thereafter. At the time she offered that warning, the day before we left Turin, she was being fitted for a new garment. When I scoffed at the notion of her being displeased, she snatched out a pin holding a corner of the sumptuous fabric. Then as I turned to flirt with Maxine, she stuck my ass with it!

I leapt and shouted ridiculously. Maxine squealed with laughter, of course. But Ilaria, wearing a wicked smile, displayed the pin and offered her warning again.

'Heed my words, you rascal. Or else beware my sting.'

'Yes dread mistress.' I groaned.

Then I rubbed my backside far more than I needed to. Ilaria and Maxine laughed at my antics. That was something for my pain.

Yet our stay in Turin, other than providing me with a pain in my ass, proved to be no source of danger at all. For our young premiere dame however, Turin was the beginning of an indulgence in every aspect of Italian culture that began to envelope her. Immediately, she seemed to relish every morsel of it. And that was merely her first taste.

From there, we pushed beyond the towering peaks that hold it close, passing through the Padan Plain and onto Novara's rich pastures. The landscapes that opened before our eyes brimmed with grains and vineyards. Then by all that's holy, the resplendent citadel of Milan rose before us. Oh sweet friends, it was a rare sight to see.

The mighty citadel lured us in, immersing the Capulets in an even more vaulted experience of culture and hospitality. And it was in Milan that Ilaria's indulgence for all things Italianate became utterly feverish. In every merchant emporium we entered or seller's stall we browsed, her penchants caught fire.

Every aspect of that fabled citadel seemed to leave Ilaria breathless. As a daughter of fabric and fashion, she swooned at the styles of couture we encountered: high, middling and low. Italian fashions in coiffure, cosmetics and jewellery, then their manners – both public and intimate – swirled about her, coaxing her interest as she and Armand browsed and caroused.

Storage trunks and cases began to brim with purchases. Maxine began to dress more elegantly as ever more garments – discarded by her discerning mistress and adjusted by her too – graced her server's form. By then, I confess, Maxine had truly become my sweetheart. For by the time we had reached Milan, our intimacy had crossed a threshold.

No I won't scandalise you here with those details. Later, if you're well behaved – even if you're not – you'll learn more anon. But despite that new intimacy, thanks to Ilaria's rampant indulgence, we began to look less and less like a matched pair. For before we left Milan, Maxine dressed more like a refined demoiselle-in-waiting to an ever more refined premiere dame who was also a Merchant Princess.

In every new citadel we entered, Ilaria adopted whatever new style, colour or fabric combinations she discovered. Then at her insistence, all in our party except Caspar and our two veterans, dressed in more resplendent Italianate garb. Armand exempted our three men-at-arms. He insisted they continue to look as French as possible. For news of our victory against the English had run well ahead of us and was greatly enhancing local respect for the quality of our warriors.

I was no warrior of course, and so I was fitted for some fanciful new doublets. Yes they were more fetching. Yet I pleaded to Ilaria to spend less on my attire to allow for the purchase of a more splendid instrument. She didn't wish to sacrifice one for the other and began to insist but I haggled the point.

'When I play before all Madame, much more attention's drawn to my instrument than my attire .'

'That may be true rascal. What do you think Maxine?'

'It is.' I blurted before a word could pass her lovely lips. 'And you've seen my old lute and battered Irish harp.'

Maxine turned to Ilaria with a supportive frown.

'His harp is quite beaten Mistress.'

Seeing my chance, I pleaded again.

'Given my main employment Madame, first and foremost my instruments stand in greater need of replacement than my attire.'

'Hmm. Where would we find such tools?' Ilaria asked.

'Oh, I've seen one lute in particular which I greatly covet.'

'Have you?' She and Maxine exchanged a glance.

'Well, yes I have. When we were in the grand market, after you retired into the fabric closet to try on those intimate garments –'

'I assumed you were peeking.'

'Oh, I peeked. But not at you. Well yes, I always peek at you when any opportunity presents itself …'

'Marcel!' blurted Maxine.

'Oh and you too, sweetheart! I play no favourites when any part of a beautiful woman's body is on display. But not that time. That time I peeked into the store across the path.'

'The alchemist?'

'Next to the alchemist is the studio of a master luthier. Even in Paris I'd heard whisperings of him. Oh, and please don't tell the master I left you for that fleeting moment.'

'You know if he asks me directly –'

'Oh yes, yes Madame Capitulation.' I dared to interrupt as she supressed a smile. 'But oh! Oh when I entered and saw his work? Oh Ilaria – I mean *Madame*.'

Both their eyes leapt open wide.

'Imbecile!' spat Maxine. 'What's gotten into you?'

'Oh sweetheart I've been hexed!'

'Don't call me that in public while I attend our mistress.'

'Yes. You're right. But truly the sights in Maestro Amati's studio have left me spellbound.'

Maxine blinked in amazement. Ilaria's face lit with incredulity.

'It must have done you rascal. I've never heard my name on your lips before.'

'Apologies. Little excites me more than my craft.'

'So it seems.' Ilaria frowned with mock concern.

'Your lovely close server excluded of course.'

'Marcel!' hissed Maxine.

'Yes! Apologies again.' I fell to my knee. 'Oh Madame! Won't you at least come and see the gorgeous thing?'

After so much ado, she did so of course. Like me, both women stared in wonder at the instrument that had me smitten. It had an ebony back and neck that contrasted sharply against a light maple sounding board. The sound chamber was filled with a delicately patterned rose, carved from belly wood with delicate patterns of ivy and grapevines.

I accepted the lute reverently from the hands of the old master craftsman, running my own hands over its flawless lacquered timbers and veneers. It was as if I had been invited to touch a forbidden master work of art. When I glanced toward Ilaria and Maxine, I felt sure I looked like a puppy who hoped to be fed a delicate morsel.

'Dear Heaven rascal' Ilaria whispered 'it is divine.'

'Oh Marcel' said Maxine reverently 'it's simply beautiful.'

Ilaria met the ancient eyes of its maker. 'I must compliment you Maestro Amati on that breathtaking piece of work.'

'*Grazi* Madonna. Your man told me you're also an artisan. Of haute couture?'

Her brows lifted high. She turned her scandalised expression on me for an instant then turned back to the maestro.

'I am, but remain a poor novice. You're a deeply skilled artisan, a virtuoso, an artiste.'

'Hmm. I'll admit at my age, some call me the king of my craft.'

'From the evidence that surrounds us, it's a well-deserved accolade ... your Majesty.' She curtsied deeply, making him smile.

'Perhaps. But it may give me some right to assess the quality of other artisans. Would you agree?'

'Of course Maestro.'

'For if I'm not mistaken –' He stood in between Ilaria and Maxine '– you wear a new creation of our very own Donna Ferrazzi?'

'Yes. She completed it yesterday.'

'And it's very lovely.' He frowned quizzically. 'Indeed Isabella appears to have excelled herself. There's no doubt she's very talented.'

'I think so. Her capability is something to aspire to.'

'Yes, for some. But standing next to you Madonna –' He turned to Maxine. '– the form of your own follower is graced by something more inspiring. A genuine masterpiece.'

Maxine's eyes lit with sparks. Ilaria's eyes lowered to the floor.

'Madame created it herself maestro.' Maxine offered.

'Yes Signorina. It's easy to tell.'

'Maestro, we've never met before.' Ilaria chastised him. 'How could you possibly tell?'

'From the instructions you gave Isabella that have made her creation more exceptional than even her capability would afford.'

'I ... made some suggestions, yes. Yet Donna Ferrazzi is –'

'False dissembler I say!' He winked and gave a smile. 'Any who know what to look for, can tell from a glance at your own choices in either creation. You possess an uncanny eye Madonna for combining colours and textures. And … you have a rare gift for *composition*.'

'Maestro you don't need to flatter me to ensure my purchase. I'm happy to confess that I intend to take the lovely thing.'

'It may be flattery if you were merely a purchaser. But to one's peer, an artisan has a sacred duty of recognition. Tell me. Are your gifts more inherited or learned from a mentor?'

'My parents are my mentors. And so I suspect the truth lies somewhere in between.'

'No doubt.' He murmured.

'Yet if I had to assess the source of my intuition, I'd say I've inherited an eye for combination from my papa and an eye for composition from my maman.'

Amanti wagged a finger of pronouncement.

'And my intuition tells me that you've surpassed them both. I know I have skill Madonna. And yes, many praise it. But I'll accept praise from you as the rare compliment of one artiste to another.'

'Oh no Maestro. Not at all.'

'Oh yes. The veteran maestro humbly accepts the praise of a budding maestra.'

She frowned with the kind of confused humility I was more use to seeing on Armand's face.

'No. No not a maestra.'

'Yes. And from the evidence before *me* it's clear you're already worthy of the accolade.'

Though I was moved by his heartfelt praise, it meant that I was no longer the centre of attention. And so I held up the magnificent instrument and cleared my throat discreetly.

'If you're done praising each other fond doters … look! It has movable frets!'

'Made from the finest sheep gut of course.' said Amanti.

'Maestro, may I play it for her?'

'Be my guest Master Poquelin. I'd never allow any to purchase an unheard instrument. But first Madonna … please take my seat.'

Quiet descended as Ilaria settled. I cradled the sacred instrument and shut my eyes. My fingertips felt the strings bend-bend-bending to my pressure and then I began to play. My mind and heart were swept through its frame, every sensual tone poured through my soul like a cascade of sweet angel song. By the time I was done, Ilaria pronounced the tone of the rare lute to be otherworldly.

All that while, our giant Caspar who'd escorted us for protection stood silently scanning for threats. Ilaria turned to Amanti and suggested, in order to test the instruments true worth, I must sing as I played. The maestro agreed. By then however I felt certain, she simply wished to spend a little more time in the old man's company.

During that encore our grim giant listened blankly. Or so I thought. For when I concluded, with no invitation to do so and much to my surprise, the towering ninny announced *his* verdict!

'Between your warbling baritone and the sonorous bass of that pretty instrument, it was a fine harmonic partnership.'

To say we were stunned to hear that critique issue from the ever-silent and foreboding man mountain, would be one of the greatest understatements of my lifetime. What's more, Armand had also stepped into the shop while I sang. But when he heard that commentary he glanced sidelong at his squire, wondering what else he may be capable of.

Then to my greater amazement, Ilaria crowned the odd experience by stepping up to the ninny, standing high on her toes and by way of miraculous reward, for merely opening his wide mouth, kissed him upon the cheek! Cupid's Balls! For the very first time I saw the giant ninny blush like a novice. I glared indignantly at her.

'I was the one who *created* the fine harmonic partnership!' I leaned my cheek and pointed to it.

'You did rascal. However I see little need to reward more utterances from one whose mouth is forever awash with sound.' Everyone smiled but me. 'Perhaps if you took a vow of *silence* for –'

'A week?' I offered hopefully.

'A month!' she retorted. 'Even *you* might earn such a reward.'

I spurted a huff of incredulity. Armand drew his arm around her as he coughed for her attention.

'Suffice it to say angel *that* payment will never be required.'

They both laughed. The Maestro did too.

'Oh yes, touché Chevalier Cough-a-lot!' That set all laughing. 'Yet I'll thank you both to leave the humouring to me!'

'To you?' he spat. 'I thought you didn't want to be our fool?'

'Ha! Less embarrassing than leaving folly to either of you!'

Though I was jealous at her show of favour to Caspar, I was happy to see my brazen reprimands being so well tolerated. Both my employers were becoming used to my want, within reason, to be able to scold them. As you may understand, to do so with relative impunity, is meant to be a sacred license afforded to one's dedicated fool.

We left Milan behind us, toting my new lute and an extra wagon to accommodate Ilaria's growing trove. Our path continued along the ancient road – the *Via Gallica* – which stretches west to east across the country. That mighty thoroughfare connects Milan to the port of Venice and would deliver us to each citadel in between, including Verona.

Armand expected the broad path to be easy to follow and brimming with travellers, making our travel safer. Soon after our exit from Milan, we found ourselves flanked by merchant and martial traffic of every description. Pilgrims appeared more often too, most crossing our path from north to south, heading to or from the sacred citadel of Rome.

As you may know, the distance from Milan to Bergamo is perhaps ten leagues. The distance from Bergamo to Brescia is about the same and the final portion from Brescia to Verona spans just a trifle more. And so, as long as none of our haulage beasts went lame, we expected the distance between each citadel would take no more than a day to transit.

With each step closer to Verona our excitement was growing. When we climbed up into the charming seat of Bergamo, high on its lofting hill, dear Heaven sweet friends it was simply beautiful. By the time we departed there Maxine was very loathe to leave. She dubbed Bergamo the *Ethereal Citadel*.

No, it didn't have the bustling allure of Milan. Yet I agreed with Maxine, Bergamo simply proved to be one of those restive places where a person could imagine spending their lifetime. Not only did I concur with that assessment, all at once I began to consider the notion of spending my lifetime with Maxine.

Oh yes, I know *what kind of potion was possessing me?* Sweet friends it was a potion called love, offered in the form of the only woman who's ever personified it to me. Oh yes, I'll move on.

From Bergamo we wandered into the Lake Iseo district to make our approach to Brescia. It would be our last stop before pushing on for Verona. A cousin of Ilaria's named Maël resided in Brescia. The day we arrived in Bergamo she sent word to ensure he anticipated our coming. Late the next day she received a reply.

The missive informed her of how excited Maël and his *famiglia* were to know of our pending arrival. He wrote of how much he looked forward to reacquainting after such a long time. Ilaria hadn't seen Maël since he left Lyon to marry. Since then his wife had five children, Ilaria's nephews and nieces. And so as we left Bergamo for Brescia, she was brimming with anticipation to meet them.

The citadel was sighted earlier than expected, which was well, for our forward team had developed a hobbler. When we approached the walls of Brescia, the guardians of the western gate looked us over without suspicion, waving us through quickly. Shortly thereafter, not a furlong from the gate, Armand sighted a post-house and called a halt.

Knowing we planned to depart early next morning to allow us more time in Verona, Armand announced his want then and there to exchange the hobbler. By the time we reached Maël and became swept up by his hospitality, the chance to do so thereafter in good time may be lost. By Armand's reckoning Maël's palazzo was not much further, so we had little reason to fear a short delay.

Attached to the post-house was a small tavern. For some in our entourage, including Ilaria, it beckoned our interest to attend to ablutions before we presented to our hosts. Liberati was directed to enter the post-house and see to the replacement. As he walked on, the Capulets turned their attention to the tavern house. Ilaria signalled for Maxine to follow.

Armand and Ilaria pressed on toward the tavern's entry while in the forecourt, perhaps twenty yards to their left, Caspar and Boccolo stopped by a well. From that vantage they could slake their thirsts and remain in sight of our wagons. Now assigned to drive our extra wagon, I was last to step down.

As my feet touched the ground and I turned, Maxine was passing. She cast a questioning glance between my legs. I looked for myself and smiled. For comfort while driving the wagon, I'd drawn the hanger holding my mace with its marionette head, to the middle of my belt. That allowed the unruly thing to hang more comfortably between my legs. Yet Maxine glared.

'That looks too suggestive.'

'Would you like to touch it?'

'Don't be saucy! Fix it before the mistress sees. Follow me fast.'

'Yes sweetheart.'

I tilted my eyes to Heaven, made the adjustment, then hastened to catch Maxine. She scurried to catch Ilaria and be ready to assist before she entered the tavern. Glancing about me as I went, I noticed Caspar. Scanning instinctively, he waited for Boccolo to drink at the well. An instant later he heard, then saw, a young boy approach.

Caspar's eye caught a glimpse of the lad as he scurried past, heading toward the door of the drinking house. He was calling for his father who, by all appearances, lurked somewhere within.

Between that moment and the next pandemonium erupted!

Caspar's eyes lurched as he glanced about frantically. He caught sight of the Capulets on the verge of following the boy inside. Armand glanced inside for safety, then held to allow Ilaria through before him. Just as she did so the toe of her shoe clipped an uneven surface on the floor boards beneath.

Ilaria reached a hand out to steady herself, grasping for the door frame. Then without warning, a massive arm reached over Armand's shoulder, sweeping him aside, as the jolting grip of a massive paw snatched onto Ilaria's wrist and wrenched her away. It was Caspar!

Assuming the grim giant had lost his wits, the unexpected assault sparked a potent reaction from our polite mistress. She flailed in the massive man's grasp, bucking and kicking. Her free hand opened, lifted and smacked with fury against his bearded cheek!

She opened her lips to scream! Yet before she could shout, the titan's massive hand clapped over her mouth. Her eyes leapt wide. He groped a massive arm about her waist, tucking her to his side like baggage and began to haul her away. The sight of her abduction left Maxine and I stupefied of course.

That astonishing transaction took only an instant as Armand stumbled and flinched and turned. He blinked in confusion at the sight of the erratic monolith, manhandling his wife and attempting to flee. Armand lurched after them shouting a command to halt!

Misbelieving our eyes, Maxine and I froze for a moment, then rushed headlong into the drama. Suddenly Caspar, assailed by a command to halt, feeling a clap on his shoulder to turn him, dumped Ilaria like a sack of grain! She squealed then landed with a thud as the giant spun on his heel to engulf the leaping Armand in his arms.

'Cupid's Balls on fire!' I squealed. 'I'm coming Master!'

Caspar snapped his massive hand over Armand's mouth too. They struggled together in a flailing mess. Ilaria flapped and floundered, trying to stand against a tangle of dirt-smeared skirts and dusted train. Still confounded by panic, Maxine and I raced in to help Ilaria to her feet.

Lifting and steadying, I could see Maxine had her, then spun on my heel to see if I could aid Armand. My eyes were aghast. Our run amok giant was leaning his open mouth toward Armand's ear. Fearing the out-of-control ingrate would bite it off completely, I drew my stout mace! I knew I must smash him first! More than once if possible!

The moment had come to PROVE my mettle. I saw Caspar whisper to Armand whose eyes jumped open wide. I had no doubt it was a threat of death or worse! I drew my mace. I loaded it high to swash a blow at the hideous monster! Then screaming for courage and shutting my eyes, I swung in anger as hard as I could.

Krumpp!

Yes! I cried triumphantly in my head as I felt the impact. My eyes leapt open to see the result! Saints mock me for a blasted Fool! I had struck Armand instead. The giant oaf was completely unhurt. My marionette's skull was all smashed apart.

Knowing that blow was meant for him the titan glared with death in his eyes. He released Armand. Surely now he would snap my neck in vengeance! I winced and crouched, hoping Armand would come to my aid as promised! But instead of turning on Caspar, he leapt toward Ilaria.

Now on her feet with Maxine fussing about, pleading to know if she was hurt, Ilaria turned to scream blue murder at Caspar. Yet again with no warning, before a sound left her lips, our elegant mistress was hauled off her feet by her now wounded husband.

Cupid's Balls! It was mid-morning madness!

Blood flowed from his hair to his cheek as Armand swept Ilaria up, squealing in fright 'til she realised who had her. He shot a warning glare at Maxine and I, shunting his head toward the wagons. Then with his mystified wife in his arms, our master ran as fast as he could. It was even more confusing than watching the fiasco begin.

Suddenly recalling the threat of our giant, I spun to face him. Yet Caspar had wheeled and was racing across to Boccolo. He skidded to a halt and held the soldier in urgent conference for an instant. Their exchange set Boccolo racing into the post-house to fetch Liberati. Maxine and I blinked, clutched our hands, and ran to the wagons for dear life. Still we knew nothing but we had seen more than enough.

Clearly something desperate and dangerous was in motion. From the corner of my eye as we ran, I saw Liberati surge over the post-house threshold, hot on the heels of the sprinting Boccolo. They leapt aboard their mounts in a frenzy, then wheeled and reached to snatch the halters of the leading beasts. They wheeled again as the teams came about, facing back the way we had come.

One heartbeat later from inside the drinking house, screams of panic erupted. All at once patrons came pouring out, stumbling into the street, cursing and crying out their alarm. We had gathered ourselves in a flurry of desperate whispering when suddenly, as if from nowhere, a sheriff appeared on the deck by the drinking house door.

By good or ill fortune he was attending to a ruckus nearby. Instantly roused by the hue and cry, the sheriff ran headlong to investigate. Despite the summer's warmth, he was robed in the fur-lined coat of his office and flanked by a lackey who toted a bell. For all the world, the latter looked like a witless ostrich.

The sheriff considered the conundrum for a moment, then ordered his lackey in to investigate. In went the ostrich with bulging eyes, buffeted by patrons lurching in the opposite direction. He vanished and time hung still for a moment. Then his warning bell burst into action. Suddenly the lackey re-emerged, flapping his wing and with a terrified nod, confirmed the source of our pandemonium.

As the bell clanged to the erratic rhythm of the flapping ostrich, the sheriff filled his lungs to utter a grim declaration.

'An outbreak of Black Death is suspected! This establishment must now be held under STRICT confinement! Summon the TEAM!'

A hammer in the lackey's other hand began to belt at his bell.

Clang! Bing bing! Clang! Bing bing! Clang! Bing bing!

Once that coded alarm rang out, everything became helter-skelter. Heads in the vicinity began peeking from doors and poking through windows. Suddenly the turmoil took on the desperate tone of a fire emergency. But the Sheriff understood that threat lurking inside the tavern may spell more disaster for his citadel than an outbreak of flames.

Moments later, the stuttering clangs summoned a floundering team of assistants. By ordering them into action, the panting official had pronounced the establishment's doom. For the reactionary band, with no time to lose, snapped doors and shutters tight, holding hard against any effort from within to resist their enclosure.

Next came a burly carpenter, trundling a barrow of stout hardwood beams before him. He disgorged the timbers in an instant. Each was lifted and shoved into a readymade holding brace. Clearly such disasters were now anticipated in public gathering places. Finally every opening was barred and the occupants locked within. With every portal shut, the wide-eyed sheriff breathed a sigh of relief. He cleared his throat as he scanned about, then saw what was missing.

On came a nervy young girl, toting an item in each hand. He barked his orders. She set her to work upon her special task. From one small hand hung a small wooden pail, filled with thick whitewash. A weasel-hair brush was gripped in the other. In a well-practiced move, up she ran to the doors and windows. Dipping and thrashing quickly, she painted rough white squares upon every shutter and door.

As she finished creating her background canvases, a second young girl arrived. Perhaps this was her sister? Who could tell? Yet the newcomer dove in fast behind with a pail of blood red paint to slash a crimson cross upon every white square. Together they had fashioned the Black Death's sinister warning mark. Never had I seen a more devilish sign from two more innocent angels.

Shouts for release and pounding on doors and windows began to sound from within the establishment. As we drew away in haste, the piteous cries receded. Then beneath the slashing crosses of her sister, the elder angel chalked a final pronouncement in white.

Lord have mercy on us.

In time a surgeon or medicus would arrive. Perhaps they'd come quickly, perhaps in a day. The timeframe depended on the amount of local expertise the sheriff had at his disposal and severity of the outbreak. When such helpers arrived, I knew that by their garb they would appear more like the image of a grim reaper than a bringer of hope for healing.

Minutes later we stood before the citadel gate we had entered not half an hour before. Just before we reached it, I saw the foreboding image of a surgeon shuffling toward the doomed establishment. As he made for the sound of the bell, citizens parted at the sight of him.

Surely enough, he was dressed in a thick black protective coat that fell to the base of his feet. Covering his entire face was a grim-looking raven's-beak mask. His image was crowned by the wide-brimmed black hat that announced his enlightened profession. But that grisly mask announced his dark purpose. I discovered much later the curling beak is filled with aromatic herbs, intended to staunch the air they must breathe when entering to investigate.

Once we were cleared to pass back through the gate, we halted at a near distance to conference and see to Armand's hurt. Though we had come so close to our destination within the walls, even if we could skirt the citadel to enter from another side, all agreed the visit should be postponed until the dire situation inside had time to mature.

And while, as sometimes occurred, such alarms proved to be unwarranted. Given what Caspar reported, Armand was now eager to put as much distance as possible between that potential threat and his bride. Who could blame him? The hobbler in our team would remain unchanged for the moment.

Before we left, Maxine tended to a large bump at the corner of Armand's skull. While she did so, Armand wincingly explained how Caspar had sighted the signs of sickness on the neck of the boy who rushed in seeking his father. His alertness and swift action, though appearing preposterous at the time, had almost certainly saved the Capulets and perhaps our entire company. As he praised our run amok giant, I cradled the broken head of my marionette.

'Caspar you warned me in the nick of time!' Armand groaned.

The giant glared at me. 'Only to allow that errant fool to lose his head and assault you!'

'I meant to strike *you* lummox!' I bleated. 'Truly? Manhandling our mistress like a whore in a cathouse! What was I to think? I'm sorry, master. I'm sorry mistress. Truly I –'

'Yes rascal, you meant well.' said Ilaria, then her brow rose high. 'But if you *ever* hit my husband again, I'll clout you with that wretched thing myself!' She glared as I cowered sheepishly. 'As for Caspar, he deserves our deepest *thanks*.'

Just when I felt I'd heard enough praise for him in Milan, to crown all my folly, she suddenly anointed the giant ninny with *another* kiss of approval. I glanced up and realised she was looking at me.

'No complaint this time at my offering a kiss of gratitude?'

'No. I admit the giant ni – Caspar – deserves commendation. Truly he saved us all.'

Maxine and I looked at each other solemnly. We had been walking toward the tavern together when his wild behaviour erupted. In truth the lummox did save us all. Despite my chagrin I felt I would never forget the debt I now owed him.

'Oh no.' sighed Maxine. 'Your marionette's broken.'

'That was expensive wasn't it?' said Ilaria.

'Yes Madame. A month's wages.'

She laid a sympathetic hand on my arm. I smiled thinly.

'You lost your head in more ways than one rascal!'

A titter of laughter ran among them. I had to admit, Ilaria had her witty moments. That was one of them.

'Next time fool' growled Caspar 'remember the golden rule of striking an opponent!'

'What's that, pray tell?'

'Hit what you *see!*'

'Oh.' I spat dejectedly. 'That's a good rule.'

Armand clapped my shoulder. Suddenly the world stopped as his blue eyes blazed in that manly, heartfelt way that only he has ever offered to me.

'Marcel I appreciate that your effort was offered in my defence. And I must say, against a threat like Caspar, that was *bravely* done.'

'But not *well* done.' I bleated.

'Perhaps. But I won't forget it.'

The compliment lifted my spirits.

'But you must heed Caspar's advice.' Armand added. 'And remember, you can't *see* what you hope to hit if your eyes are *shut*.'

'Yes Chevalier. Next time I'll try to keep my eyes open.'

'Let's hope we don't have a next time.'

Another hand reached for my shoulder. Ilaria's eyes held me. 'Perhaps rascal, we can find a new bauble to disguise your fearsome weapon in Verona tomorrow.'

'Or ...' I smiled. 'perhaps replace it with a shiny dagger?'

'Cupid's Balls!' she spurted in mimic of me. 'Imagine if it had been a dagger?'

With smiles, snickers and slaps on my back, we moved on to leave Brescia behind us. Now it seemed we'd reach Verona sooner than expected. Once there, we hoped to make up for this unexpected turbulence and enjoy the warm familial welcome that awaited us.

Oh dear Heaven how I wish now we had turned about instead and headed back to the safety of France.

Chapter 10 Premonition

Despite the turmoil we had just experienced, thus far we had safely traversed the northern end of Italy through Turin, Novara, Milan, Bergamo and Brescia. Yes, we were departing the last not long after noon and without staying. And yes, the distance to reach Verona from Brescia was fifteen leagues, not eight or nine or ten. That stretch would be the longest to travel between citadels we had planned on our journey. Now we had far less time than needed to reach it.

We had entered Brescia by the western gate before noon. By the time we exited the way we came, traversed around the township, then halted on the eastern side to consider our way, we heard their civic bell strike two. The hours left for safe travel that day were waning. Yet even if we couldn't reach Verona before nightfall, there was still time enough to reduce our distance to it considerably.

We pressed on firmly for two more hours, then halted to one side of the wide road to conference. Traffic and pilgrims and pastoral rustics ogled us with interest as they passed. Ilaria arrived at Armand's side as he hailed Caspar to wheel and rejoin us. Quickly they agreed Liberati and Boccolo were needed.

The veteran pair arrived. Given Liberati hailed from the region we were entering, he stayed while Boccolo went forward to stand in for Caspar. Fabrizio dropped back to our rear. It was better to have a junior squire sound the alert from there than have no warning at all.

No, I still didn't call him Fabio! I can't explain why, but I've always preferred speaking full names rather than shortened pet versions. Particularly those that have more than two syllables. Yes, that may seem perverse, given most pet names appear designed to save tongues and lips from doing more work. Yet I digress, where were we? Ah yes, literally by the side of the high road.

And so, with us gathered and ready to confer, I held close to Maxine. Since the incident in Brescia she refused to allow Ilaria to wander a step without her. From the talk of our betters, I gleaned they were beginning to accept the possibility we may need to stay overnight in a village or, if absolutely required, camp by the high road.

Ilaria stoically insisted she'd relish another chance to sleep *under the stars* with her husband.

'Don't fret for my comfort. It was wonderful last time.'

'Wonderful?' Armand replied sceptically.

'Yes my heart. It was very romantic.'

'That was in France angel. We must be far more careful now.'

I offered my opinion. 'I can't for the life of me see how taking one's repose in the dirt, even amorous repose, can be *romantic*.'

'Rascal hold your tongue.' snipped Ilaria.

Hearing my complaint, Liberati cocked a questioning brow, pushed his lower lip into his upper. He didn't appreciate the license I was offered to give blunt rebuttals. The old soldier turned to Ilaria.

'Madonna if you please.' Since Milan he had taken to addressing her so. 'You carry a trade map of the high road?'

'I do dear Liberati.' she replied with warm smile.

I huffed and snapped my hands by my sides.

'Why is he your *dear* –' I objected. '– yet I'm your *rascal?*'

Liberati pressed his lips with impatience. I knew the answer of course. His service in the hallway at Grenoble had endeared the no nonsense veteran to her greatly. He ignored my interruption.

'May we peruse it Madonna?'

'Of course. Maxine, please fetch the map.'

With a nod and curtsy my sweetheart ran to rummage and fetch. As she went, Liberati requested Boccolo attend us again. Deciding it was better to risk no watch over the direction we had come than have no eyes for what lay ahead, Fabrizio was sent forward to replace him. Soon Boccolo stood with us and Maxine arrived with the map in her hand. She offered the rolled parchment to Ilaria, who passed it to Liberati.

As soldiers tend to do of course, without thinking, the veteran knelt to spread it over the ground. All in our company lifted their brows. For an instant, Ilaria pressed her lips in a wry smile. Yes, she could have insisted any of us bend our backs to spread the chart for her comfort. But to continue the parley, and I believe, not wishing to make Liberati feel clumsy, she lowered to her knees by his side as her gorgeous garment pressed into the dust.

'Dolt!' screeched Maxine 'Where are your manners? Do you expect my mistress to lay in the dirt like a *chicken* while you utter your *doubtful* wisdom?'

'Oh Madonna I beg your pardon! Pure instinct.' He moved to assist her but her own hand stayed him.

'Thank you Liberati yet, I'm here now. We're all soldiers on this adventure together.'

'Spoken like a true Capulet Madonna.'

That made her smile. 'Please continue.'

Armand's smiling face appeared beside her. His grin was infectious. Suddenly Caspar, Boccolo and I were on our knees, leaning into the circuit of conspiracy. Maxine tilted her eyes to Heaven, then lowered into the dirt with the rest of us. Once again, with no warning at all, the Angel of Lyon had cast her infectious spell on us, just as she did in the early morning conference at Grenoble.

Liberati winked at her and twirled his greying moustache. He had the kind of bright eyes one so often sees in a wiry, weathered old soldier. For the love of folly, she grinned from ear to ear. So did we all. All but Caspar of course.

'If it please you both?' Liberati ran a gnarled finger over the map. 'This crossroad ahead allows travellers to turn south to Mantua, Modena, all the way to Rome. Or else to turn north-east to the Lake Garda district which is ... ah yes. There it is. Peschiera del Garda!'

Ilaria's eyes lit up.

'Armand I've heard of that lake! My parents visited there. Maman said it's lovely.'

'It's a pretty place Madonna. And a mighty fortress sits at the south end because ...' His finger traced the map. 'it's also the gateway north to the alps and the Brenner Pass beyond.'

'That pass leads into the Germanic Kingdom?' asked Armand.

'Yes Chevalier. One of two alpine pathways that run from Italy to Germany. The other is north of Milan and now behind us. This one ahead runs north from Verona. It's travelled in great numbers by merchants trading from Venice through Verona to Germany.'

Ilaria drew an arm over Armand's shoulder. 'I'm sure this lake is the same my parents visited. Papa said it's enchanting. Oh Armand' she implored 'we must see it. This is our marriage tour after all.'

'Even a small glimpse would be memorable.' Liberati agreed. 'However Madonna, as Boccolo may attest, all the approaches from here towards that crossroad ...' His finger traced the path again. '... which we we'd need to travel along toward dark, are also infamous.'

Ilaria glanced at Boccolo. 'Infamous because?'

He tipped his head then pouted with a frown. 'Because all roads approaching it from here Madonna are foul with bandits.'

Brows lifted and heads inclined to hear the sobering answer.

'The merchant traffic attracts them?' Armand suggested.

'Yes Chevalier.' said Liberati. 'And on this tour so far, with just one exception while we remained in France, to avoid that danger we've managed to be off the high road well before sunset.'

Boccolo scratched his chin. 'Sunset's when they begin to lurk at the edges of the high road. They wait for any who have mistimed their run, forced for lack of light, to halt before they find good shelter.'

'I see.' said Ilaria.

'And ...' Liberati added 'after sunset they set upon any who risk the high road at night to reach better shelter.'

I huffed an incredulous gasp and bleated.

'That sounds more like folly than adventure!'

'Caspar?' said Armand.

'Pushing forward safely after dark requires *stealth* Chevalier.'

'Agreed. That may prove difficult now with three wagons.'

'Even if we dismount ...' Caspar added 'and cover wheels and hooves with cloth to dull the sound.'

Armand cast a sideward glance at me.

'Not to mention one wagon driver who *jabbers* incessantly.'

'And ...' added Ilaria 'a quivering junior squire who *squeals* at the hoot of every owl.'

Suddenly all were silent with thought.

'I can be quiet master!' I pleaded. 'If my *life* depends on it.'

'I'm not so sure.' muttered Liberati frowning with doubt.

While some in our conference managed to smile, most still wore looks of sober consideration. Caspar broke the silence to suggest, if we must make a camp for shelter, we should travel a shorter distance and halt soon to allow time to fortify it. And though Liberati agreed, he rubbed his grizzled cheek, twirled half his moustache, and offered another solution.

'The Squire's suggestion is prudent. But now with the late set of the summer sun, if we push on immediately and make haste, we're likely to reach an outer post-house of the lake fortress ...' Liberati gestured to the map once more. 'no later than an hour after sunset.'

'Later than usual.' said Ilaria hesitantly.

'Yes Madonna. Yet if we're close enough to see the fortress walls by then ...'

'We'll be too close for the comfort of bandits.' said Armand.

'I believe so Chevalier. And with a little luck, not too late to secure decent lodging.'

Before it was finally decided, Ilaria reassured Armand she still had no objection to camping under the stars if needed. However, just as she said so, the sound of Fabrizio squealing at the sight of a rodent, broke our concentration.

'Dear Heaven my heart, perhaps it's a sign?'

Armand knelt and offered her his hand. They stood together.

'Angel at least it's a reminder that Caspar should be minding our way forward.'

I stood, then looked below me to see Maxine glaring upward. I knelt again and she rose with my assistance. Without further ado, Ilaria and Armand agreed to press on for the lake fortress. For the sake of speed, we would make no attempt at stealth, and in a matter of moments had set out upon the second-to-last leg of our journey to Verona. If we reached the lake that night, our most anticipated destination would be reached by noon the next day.

Despite our dark talk in the dirt of bandits, owls and rodents, the Capulet's decisiveness rewarded them. Next morning they awoke in the rustic but comfortable chamber of an outlying post-house. The magnificent fortress stood off in the distance, too far to reach with tired teams the night before, yet close enough to ensure our safety.

When we realised the first post-house we had reached in the dark offered room enough for all, we gratefully halted. The morning light revealed it was nestled hard by the lake shore upon a gentle rise. After we awoke, it's outlived comfort was more than offset by the breathtaking vista that greeted us beyond its windows.

On that clear summer morning we broke our fast early, then stepped out to fill our lungs with lakeside air as all made ready to depart. As for myself, I was more pleased than I expected to have avoided a night under the stars. For despite our late hour of arrival and lateness to retire, the Capulets spent hours making love for all to hear through the thin walls of the closely set bedchambers.

No, that isn't what I celebrated next morning!

Half an hour before their antics began, as had become their custom on tour, they had me play in their chamber for ambience while they continued to drink and chatter. Maxine remained for a time to fuss with food and drink. She even applied her scented oil to the shoulders and necks of both this time.

After she was dismissed, I exchanged my lute for my harp and lingered for a time. Since our tour began, little by little, they had grown more used to my presence during such interludes. It still baffles me to this day how much the sound of continuous music in intimate environments seems to make fond duets forget my presence.

A familiar moment arrived in their bedchamber when I realised I was no longer heeded or needed. Watching them engulf each other caused me to consider what I may be missing on the other side of the wall. Oh yes, as usual I had been given a billet in the *stable*. Also as usual Maxine was assigned to the bedchamber beside them. I assumed she would be there and in bed by now. But by the sound of the Capulet's indulgence, I suspected she wouldn't yet be able to sleep.

And so while I continued to play, I stood and began to exit. Alone in the hall, I played for a moment before ceasing. Wavering there, I wondered if I should venture to knock softly on Maxine's door. I wanted to do it. I told myself to do it. But discretion allayed my amorous desire. I don't know why. I wouldn't normally have been so faint-hearted.

I turned to head for the stable where I would share my repose with men I knew would keep me awake with their snoring. However as I stepped on with a heavy heart, I heard a door creak behind me. I turned and saw Maxine's enchanting face. Her smile beckoned, then her finger. Only twice before had we been intimate in that way.

The first was when we camped on the road and slept under a fig tree together. The second was on the way to Bergamo when we halted to change horses. Quite by accident, we ended up together in the baggage wagon rummaging for items. Yes that amorous escapade was quick and perhaps uncomfortable. Yet it was unforgettable too.

This time however, was our first chance to share intimacy in an atmosphere that didn't expose our waking bodies to cold morning dew or force us to bump and shift for comfort, more than such intimacy should require. In very short time we were lying naked together in a comfortable bed built for two.

We began to turn our attention to each other. Then through the wall, the sound of the Capulets began to rise. As our tour had continued, Maxine and I agreed their antics had grown more noisy and volatile. Despite that distraction, we attempted to concentrate on arousing each other. But, for the love of folly, we just couldn't help smirking and giggling at all we could hear.

'Hush!' I whispered with a grin.

'I can't help it!' Maxine squealed huddling in closer. 'She's more animated than usual.'

'I know!' I muttered. 'And he's offering harmony to match it.'

'Oh. Perhaps it's a reaction to the danger in Brescia?'

'We were in danger too.' I whispered.

'Yes. Does that mean ...?'

'We should attempt to outdo their effort?'

'A competition,' she said with a kiss.

'That means they'll hear us.' Kiss.

'That will feel dangerous too!' Kiss.

We rolled in our embrace. I felt her thighs separate.

'So, lover ... oh!' Her eyes leapt open. 'That's very ... hard.'

'And you're ... oh! Sweet elation you're very soft and ...'

'Oh it's ... it's bigger than I remembered.'

'A big noise requires a big ... ah!'

'Just ... oh ... how much noise? Ahhh ... we willing to make?'

'Enough ... enough ... to make them giggle too!'

With comfort and a willingness to lack caution for being heard, our intimate ritual began to create a signature of its own. I can't attest that our passion was more potent than theirs. I can attest, that as our bodies and minds engulfed one another, we felt the lure of a deep-soaking rapture immerse us like never before.

What's more, to crown our accomplishment, before our own crescendo was reached, we heard giggling on the other side of the wall. Then the competition began in earnest! Some people say love can spark in an instant. I felt I'd seen that in the case of my late master Toulon and Countess de Viviers. However I believe that for most, only *interest* can spark in an instant and *love* requires something more. By the time we fell asleep in each other's arms that night, I had no doubt I was in love with the woman I wanted to spend my life with.

Such were our antics of the night before after a day of unexpected excitement. And now, having only seen the enchanted lake for the first time that morning, we were already leaving it behind. And to ensure our efforts that day would deliver us to our final destination without fail, we stepped out soon after sunrise. I stood idle for a moment, basking in the suns warming glow.

Armand and Ilaria emerged in a state of contentment that was written on their faces for all to see. Yet despite their blissful mood and our idyllic locale, no sooner had I seen them together, then just as I did in Grenoble, I began to feel uneasy. They appeared so unwitting once again, so distracted by each other that neither seemed to care a fig for watchfulness.

That uneasiness caused me to scan about. The rest of our entourage was busy in preparation. I spied nothing out of the ordinary and turned to admire the lake. Even so early, along the idyllic shore, the business of its water-living folk was already stirring. I became distracted by the sight of a fisherwoman stepping from a small craft. She hefted it onto the pebbly beach as a young girl emerged to hold it by a tether. The image reminded me of my childhood years in Calais.

Just as I thought so, my sense of foreboding increased.

The woman hefted two wooden pails filled with fish. Barefoot with skirts tucked at her thighs, she trundled toward the post-house. As she came on, the bodies of her catch flipped and flapped at the top of each bucket. Just as she breasted me, a flapper from one pail flipped free. It hit the ground at my feet. I stared in astonishment and knelt. Suddenly Ilaria was kneeling beside me, her bright eyes inspecting the lively spectacle.

For an instant, to allow the woman to free her grip, the bucket descended to the ground. A second flapper flipped out and lay floundering next to its mate. The first was large and dark with bulbous eyes and a grim mouth. The second was smaller with sharp teeth and shiny scales that flickered with lively colours.

'He looks gruesome!' I pointed at the first, pulling down the corners of my mouth and bulging my eyes to mimic it.

'Yes. But that one's pretty in the light.' Ilaria pointed.

She stared smiling for a moment, green eyes transfixed. But then slowly a clouded thought seemed to scatter her mind.

A hand drove down so fast, it shocked us with a start. The flash of a knife point plunged to skewer the grim flapper, driving into the turf below. The blade drew up with a tilt. The impaled creature lifted for an instant, then turned to be thrust mercilessly against the second.

The hand turned up to display them both. Flicks and flaps of stuttering life gave testament that the spark of life in the smaller fish wasn't yet spent. As it lay there, hung against its larger companion, a trickle of blood ran to mix with the glistening sheen of its scales, reflecting glints of the early sunshine.

'Ironic Master.' mused the wench mistaking me for a husband.

I stood to face her, surprised to see a face and smile that was far more kindly than I expected.

'How so?' I asked politely but felt a sudden shudder inside me.

'Territorial. They hate each other.' She gazed at them for moment. 'Now they're skewered side by side.'

The wench turned them over and drove them, knife and all, onto the brimming bucket.

'Yet their dislike of each other won't spoil the post-master's taste for them. He and his wife are my best customers.'

'Then your work's well situated here.' I said numbly.

She glanced at Ilaria, still staring at the bucket. 'Would you like that pair for your travels Madonna? For you, no cost at all.'

Ilaria blinked with belated comprehension.

'Oh that's very kind.' she smiled. 'Bless you but no thank you.'

'Ah Français? As you wish.' She halted to stare at Ilaria for a moment. 'Hmm. I've seen *that* look before Madonna.'

Ilaria glanced. 'What look is that?' A tremor was in her voice.

'You've *seen* something.' said the rustic. 'Just now. A vision.'

Ilaria's eyes opened wide. 'How did you ...?'

'You need to be careful Madonna.'

'You have visions?'

The fisherwoman looked about cautiously and stepped closer.

'Of my husband Madonna. He was drowned in that lake. Murdered last season by the emperor's soldiers in a drunken rage.'

'Oh mercy, no.'

The fisherwoman's eyes stared coldly.

'Mercy had nothing to do with it Madonna. Now I'm alone with three children and must tend the fishing myself.'

'Oh dear Heaven. I'm so very sorry to hear that.'

'God's will ... so they say.'

'You must miss him.'

'I do. I also miss not doing his work for him.' She cocked her head to indicate behind her. 'That's my youngest.'

We glanced to the shore, the winsome girl stood by the craft.

'She's the spitting image of Alto.' she sighed. For an instant the wench wavered, looking as if she may go. 'Madonna ... be cautious of what you *think* you see.'

'What do you mean?'

'Some signs are lures to *warn* you. Some are lures to *deceive*.'

'How can I tell ...?'

'You tell me Madonna and we'll both sleep more soundly. Are you on to the fortress this morning?'

'To Verona. My new sister-in-law lives there.'

'If she's as refined as you, I'm sure I don't know her at all.'

'Her name's Aurelie.'

'Ah! Also Français.'

'Aurelie Cortellani.'

The Fisherwoman's eyes widened with surprise. 'Cortellani? *That's* not a name to be trifled with.'

'You know her?'

'Why would I know such an exalted signora? Fare you well good people.' She glanced at me. 'I bid you safe ...' she halted in confusion. 'But this is not your ... a moment.'

She scanned about. Armand stood in conference with Caspar.

'Ah, there's your husband.' Ilaria and I stood blinking. 'Hmm. he's Cortellani Madonna?'

'Capulet.' she whispered.

'Ah Capuleti. Then Donna Aurelie was ...?'

'Capulet but now Cortellani. My name's Ilaria. What's yours?'

'Fausta. Yet most just call me the *Widow of the Waves*.'

Ilaria frowned. Her eyes lit with a notion. She scanned about.

'Fabio!' she called.

He hastened at her summons. She held three fingers to signal the withdrawal of three gold ecus from his purse. He pressed them to her hand. She offered them to Fausta.

'No, no, no. I'll be dead before vespers if you give that to me here Madonna. No, no. Keep it."

'But I want to help you Fausta. I may never be back this way.'

'Mmm?' Fausta closed her eyes slowly as if to shut out the world. 'Not for a long time.' Her eyes opened. 'But you *will* return to me Madonna. Once. I'll be here.'

'We discussed stopping here on our return –'

'No Madonna. You'll return to me *alone*. Your husband ...'

'Armand?' Urgency lit up her eyes. 'Oh Fausta what did you see? Please tell me?'

The widow held cautiously considering her words.

'I see that he is ... unique. So are you. Take care dear Madonna. Enjoy every moment together.'

Ilaria was growing more troubled. I hoped by delaying the mouthy wench I'd cause her to say something else to diffuse the turmoil those pronouncements were causing.

'What about me soothsayer?' I blurted.

She halted and turned, narrowing her eyes, then knit her brows and pouted. 'You?' Eyes shut. 'You clever man are so *fickle*.' Eyes open. 'Even fate can't assure *your* path.'

Ilaria smiled, which relieved me. I glared antically at the mystic.

'No advice for *me* to take care?'

'My advice to you is ... to keep your *wits* about you and ...'

'Yes?'

'Keep your *pants* on.'

I shrunk with embarrassment. Ilaria's brows lifted as she smirked and leaned on my shoulder. Without another word, the widow turned to spurn our company and haul her catch away to the post-house. Watching Fausta walk on, Ilaria stood in thought. She turned her eyes to the girl, who was perhaps five years old, holding the tether of the craft. They shared a smile from a distance.

Ilaria turned and beckoned Fabrizio closer. She told him she was going to pretend to give back the ecus. He must pretend to replace them into the purse and return to the wagons. After he did so, she turned for the lake, wandering innocently toward the craft.

Passing by the quiet urchin, Ilaria glanced then knelt by the craft, pretending to search for a pebble. As she did so with one hand, she discreetly reached with the other to deposit the ecus on the floor at the rear. She stood with a large pebble, feigning to inspect it. Then catching the girl's eye, she tossed it lightly, watching it rise and plunk.

Ilaria turned and knelt with a smile, tapping her forearm.

'What's your name little one?'

'Fontanella Madonna.'

'Oh dear mercy what a *lovely* name. My name's Ilaria.

'Your name's lovely too. Such green eyes. Like my papa.'

'And like you Fontanella. He must have been handsome? Please tell your maman Ilaria said thank you and farewell.'

'Yes I will Madonna.'

'Farewell Fontanella. God keep you safe.'

As we departed, my sense of foreboding lingered. Yet I believed the widow's flippant words to me, along with Ilaria's gesture of gratitude, had lightened her mind. And the thought of that rustic's face discovering gold coins in her rickety boat, was enough to inspire me to compose a song celebrating the generosity of *Madonna Capuleti*.

As for the generous woman herself, I hoped the mischief of how she managed to do it would draw her mind from the darkness that loomed just moments before. I didn't know if I should consider the mystic's words too soberly or dismiss her as a charlatan. Perhaps she had some insight. After all, she did call me *clever*.

I felt it was clever how, after that moment of darkness with Ilaria, an instant later Fausta managed to lighten Ilaria's mind with her antic quips to myself. Then, as I considered it further, I became mindful that it was I who had initiated that interaction by holding Fausta back to talk a moment longer. It hadn't been her instinct to stay. Yet, once Fausta did stay to offer more, I realised she could have said something more dire.

As usual, it was hard for me to draw a resolute conclusion.

Glancing about, I saw we were all but ready to depart. I gazed toward the path we were set to follow, and suddenly the cloud I had seen darkening Ilaria's mind felt like it was hanging in mine. By all the saints who pray in the safety of Heaven, I felt sure we were heading into danger. I looked all about me for a sign. The sky was blue. The lake water was placid. The air was clean and our setting was tranquil. But the fear rising in me was so palpable that my palms were sweating.

Cupid's Balls! What was happening?

In summertime, Lake Garda looks like Heaven on earth, a gorgeous, sprawling body of water. But the upper reaches of that vast lake stretch far north into the freezing alps beyond. If a pilgrim makes the journey from the fortress, up through the alpine trails into the mountains, they'll trek through *Roverto* to *Trento* and finally to *Bozen.*

Those towns lie at the northernmost reaches of the Italian kingdom. Just beyond them, sits the border gateway that Liberati had mentioned the day before. He called it the *Brenner Pass*, one of two great crossings that separate the Germanic and Italian kingdoms. Beyond the Brenner Pass on that very day, the German King Frederick was holding court and marshalling his power.

And you must understand my friends, Frederick was not only the German King but the newly elected Emperor of our Christian World. Yet though Frederick had been elected Emperor he was not married. Even as I write this, I still know little of politics. Back then I knew nothing, nor did any in our company, save old Liberati. In hindsight, I understand more clearly: the fact Frederick was *not yet* married was rather important.

For you see, while an elected Emperor remains unwed, he cannot be crowned. However, for some time already, an effort had been in motion to broker a marriage for Frederick. By the time we arrived at the lake shore, indeed since the day we crossed the border to enter Turin, news began to filter through to the emperor's allies in Italy. His marriage was finally agreed.

That single factum would change many lives forever.

For you see, once he wass married, no obstacle would remain to stop Frederick from claiming the right to be crowned, not only Emperor, but King of Italy too. Both notions made many people nervous. Indeed, by that moment, Frederick had already laid plans to claim all three at once. In less than a year, he hoped to ride south to Rome to claim his Portuguese bride and be both married and crowned by his Holiness.

And in little more than a year, that hope would come true. More importantly for our story, in Frederick's haste to arrive in Rome he would choose to travel by the fastest route possible, down the Brenner Pass and through Verona. And, despite any agreements that would arise between his Holiness and the emperor to allow so much to happen, you've already heard tell how relations stood between them and their political factions: the Guelphs and Ghibellines.

And so, given all that was stirring as we departed the lovely lake district, a politically minded person would have described that relationship to be like a smouldering volcano, waiting to erupt. Little did Ilaria or I understand, the recent death of the Fausta's husband had been the result of an early tremor. It was a warning of the chaos that had been unleashed so often in northern Italy, whenever new hope was offered to members of the emperor's faction, that his power was set to rise again.

For our sake, I wish I could say the tremor was nothing, that the volcano dormant. But it was not. The threat of fighting between the Guelph and Ghibelline factions was bubbling again, and we understood none of it. For generations the Capulets had been loyal to the Guelphs. Above their familial crest, three gold fleur-de-lys on a field of blue, declared it to be so. Yet neither Armand nor Ilaria had given so much as a thought to the meaning of that symbol.

In far off Lyon, the impact of that feud hadn't been felt for years. And even if a new Emperor was crowned, with the English finally defeated, his impact wasn't expected to reach into France again. Living in Verona however, were the members of another powerful House who were not just aligned to the emperor's Ghibelline faction, they were seen as leaders among them.

The name of that mighty famiglia was *Montecchi*.

On the day that lay ahead of us, the paths of the premiere Sieur and Dame of Capulet would cross for the very first time with the primo Don and prima Donna of Montecchi. From that day forward, none of our lives would be the same. And my dire friends, by the time the sun rose on the day thereafter, the fateful words of the Widow of the Waves would echo in our minds and haunt us all.

Chapter 11 Sycamore upon the Hill

Knowing she would soon meet her sister-in-law for the first time, Ilaria had dressed to greet her in resplendent fashion. She chose a French gown of her own design rather than an Italian one, assuming Aurelie's life would be steeped in the latter to the point of finding it mundane. She also chose something she felt struck a balance between sophistication and feminine allure, expecting the prima Donna to be both and powerful too.

The landscape of the lake district fell behind us. Ilaria rode side-saddled on Tempest again. The light grey mare with four dark feet had a smooth delicate gait which barely disturbed the fall of her gown over its flank. Maxine had draped the sapphire-and-silver silk damask to perfection. Ilaria's creation included fine gauze trims, as thin as gossamer, light enough to ruffle and flutter in the playful breeze.

Armand rode beside her on Victoire, looking every inch a bold chevalier on that mythical creature. Even before the sun had risen that morning Victoire's long mane and tail had been combed to hang and oiled to shine by Fabrizio. After such a long separation from his little sister, Armand also wanted his arrival to make a lasting impression.

I watched them enjoying the tranquillity together as I ambled behind on my mule. Yes, *my* mule. Oh I know it sounds dizzy. But after our emergency in Brescia, Fabrizio came to me before he slept. He confessed to feeling guilty that during the fiasco he had been of so little assistance. He insisted that he must become better prepared to serve the needs of our security.

'I can't do that if I don't become verore fit and able.'

'You understand that means doing more and digesting less?'

'Yes I do. And I'll never become senior squire if I fear to ride a stubborn beast.'

'And so?'

'And so the ass is yours. I'll take on the rouncey. I must show that gelding that I'm the master.'

'Bravo little man. Toulon would be proud to hear it. And I'm … feeling a little tired.'

His eyes widened with comprehension.

'Ah! You were going to say that *you* were proud too!' He grinned much too broadly.

'Don't be ridiculous. I'm not proud of you at all. I'm … I'm …'

'And lost for words! I must tell Mistress Maxine.'

'Oh … go sniff Lucifer's ass! Be gone daft malingerer.'

He told Maxine of course, who told Ilaria. Yes, they'd teased me relentlessly. Despite that mental discomfort however, fate had intervened for my physical comfort. For without regret, Fabrizio gave up his claim to the she-devil. Now as we went forward toward Verona, I felt her under me again while I watched the blissful newlyweds riding on before me.

Ilaria glanced at her husband. He'd become a picture of health again, with the exception of that accidental blow to his head, of course. The wound to his chest from the siege of Carentan was healed. The wounds taken at Formigny to his rib and thigh remained tender. But thanks to Maxine's potions both looked much healthier too.

With every passing day of our tour, the muscles around each wound had become more limber and strong. Yes, perhaps that was the result of engaging in so much romantic intimacy. It appeared to be a newlywed compulsion. One week before that morning however, I noticed Armand had also resumed his dawn ritual of martial exercises. I knew Ilaria also practised a morning ritual of physical exertions. Maxine confided she had been inducted to them while serving with the Countess. Though Ilaria's ritual exertions were performed alone and indoors, away from prying eyes. Armand's martial exertions were performed out of doors and often in partnership.

Just two days earlier he'd been sparring with Caspar, both stripped to the waist in the warm Italian sun. It reminded me how strong and capable Armand was at his calling, how little he feared the size of an opponent. And he was so fast and difficult to strike or grasp. At one point, when I felt sure Caspar had him in his clutches, in a flash Armand slipped his grasp. Then somehow, from a standing position in front of Caspar, he spun on his heel and vaulted, sweeping his body in an arc, to wrap the giants neck from behind like a python!

It looked like martial sorcery. And despite all Caspar's violent twisting and turning and striking and grappling to shake his captor, in less time than it would take me to bite and chew and swallow an apple chunk, Armand brought him to his knees for want of breath. Or so I thought, until he explained it was actually for want of blood! Somehow he had managed to cut the flow of blood to the giant ninny's skull.

I wondered if I could learn to do that!

At any rate, the sight of Armand returning to such health made me hopeful for our safety. And I knew that when we reached Verona, he would finally be staying in one location for more than a few weeks, rather than a few days. Finally both Capulets would have a generous period of time to allow for any indulgence required, to rest, revel or recuperate.

I now also understood, this much anticipated sister did not live within the walls of Verona. Liberati explained that the northern foothills, where their estate was located, lay more than a mile beyond the citadel walls. Soon we'd see that idyllic landscape. But as we drew beyond the lake district, Ilaria swore it was the most enchanting vista she'd ever seen.

'Promise me my handsome we'll stop again on our way home.'

'If we have time angel.'

'No Chevalier.' she teased him. 'I'll take nothing less than your sworn promise.'

'Marcel I know you're idling behind us. What should I say?'

'Well dread Chevalier as you always say, any vow is sacred and should not be given lightly.'

'Agreed.' said Armand.

'And Chevalier you've reminded me more than once that once a promise is *given* – unless *forgiven* – it must *never* be broken.'

'Hmm. I do recall saying that.'

'A great many times.' said Ilaria smiling, reaching for his hand.

'And so?' he asked me.

'And so the advice of a fool to you is ... give in to every demand that your dread wife makes.'

'Ah! Dear mercy.' she cried. 'That's the first sensible thing I've *ever* heard him say.'

I thought she was being witty until I saw her head turn. Her look of sincerity made me wonder if I was really so contrary as to deserve it. Or was she becoming more skilled as a comedienne? In the end of course, Armand did *promise* Ilaria they would return to the lake.

And while that was the only detour she made him *promise* to or the only detour she asked to consider, within half an hour he'd also agreed to visit the port of Venice before we turned back for France. What's more he agreed, once we reached Grenoble again, to detour south so Ilaria may visit the fabled port of Marseilles!

Indeed, she requested making so many significant diversions, and I feared more may come, that I couldn't see how they would fit them all in and still return home before winter fell. Moreover, their swelling itinerary meant that despite the visit to Aurelie being our entire reason for coming so far, to accommodate those changes they would not be able to stay in Verona for any longer than two weeks. That calculation concerned Armand and he said so.

But Ilaria was so enthused by her plan she made a declaration.

'If a shorter stay to ensure it all is required my heart ... then that's just what it *must* be.'

'Let's see how we like Verona angel, then commit to a plan.'

'Oh Armand we must see it all. This *is* our marriage tour!'

No, it wasn't the first time Ilaria had used that magical phrase to end a debate. Indeed she was using it to sway his reluctance ever more frequently. And it was becoming clear: our young premiere dame was adept at turning our premiere sieur's resistance. However, I don't mean to suggest that Ilaria was peevish. Not at all. It's simply that her green-eyed enthusiasm for things had a way of being ... irresistible.

'Armand' she sighed 'we don't want to return to Lyon and regret that we stayed overlong in one location at the expense of others.'

'We don't?' he said innocently.

I'd learnt that when Armand wasn't completely convinced of a thing, he had a way of pushing his pout sideways and tilting his eyes to Heaven. He was doing that as he said the last. By then, I understood what that particular expression meant. But so did his wily negotiator.

'Of course not my heart.' she pleaded earnestly. 'And who knows *when* we'll have a chance to return to make good on missed opportunities? Perhaps never.'

Armand was smitten of course. And when the smitten smile at those who smite them? It signals surrender.

Yet before he did so, he looked back the way we'd come, considering the mountains and the season. Quietly both agreed that, for our safety, no matter the final plan, our return home must be under way long before the chill descended into the alpine pass.

'For the moment however' He smiled. 'summer lies before us.'

'It does my heart.'

'Marcel you insensible cretin!' Armand cried. 'Earn your keep and strike up a travelling tune.'

I did so. Ilaria, Fabrizio and I smiled. That was the same command our old master Toulon bellowed to me on the morning we rode away for Normandy. Yet unlike that day, instead of two instruments to choose from, my old weathered lute and battered Irish harp, I also had my new ebony masterpiece from Milan. But we were outdoors and mounted. I'd never risk that beautiful thing to the elements. So I hefted my old lute, tuned for a moment and began to pluck a fanciful air.

As the music began, Armand leaned across the gap between their mounts. Ilaria leaned a little too, held more firm by the surge of the side-saddle on her offside. Victoire and Tempest drifted together. Both lovers leaned in again. Two pairs of pouting lips met and held for one step, then another and another, until a smile began to crease between them.

Their lips parted but their eyes held each other, blue blazing into green, as if the world around them had vanished in a blissful haze of nonchalance.

'Did I tell you I love you?' he whispered.

'Once or twice.'

He frowned. 'That doesn't seem enough for one morning.'

'Perhaps I could stand to hear it again. Yet not before ...'

'Before?'

'Not before I say ...'

'Say what?'

'How much you love to hear *me* play, madame?' I interrupted.

'How *much* I love my husband you rascal.'

'Oh? How much is that, pray tell?' I teased her.

'*Desperately.*' she confessed as if I didn't exist at all.

'Desperately?' he whispered.

'Yes.'

'Hmm. Then I must confess that I love my *wife* –'

'Be warned Chevalier, now at the very least you must love her desperately too.' I advised.

'Hmm. But I love her *more* than –'

Before he could say how much, Ilaria launched an impulsive kiss that spoke more passionately than words could ever tell. Finally, they parted, yet their hands were still reaching. Tethered at the fingertips by love's fond touch, they rode on quietly together.

After a spellbound minute or two, Ilaria broke the lazy silence.

'I can't wait to see Verona.'

'Liberati says it's bustling and beautiful. But for today he advised we skirt the citadel and bear north directly into the hills. That will ensure we reach Aurelie's estate well before sunset.'

'Oh? That seems a shame.'

'We'll see Verona tomorrow but may catch a glimpse as we go.'

'What's that lovely name of their estate?'

'*Valle del Nocciolo.* Vale of the Hazelwood.' he translated.

'Gracious me, what an irresistible name. It sounds like Heaven.

Don't you think so, Maxine?'

Until that moment my sweetheart had been quietly driving the carriage wagon behind us.

'Everything in this region sounds enchanting Mistress.'

Ilaria turned in her seat to grin, then glanced at Armand and reached again.

'I'm so glad we came this far to visit her my heart.'

'Yes angel so am I.'

'Even if she *doesn't* like me at all.'

He frowned, turned his head and arched a brow.

'You'll cast your spell over Aurelie as you do upon everyone.'

Her own brows lifted. 'Hmm. Women aren't so easy to charm as men. Are they, Maxine?'

'Not at all Mistress.'

'Ah!' he declared. 'So all this time, my bride and her accomplice have been comparing how well she can charm all the men that she meets compared to –'

'Hush Armand! This is your *sister*. Not a cousin or associate. And by all reports she's now a very grand lady.'

'Little Aurelie? By whose report?'

'Even a fisherwoman at the lake knew of Aurelie.'

Though my strums ran uninterrupted my thoughts did not. I hoped not to hear any mention of our tryst with that fortune tattler.

'When, during that very short visit, did my glamorous wife find time to keep company with fisherfolk?'

'Oh it was just for a fleeting moment by the lakeshore. Before we departed.' Ilaria glanced at me. 'She said that Cortellani was not a name "to be trifled with." '

Armand widened his eyes with a smile. 'Well, who am I to fault the sage mumblings of a fisher wench?'

'Nor should you. But I liked her Armand. And her lovely daughter. Marcel met her.'

'Did I?' I lied. 'Oh yes. I seem to recall that she was skilled at skewering fish with a *very* sharp knife. So skilled indeed, I was glad to have a short acquaintance with her.'

'Well I pitied poor Fausta. She had suffered great torment.'

'Fausta? Hmm. What kind of torment angel?'

'Her husband was recently murdered by Imperial soldiers. Drowned in the lake.'

'Oh. That's very unfortunate. One wonder's what Germanic soldiers were doing so far south.'

'How would I know. But now Fausta's alone with three children. She's learning to survive it. Yet her daughter Fontanella –'

'Is this why you insisted we must return to the lake?'

'That's part of it. Yes.'

'I see. Well for now angel please, don't let her troubles distract you too much. Smile.'

Ilaria stared at him for a moment, drawn back from a reverie she had begun to succumb to. She blinked and smiled. I could see she did so to ease his own mind.

'Oh the thought of meeting Aurelie is far more distracting. I must confess I'm *very* nervous.'

'And she'll be *more* nervous. Don't fret Ilaria, she'll love you.'

'Yet even if *not* –' she began.

'Yes she *will*.' he insisted.

'No matter the outcome my heart, I'll never forget this tour. After my fear of the war –' She pressed his hand to her cheek. '– it's so good to know you're safe. That we're safe together. We can take our time and just enjoy this journey.'

Silence fell and continued for a time. As I continued to play and began to hum, the sights and sounds of the Veronese landscape drew us all in. Then, they began to chatter again about every little thing they saw, while Victoire and Tempest tossed their heads flirtatiously at each other.

Sometime later, Liberati appeared, falling back from the fore to approach the Capulets. Given his local knowledge he was leading us that day in Caspar's company.

'Chevalier. Madonna.' He tipped his head in acknowledgement. 'Just ahead, we'll begin the ascent into the northern hills.'

'Armand said we may catch a glimpse of Verona?'

'Many glimpses Madonna. And if you look closely to the south, just inside the centre point of the furthermost walls, you'll see the tall form of the ancient Arena.'

He wheeled to return, leaving us in a state of anticipation.

'The arena sounds exciting. Oh Armand it's not too late. I'd love to see it today. Perhaps we *could* ride through Verona after all.'

'Well I confess, I'm rather ... oh. Oh I see. You're still fretting.'

'Just a *little* detour Armand, to steady my nerves.'

'Just a *little* detour?' I mimicked, batting my eyelashes, which was rather ridiculous for that was not something I ever saw Ilaria do.

'Oh rascal tais-toi!' she warned.

By then I had learnt that being told to shut-up by Ilaria was the *second* sign she was growing impatient with me. Being called *rascal* in a particular tone was the first.

'Normally angel I can deny you nothing. But you know I want to see Aurelie. And I know you agree that famille must –'

'Come first. Yes of course.'

'It's Saturday. We'll visit Verona tomorrow.'

'Yes, you're right. Very well.'

'Let's attend the cathedral tomorrow, spend the day browsing.'

'Ooh. I could wear the gorgeous grey damask from Milan.'

'Even in dull sackcloth your entry to Verona would be nothing short of spectacular.'

'After *we* arrive my heart I'm sure they'll speak of nothing else.'

I was glad to hear her confidence rising. Ilaria wasn't a boastful person of course. That boast simply came from a need to bolster her confidence for Armand's sake, and from the growing strength of their marital bond. Suddenly I realised, when our visit was done, our tour would turn about. Sadly that meant that this great adventure they were sharing together, would start to end.

All at once, I understood why Ilaria seemed more aware of relishing every second left to spend at their leisure. It wasn't just the foreboding words of a fisherwoman. It struck me that any young wife, who sensed the tide of such a blissful period was about to turn, would have felt the same. And then finally, returning to their lives in

Lyon would mean altering that gorgeous rhythm they had settled into.

After browsing through the pretty region for perhaps an hour more, we finally stood just half a league from our destination: Vale of the Hazelwood. Just as Liberati had promised, while meandering through the foothills we caught tantalising glimpses of the citadel below. And the interest created by each glimpse had considerably slowed our progress.

Then at the base of a formidable hill, we drew around a wide curve and a gorgeous grove of sycamores fell into view. The spread of majestic trees ran ahead to either side of the wide road, forming a wondrous tunnel that seemed to beckon us on. Despite Ilaria's doting reaction to the lake vistas that morning, as she looked up from this vantage, she suddenly became transfixed.

Perched on the crest above us was a hillside estate. A roadside post with a clutch of orange lilies growing at its base, declared its name: *Villa sulla collina del sicomoro* - Villa Upon the Hill of the Sycamore. What's more, the sign suggested that just around the curve beyond our sight, some manner of formal entry would be found.

'Dear mercy my heart, what a delightful name. Oh my word! Oh Armand look at it. Have you ever seen such a beautiful estate? What a wonder it is. And look on the hills. Vineyards, olives and more. Maxine, Marcel look! What do you think?'

'It's very pretty Madame.' I declared.

'Pretty? Gracious me it's a jewel. A rare, rare jewel!'

'Oh yes Mistress.' Maxine sighed 'It's such a beautiful thing.'

'The hills roll and slope. The colours are ... oh Armand look down there, at the river. See how beautifully it curves around.'

'That must be the Adige.' he said gazing down.

'Oh dear Heaven. And that villa on the hill in the ancient style? It's simply majestic. What a commanding view they must have. Perhaps of the citadel itself.'

'Very likely angel, yes. They're very lucky people.'

'Oh Armand. My heart –' I saw the glint in her eye before she said the next. 'Wouldn't this make a fine summer estate?' Her brows lifted in anticipation.

'Hmm. A fine summer estate?' He said soberly. 'No.'

Her brows knit in consternation.

And though Armand responded with a patient smile, I could see he was concerned that her rapture was rising. Since Lyon, we had all come to know that tone in Ilaria's voice presaged her merchant passion to investigate a purchase.

'Now angel wait just a moment. Before you say anything more. We agreed not to purchase more than we may carry home in a *wagon*.'

'Unless it's a beast to *pull* a wagon!' I quipped.

'Oh yes Armand ...' She ignored me completely. 'but just *think* for a moment. No more than half a league from your sister's estate? Surely this must be her closest neighbour?'

'Quite likely, yes.'

'Then I'm *certain* they're wonderful friends.'

'How could we know that?'

Oh my *love* ...' she purred. Maxine and I glanced at each other. We'd come to know that term of endearment was an advanced weapon from Ilaria's persuasive arsenal. 'we can purchase garments and trinkets to our soul's content.' she ran on. 'But to return to Lyon and report the purchase of an estate such as this –'

'Angel?'

'To enrich our holdings' she pleaded 'and so near to Aurelie.'

'Angel?'

'And the port of Venice too.' she added excitedly.

Armand tilted his eyes to Heaven. 'Yes, you're the daughter of great merchants. But your famille trades in fabric and dye! And so yes angel, it's very beautiful, yet all I see are *wine* and *olives* and –'

Despite his effort she ran on impulsively. Cupid's Balls! I'd never seen her so passionate. Oh yes, she loved to browse and purchase. But her merchant instincts usually guided her to remain aloof. Indeed our experiences to then suggested – with the exception of her errant attempt to run away to Normandy – our mistress was *not* an impulsive person.

Nor did Armand ever, other than in jest, suggest that she was. On the contrary, he already considered himself to be the impulsive half of their match. And since their marriage, when it came to impulsive decisions, more often than not Ilaria proved to be his prudent rudder, not the other way around. To have the roles so suddenly reversed, took Armand and the rest of us, quite by surprise.

But in truth, there was just something about *Sycamore Hill*, as the natives called it, that made the pulse of our young premiere dame run so feverishly. I saw it in Ilaria's eyes. So did Armand. Suddenly a request issued from her lips.

'Before we travel on let's venture in to investigate its purchase.'

'But angel –'

'Armand, with only two weeks to visit Verona, time will be of the essence. If we wait to attend the cathedral on Sunday, become caught up in social engagements ... the time needed to pursue this chance may slip away from us.'

'Yes but angel ...'

'While we're passing right by it however ...'

'Ilaria de Capulet. Premiere Dame. This sounds more like unbridled passion than bridled prudence.'

'Oh *my love* I'm just saying –'

Hearing that again, Maxine and I exchanged a knowing glance.

'Be careful Chevalier.' I warned.

'Oh rascal tais-toi!' she snapped.

'Yes Madame.'

'While the day's still young, let's take the time now to see if we can peek in. And who knows, at closer inspection we may not like it so well, or they may have no interest at all to sell.'

'That's true.'

'But before the time to even enquire may be lost, let's at least make the effort right now to simply announce ourselves, present to the friendly owners, and make some kind of a start.'

'Well ...'

'And imagine Armand. Imagine if they agreed.'

'You know I'm not very imaginative.'

That made me laugh outright and drew a stern glance, of course. She caught him in the grip of her emerald eyes again.

'Tush my handsome. Imagine what a wonderful surprise it would be to greet Aurelie with the news we'd already entered into an agreement to purchase a neighbouring estate.'

'I'm sure she'd be very ... surprised.'

Oh yes, I desperately wanted to laugh out loud again.

'Then from the very first moment we met, she'd know her new sister-in-law is no shrinking violet in matters of trade and negotiation.'

'Is that what this is all about?'

'Oh no, not at all. Well yes, in part ...'

'Ilaria.'

'But wouldn't that be a delicious reward for our trouble.'

'*Trouble* is the word for it.'

Pushing his pout aside and tilting his eyes to Heaven, Armand pleaded again for Ilaria to wait. He offered a promise that after they arrived to greet Aurelie and Sabatino, he'd seek an introduction to their neighbours as soon as possible, then return in a few days.

Just as he concluded, Caspar and Liberati arrived to investigate why we had halted. As the Germanic hulk listened, he realised a visit to the crest of the hill was being considered and offered blunt counsel.

'With our final destination so close Chevalier, for the sake of resting the train, I suggest we press on without further delay.'

Liberati glanced up at the villa on the crest. 'That hill's quite a climb for tired beasts to haul our wagons.' he added.

But Ilaria was smitten by a surge of curiosity. In truth, had she merely protested like a spoilt child, Armand may have appealed more successfully to her patience. Had they been married a little longer – time enough for him to devise more tactics to resist her in such moments – the result may have been different. But her will seemed irresistible. And as many had observed, Ilaria de Capulet was the personification of charm.

In that moment however, I thought her charm may have found

its limit. Indeed for an instant, still assailed by Armand's hope to deny, her impact began to wither. Then to my great surprise, just when her charming assault was threatening to flounder, our young premiere dame revealed her willingness to unleash a more potent weapon.

In a sly trick of couture, which I still don't fully understand, as Ilaria continued to speak she drew down the shoulders of her gown. Like a curtain lifting to reveal an irresistible image, except in the opposite direction, her bare shoulders appeared on seductive display to accentuate her lovely neck, revealing more of the swell of her chest as she leaned toward her susceptible target.

'You realise my heart, nothing's more exciting for a merchant's daughter than to attempt this kind of thing.'

She kissed him gently to punctuate the suggestion. I glanced at Maxine. Her expression suggested the end was nigh.

'Is that so?' he replied.

'Yes.' Kiss. 'And nothing could make you more irresistible to me ...' Kiss. '... than knowing how utterly ...' Kiss. '... you support my want to attempt it.'

Cupid's Balls! If I didn't know she was talking about purchasing an estate, I'd have felt certain they were discussing the attempt of something more debauched. Yes, Maxine and I had heard her in rapture behind the coverlets. But not until that moment had we seen her behave so seductively with our own eyes. Had she asked me in that manner to murder my cousin, I feel sure I would have attempted it! Even though I have no cousin!

None of us were surprised at the result she gained from Armand. The instant the tactic emerged, I knew he would be vanquished. Not just because he was tempted by an alluring woman, but because he was tempted by the alluring woman he singularly adored. And at no point did she shout or squeak her voice at him. Nor did she pout or avert her eyes. Quite the opposite.

Without any sudden adjustment, she fixed her bright eyes on him and her voice sank into a deeper, softer tone. Earnestness and soothing care were Ilaria's most alluring qualities. Mixed with that passionate surge of heat, they became her most potent weapons. Those of us watching it unfold, waited to see if our mighty leader may shock us all with a display of stubborn resistance or display the fatal sign we had all seen before.

For you see, when the moment of defeat at Ilaria's hands was upon him, just before Armand surrendered, he always reached his hands to take her shoulders and gazed into her eyes. That was the signal of capitulation, his white flag waving on the marital field of battle. Their eyes would meet, green beckoning blue. Then he would lean forward to press his lips to hers.

We held our breath, wondering what would follow. Would he offer that sign now? After a lingering kiss, to the surprise of none at all, he leaned away and reached for her shoulders, staring into blissful oblivion ... then agreed to it all!

Not only did the ninny agree to enquire to purchase but to properly satisfy the urgent need of his seductress, he promised that before we drove on, he'd make them an offer *so generous* it would be difficult for any but a Prince of the blood to resist it. Cupid's Balls!

Oh my sweet friends, with the gift of hindsight I say to you all: Heaven help all young men in love. For in reply to that offer Ilaria said those words no young man in love can ever resist.

'Thank you my heart, *that's why I love you so much.*'

Yes, she kissed him again! Armand was beyond refusal.

'But angel you must promise me ...'

'Yes my heart?' she purred and kissed.

'Not to raise your hopes on this fancy. And –' She kissed again. 'No matter what transpires –' Kiss. 'If our host –' Kiss. 'Shows *no* interest to sell –'

'They won't.' She reached to kiss again but he held her at bay.

'If they show *no* interest then promise me, we'll not press or linger, just graciously thank their hospitality and take our leave.'

'Maman has a saying.' she purred to avoid that promise.

'I'm sure she has many.' He smiled. 'Dare I hear *this* one?'

'*If one seeks not to venture – one stands –*'

'*Not to gain.* Yes charming coaxer I've heard it said.'

'By many a merchant's daughter!' cried Maxine on her perch. Ilaria was delighted to hear the voice of an ally at last.

'Max!' Armand warned. 'I'll not have a duet gang up on me.'

'Yes Master.' She grinned.

'And so angel if they agree to meet us on such a lack of notice, then I promise in return to make them an *irresistible* offer of purchase.'

'Chevalier.' I cried. 'I fear you'll promise her anything under such potent influence!'

'Hush rascal!' said Ilaria softly. 'He knows I love him for it.'

Then just to spite my influence, she kissed him again.

'Almighty Venus!' Armand cried. 'Don't kiss me again! You'll make me promise to storm the citadel.'

'Well' She smiled. 'if time permits how long would that take?'

She glanced at her nails then winked at Maxine. My sweetheart smiled and glanced at her own lover, yes myself, seeking inspiration. I rolled my eyes and pouted my lips in mock disdain. It was hard to compete with our muscular chevalier.

'Very well!' Armand declared. 'Let's call upon these strangers.'

'Armand we're calling uninvited. We need a moment to prepare.' He rolled his big blue eyes. 'To avoid being spurned I must ensure we'll make a showing to impress.'

'Very well. Yet no more than a moment. Caspar! How far?'

'By my reckoning the entry lies just beyond the bend.'

'Take Liberati. Investigate and return. *Allez!*'

'Yes Chevalier.'

Both men dipped their heads, mounted, wheeled and rode on.

'Squire Cavoli!'

'Yes Chevalier.' snapped Fabrizio.

'Fall to the rear. Inform Boccolo of our plan. *Allez!*'

'Yes Chevalier.'

He leapt aboard the gelding in one vault, then wheeled as those left set upon their tasks in haste, with the exception of myself. To offer the impression I was busy, I pretended to tune my old lute. Moments later, Fabrizio returned to perform the duties of a page once more. He joined Maxine and Ilaria with their fussing and fumbling, then a hasty inspection of the servers was turned out.

Ilaria glanced at me. She insisted I use my exquisite new lute just as Caspar and Liberati were returning. Wearing sober expressions the warrior duet drew rein and leapt down together.

'Report.' said Armand as Ilaria joined him.

'Chevalier' Caspar began 'just beyond the curve two men-at-arms guard a wide entry plaza. Liberati recognises their crest.'

Armand and Ilaria glanced at the veteran.

'Chevalier. Madonna. I'm sorry to advise you but ... this is a *Montecchi* estate.'

That was the first time we ever heard that volatile name.

Chapter 12 Rampant & Screaming

'Montecchi?' echoed Ilaria looping her arm over Armand's. 'They're an exalted famille?'

Liberati bowed his head. 'Very much so Madonna. And if memory serves me correctly, this particular estate is their familial seat.'

'Indeed?' Armand cast a thoughtful glance at Ilaria.

'Yes, and the Montecchi are led by a warrior of wide repute.'

'A *Cavaliere?*' Asked Armand.

'A *Condottiere.*' Liberati said soberly.

Caspar's eyes widened to hear it. 'A mercenary.'

'Not just a mercenary. Their primo Don retains many Condottieres under his command.'

'A leader of mercenaries.' Armand creased his brows.

The giant's expression grew dark. For the very first time I saw Caspar, perhaps unwittingly, cast a dark glance at Ilaria. Yet it surprised her enough to unsettle her.

'Chevalier' said Liberati 'you should also know, last night at the post-house, in the hope of foraging for some local information Boccolo and I shared a drink with the ostler.'

Armand wore a wry smile. 'My father chose you wisely.'

'The ostler and a serving girl confirmed that a new *Podestà* now governs in Verona'

'*Podestà?*' asked Ilaria.

'Chief lord of law and politics Madonna. The new man's said to be a prince of the blood named *Escalus.*'

'Escalus.' said Ilaria. 'Like the ancient Greek poet?'

'Yes Madonna. In older times our Podestà was chosen by the local elite. Now Verona is controlled by the Republic of Venice.

'Yes.' muttered Armand thoughtfully.

'And so now, to reduce the risk of corruption, he's an imported man. Venice has sent Prince Escalus here to maintain order.'

'Well?' Ilaria had begun to strain for patience at the delay.

'I can't swear it for a certainty Madonna. But the serving girl had an extra morsel of gossip. A recent marriage among the Montecchi has bound this Prince to their House.'

'Ah!' She smiled. 'There Armand you see? These people are exalted at least, perhaps noble at best.'

'It seems so angel.'

'Either way my heart, though our arrival's unexpected, as fellow elite they're bound to receive us with a civil welcome.'

'I beg your patience Madonna, but I have something else that may auger more *caution*.'

She huffed at the sound of more words that suggested delay.

'Dear Liberati I know you mean well.' She placed a placating hand on his forearm. 'But if we wish to make this call, time's no longer our friend.' She glanced at Armand. 'Perhaps we've heard enough –'

'Angel please.' He sensed concern in Liberati's face. 'Just give him a moment more. Go ahead Liberati. Speak your mind.'

'Forgive me Madonna. But on the guard's crest I recognised something more, which also appears in the emblem above their gate.'

'What is it?' asked Armand.

'The Montecchi crest is displayed there of course, a silver annulet encrusted with seven white roses.'

'Oh how pretty.' said Ilaria.

'Less pretty Madonna, is the rampant black wolf at its centre, clutching at a castle.'

'Well yes. But a circlet with seven would usually signify seven unbroken generations.'

'Yes it can Madonna.'

'And a castle declares they control substantial holdings.'

'Indeed they do. Unfortunately, it's what sits above their crest that concerns me more deeply. The sign of the Ghibellines.'

'Ghibellines?' Her brows knit in confusion.

Caspar however, was frowning again and found his voice.

'Their the emperor's political faction Madame.'

'Aye.' said Liberati. 'The symbol is there for all to see. A two-headed, screaming black eagle. And Chevalier, that's a crest that one such as yourself, should not take lightly.'

'An open declaration' said Caspar 'they support the Emperor.'

'Tush Caspar!' Ilaria pouted. 'What's that to us? Surely nothing at all.'

'I beg your pardon Madonna.' said Liberati. 'But it means a great deal to the chevalier's father. His famille, now your own, have sworn allegiance to the Guelphs against the Ghibellines.'

Ilaria blinked in surprise and frowned.

'Well ... that may be. But how would anyone in Verona know what faction the Capulets do or don't support?' she insisted. 'Even I knew nothing of it until this very moment. I certainly don't expect it to be a topic of social conversation with our hosts today.'

'Perhaps you don't recall Madonna' said Liberati 'that the sign of the Guelph is three golden lilies on blue.'

Quiet descended for a moment. Every eye scanned.

Caspar looked at Ilaria soberly. 'Even a glance reveals the image on the livery of every server, our master's new standard and –'

'And' Armand added 'to proclaim your entry into our House, it's pressed in the coverlets of the wagons your parents provided.'

My own eyes scanned thoughtfully. There above the ancestral emblems of Capulet – the cape, hat and sword – sat the three golden lilies on a field of blue. We'd seen them every day of course, I often admired them, yet with no real appreciation of their meaning.

Caspar turned to Armand.

'Chevalier. If we climb that hill displaying that emblem ...'

'Yes.' said Armand. 'I assume they'll recognise it.'

His eyes met Ilaria's. Liberati shook his head doubtfully.

'I fear Madonna' he said 'your welcome may not be so civil.'

Quiet descended again. To me it seemed food for sober thought. But Ilaria was young and lacking experience in the wider world. So was Armand. Moreover our new premiere dame was hopeful by nature. And she had become more confident since we'd visited

Grenoble and Milan.

She expected to reveal the best in new acquaintances until experience proved otherwise. And I believe that in all probability, until that moment - with the exception of a nasty prioress in the abbey in Lyon - Ilaria had never met a person who didn't take to her kindly.

'Tush and nonsense!' she scoffed. 'Guelphs and Ghibellines! That's old, forgotten politics. I know nothing but the *echo* of it. I'm sure the two haven't been at odds for years.'

'I believe that's true in the world we left behind us angel.' Armand said doubtfully. 'Yet I confess that recently during our feast, our fathers spoke with concern over the Emperor's election.'

'Did they my heart? I heard nothing. No talk of it at all.'

'No. Nor should you on such a night. But I recall one feared that trouble may be stirring again between the factions.' He shrugged. 'Alas, with my own distractions that night, I paid little attention.'

'Nor should you now.' She kissed his cheek. 'Politics is far too dull and wearisome.'

'With respect Madame.' said Caspar. 'Politics has the power to help all your own pursuits or hinder them. Even a smattering of pointed knowledge can make a great difference.'

'Oh Caspar. Do you have *pointed* knowledge here and now that'll make a difference?' Her impatience was rising, but our giant ninny remained nonplussed.

'Madame, Frederick's the German King and now the elected Emperor. He aims to be King of Italy too. However, he's not yet *wed*.'

Ilaria tossed her hands in the air and sighed with exasperation. 'Well Caspar?' she spat. 'Do you want me to find him a fiancé?'

Even the giant was forced to smile. 'The King of Naples has already found him a fiancé.'

'Oh! Then I'm so glad he spared me the trouble to do it!'

'I mean to explain that until he's wed he can't be crowned King of Italy or Emperor. One must occur *before* the other.'

'And so Caspar?' she huffed. 'None of that will occur before sunset *today*! Armand please we must go?'

Caspar's words had set Armand's thoughts moving.

'Angel I recall the emperor's betrothal was also mentioned. Your father said many in Italy were opposed to both coronations. I recall that Milan was opposed.'

'I wonder where Verona stands?' asked Caspar.

'Verona is now ruled by Venice.' said Liberati. 'Venice is *neutral and so –*'

'It's safe to assume Verona's neutral too?' Armand asked.

Ilaria's frustrated glances followed their debate.

'Well?' she spurted in frustration. 'I can tell you all that I'm *not* neutral! Heaven give me patience with you men! This talk grows more tedious by the moment!'

'Angel ...'

'Darling husband. Shall I tell you where I stand in the matter?'

He tilted his eyes to Heaven.

'I feel certain you shall.'

Every eye of every man met every eye of every man.

'Wherever you stand Mistress,' cried Maxine 'I stand with you!'

'Thank you Maxine. At least one is loyal!'

'I prefer to *sit* rather than stand!' I blurted.

'Tais-toi you rascal!'

'Yes Madame.'

'Armand.' Ilaria swirled to face him. 'I stand in this gorgeous landscape with my gorgeous husband, eager to meet the gorgeous neighbours of your gorgeous sister.'

'As do I.' Armand replied patiently. But then .... he embraced her, held her shoulders and looked into Ilaria's eyes.

Yes, we all saw the ominous sign again. Yet this time old Liberati dared to resist on Armand's behalf!

'Chevalier. Madonna. I'm just an old soldier. But I grew up in these parts. If all that's been revealed is true, Verona may be in for troubled times ahead.'

'Agreed!' snapped Ilaria. 'Trouble *ahead* but not *today!*'

Liberati stood contrite as her look softened.

'Come.' she insisted, like a parent scolding children. 'Come all of you!' She laid a hand on Liberati's shoulder. 'You old coaxer! I won't allow you to douse my grand plans with your foreboding. Armand? This Emperor Phillipe –'

'Frederick.' corrected Caspar.

'Fiddlesticks for all I care!'

Despite myself, I burst into laughter to hear her say it.

'He's not yet *crowned*? He's not yet *wed*? Therefore, this Emperor and his Holiness are not *yet* at odds *because* ... he's not yet crowned or wed!'

'That's very logical angel.' Armand smiled.

'Thank you my heart. And Caspar? Should Emperor Fiddlesticks *soon* be crowned or wed, I gather it shall be by the hand of no other than his Holiness. Yes?'

'It must be so.' the giant agreed. 'Or else he will not –'

'Of course!' she interrupted. 'And so my handsome husband, an Imperial wedding, if and when it happens must occasion *peace* between them, not rekindle their feud to spoil my schemes of merchant conquest.'

Silence expanded like a bubble that was fit to burst among us all, when a hearty laugh suddenly broke from Armand. He picked Ilaria up and whirled about as she beamed a girlish smile.

'Not just a merchant but an orator too!'

'Madame de *Cicero*!' I cried.

'Angel you may be right about it all.'

'Of course I am! What's more, if we forge a link today with this *famille*, it may become an alliance with this Prince who rules in Verona. What was his name?'

'Escalus Madonna.' said Liberati.

'Yes. After the poet,' she cried.

'The *tragic* poet!' I added soberly.

'Then we're decided.' Armand declared and glanced at Liberati. 'Old soldier, anything more?'

'Oh Heavens Armand, no more!' spat Ilaria.

'Madonna please. Just one thing more that may *assist* your interest to purchase?'

'If you're truly my ally now, I shall allow it.'

He reached to pluck an orange lily stalk from the base of the sign, offering it to Ilaria.

'I'm forever your ally Madonna. Never doubt it. I recall a brother to their famiglia named Aldobrando. The second heir. He holds a bevy of estates to the south.'

'That *is* of interest.' said Ilaria, twirling the stalk.

'But unlike their primo don upon that hill, Brando lives in the citadel. Any of the estates he holds Madonna are much larger than this. Though not as pretty, of course.'

'Nor as close to Armand's sister.' she replied.

'Beyond any spoils the Montecchi have gained from Onorato's many conquests, those southern estates have always been their main source of their income.'

'That's valuable information.' Armand clapped his hand on the veteran's shoulder.

'And so' Ilaria began 'while we visit our new friends, we must seek an introduction to that brother who ...'

Armand's wide fingertip had laid against her lacquered lips.

'Angel ... I've promised to climb the pretty hill with you.'

'You have.'

'I always keep a promise?'

'You do.'

Green eyes gazed into blue.

The kiss of compliance followed.

Armand assisted Ilaria to mount Tempest.

He vaulted lightly into Victoire's saddle with a smile.

The avenue of sycamores sat beckoning before them.

Fate leaned closer.

Around the next corner our destiny waited.

Chapter 13 Madonna Montecchi

We ventured around the curve along the sycamore-clad road. After a short distance a guarded gate appeared at the foot of the hill, recessed by the roadside. As we approached a bell was struck in a coded manner to alert those in the villa above. Then from the hill crest we heard a sequel sound in reply. Caspar, Armand and Ilaria dismounted. The giant led the Capulets forward to speak to the guardians.

From my perch I could see the Guards were smartly dressed in Montecchi livery. Yet they were also armed to the teeth with sharp-bladed polearms, swords, daggers and shields. As idyllic as the villa above may appear, the gatekeepers made the notion of entry appear foreboding. Armand took the lead to converse. Yet as I suspected, it was Ilaria's charm that seemed to sway the reluctant warders into delivering a message above to request an audience.

With a golden ecu in his palm, the elder guard sent his junior up the hill while he remained below. I think one look at Caspar was enough to make any guardian cautious. At any rate, the senior man wouldn't leave his junior to mind their gate against a potential threat such as ourselves. And so his fellow retreated up the hillside path at a brisk trot. While we waited, the senior man stood alert, hand gripped on the rope that was hitched to the bellringer.

I have to admit, until that moment in our travels throughout France and Italy, I'd never seen such caution taken against unwanted entry to a private estate. It felt more like the atmosphere in Normandy during the war. Yet despite that first impression, the junior man returned in less than a quarter hour to present a brief missive. It was penned in an elegant hand and perhaps for the guardian's sake, Ilaria read it aloud.

' "*Signora Esmeralda da Montecchi.*" That's an elegant name. "*Expresses her delight at the opportunity to meet Chevalier and Dame Capulet.*" There you see I told you so. "*For a brief introduction and making of acquaintance."* Oh yes my heart, that's perfect.'

While no mention was made of *Signore* Montecchi, the missive sounded convivial to me. That was a relief. Ilaria smiled in triumph, of course. And nothing had been said by the gatekeepers to deepen any of the fears we had discussed before. Yet while we had waited for that reply, I felt sure the elder guard had continued to glance at the golden lilies on our wagons and costumes.

I couldn't be certain, however. Left alone, he looked hesitant of every living thing. I thought to myself, *perhaps that's what makes for a good guardian.* From our side however there was no mistaking the emblem which Liberati had described to us. There it was, a screaming, black, double-headed eagle with red beak and talons, declaring the Montecchi were indeed Ghibellines who supported the emperor.

But I must confess, it made me smile to see it. For the iconic bird with its two screaming heads looked as if it was caught in a fit of apoplexy. Cupid's Balls! I felt the urge to mimic the antic sound it seemed to be making, like a screaming chicken being throttled for supper! Oh yes, I thought better of responding to that urge. But as I think you understand by now, I'm rarely so discreet.

Yet something about this encounter was already taming my instincts. Ilaria drew me aside in haste before we ascended.

'Now rascal, during this visitation, less of the fool from you and more of the musician.'

'Yes Madame.'

'Perhaps ... play from the very start, as we ascend.'

'Yes Madame.'

'Something friendly and festive.'

'Yes Madame.'

'Please stop saying *yes Madame* it's making me anxious.'

'Yes little bitch.'

'Marcel!' she hissed.

'I couldn't resist. But see? *Not* so nervous now.'

'Rascal how do you do that? Don't answer me! Just play.'

Moments later, I struck a breezy melody from atop the she-mule. And though as we rose, she strained against the hills steepening rake,

I dropped the rein to let the stout creature have its head while I hummed, strummed and whistled.

Yes, I sometimes whistle. No, not often.

Soon the enchanted villa fell in sight. Even from where I sat, I could tell that the closer we came, the more it seemed to weave its spell around Ilaria's heart. With no whit of exaggeration, it was the kind of paradise only praised in poems or songs by such as myself. The long sloping path had delivered us up to a wide-open seat that boasted a breathtaking view in every direction.

And as the vision of the villa revealed itself, standing before it we saw the hallowed icon from which the estate drew its name. It was the loveliest of lovely old sycamores, a towering giant. It spread its roots so broadly, held itself with such ownership upon the hill that even the ancient path we rode was fashioned to wind around its base in homage to that rare artefact of God's creation.

One glance made me suspect the venerable giant was standing before the villa had been constructed. Yes, perhaps it was the offspring of an ancestor. Either way, it seemed experienced enough to tell of many generations that had lived upon its hill.

We drew into the turning circuit that stood before the formal entry while the sight of the villa continued to burst on our eyes. Its front was layered in ornate marble and flagstones. Majestic columns rose to frame the entry portal. Like a hidden temple, it was hardly what one expected to find nestled on a hilltop in the Veronese hinterland.

Standing before the magnificent structure to receive her unexpected guests, stood its high priestess Signora Esmeralda Montecchi. She was flanked by a retinue of six liveried servants that included a grim faced major-domo, while two massive hounds sat lounging at her feet.

Cupid's Balls! For a woman who resided on a pastoral estate, expecting no visitations on a Saturday noon, their prima donna looked ready to mingle at an empirical ball.

Unlike Ilaria, who was of modest height with golden hair, their prima Donna was tall and statuesque; a raven-haired Signora of Portuguese descent. For the Italian summer, Esmeralda adorned her lithe figure with light fabrics of stark, bold colouring that wrapped her form closely. I knew nothing of it at the time, yet this was the same Esmeralda who Queen Marie described to Yolanthe de Paris before she departed east upon her own great enterprise.

The burgundy silk damask that gripped her body was finely piped and laced in black and gold which seemed to lift and explode above her. That flourish of fabric drew the eye to a headpiece that wove her black tresses through and about a mesh of fine gauze webbing. Her braids were wrapped with cloth of gold and decadently studded with pearls.

Esmeralda's lips were lacquered with a burgundy gloss that matched her nails and couture, while lashes as long as a doe of the forest curved elegantly above and below her wide dark eyes. Whatever the House of Montecchi may be, by the image of their prima donna and the villa she stood before, they were not poor or miserly.

Pleasantries were exchanged at once, each kissing thrice in the Italian fashion. All agreed to address each other by their forenames. The prima donna revealed her husband was ranged over the estate. And so, without a chance to consult him, she agreed perforce, though eagerly, to the unexpected request for visitation.

'Oh Armand. Ilaria. I didn't want to miss a rare chance to greet exalted travellers.'

'That's very kind Esmeralda. Our deepest apologies for surprising you this way.'

'Not at all dear. Let's step into the shade while we chat.'

They wheeled slowly together to step into the shade of the magnificent old tree.

'And when your note explained your connection to the Cortelannis, I assumed that Onorato would have no objection.'

'If it proves inconvenient in any way ...' offered Armand 'we'll just stay to greet him and press on.'

'Oh yes Armand, we'll see. At any rate I feel sure that before your stay ended, Aurelie would have planned for us to meet. I've sent a man to the western vineyard to fetch Onorato. He's inspecting the corvina with the master vintner, and a new wine press installed just this morning.'

'I'd love to see the vineyards.' Said Ilaria with a broad smile. 'They looked so lovely from a distance.'

'Then you *must* see them when Onorato comes dear. He'll have heard the bells of course. When he's in residence, he always comes personally to investigate if they're sounded.'

Armands brows lifted. 'He sounds very prudent.'

'He's certainly cautious Armand. Soldiers who hope to live long enough must learn to be. But like many mature soldiers, Onorato's no longer a very social man. So Ilaria, you'll have to forgive him if he seems detached when he comes.'

Ilaria knitted her brows sympathetically. 'Oh no Esmeralda, I'm sure he's delightful.'

'When we were first married he was very social.' she glanced at Armand. 'As squires dear, they're taught to dance and mingle.'

'Oh we love to dance.' she tilted her cheek to Armand.

'And so you should, pretty people. But we've rarely danced in the last five years or indulged in much social company.'

'No. That's a pity.'

'I think so too. Which is why I was so glad to hear your man playing as you arrived. He sounds very talented. And now that I see him, he's quite handsome. I do like lankish men.'

I smiled in recognition. That made me warm to her at once.

Esmeralda glanced at Armand again.

'Did he come to your match from Ilaria's side or your own?'

'Esmeralda I plead guilty to inflicting him on my wife. Yes, he's talented and clever. But he's also a handful.'

I tilted my eyes to Heaven as they all looked me over.

'Is he?' Esmeralda's immaculate brows lifted with interest.

'Fortunately, Ilaria seems to manage him with a steady hand.'

'Bravo dear. You have a rare treasure in him. And if he's as talented as I suspect, he'll impress a great many.'

I smiled again as she looked me up and down, yet now with discomfiting interest. Indeed I had begun to feel like a lump of prize livestock at a beast market.

'If he is a handful dear' Esmeralda added 'I'd be happy to take him from you for any price you feel is reasonable.'

The offer took Armand by surprise but seemed to startle Ilaria. I gulped at the thought as Esmeralda's dark eyes held me in their grip.

'He'd learn to behave in my company.' She turned back to them. 'When I first came to Verona we lived in the citadel of course.'

'We saw glimpses.' said Armand. 'We hope to visit tomorrow.'

'It's lovely Armand, and lively. At our palazzo there we retained a minstrel and a buffoon.'

'Marcel's a little of both.' said Ilaria with a grin.

I pressed a thin smile, tilting my head in childish affirmation. Yet I began to harbour fretful thoughts of being offered to the staring prima donna in an attempt to secure the purchase of her estate.

'And we used to travel far and wide, attend exclusive masquerades. Many were quite daring.' She glanced at Armand for an instant again. 'Onorato loved them. Particularly those in Venice and Rome. Oh Ilaria, they were so extravagant and decadent.'

'Rome? Yes Esmeralda, that's sounds thrilling. I'd love to see Venice too or attend a masquerade.'

The prima donna met Ilaria's eyes and stared thoughtfully.

'Hmm.' She purred. 'Be careful what you wish for dear. But yes Ilaria, they are thrilling. And utterly addictive.'

'We certainly hope to visit Venice on this tour. Perhaps we'll have the chance to attend one there.'

'Ah that would make me jealous.' Esmeralda flitted another glance at Armand. 'My existence is more isolated since Onorato decided to withdraw to Sycamore Hill. And much less thrilling.'

'Oh Esmeralda that's such a shame.' Ilaria pouted.

Although Ilaria's comment to Esmeralda's reaction seemed sincere, for the sake of her undisclosed interest to purchase the villa, I felt she was pleased to hear Esmeralda say she pined for the citadel.

'You're so elegant and convivial Esmeralda.'

'Oh no. You can't say that dear.'

'Yes it's true. You mustn't be kept from the world to languish.'

'I'm flattered to hear such a pretty young woman say so.'

'No, not at all.'

'I am. And this villa's gorgeous of course. I was mesmerised when we first came here. But now I confess, for me, it all feels a little too ... old and austere I'm afraid.'

'Yes. I understand.'

'Do you?' she asked with playful condescension. 'And yes, it's too far from the citadel. Once Onorato was social and courtly. Indeed he was quite flirtatious.'

'Oh, no?'

'Yes. I've found most successful soldiers are.' she warned and glanced at Armand. 'When Onorato wasn't on campaign we moved in delightful company. But that was during his rise Ilaria.'

'I see.' she replied soberly.

'You will dear. Once they gain a certain status and it appears to be secured Ilaria, some military men can become far too sedate.'

Ilaria smiled and glanced at her husband. 'I can assure you Armand is anything but sedate.'

'I'm sure that's true dear.' said Esmeralda.

She glanced at him again. This time her eyes settled. I swear to you sweet friends, if I had held a drink to my lips at that moment, I would have spurted the mouthful back out.

Esmeralda turned on Ilaria.

'Nor should he be sedate with such a tempting bride.'

Ilaria began to blush. It seemed to mean something to Esmeralda that she had managed to solicit that reaction.

'Now lovely people.' She smiled charmingly. 'Until Onorato arrives, come in out of this heat and bring your warbler too. I need to hear him and more from yourselves.'

Ilaria smiled in quiet triumph to Armand.

'Perhaps for half an hour.' he said. 'We promised Aurelie to arrive well before sunset.'

'Of course. She'll be jealous if I keep you at her expense. Aurelie's a fiery woman.'

Ilaria's brow lifted to hear her say so. I guessed her anxiety to meet her sister-in-law was goaded by it. All at once, the notion of greeting Aurelie with news of a triumph from this visit, loomed more importantly as the trio reached the base of the wide entry stairs.

'I like Aurelie greatly. She is gorgeous of course Ilaria.' Her eyes settled on Armand. 'Just like her brother. Now come up pretty people.'

Before Ilaria could reply or do more than blink, Esmeralda swept toward Armand. In one fluid motion, she offered a hand to be led, then swept on to draw him up through the centre of the wide casement of stairs. She leaned as she smiled, lowering her free hand to draw up the swathe of fabric below and allow her unimpeded progress.

I moved to follow, turning to glance at Maxine. She looked vexed, drawing her top teeth over her lower lip as she hovered in confusion, wondering if she was at liberty to follow Ilaria. Swept up in the confusion, Ilaria hadn't directed her one way or the other.

As I approached the base of the stair a short distance behind Ilaria, I spun on my heel to look again. Maxine was teetering still, glaring, unsure if she should stay or come. I shrugged my shoulders naively, blew her a kiss and pressed on. Unfortunately she stayed!

For just as Esmeralda reached halfway and I noticed the gathered fabric of her gown trailing neatly behind her, a thought came to me. She had secured Armand's arm to assist her ascent. Ilaria coming behind, watching the prima donna's hips sashay ahead, must either swoop to the side and hold the rail like an invalid, or curtsy like a serving maid and heft her hem with both hands to ensure her feet wouldn't falter.

By the time I had dealt with Maxine's conundrum, then thought to assist Ilaria myself, it was too late. Armand and Esmeralda had already reached the top and turned to watch Ilaria rising through the centre alone. Yes, she did it very elegantly. But as we arrived to join them, something in Esmeralda's smile convinced me this was a little game she had played with young feminine guests before.

'Bravo again Ilaria. Elegantly done. But I didn't mean to steal your husband at your expense.' She glared at Maxine. 'I felt sure your server would follow to assist you.'

I glanced myself. Maxine looked mortified. Ilaria could see it.

'Yes.' Ilaria began awkwardly. 'Yet in my hurry to follow I neglected to instruct her.'

'Dear me Ilaria, she should need no instruction.' Ilaria flitted a nervous glance to Armand and back again. 'These stairs are fickle for a donna with a train to manage unassisted.'

'Well yes, a little.'

'Of course you agree. Shall we wait while you deal with her?' Esmeralda asked bluntly.

'Deal with her?' Ilaria murmured.

Esmeralda's brows lifted innocently. 'I'm not sure what French protocol demands for an errant server these days, but in any Italian citadel ...' she glared at Maxine 'such dereliction of duty before a social audience would draw a swift response.'

'Indeed. What manner of response? Yet perhaps –...'

'I know you're young dear, and newlywed. Allow me to demonstrate?'

'Well I –'

'Oh it's no trouble Ilaria.' Esmeralda's dark eyes fixed on Maxine. 'Girl.' She hissed. 'Come here at once.'

I frowned to hear my sweetheart addressed as if she were one of the hounds that had sat at the prima Donna's feet. Maxine scurried toward us, gulping with anxiety. Then just like Ilaria, she bent and hefted her skirts to ascend. Head down, she lowered in a curtsy.

'My name's –'

'I don't care to know your name girl!' snapped Esmeralda. 'I care to see you do your duty. You've embarrassed your mistress. Why didn't you follow to assist her?'

'Well I –'

'The only possible answer is ... "I'm sorry Madonna. I have no excuse Madonna. It will never happen again Madonna."'

'Yes mada- Madonna.' sputtered Maxine on the verge of tears.

'Learn it for next time.'

'Yes Madonna.'

'Look at me when I speak to you girl.'

Maxine's face lifted in fear.

'Do you think you'll remember it?'

'Oh yes Madonna I–'

SMACK!

With no hint of warning Esmeralda's hand had lifted and launched. Without flinching or showing any sign of heat, she slapped Maxine's terrified face. It sent her sprawling onto the casement of stairs. I winced in shock, shunted to assist. But a broad hand held me back as Armand, though clearly incensed, glanced in warning not to intervene.

'That will ensure you do.' said Esmeralda, as if completing instructions for a menial task.

Ilaria was greatly distressed yet attempted to mask it. She had no notion of what to say or do. Armand stood stoically. He understood that in elite circuits, such protocols were not meant to be challenged, particularly in this instance. Not only were we visitors to another culture, but when asked, though Ilaria stumbled to reply she hadn't expressly declined Esmeralda's offer to discipline Maxine.

The prima donna sighed and turned her guests.

'And so pretty people, that's settled. Come in, come in.'

This time Esmeralda reached for Ilaria's hand. Yet she offered her such a convivial smile, it stunned me to see how little the incident appeared to mean to her.

'At least now Ilaria, before you and Armand venture with your girl into Verona's elite circuit, you'll know what's expected.'

'I see.' said Ilaria attempting to regain her composure.

However, the heave of her chest above her daring neckline, betrayed that Ilaria had been rattled by the harsh lesson. By that time I understood, that the stutter in her heart was triggered by anxiety. The tell-tale sign of it – pressing a hand on her heart to settle herself – hadn't yet appeared. Though I felt it must be near. And by then my own heart was galloping of course.

'It may seem like a small thing Ilaria. But I wouldn't want lack of understanding to embarrass you in front of an important audience.

Armand did say you hope to attend at the cathedral tomorrow? Yes?'

'Yes.' he said. 'Yes we are.'

'Well *darling*' she whispered, leaning to him and glancing to both 'Prince Escalus and Princess Florentia are certain to be there.'

Ilaria's eyes widened at the revelation. Yes, she noticed Esmeralda's intimacy appeared to warm with the use of that word. Yet she assumed it was a tactic to impress the importance of her point.

'Oh. Oh yes Esmeralda I do understand.' she said sincerely. 'Thank you.'

I couldn't believe my ears, of course. Her agreement felt like a betrayal to poor Maxine. Yet in truth, I also couldn't quite see how Ilaria could have said anything else.

'Not at all Ilaria.' Esmeralda smiled and glanced at Maxine, still hovering contritely. 'Now dear, you can dismiss your girl. She won't be needed inside. My people will see to our every need, even intimate ones.'

Ilaria turned to face Maxine who had stumbled to regain her feet on the stairs before she stood contritely with her head bowed. Clearly it was hard to pretend nothing difficult had transpired, as the bright red welt upon Maxine's soft cheek declared otherwise.

'Maxine.' said Ilaria with uncharacteristic detachment. The tone made Maxine scurry in. Her eyes lowered as she dipped a curtsy.

'I'm sorry Madame. I have no excuse Madame. It will never happen again Madame.'

'Yes, very well.' It was clearly a difficult moment for both. 'You're dismissed Maxine.'

Without lifting from her curtsy, my sweetheart turned a demi-pirouette and descended silently. Filled with pity I watched her go.

'But you musician' I turned to Esmeralda as she purred 'must follow us and play for me.' I saw her consider the retreating form of Maxine for an instant. A hint of a smile lifted on her lips before she considered me again. 'I like him Ilaria. He's interesting.'

From the corner of my eye, I saw Maxine halt on the stair. I knew she had heard that comment, sensed her want to turn and look. She didn't of course and stalked away. Suddenly I wondered if the prima donna had seen me blow Maxine a kiss before I ascended. Now I suspected she was toying with the feelings of both young women. I also began to fear just how easily she had managed to do so.

For the moment however, she displayed no outward sign of malice. And so I still offered her the benefit of my doubt. Looking back now on my life and time among the Capulets, that was perhaps the most naive thought that's ever entered my mind. Cupid's Balls! If I'd never been a fool before then, I certainly was at that moment.

Passing through the wide portal entry we drew left into a sumptuous receiving chamber to settle and await the primo don's arrival. I casually leaned against the sill and turned. It offered an open view of the forecourt below where our company was settling in to wait. I caught a glimpse of Maxine. She was still visibly distressed as young Fabrizio attempted to console her. No, she didn't look up at me. I wished she had.

Behind me a flurry of chatter began to sound. And so, much to the prima donna's rising anticipation, I set to tuning my lovely new lute. While they were settling together, it gave me a moment to consider our potent hostess more closely. I judged her age to be more than thirty, perhaps thirty-five or six. And even while reclining at her leisure, Esmeralda was beautiful in a statuesque way, with an unmistakable feminine sophistication, yet defined by hard edges rather than soft.

I felt it would be sobering for Ilaria to hear an elite married woman, who was still younger than her mother, speak of feeling isolated while living so close to a thriving citadel. I assumed that as a newlywed considering her own future, that confession would strike a chord in Ilaria. It may sound like a note of shared experience to come, cause Ilaria to feel more immediately aligned to this powerful woman.

And yes, the incident with Maxine had shocked Ilaria momentarily, jolted her out of alignment. But the guileless explanation that it was done for Ilaria's own benefit, seemed to have been effective. It seemed to instantly rekindle her interest and a sense that, despite being cultures and years apart, Ilaria and Esmeralda were now compatriots in a world of *elite marital experience*.

For her life ahead with Armand, the insight of a woman like Esmeralda, also married to an elite warrior, may prove valuable. I already felt hope rising in our young premiere dame, that she and this experienced prima donna may become friends. Indeed from the moment they met outside, with the exception of Maxine's incident, Esmeralda seemed to warm instantly to Ilaria's youthful charm.

That's how it began.

Once inside however, I noticed the prima donna was also warming to Ilaria's youthful husband. Outside Esmeralda had glanced at Armand in flits and glints but kept her eyes more firmly on Ilaria. Once inside and settled at her leisure, with refreshments in hand, her dark eyes not only sought her male guest, they began to linger on him. It was clear her interest was rising, though Armand offered it an unwitting facade.

Oh no, I didn't need to do the same. Once inside, Esmeralda's interest in me appeared to wane dramatically. That left me free to observe her more baldly. I felt sure however that Armand couldn't misunderstand the nature of the looks our host was beginning to offer him. In a rather short time they had expanded from disparate glances to doting interest.

Yet despite how obvious that seemed to me, still settling after their incident, Ilaria hadn't noticed the same, or if she had, was refusing to take it to heart. Yes, Esmeralda was elegant and attractive. But she also seemed starved for any chance to be charmingly social. Ilaria's social life as a married woman had barely begun. As new people were drawn into her company with Armand, she was still learning to assess the nature and intent of their interest. Was a new acquaintance drawn more particularly by an interest in one or the other, or in them together as a couple?

What's more, I gathered from Ilaria's behaviour during our travels so far, she didn't yet consider any woman older than Armand, to be capable of presenting herself as a romantic threat. Speaking for myself at that moment, as a young man closer to his age, I confess that I could feel the lure of Esmeralda Montecchi.

Well bite my bare ass! Yes I could!

Oh yes I know, my sweetheart was crying outside with a welt on her face. I know it makes me sound like a callous brute. Yet I'd be lying if I said the charismatic woman's glances and statements of interest hadn't affected me. I was young and vain. Ilaria wasn't the only person who watched the prima donna's ass sashay up the stairs.

My point being, if you care to stop cursing me for a moment, that I wasn't so sure this woman's interest in Armand should be dismissed as no threat at all. Imagine if we had been back in Lyon, and Esmeralda was a new neighbour they had come to call on together? Unless she was as plain as the bark on a birch tree, I'm sure her emerging flirtation would have been treated with more concern.

I was suddenly reminded of something the gossips love to say.

Proximity promotes promiscuity.

Yet even as I began to fret that notion, my mind began to dismiss the danger. For the truth was, we were *not* in Lyon. We were far from home. And, this may quite possibly be the only time we would ever encounter this woman. That's what I told myself. I even began to assume the lonely prima donna must have felt exactly the same way.

Surely to Esmeralda, these flirtations, even those aimed at myself, were nothing but harmless play, a welcome distraction from her isolation on top of Sycamore Hill.

Ilaria drew her attention back. ' Perhaps your husband's need for tranquillity is just a phase? It may reverse in time.'

'Heavens Ilaria.' She sighed. 'I only wish that were true. I think active soldiers who reach a certain age, tend to become this way.'

Armand's eyes reacted to the suggestion that Esmeralda's husband wasn't just a stagnant retiree.

'And Onorato's grown even more reclusive of late, unless Venice sends him away to douse some angry territorial dispute.'

'Is that often?'

'Oh every few months Armand. But for weeks on end Ilaria.'

'That is often.' Ilaria replied, glancing at Armand.

'No dear. I fear that unless a sweet pair of newlyweds like yourselves stumble through my gate accidentally, I'm doomed to keep company with none but domestics.'

Ilaria considered her for a moment then turned to Armand.

'Perhaps my heart.' She reached for his hand. 'We can seek an invitation through the Cortelannis to dine with the Montecchis?'

Esmeralda's eyes lit at the suggestion and she smiled at the mention of Ilaria's pet name for Armand. 'Oh yes Ilaria, please try. Yet I doubt the outcome. I thank Heaven for Aurelie's close presence however, and the distraction of Sunday mass. At least the fear of God still has some power to summon my husband's attention.'

'As you know, we hope to attend service in Verona tomorrow.'

'Yes dear at the cathedral. But tomorrow I insist you must attend at Saint Fermo instead.'

'Saint Fermo?' Armand echoed.

'It's in the citadel too, darling. But my sister-in-law, Donatella, is returning to mass tomorrow after the birth of her first.'

'Oh a baby.' chirped Ilaria. 'That's exciting.'

'It is. Aldobrando *finally* has an heir.'

Esmeralda's tone and expression suggested deep relief. A sly second smile of triumph passed from Ilaria to Armand. Just as she hoped, an invitation to meet the wealthy second brother seemed all but secured. Indeed Ilaria seemed so distracted by her triumph, she appeared not to notice Esmeralda use of the word *darling* again.

'A boy!' Ilaria grinned with enthusiasm. 'Oh my Esmeralda, what a wonderful blessing.'

'More than you know dear. Brando's first wife Mariana, who was very lovely, was also barren. Sadly she died two years ago.'

'Oh no that's so sad.'

'Yet beautiful Donatella's already given him the son he so greatly desired.'

'A child of early summer' said Armand 'born under the ram?'

'No darling the bull.' she corrected with a warm smile. 'Yet ram or bull he's a Montecchi. Any stubborn creature is appropriate.'

Suddenly the chamber filled with laughter that drowned the plucking of my lute. Esmeralda glowed to see her quip had hit the mark so neatly. Even I smiled, especially to feel Ilaria's bold plan seemed to be making progress. She was enjoying the sense she could enrich their world with potent connections and show Armand just how to it may be done. Her hope to discuss their interest to purchase seemed ripe to initiate.

'However the ram's a fighter while the bull is … a lover?'

Esmeralda's arched brows, lifted in surprise.

'Yes darling. Heaven's Ilaria. What man knows such things?'

Esmeralda shot her an envious glance as Ilaria smiled. Then she scanned to rest her deepening gaze on Ilaria's husband.

It made him self-conscious as the silence lengthened.

'Do you have children Esmeralda?' he asked a little hastily.

'No.' Armand's eyes widened with discomfort. Esmeralda glanced at Ilaria. 'I confess we had son at the very start. But I miscarried him and –'

'Oh no Esmeralda.'

'Yes dear it's true. After that experience I've never been able to … well we were both heartbroken. Onorato was bitterly disappointed. And so we've filled our lives with other distractions. Now at least we a nephew to spoil. Onorato will want him to be a great warrior.' She leaned to Armand and lowered to a whisper. 'But I promise you my beautiful nephew *shall* be a lover instead.'

'Oh yes.' Ilaria agreed. 'He must be.'

'I'll leave him no choice Ilaria. My life's had its fill of harsh fighting men and their gruff ways –' Suddenly she halted. 'Ooh that lute is divine. Bravo talented man.'

'Marcel's very gifted.' said Ilaria beaming a smile at me.

As she did, Esmeralda gazed more deeply into Armand's eyes.

'Now … where was I? Oh yes. My little nephew.'

'A lover not a fighter.' Armand reminded her politely.

'Yes darling. And if the stars don't see to that, I'm determined to do all I can to encourage him to hate less and love more.'

'As you must.' said Ilaria. 'What have they named him?'

'Romeo. Romeo Amicus.'

'Romeo Amicus Montecchi.' said Armand.

'Amicus for *friendly*.' added Esmeralda.

'What a lovely name.' Ilaria mused. 'And so he'll be with you tomorrow at Saint Fermo?'

'Yes for a change. Onorato and I usually attend at the cathedral with the Prince.'

'His name is Escalus?' asked Armand, hoping to alter the topic.

'Yes. And oh Ilaria, you must see him. Escalus is such a *beautiful* man. He and Florentia –'

'The princess?'

'Yes dear she's divine. They always attend at the cathedral. Yet for Brando and Donatella, Saint Fermo's closer to their palazzo.'

'Of course.'

'Saint Fermo was Benedictine 'til the Black Friars moved over to the western quarter. Now the Franciscans occupy it.'

Armand knit his brows with interest.

'We've seen many Franciscans on this leg of our tour.'

'Oh yes darling. I like the Franciscans.' Esmeralda lit with inspiration. 'If you can't make Saint Fermo or the cathedral, you must attend the church of the Franciscan sisters on the north riverbank.'

'Is that close by?' asked Ilaria.

'Not far. The closest to Sycamore Hill is Saint Peter's on the hill. But Aurelie and I prefer the abbey church below on the riverbank. Whenever Onorato's away, I attend there with Aurelie and Sabatino.'

'Not to the cathedral for more exalted social company?'

'Oh, we always cross into the citadel thereafter. But in that little church we can listen to our favourite, Father Lorenzo.'

'Lorenzo?'

'Most call him *Friar*. He prefers it. He's our confessor too.'

'Yours and Aurelie's?'

'Yes. And he's tall Ilaria. Oh, so tall.'

'He sounds interesting.' said Ilaria with encouragement.

'Very interesting. He's a towering, brawny man with a wild beard. Unlike the clean-cut Dominicans at Saint Anastasia. That's our most *prestigious* church.

'Not the cathedral?'

'The Cathedral's lovely of course. But Saint Anastasia is larger and more glamorous. The basilica that adjoins it is sprawling. Whenever the emperor transits through Verona, his court resides at Saint Anastasia.'

'The emperor?' said Armand. 'When was the last –'

'Oh years ago *my* darling. Though rumour has it another visit may be imminent.'

Esmeralda's eyes widened, glancing between them, excited by the prospect. Then she rested her attention on Armand and lingered again. A doting pause began to lengthen.

At last Ilaria seemed to be mindful of Esmeralda's attentions. Perhaps she spoke next to escape the topic of politics, but I felt sure she was moved to greater caution after Esmeralda addressed Armand as *her* darling. The interest of our hostess was becoming more possessive.

'And so tomorrow' Ilaria began 'we have the cathedral or Saint Fermo or Father...?'

'Friar Lorenzo's little church on the riverbank. It's modest of course. But he has such a marvellous way with words. And he's very, very humorous.'

'I like the sound of that.' Armand flashed a grin to Ilaria.

'Oh Armand' Esmeralda purred 'you have the same gorgeous smile as your sister. Yes my darling, you'll like Lorenzo immensely.'

Ilaria blinked in confusion to hear that more intimate term of endearment again. Then her perfectly plucked brows bent into a frown. It didn't appear Esmeralda was paying attention to Ilaria, but the hint of a smile played on her glistening lips, as if she had caught sight of her frown and was satisfied.

'I only attend when Onorato's away. But I wish I could see Lorenzo more often.'

'Well Esmeralda why don't you?' Ilaria smiled less warmly.

It seemed clear she was trying to supress her chagrin at the growing evidence of flirtation. But suddenly with that last question, a look rose in Esmeralda's eyes that was difficult to read. I assumed it was a flicker of incredulity at Ilaria's assumption that, with her husband away, she enjoyed the freedom to attend wherever she pleased. We would soon realise however, it indicated something more.

'Oh no dear.' she scoffed tiredly. 'By rights we should attend Saint Anastasia where the emperor's patronage holds sway. Most of our faction attend there.'

'But you don't?'

'Not at present. Verona's ruled by Venice now Ilaria. They sent the prince to rule in Verona. And so for now, Onorato insists that we keep company with the prince.'

'I see.' Ilaria flitted an ironic glance to Armand. 'That sounds very ... political.'

'Oh it is dear. And what could be more tedious?'

'Yes Esmeralda, I agree completely.' She smiled at Armand.

He smiled patiently back at her.

'But I can't complain Ilaria. Any excuse that draws us beyond the sycamores is welcome for me.'

'And the prince?' Ilaria probed. 'What sort of man is he?'

As I listened from my perch, I was reminded of that special skill most women seem to possess. It's an uncanny ability to create flow in conversations, simply by questioning every modicum of everything either one may think to say. It makes me feel as if the detail of any topic has no bottom or boundary at all.

'Escalus is imposing, of course. But in an alluring way. Aurelie's utterly smitten by him, along with every other woman. Princess Florentia however, oh she's a saint. Such a caring, patient woman. And despite being from Venice, she's not at all aloof.'

'Are Venetians aloof?' asked Armand.

'They're our new masters my darling, of course they are.' On the pretence of leaning to chatter with both, her hand reached to lay on his forearm. 'Oh my you're strong!' she gasped and stared at Ilaria. 'Mercy, dear, this beautiful man must crush the life out of you.'

Esmeralda had managed to make Armand blush. I'm sure she hoped to cower Ilaria too. But the unabashed tactic finally firmed Ilaria's determination to hold Esmeralda's gaze and match her bluntness. Now her green eyes were glowing with resistance.

'Yes Esmeralda he does.' She glanced at Armand and back again. 'And now that we're wed … he does so every single day.'

Esmeralda didn't flinch, nor did her smile falter. ' Newlywed bliss dear. Mmm I remember it. Lucky for you. Yet where was I?

'In Venice Madonna.' I declared politely with a bow.

I felt it was time to risk being heard. She glanced at me.

'Yes. Verona's new masters. I've known no others during my time here. But before Onorato's father died, he detested being under the thumb of Venice. In his day Verona was its own master. Though just one generation before, it was ruled by the emperor.'

'How are things here now Esmeralda?' asked Armand.

'Well my darling …' She glanced at Ilaria more consciously, seeming to know that term of endearment was goading her. 'the emperor's election has stirred the political pot, along with recent talk of his marriage. And though Escalus is our new Podestà and is very much liked, some consider him to be much too soft.'

'And you?' asked Ilaria.

'Soft or hard, until the Emperor's coronation is final, just to be safe the powerbrokers in Verona still vie for the Prince's interest.'

Armand glanced thoughtfully at Ilaria. It took her a moment to respond. Perhaps she was more distracted to know if she'd hear *my darling* uttered again. Ilaria looked at Esmeralda and sighed.

'I fear this talk of *politics* is a little too much for me.'

She glanced at Armand, hoping that statement had indicated her desire to direct their attention onto the topic of the estate.

'And so it should be dear.' Appearing to abandon flirtation, Esmeralda turned her attention to Ilaria. 'Now pretty people, after mass we usually visit the markets in the civic square.'

'Yes.' Ilaria smiled. 'That sounds interesting.'

'It is dear. And you need to know that Escalus and Florentia usually wander along from the cathedral.'

'That sounds more interesting.' She glanced at Armand, sparking with enthusiasm.

'And so lovely woman' Esmeralda purred 'if you come to Saint Fermo to bless little Romeo and meet Brando and Donatella. Then you can stroll with us into the market where I'll introduce you both to the Prince and Princess.'

Ilaria was caught by surprise. She hadn't expected the conversation to lead so quickly to such a potent offering. Her face was suddenly flushed with excitement. She glanced from Esmeralda to Armand and back again.

'Oh. Oh Esmeralda ... oh that would be lovely!'

I listened with foreboding. It felt as if, right before Ilaria's eyes, Esmeralda had lifted a pretty leash and was winding it slowly around her neck and fastening it with a smile.

'Mercy Armand, isn't your wife's enthusiasm contagious?'

'I think so.' he agreed with some caution.

'Then pretty people we *must* ensure it's done. I'd love to introduce the newlywed Capulets into our exclusive circuit.' That offer seemed tantalising enough, then she added more. 'Why Ilaria, even Aurelie hasn't yet been able to gain the Princess's attention.'

Ilaria's eyes glowed with enthusiasm. 'Oh Esmeralda that would be wonderful. We'd be so *very* grateful.'

Emeralda's dark eyes held Ilaria firmly.

'Not at all dear.' She flitted a glance at Armand. 'And who knows, perhaps with such valuable social connections assured in Verona, you'll make it a habit to visit here *every* summer.'

All at once I felt I understood why the prima donna seemed so willing to solicit Ilaria into her circuit. No young wife could travel so far to attend a yearly retreat for weeks or months without her husband. His *proximity* would *promote* Esmeralda's *promiscuity*. Yet I could see by the look in Armand's eyes, he was not so certain the Montecchi circuit would be the best company for Ilaria or himself to be immersed into.

'Obviously for tomorrow Esmeralda ...' he began cautiously 'we still need to see what Aurelie has planned for us.'

'Yes of course my darling.' Her eyes found him again. 'But I know Aurelie adores the prince and dreams of being drawn into the princess's circuit. She'll be very excited by the prospect.'

'It seems strange they're not yet acquainted?' said Ilaria.

'Oh the prince knows the Cortelannis by name and reputation. I believe he's met Sabatino directly. But Aurelie's been so smitten by him at a distance, she feels uncomfortable approaching the princess socially.'

'Dear Heaven' said Ilaria 'that seems strange.'

'It is dear but she's obsessed. Harmlessly, of course but she never stops talking about him.'

'How does her husband ...?'

'Sabatino? Oh dear it's just a flirtatious game. He's quite a bit older than Aurelie. And she loves teasing him with it, pining for the prince. He mockingly protests but they both think they're hilarious. I think its adorable. Older husbands and lovers can be very patient dear.'

Ilaria's brows lifted at her casual mention of husbands and lovers in the same breath, as if in Esmeralda's world they held the same value. Given the situation and company, even I was flabbergasted for an instant. By then however, little that passed that prima donna's lips had the ability to surprise me. And now her eyes rested more confidently on Armand.

Esmeralda sighed and leaned forward to lay a hand over his.

'I fear my darling, Onorato only attends mass to stay apprised of politics, not to keep my company.'

Ilaria was caught in a tantalising trap. Just a moment before she had gushed and admitted her debt for the offer to introduced them to the prince and princess. Now, in the wake of the enticing offer, her creditor was already claiming a down payment, by expanding the boundary of familiarity toward her young debtor's husband.

'Well Esmeralda' Armand said soberly 'keeping abreast of politics is important.'

Ilaria sputtered her wine in reaction to the ironic comment. I wanted to giggle myself. Yet as distracting as that should have been, Esmeralda ignored it completely, latching her eyes onto him.

'Not more important than paying attention to me Armand. Even in the Archbishop's presence, Onorato rarely remains for the entire service.'

'Well ...' He glanced at Ilaria. 'mass can become tedious.'

'You're being polite handsome man. But no, he no longer cares what any think.' Armand frowned sympathetically. Ilaria did not.

'Oh yes' she ran on. 'He complains of an old wound to his knee.'

'His knee?' echoed Armand.

'It does bother him greatly. But any excuse to escape will do. Tomorrow however ...' Her hand withdrew and she faced Ilaria again. 'both you pretty people will sit with me.'

Ilaria was held like a startled dear not wishing to flinch.

'Won't you Ilaria?' she coaxed. 'We sit right in front of Brando and Donatella. You must meet them all tomorrow. You simply must.'

Ilaria was muddled, surprised from too many directions at once. 'Why ... yes.' she said hesitantly. 'Yes we'd love to meet them.'

Esmeralda's eyes had transfixed Ilaria again like a siren's call to an unwitting lover.

'Of course you would dear. I knew you were clever. Of all the important famiglia in Verona, the Montecchi are the most influential. Even their highnesses appreciate how important it is to remain close to our circuit and in our good graces.'

Since I'd spoken before, Armand had begun to glance in my direction. Now he did so again. He was clearly unsettled at how Ilaria had been lured to agree to that arrangement. I lifted my brows hopelessly as he turned his attention back to our hostess.

'I understand the Cortelannis are also greatly respected.'

'Of course they are my darling. Why do you think I've opened my life so much to your gorgeous sister. But most importantly for me tomorrow, with you both in our company, I won't be left sitting by an empty space when Onorato makes his excuse to exit.'

'Of course.' he replied. 'But for now, to be clear, we can only agree to this plan so far as it doesn't *disagree* with anything Aurelie's planned before time.'

Though she tried to mask it, Ilaria was greatly relieved to hear him repeat the warning.

'Of course my darling. But you'll have every day to spend with your sister.' She pouted coquettishly. 'And she and Sabatino usually meet us in the market after mass. So even if you attend Saint Fermo, you won't miss them tomorrow at all and we can explore Verona together. There's so much for you both to see.'

Esmeralda hung on his reply, hoping to secure agreement.

'From the road we saw an *arena* down in the citadel?' said Ilaria hoping to delay the response.

Esmeralda blinked in surprise. 'An ...? Yes dear. It's ... there. One of several ancient landmarks.'

'It sounds very interesting.' she chirped. 'What's it like?'

'It's ... majestic. Haunted by blood, death and the ghosts of gladiators.' Her eyes sparked. 'And you must see it Armand. Every warrior who comes to Verona visits the arena of course.'

'I'm sure they do.'

'And darling' she chirped to mimic Ilaria 'I'll be your guide.'

Despite herself, Ilaria rolled her eyes in frustration. Esmeralda was so fixed on Armand however, she failed to see the response.

'I know the arena so well.' she ran on. 'When I arrived I spent a great deal of time there studying its architecture, drawing for hours.'

'Drawing?' echoed Ilaria.

She desperately hoped to avoid any more offers to spend time in the company of this overconfident woman. And, given her husband still hadn't arrived, Ilaria began to wonder if it was time to broach the topic of their interest and depart without consulted reply.

'Yes I know every nook and cranny there intimately.' Esmeralda gazed at Armand. 'I still draw on occasion, when I find something inspiring enough to capture.'

Cupid's Balls!

If Ilaria's imagination wasn't running by then mine certainly was. Between one invitation to sit beside Esmeralda in mass and another to venture into every intimate nook and cranny, even I felt her overtures had spilt beyond the rim.

Ilaria's lips began to move to respond. I felt certain she would prompt a suggestion to depart. Yet before she could utter a syllable, an assortment of sweetmeats arrived to accompany the wine. Ilaria glanced at Armand. He stared back stoically. I felt their frustration.

Now, so as not to seem ungrateful for that effort, they were obliged to remain for at least a little longer before they could politely announce a need to go. In just a moment however, we would all begin to regret they hadn't done it sooner.

Chapter 14 the Black Wolf

The delicacies were served by a pair of noiseless slaves.

I felt they may be Slavic, yet without a word from either it was difficult to tell. Their service was overseen by the grim major-domo. Seeing him again made me wonder why he hadn't moved to assist Ilaria on the stairs. Just as my suspicion to indict him as a conspirator began to rise, I was distracted by a server passing with a tray full of temptations. Yes, I distracted him to purloin a morsel for myself. The tasty fare included a selection of suckets, marzipans and comfits softened with honey.

'Oh Esmeralda these taste delightful.'

'Thank you Ilaria. Do you like them Armand?'

'This one's interesting. What's that exotic taste?'

'Coconut darling.'

'Of course.' said Ilaria. 'We have very little access to it in Lyon. Does it come here through Venice?'

Before the prima donna could answer, the sound of pounding hoofbeats announced an approach. I didn't have to be a soldier to recognise the heavily shod tread of a sizeable battle horse. As the war-like hoofbeats halted, all eyes, including the servers, fell upon our hostess. Her voice had fallen silent, her face became still.

The charm in Esmeralda's smile had vanished under pressed lips that reined in her warmth. In an instant, the confident woman appeared less confident and her grim major-domo had vanished without a sound. Then we heard the light footfall of his heels out upon the marble entry plaza. His feet stopped suddenly. A muttered voice, I assumed it was that grim server, burbled something. Beyond our seeing came a throaty reply.

'Yes I *see* it!' snapped the sullen voice. 'Well you dolt? If we have guests then *announce* me!'

The server's hurried footfalls came clicking back to our chamber to do as he was curtly bidden. Now the duet of slaves who served us looked on nervously, glancing at each other in trepidation.

The major-domo reappeared clutching a pair of battered gloves.

'Don Onorato's *arrived* Madonna.' he announced. 'He'll be with you momentarily.'

'Yes Sampson. Thank you. Stay close.'

'Of course Madonna.'

Armand and Ilaria lifted to their feet in anticipation, then into his receiving chamber strode the primo don of their mighty House, Onorato Domitzio Montecchi. He entered like a man who enjoys suggesting he owns everything in sight and who wields the power to possess anything that may fall into his sight. I swear to you all, by every nervous saint who prays and every quaking angel who sings in Heaven, from the moment I saw Onorato I disliked him.

The major-domo hovered anxiously, perhaps with an expectation of being handed more to tote. No more was forthcoming. He bowed, scraped and vanished again like a scalded phantom. Yet I felt certain, just as he promised Esmeralda, he would remain close by. All at once I began to feel there was a reason she presented such a strong front to strangers.

As her foreboding husband entered, the dark glare he shot his elegant wife startled me. After all her effortless charm and chatter before, this sudden metamorphosis in Esmeralda was unexpected. Yet now in his presence it was instantly understood. Moreover from the primo don's reaction, the prima donna sensed at once, she had made a grave error to receive such visitors.

Yet as palpable as his anger appeared to be in that first moment, in the blink of an eye it appeared to vanish when his head turned and he saw Armand. Suddenly the man known to all – though not yet to us– as the *Black Wolf of Verona* offered the unexpected stranger an affable smile. Then Onorato Montecchi prowled forward to greet his guests.

His wife attempted to regain her composure. She wafted to his side, her elegant manner apparently restored. Before he said anything to Armand, Onorato turned to Esmeralda. His hand didn't reach for her hand, nor her waist or even possessively about her neck. Instead, as their eyes locked together, he played his thumb and forefinger along the sides of her jaw, sliding down to rest her chin between them.

Esmeralda smiled, puckered and kissed his full lips softly, even indulgently. After her bald display of confidence with the Capulets, to see such a sense of obedience become so suddenly visible in her form, in her intimacy with him in front of complete strangers, made me feel more uneasy. It was one of those shattering moments I fear we've all experienced, when in an instant, the momentary image of two people together suggests an entire story.

Ilaria flinched under the impact of their display as she and Armand waited on the primo don's leisure to introduce themselves. Just moments before, we'd been losing patience with his bold prima donna. Now we felt a surge of sympathy for Esmeralda, perhaps even fear. I suggested before that she was tall. Yes, she was. But her husband was a towering, muscular hulk who made her appear diminutive.

No, he wasn't as tall as Caspar. Very few are. Yet suddenly I understood what manner of man it may take to lead hard mercenaries as their primo condottiere. I glanced at Armand, a man I considered imposing for his muscular chest, shoulders, arms and thighs. Yet this man, perhaps fifteen years his senior, made our warlike chevalier seem like a youth in comparison.

Onorato's demeanour remained as blunt as his manner. Perhaps it was an instinctive response for one of his kind when he didn't know just what to expect. That made some sense. As his wife's sensual kiss withdrew, he scanned with eyes of brown so dark I can only describe them as black. They fell on me for an instant, then dismissed me utterly.

Esmeralda began to present Armand. Her husband had squared himself to size up the young man before him, when the image of the young woman behind struck him like a bolt of lightning from a cloudless sky. If ever there was a moment in my life when I saw a person mimic the kind of primal instinct one only expects to observe in a wild animal, this was that moment.

After an inconsequential greeting to his male guest, with the hungry eyes of a predator salivating at the sight of a stray lamb, the Black Wolf of Verona gazed into the eyes of Ilaria de Capulet. He stalked forward to receive her rising hand. Black eyes devoured green. She dipped a curtsy. Despite the fact they were social peers, her eyes lowered instinctively to avoid his voluble stare. From my vantage to the side of them, leaned against the sill, I watched and saw it all clearly.

As he stood in front of his own wife and the husband of his prey, Onorato took advantage of remaining unseen by both to leer provocatively. While Ilaria knelt to curtsy before him, I suddenly realised how much her neck, shoulders and chest were revealed by the sensual cut of her gown - created by herself to tempt Armand's romantic interest.

Maxine told me she loved the daring design for the way it made her more alluring to Armand. Of course, she hadn't expected anyone of significance but himself and the Cortelannis to see her in it that day. If I was regretting her choice of it now, I feared Ilaria was too. One who revelled in it however, stood right in front of her, devouring every eye catching inch it revealed.

Ilaria held for a moment, resisting the expectation to rise. Onorato hung in wait, knowing she must lift again and tilt her face to him. As she did so, his hungry stare challenged Ilaria. She tried not to flinch, to show she wasn't intimidated. Yet try as she might, I was certain the prowler not only sensed her anxiety but revelled in it.

No, he didn't bother to glance at me. He was so unintimidated by my view of his provocative behaviour that he didn't take his eyes off Ilaria for a moment. Suddenly every word that Armand's parents had spoken in warning came flooding back into my mind. As the pair remained locked together, I stared at him staring at her.

Then with no hint of shame, Onorato lowered his eyes again to let them linger, grazing over Ilaria's neck, collar, chest and shoulder then back again. In just a matter of moments, the brazen tactic had tipped the balance between them. Behind the defiance he first met in her eyes, knowing Esmeralda and Armand couldn't see, Ilaria's anxiety was already tipping into fear. I was shocked at how quickly he rattled her resistance. Then suddenly, against the intimidation of his shameless show of intent, her lower lip began to tremble.

Though the venal exchange felt like an eternity, it took only moments. It was long enough for Armand and Esmeralda to exchange a look of confusion, but not long enough to openly question. Watching it unfold had left me breathless. The behaviour of this man in the presence of others, moments into a social greeting with a complete stranger, was dominating in the extreme. I wanted to be brave, to demand the leering dog take his eyes off her! But the experience before of being held back by Armand and the sheer threatening presence of this brute in the flesh, a hulking professional killer, had cowed me into submission.

As a musician working in taverns and cat houses, I was used to seeing brazen displays of carnal intent. Indeed I was used to seeing much more than just intent. But in this manner of setting, aimed at someone I cared for, what I saw in that moment left me dumbstruck. And I knew, against Ilaria's own expectation of a polite social greeting, she would never have encountered anything like it before.

It was clear Onorato's silent assault was calculated to shock her. What's more that element seemed to entertain him as, feeling he had succeeded, his lascivious smile widened into a grin. Then I saw the sign. Ilaria's hand lifted to her chest, not to cover her exposure, but to quell the lurching rhythms of her heart.

Just days before I had heard her describe the sensation to Maxine. When her anxiety rose too sharply, the beats became erratic, skipping and leaping wildly, even causing her head to feel light. It was afflicting her now. I wished Maxine was still by her side. I felt sure if she were, she'd instantly snap harsh words at the salivating dog to put him in his place.

But Maxine was whimpering in the forecourt with an imprint of his wife's hand painted upon her cheek. It was a reminder of what to expect if one inspired the Montecchi's displeasure. Keeping Ilaria's offered hand, Onorato turned, drawing her with him. He glanced at the sweetmeats offered about.

'Esmay, this fare's not fit for such welcome guests.'

To mask what I'd witnessed so clearly, suddenly his tone was soothing and playful. He turned and smiled at Ilaria, showing a wide mouth full of strong white teeth. I could see that for all his hope to charm her with his voice, that carnivorous smile did nothing to quell her anxiety. Back in full view of Armand and Esmeralda, Ilaria tried to regain her composure. It was an ironic mimic of our hostess's behaviour from just moments before.

And despite Ilaria's attempt to do so, she knew the predator had seen her first trembling reactions. Moreover she knew that so far, Armand and Esmeralda hadn't witnessed a thing. I doubted however the now obedient Esmeralda would have been surprised to see it. In all probability she may have assumed something like it had occurred.

'Let's take them through to see more of the villa.' he insisted. 'And surely Esmay, more sumptuous fare can be offered.'

Remarkably his words began to muster an air of genuine hospitality. I assumed the effort was aimed at Armand to lull him. Cupid's Balls! It didn't lull me! And surely the lecherous swine didn't expect it to put Ilaria at her ease? The wolf lifted the delicate hand of his prey and wrapped it over his massive arm, turning in the same moment to leave no time for a response as he drew her away. It was identical to the manner in which Esmeralda had drawn Armand from Ilaria. Now she had to watch as her husband did the same with another woman.

Though unbidden, I followed them of course. But as I watched them go, Armand looked very ill-at-ease, that this hulking stranger had drawn his young wife away so easily. Yet it made me feel safer to know he was uneasy. But that feeling also caused me, of all people, to reach and ensure that my stout mace which he insisted I carry, was still hanging on my hip. Yes, it was!

The marionette's head, broken since, no longer covered the top to disguise its purpose. Yet I felt sure that from where he'd seen me, the wolf didn't realise I had it. I hadn't expected to need it. I prayed to all the saints in Heaven that I wouldn't, then scurried in pursuit.

Onorato seemed to be guiding Ilaria toward the centre of the villa. Esmeralda was now upon Armand's arm and following behind.

Following I had the chance to observe the brute more closely. Montecchi was a large fortified man, muscular yes, but hefty muscles rather than lean. His skin was browning, baked by the north Italian sun. He'd come from the vineyards in a loose untied shirt that revealed his hard upper form. And his unbuttoned cuffs were shoved to his elbows. He seemed like a man who enjoyed the excuse of heat and work to display the intimidating shape of his body beneath loose attire.

Below his waist, soft leather breeches strained against strong wide thighs. His massive calves were encased in rough hunting boots, entwined to the ankle with straps of leather. And while his hairline was beginning to recede, his thick black hair, unbound and swept from his ride, ran grey in streaks. Against Armand's youth and formality of attire, the pair cut a stark contrast of character and couture.

We arrived at an entry to the villa's centrepiece: an open and sunlit courtyard. Even from the threshold we could see it was adorned with immaculately cultivated plants and broad water beds. The latter were alive with bright spreading lilies and vibrantly coloured fish. Yet even before we entered the exotic chamber, Armand attempted to lay a path for our imminent retreat.

'I can see why you hide this beautiful centrepiece.' he said casually. 'It's enhanced by the surprise of discovery. Very impacting.'

'Yes, just so. The element of surprise is a potent thing.' Onorato glanced at Ilaria who stiffened. 'Come along inside. I can't wait for you to see what's hidden in the centre.'

Though his tone was childlike with enthusiasm, I wasn't convinced any surprise lurking within would be welcome to see. I imagined a pit of vipers to tip the unsuspecting into. Or a private gallows to watch the unwitting hang for his entertainment.

Well bite my bare ass, yes I did! Yes, I know that sounds grim. But if you had seen what I'd already seen, you'd have imagined it too.

Before we ventured in Armand began to offer their apologies.

'Sadly Don Montecchi I should warn you – as we explained to

Esmeralda – since our arrival at the gate nearly an hour ago, we now stand in danger of being late to greet Aurelie.'

'That's true. The Cortelannis expect them.' said Esmeralda.

'And so' Armand added 'we can only stay a little longer.'

'Oh I understand completely.' Onorato smiled. 'You've come a long way. Now you're so close to their sanctuary and ... I apologise for taking so long to come in from the vineyard.'

'Not at all. Business waits for no man.'

'Well said. But please I insist, remain just long enough to sample the early corvina we inspected and to see my surprise. Esmay's very proud of it. Aren't you *vita mia?*'

'Why ... yes. Yes dear.' she said nervously.

'Esmay. That's no way to address me in company. Is it?'

'No. No it's not vita mia.'

'Much better.'

'*Vita mia?*' asked Ilaria soberly.

'My life.' Onorato stared far too innocently.

'Oh.' Her brows lifted in surprise. 'Oh that's charming.'

'I'm glad you think so Ilaria. Since the moment we met, when she first arrived from Portugal I insisted that she call me *vita mia*. Didn't I?'

Esmeralda stared. It was clear her mind went back.

'Yes. You did.'

'I reciprocate of course. Yet from that very first moment I wanted her to have no doubt that her life belonged to me.' I saw Ilaria's brows knit as her lips pressed. 'What do you say to that Esme?'

Esmeralda lifted her eyes to Onorato. Somehow she managed to convince all watching they were lit with genuine desire for the brute.

'I say ... *yes* my love *utterly.*'

'Hmm. I never tire of hearing that. Or that look in her eyes.'

'I'm sure that's true Onorato.' Ilaria dared to say. 'Do you reciprocate with that too?'

His black eyes confronted her. 'Never.' His mouth curled in a wry smile. 'And now, come in for a moment and sample the early harvest. Then when you meet Sabatino, you can give him your verdict. He's always been envious of it.'

I confess as I watched silently, though he treated his exalted wife like one of his enslaved servers, it was becoming difficult to tell the brute wasn't less of a threat than his initial antics had made him appear. Clearly he was an inveterate dominator of women, or perhaps *any* person that had the misfortune to appear in front of him. Yet I began to suspect that as their primo don, despite his brutal instinct to intimidate and control, perhaps the boundaries of social protocol would now hold him in check.

For it seemed every other aspect of his manner was becoming more conventional. And perversely, even his want to kiss his wife so sensually and draw her confessions of devotion, compelled or not, seemed to suggest he had as much interest in her as any woman. Yes, that shows how little I understood such venal brutes and their victims at that time. But it made me hope his leering attentions may be nothing more than a perverse entertainment, one that had finally reached its limit.

Just as I debated that notion in my stirring mind, we stepped into the courtyard, where a new distraction claimed our attention. I heard Ilaria gasp as she saw it. The sound drew me faster and I halted. There in the centre was an extraordinary sight. Sweet friends it was just a tree, yet none of us had ever seen it's like before. Despite the vision of the ancient sycamore that greeted us before the villa, this much smaller totem was a more miraculous thing.

'Dear Heaven.' said Ilaria. 'I confess that I'm ... thunderstruck. Armand have you ever seen one like it before?'

'No angel never. But it's ... extraordinary.'

'Esmay, tell them something about it.'

Finding her voice with some effort, Esmeralda began to explain. 'Some call it a *Sun Tree*.'

'Yes I can see why.' whispered Ilaria, reaching for a blossom.

'Some call it a *Gold Fountain*.'

'That's equally fitting.' said Armand.

'It's from a territory far to the east of Constantinople.'

'Did a local merchant acquire it for you?' asked Ilaria.

'No dear. We were in Constantinople on the final leg of our marriage tour when I saw it in a market.'

Onorato was quick to use that reply to engage with Ilaria again.

'I'll never forget it. Esmay was instantly smitten. So was I.'

So were we all, as far as the astonishing tree was concerned. Not unlike a willow it had a broad trunk with long whiplike branches. But the closely massed heads of bright golden flowers appeared to drip along each drooping stem. The effect was otherworldly. For a moment the miraculous thing held us transfixed and all else was forgotten.

Indeed for that moment as I listened to their story, though I was loathe to think well of them – particularly of that beast – for a sliver of an instant I imagined there was a time when they behaved very differently to each other. It made me wonder what life had done to them to bring them to where they were. But in the same instant, I felt a twinge of caution tug at me and recanted the thought as quickly as it had come.

I suddenly realised that, even if there was a time when he behaved more respectfully, by his own description of the moment they met, his good will was predicated on an insistence that Esmeralda submit to being treated like a slave to deserve it. I couldn't imagine Armand behaving in such a way. I couldn't imagine Ilaria submitting to such a person.

As they gazed at the tree, that realisation caused me to glower at the beast. To my great relief as I did so, Ilaria used the distraction of that wondrous sight to draw over to Armand's side. Onorato's eyes followed her of course. When she turned and looped her hand through her husband's arm, the wolf began to chatter as he stared.

All at once he launched a curt enquiry at his male guest. He understood Armand was a chevalier, but probed for details of his war service. Very little was offered in return. Then Onorato suggested, as an employer of soldiers he was interested to know Capulet's plans for future service. He even sifted for political news from France.

In reply Armand quipped he paid scant attention to politics.

'I confess Capulet, I'm also curious to know how that giant out-side, who is your squire?'

'Yes.'

'How a man such as that came into the service of such a recently risen chevalier?'

'Purely by chance Don Montecchi. We met during the siege of Carentan. He lost his master on the same day as myself but I was granted my rank in the field.' Onorato's eyes narrowed. 'Next day the siege lifted. He was at a loose end. I found myself in need of a squire.'

Oh yes, all that was true! If *being at a loose end* means Caspar found himself chained to a dungeon wall! Not to mention the omission that Armand slew his former master!

'You earned your spurs in the field?'

'Well yes but to be fair, that may have been greatly due to our urgent need for more numbers to meet the enemy.'

I held my tongue, even though I knew his rank was awarded for killing five men singlehanded!

'And so' Armand added 'as time was short, with our Duke leaving to chase the English, I asked if he had any interest to follow me. Misery loves company they say, so he accepted.'

Oh yes, the rest was very loosely true! At that moment, I wasn't sure if Armand's version was due to his inveterate humility or a matter of tactical restraint. By then I'd learned to trust his instincts. If he appeared to want to play his cards close to his chest, I'd go along. So for the first time since taking up his service, I didn't make bold to boast on his behalf.

For his part, Onorato seemed unimpressed by it all. I was glad to feel that was the result Armand hoped for. However as Ilaria listened, feeling safer on his arm, I sensed she still reeled from the galling experience suffered before. I could tell it rankled her to hear Armand offer that beast such a modest report of his time in the war.

Even when Onorato pressed him for more details, Armand referred vaguely to his brave service at Formigny. Other than his admission of meeting Caspar in Carentan, he completely omitted his exploits in that victory. By then I felt sure his omissions had a sound motive that I shouldn't undermine. But for Ilaria, forced to endure Onorato's stifling presence and veiled looks, she felt reduced by Armand's humility as the men spoke back and forth.

And so regretfully, though I held my tongue and refused to boast, Ilaria decided to salvage the potency of her husband's tale. Nor was it mere vanity to do so. She hoped, for their safety, that a clearer suggestion of Armand's martial skill would intimidate Onorato and decrease any likelihood his unwanted attentions would rekindle.

That's what Ilaria hoped.

Starting nervously, she began to sing his praises. 'Armand received his rank before time for *conspicuous* bravery.'

Onorato's brows lifted. Armand stared stoically.

'Did he?'

'And he was dubbed by the hand of our Queen in person.'

'Well, well, well. That's not ordinary at all.'

'No. I believe it's not.'

'Indeed it shows *very* great favour?'

'I feel it does. I'm *very* proud of him.'

As Ilaria shared more, in an effort to cower Onorato, I noticed that not only did Armand appear troubled, so did Esmeralda. Then when Ilaria mention Armand's injuries, it raised a wry smile and a lifted brow of interest from the mercenary warlord.

'That's very interesting. Yes Ilaria, I can see he was just being humble. You must be proud of your strapping young man.'

He smirked as he stared. It seemed clear Onorato understood Ilaria had hoped to intimidate him. But as her story had unfolded, I noticed Esmeralda's glances flitted more furtively between them, as if she was no longer certain of anything. The wolf scanned his silent wife and then his gushing guest.

He glanced and held in thought on Armand for a moment. 'Wounds from arrows and crossbow bolts can be nasty.' Armand lifted his brows and pressed his lips in casual agreement. 'But in my time chevalier' he said acidly 'I've found myself at the start of an engagement wearing three or four arrows in my armour before the fight even began.'

I felt that was not hard to imagine. Ilaria's eyes widened. She began to wonder if all she said had done nothing more than encourage the braggart. Esmeralda's dour expression suggested it was so.

'Nor' he ran on 'would I halt to extract them 'til I sat for supper in my enemies house with his wife and children tethered at my feet.'

His glance swept onto Esmeralda. She was stone-faced. Then his prowling eyes found Ilaria again, as if imagining her just as he described. A stare punctuated his boast. Incredibly it seemed he hoped that grisly commentary would draw a glance of admiration from her. Like his own wife however, Ilaria stared blankly, now beginning to sense it may not help our situation to more openly reveal the disgust she now felt for him.

The venal man turned to his wife with an unwitting look.

'Oh no Esmay, was that too crass?' He turned to Armand.

'Apologies Capulet. Perhaps in the comfort of my own home, the blunt soldier in me has taken too much licence.' He purred with mock sincerity.

Armand met his eyes with emotionless candour. 'Better to hear the hard truth from a soldier than soft lies.'

Onorato's lips creased in a smile, then expanded into a grin.

'Well said my *boy*.' It was clear he had calculated that word. 'Some say I'm not really a soldier at all, just an inveterate gambler. Perhaps I am. But many hard men have taken up the challenge to gamble their lives against me ... and lost.'

'I'm sure. You're *old* enough to have the right to boast it.'

Ilaria's eyes widened. My heart began to beat faster.

The temperature had just risen between them.

Subtly Armand suggested Onorato was long in the tooth. That would prick his vanity as much as it goaded Armand to be called a boy. Yet in the same utterance, without offering an open insult, Armand also suggested Onorato was a braggart by saying he had a right to boast for the sake of his age. Cupid's Balls!

I'd have hailed that effort as a witty retort if it hadn't scared the shit out of my asshole to hear it! Instead my mouth was dry as we hung on a response. I glanced at Ilaria and Esmeralda. Each held their breath, glancing back and forth between their husbands.

The wolf narrowed his eyes.

'When a soldier sallies forth he should know his capability.'

'And his fallibility.' Armand replied bluntly.

'He should gamble nothing.'

'Agreed.'

'I know my capability Capulet. Whenever I fight, I *always* win.'

'So far *Montecchi*. May fate ordain your luck continues to hold.'

My mouth was not only dry, my heart had leapt into it!

Ilaria's hand was pressed on her chest. Esmeralda's eyes bulged with anticipation. Until that moment, though Onorato goaded him with subtler terms of belittlement, Armand addressed the cretin more civilly, prefacing his title ahead of his familial name. That sudden omission was a less subtle declaration. Even though Armand stood in their house as an invited guest, by the rites of protocol, he was finally willing to accept he had a right to treat his host's behaviour as uncivil.

Goaded by the presence of their wives, suddenly the volatile men stood like uncorked kegs of powder. It felt as if a pair of flint's were spitting sparks that danced about the openings, flirting with the danger one stray flash would cause either to explode at any moment.

My spine leapt as Onorato's hand reached! Cupid's Balls!

Yet he smiled heartily, slapping Armand's shoulder. For the first time he let loose a genuine burst of laughter. Perhaps it was a gruff, playful gesture. But having heard tell of Armand's injuries, I felt sure the elder soldier was sizing up the strength of his younger rival. From the heft of the smack I knew it must have hurt Armand. Ilaria winced. Esmeralda caught her breath and shot an uneasy glance at her.

Armand didn't flinch at all and smiled as the braggart ran on.

'Many talk of fate and luck. For myself, I feel I was *born* lucky.'

For the love of folly it irked me to hear him say so when it was something I had always said of myself! I hated to think we shared such a thing in common.

'I'm sure you'll agree Capulet, for a soldier to win they need more than luck. Take your *skirmish* in Normandy. Was it lucky?'

'I believe there can be an element of luck in all combat.'

I knew that by *luck* Armand was referring to *the will of Heaven*, which he so strongly believed watched over him in dire moments.

'Recently we've heard tell of your fight with the English in some detail. Just last Sunday after mass, I discussed it with the prince.'

'I'm glad it provided some distraction.'

'It did. Oh yes, there's luck. Yet our report has it that their king was absent. Yes?'

'He was.'

'That means the English were likely *misled* by an underling, which caused them to lack *motivation*. And we also heard tell that their numbers were *greatly* lacking –'

Ilaria's eyes leapt. She interrupted him, revelling in the chance to address him dismissively. 'Forgive my correction Signore but that suggestion is *grossly* errant.'

Encouraged by Armand's apparent lack of intimidation, Ilaria decided to stomach no more from the brute without offering response.

'My *husband* fought in a host outnumbered two to one.'

She delighted in using that term as her eyes challenged him.

Armand laid a hand softly on Ilaria's.

'I confess Montecchi' he said quietly 'that *is* the truth of it.'

Ilaria felt the strength of facing the brute together. Onorato glanced from one to the other, smiled and inclined his head politely.

'Well it may have been so. All-in-all I'm sure the outing made for good experience. You won your spurs and took your first *real* wounds in a *significant* battle.'

'That's a fair assessment.'

'But were you *lucky* to survive Capulet? I suspect capability played a *larger* part. Either way, I applaud you for rising to the surface.'

For a moment I was flummoxed. That was clearly a compliment. Was the beast in retreat from his bullish stance?

'You've made a decent start.' he added. 'But it's not so easy to continue my boy.' There was that word again. 'I've had years of hard campaigning. Over time, it can take it out of you.'

'I'm sure that's true Montecchi.' said Armand.

'Unless like myself, as Esmay knows, you remain in constant service and practice.'

'Agreed.'

'Tell me, was your hurt at Formigny very great? Are you ably recovered? I only ask to suggest that if not, perhaps to regain some vigour during this visit you'd like to take to the hunt with us.'

'The hunt?'

'Yes, what's your preference? Fox, boar, wolf, stag, bear? We have them all. Ilaria what about yourself? What beast gets your blood up to chase it and kill it?'

'I would never kill a poor creature for sport.'

'Oh? Perhaps that doesn't surprise me. Esmay however, loves the thrill of the hunt. Don't you my little morsel?'

'Why ... yes vita mia.' she murmured. 'Yes of course I do.'

'She's deft with a bow and has a fine new falcon.' He reached for Armand's other shoulder. 'With Ilaria and yourself we'd make an elegant party. Perhaps Sabatino and Aurelie would come along.'

Remarkably as Onorato said so, he reached for a pitcher of wine, then leaned to fill Ilaria's beaker himself! I presumed with that effort he hoped to restrain her clear want to be gone.

Yet despite Onorato's pretence of retreating behind a mask of cordiality, veiled through all his waffling before was the suggestion Armand's martial status was that of a *novice*. Moreover he added the reminder Armand was his junior. And though strictly true, in military terms his use of the word *boy* to do so, insinuated although Armand was a chevalier, he hadn't earned the right to be treated as such.

By my reckoning, the cup of veiled insults Armand had been served by that cretin was brimming full. Even the invitation to join the hunt was devised to rankle them both, if for no other reason than it suggested Ilaria would be forced to suffer his company again.

Yet as I heard and saw it all, the most remarkable thing that still struck me, was how much the lascivious don seemed to hope to impress Ilaria with it all. By dominating his own wife before her eyes, denigrating her warrior husband without fear, the beast hoped to make it clear to Ilaria she could do better, and he expected that revelation to thrill her. Cupid's Balls!

The salivating beast was vanity and perversion incarnate. He expected Ilaria to realise, he was more of a man than she could hope to find in her lifetime. Yes, that appeared to be his hope for her hope. Unfortunately for Onorato, Ilaria's contempt for him had lit up in her eyes like a wild grass fire.

Armand however, though he had dug his heels in more firmly, still showed no real sign he would rise any further to bite at Onorato's bait. Yet I knew he had his limits. I saw them reached on his wedding night, when he struck his own father for crossing a line he finally couldn't tolerate. Thus far in Onorato's presence, he had deflected the slights more easily, or at least with a greater sense of caution.

But we were no longer in Chateau de Capulet. We were now deep inside the wolf's lair on top of his lonely hill. And Armand was beginning to lose patience with a more unsettling problem. During the last few exchanges Onorato's leering attention to Ilaria, began to display more openly while Esmeralda, suffocating with shame, was forced to watch on.

All throughout his babbling Onorato had permitted himself to stare at Ilaria and smile suggestively. His bulbous eyes grazed all over her as if her husband, a blooded chevalier, wasn't present at all. Armand was noticing it for the first time. Ilaria wasn't experiencing it for the first time. It had become impossible for anyone present to misunderstand.

As a guest, Armand was not just being baited by a disarming braggart, but in the company of both women his manliness was being mocked. Into the bargain, for the sake of the wolf's grinning enjoyment, the sensitivity of both women was being grossly assaulted. It was clear he revelled in exercising the power to spur their reactions.

It made me want to draw my mace and thump the life out of that lecherous pig! I hoped Armand would burst in a fit of anger and do it for me of course! At that moment however he understood, the grinning primo don had not only lured us deep into his villa, but in doing so he separated us from the protection of our people. And so, despite his leers and leans and hideous goading, Armand must remain calm, or at least appear to be so.

To add to our danger, being away from all sight of our people, we had no idea what kind of predicament they may now be in. Based on the behaviour witnessed thus far, like myself, Armand suspected that on his own estate, with resources at his disposal, to gain possession of anything he set his mind to Onorato may be capable of deep treachery.

Our situation had reached a critical moment, when even a patient man like Armand had to accept we were no longer genuine guests protected by elite social conventions. We may have been so when Esmeralda first greeted us. But in her husband's company we were not, or at least Armand was not. Clearly Onorato hoped to see more of Ilaria. And now in full view of Armand, she was clearly distressed by Onorato's drooling attention.

I glanced at Esmeralda and my mind leapt back. Her own flirtations with Armand had vanished the moment the beast arrived. Ironically now, she was paling in shame at his interest in a younger guest. Not half an hour before she seemed to pine for a time when her husband was more social and flirtatious. Yet as I glared at him again to no avail, flirtation wasn't the word that came to my mind.

My eyes began to dart desperately, wondering what would happen. Cupid's Balls! All of this was being endured for the sake of hoping to purchase a heavenly shrine that now seemed to house the spawn of the Devil. A flicker of decision lit in Armand's eyes. I couldn't tell if he still had any notion left to make an offer to purchase. I felt sure Ilaria had forgotten it completely or no longer had the stomach for it. Clearly the discomfort of lingering was unthinkable.

During the moment before, in an attempt to avoid Onorato's insufferable staring, Ilaria had moved to a chair and lowered herself to the edge of its seat. Before Armand could follow her, the salivating beast crossed his path, spun on his heel and lowered himself onto the arm of it. He sat and reclined and leaned, towering over her.

Ilaria's eyes lifted in a panic to Armand. He smiled reassuringly, emptied his elegant cut-glass beaker, placed it on a tray and stepped over to face the lounging, leering beast. Armand reached in with a smile to draw Ilaria to her feet, glancing at Onorato and Esmeralda in turn.

'And now good people, we must take our leave. Aurelie expects us. And I know Ilaria will require time to rest and prepare before dining this evening.'

'Oh' said Onorato with a mock frown 'stay just a *little* longer?'

'Alas we have no more time left today.' He glanced at Ilaria as if recalling something, then back to the wolf. 'However in one of our wagons, we do have a gift from France we intended to offer you both.'

I assumed it was a lie, or at least a ruse to lead us back to the safety of our entourage. Suddenly I felt that I would never be so grateful to see our giant, threatening, ninny Caspar! And indeed Armand's announcement put the party on their feet.

Then without warning, Armand drew Ilaria's hand through his arm and swirled to gather Esmeralda to spirit them away. Both women were desperate to depart, so the trio pressed on at a lively pace. It made me grin to see the wolf's tactic used against him and to see a Montecchi conspirator offering her assistance. They drove on through the hall that connected us back to the reception chamber.

After plunging on together, before he could think to follow them, the pompous condottiere sat gaping in their wake. He blinked at me for a moment, the gall appearing to rise in his throat. I bowed to offer him before me. I dared not look as he swept past. Then I followed his sour form at a respectful distance.

Yes, as I went I kept my hand on the neck of my mace, ready to have at him. I thought – *at least he won't see it coming if I have to clout this fucking brute!* No I didn't feel ashamed to think so! As far as I was concerned that lecherous toad would deserve it!

The bustling trio ahead of us reached the receiving chamber's threshold and entered in quickly. Armand halted and turned between his escorts, ready to offer his final thanks to the stalking primo don. Then an interesting set of objects laid upon a mantle caught his eye.

'Hmm. What do we have here?' he said casually.

The well used objects contrasted starkly with the smooth white stone they sat upon. One object was a rather beaten pewter pot the size of a fist. It lacked for a handle. And it was decorated with pagan images of Fortuna and Bacchus. The images were framed by etchings of grapevines and amphorae. Next to the pot, upon a hardwood disc, sat three gambling die all carved from bone. The disc appeared to be an improvised lid, the pewter original broken off and lost to time.

I saw a glint light in Armand's eyes. I'd seen it before.

'*Passé dix* Montecchi?' He said playfully as Onorato followed them in. 'And you said you didn't believe in luck.'

'I confess that Past Ten is a weakness of mine. One of the few.' His grin at Ilaria chilled her spine. 'That set was a gift from the captains of my first campaign.'

'I fear in time Ilaria' said Esmeralda 'you'll discover that soldiers and gambling are inseparable.'

Esmeralda seemed to hope that she may still have an opportunity, before it was too late, to dispel some of the awkwardness.

'That particular game is *special* is it not?' Ilaria replied.

'Yes dear, Past Ten is mentioned in scripture but *infamously* so.' Esmeralda rolled her eyes.

Now it appeared both women felt sure their ordeal was ending and hoped to redeem their social footing. Perhaps in future, away from her husband and in the company of other women, this contact made with Esmeralda may still prove to be a boon for Ilaria.

'It's the notorious game' Esmeralda continued 'the Roman soldiers played at Christ's feet when they crucified him.'

'Oh dear!'

'Oh yes.'

As I watched from behind, to hear them chattering more comfortably, even the beast appeared to be put more at ease. Esmeralda glanced at him, lifting her brows reproachfully.

'I'm surprised the new inquisitor hasn't declared it a heresy!'

'On a long campaign, it's harmless fun for my men.'

'I'm sure my tone betrays me Ilaria. He knows I don't approve.'

'I'm not a gambler myself.' Ilaria said smiling with relief.

'I don't mind gambling to a point, but *that* game. Onorato?'

'That's why I only play it far from your presence on campaign.'

His hand lifted to her face as it had before. He drew her in to kiss. She responded as before yet this time he returned her interest more than we expected. It appeared even in the midst of a parting ritual, Onorato's venal instincts couldn't be denied. Seeing that rite repeat again, it occurred to me that sadly, Esmeralda had developed an instinct, surely for her safety, to indulge him convincingly no matter what manner of moment he beckoned her to respond.

As he drew his full lips from hers, the wolf turned to stare.

'That game's great sport among real men. A test of nerve.'

'Yes we play it too.' said Armand. 'The risk can be daunting.'

Though I rarely heard him discuss gambling, the latter part of his comment was utterly uncharacteristic. Yes, I'd heard him suggest that a risk may be high or low. Never before had I heard Armand suggest that a risk appeared *frightening*.

Onorato's brows lifted with interest at what sounded like clear reluctance. 'I don't want a captain under me Capulet who has no stomach to risk all in a single toss.'

'Agreed.' said Armand quietly.

Onorato's interest sparked. He glanced at Ilaria. 'You see ladies, many claim the blood of *real* warriors runs in their veins. Yet how many have the balls to risk everything in a single moment.'

'Very few I suppose.' Armand replied with a frowning pout.

'You'll discover my boy, that in a game of chance or upon the field, that's often the difference between victory and defeat. If you venture nothing, you gain nothing.'

I blinked in surprise at the comment. Ilaria did too. Hearing the words she used to encourage Armand to call upon these people spring from the mouth of that beast, seemed more than ironic. It was a presage of fate. And it sent another chill down Ilaria's spine.

'But we digress.' she said bluntly. 'Now we really *must* be gone.'

It was a fitting moment to take our leave of that devilish man who lurked in that heavenly place. I hoped our exit would follow fast. And I prayed that we'd never keep company with that insufferable Signore or his suffering Signora again.

'Yes angel.' Armand agreed with a frown of mock regret.

He moved as if to take her hand and turn, then halted.

My heart froze.

'However ... before we depart' he said as the expressions of both revealed their surprise to hear more 'forgive me Onorato, Esmeralda, but Ilaria made me promise if we met that I would ask something of you.'

I couldn't believe my ears of course. Ilaria's breath drew in, her brows lifted. Clearly she had no stomach left for any kind of delay.

'Ask something?' Onorato blinked in confusion. 'Ask what?'

Given Armand suggested the request was prompted by Ilaria, Onorato smiled hopefully and began to leer. It seemed the vanity of the bold was inexhaustible. Armand glanced and couldn't fail to see the anxiety rising in Ilaria's face. Now realising his intent, she regretted having pressed him to *promise* to make them an offer.

'I know in all probability, it won't be a consideration for either of you. But would you have any interest at all – and forgive me for asking – to *sell* this estate?'

'To ... to *sell*?' Onorato stammered. 'You want to ...?'

He halted as his face went slack. He was surprised. And it was clear the beast didn't like surprises. Esmeralda's eyes leapt in panic. She reached for his arm, smiling to placate him.

'Oh Armand' she said hastily 'if only he *would* sell. Don't mistake me, Ilaria. Sycamore Hill's beautiful of course. But Onorato knows I'd love nothing better than to live in the citadel again. The rest of his people are there. And we see them so little.'

The Wolf was still blinking, glancing and thinking.

'You know Esmay ...' he stuttered 'in time, that's my want too.'

Onorato looked soured that his own wife had been so quick to add fuel to the unexpected fire.

'You see' Armand said innocently 'we understood from a local source and – apologies if the information is errant – that this is not your *only* holding, nor your *largest* holding.'

The beast frowned with indignation.

'Of *course* it's not!' he spat still chasing the tail of their exchange.

'Of course.' Armand replied calmly. 'Naturally we're interested in obtaining a pretty estate on *this* side of the citadel to allow us to spend each summer close to my sister.'

'Are you?' he growled.

'Yes. And we're willing to pay much more than a *reasonable* price. I mean you no disrespect in offering. I hope it's *clear* this was merely an impulse, created by seeing your villa as we passed. We understand you weren't *seeking* to sell it.'

I knew very little of trade or negotiation at the time. Yet I understood that comment was necessary to allow the Montecchis, regardless of their shortcomings, to deflect any suggestion they stood in financial distress and so *needed* to sell.

'You're right Capulet. This estate isn't large by my standard.'

'Of course.'

'And yes. We have *many* more ranged on every side of Verona.'

'So we were told.'

'Indeed I consider this a small holding.'

'I'm sure you do.'

'As for how *pretty* you find it to look at?' He leered at Ilaria. 'If I were you I'd care more for its ability to generate wealth.'

Armand frowned. 'I understand that logic of course. In this case however, that aspect of its value has no bearing on *our* interest.'

'Perhaps not.' He narrowed his eyes. 'You should also know, that value has nothing to do with why it remains in my possession.'

'No?'

'Without compunction we gift more of Sycamore Hill's produce to the church than is compulsory. I keep this estate –'

'Because it has *sentimental* value?'

'It does. This is our familial seat, held by my father and six generations before him. This is the spiritual home of our *albergo*.'

He spat the last with rising heat. It was the first time I'd heard anyone use that potent word, their native term for a House, a network of familial strength and associates.

The beast ran on. 'Every year, with Esmay and I at their head, several hundred from several citadels attend on the crest of this hill for our Christmas feast.'

'Of course Montecchi. I understand completely.'

Armand said it casually yet his eyes rested firmly on the wolf.

Hearing him use their familial name again, Ilaria's brows knit with concern. So did mine. It sounded and looked like a prelude. For the second time in less than half an hour, as the first men of Capulet and Montecchi faced each other, my heart leapt into my mouth.

Armand spoke again quietly. 'Much like the prima donna hanging on your arm, this villa's a pretty bauble for you to dangle and display. Both are beautiful, to be sure, but mean no more to you than secluded tokens of vanity and possession.'

It didn't take a moment. That breathtaking insult had launched so slowly that by the time it was done, the fuming beast was left in no doubt. Bright blue eyes blazed into black. Ilaria's hand lifted for her heart. From the heave of her chest I knew her heart was already racing. Esmeralda appeared shocked to her core but also seemed utterly spellbound.

Suddenly I feared what kind of retaliation that monster may unleash in response to such a clear affront, and wondered how much power was lurking nearby to help him ensure it. Ilaria reached for Armand's hand. The wolf's black eyes darted at the motion but Armand's calm expression drew him back.

'Onorato.' He said firmly. Armand stepped forward to grasp his shoulders. 'Good fortune to you.'

He kissed his cheeks in an embrace of farewell. It took Onorato by surprise. I held my breath. Could this be all? Armand turned to the staring prima donna.

'Esmeralda at *least* you've attempted to be a gracious hostess.'

The prima donna stood speechless, dumbstruck by his temerity to offer that parting quip in front of her dangerous husband.

Armand took her shoulders gently, offered a sympathetic smile and kissed her thrice. Then he turned to offer his hand to Ilaria, feeling sure she would offer no formal farewell to either host, nor would he offer any hint that he expected her to.

As if in a courtly dance, they turned on their heels as one, hands disconnecting and re-connecting in perfect synchronicity. Ilaria hoped that was all. I hoped that was all. They began to make their exit.

That was not all.

Chapter 15 Stiletto

Her heart was still leaping erratically.

With no further ado and summoning as much elan as possible, Ilaria attempted to exit the villa on her husband's arm. And though grateful to be outside, to feel marble treads beneath her descending feet, the confusion of what just occurred was reeling in her mind. In an effort to follow I bowed and scraped in dutiful farewell to the beast and beastess. Yet despite my grovelling I wanted to burst into an antic fit of laughter.

I didn't of course. Instead I kept my frightened mouth shut!

Finally turning my back upon them, the sight of stunned Montecchi faces still hung in my mind. Following the Capulets, I passed through the lofting columns that framed the portal and down the wide casement of stairs. This time, Ilaria had the assistance she lacked when we had entered an hour before.

There below us at last, watching and waiting, stood our brave little company. There was our wonderful giant Caspar! The sight of that lummox made me sigh with intense relief. Then I noticed a sight that gave me pause. Seven or eight Montecchi men-at-arms were ranged casually about our people in a loose, wide circuit. I glanced at Maxine. Her eyes were filled with anxiety. I glanced again at Caspar, Liberati, Boccolo and even Fabrizio. Each man looked gravely alert with one hand or both resting upon the hilt of a weapon.

Gliding gracefully ahead of me, still hand in hand, Armand and Ilaria had all but descended. Then from the top of the stairs, behind and above us, came Onorato's livid reply. The beast had floundered moments before, caught by surprise with the bluntness of Armand's parting quip. Then Ilaria's decision to make no attempt at a formal farewell to himself or Esmeralda, had stung him into silence.

But now, perched at the top of the entry plaza looking down on our attempt to retreat to safety, only to discover we were surrounded by his henchmen, the volatile beast found his voice.

'And ...' he bellowed holding for effect.

His bark was startling enough to send a shiver through Esmeralda. The Capulets had reached the bottom as it halted them.

'Never while I breathe air Capulet ... will any Montecchi possession be offered to one who displays that effeminate lily of the Guelphs! Certainly not a French marmot like you, a green military novice with no credibility to count himself among real men, let alone keep social company among real soldiers.'

The beast had stumbled at receiving an offer to purchase.

Next he failed to respond to the foreigner's parting insult.

Then he stood mutely as his prima donna suffered the indignity of being offered no farewell by the little French bitch.

Yes! I thought it was all so satisfying to witness.

But now the fuming warlord felt he had recovered in time to have the best of this polite popinjay and his nervy harlot. I felt sure Onorato was expecting to see the Capulets attempt to walk on, to watch Armand try to slink away in shame with his fretful wife on his hand and his tail between his legs. The glowering Black Wolf of Verona stood gloating. He looked certain this smarmy boy lacked the stomach to turn, let alone to respond any further.

And may the Devil curse me for a coward. I hoped he was right. I hoped Armand would remain silent and depart. I felt sure Ilaria did too. But Onorato was very much mistaken. For the premiere sieur of Capulet turned upon his heel and offered the primo don of Montecchi a wry smile.

'Now Onorato' he began amiably 'by Esmeralda's invitation to attend here, we're officially your *guests*. And I fear somehow, unintentionally, that I've drawn your anger.'

'Best leave here *chevalier* while that's all you have drawn.'

He spat the title as if it were a worthless trinket he had tossed to a beggar. I crossed my fingers, hoping Armand would take the offer and let us go away as fast as we could.

'Wise men and *cowards* know when to retire.' Onorato added.

During his first volley, I had scurried down the steps and turned.

Now looking up at the face of Esmeralda beside him, I felt sure she stood in grave fear for our safety.

'Onorato ...' she stammered 'vita mia please...'

'Esmay my little morsel' he growled 'shut your fucking mouth.'

Armand's eyes narrowed for an instant.

'I wonder Montecchi.' he said gazing up calmly. 'Although you don't wish to *sell* your pretty estate to me –'

'Perhaps I *might* sell it Capulet.' Onorato glanced at Ilaria and smiled wickedly.

Armand feigned a look of surprise. 'Interesting Montecchi. Unexpected.' He knit his brows and pushed his lower lip to his upper. 'Upon what terms?'

'A sum *four* times its worth in yearly production.'

'Hmm.' Armand considered for a moment. 'Agreed.'

'And of course in return for my pretty estate ...' His eyes locked upon Ilaria. 'I'll expect you to throw your pretty wife into the bargain.'

Ilaria's eyes leapt in anger as her hand gripped Armand's. Onorato's black stare was locked onto her.

'We have an empty stall in the stable Ilaria. I'll teach you what it feels like to be serviced by a real stallion. I'm sure you'll enjoy it for a change.' His hand drew around Esmeralda's waist. 'Esmay may have to instruct you of course. I doubt you've learnt enough from that boy to know how to satisfy me.'

As he grinned, every man of his posse belched in ribald laughter. Esmeralda blanched. Her body went rigid, her expression a torturous blend of bitter shame and rising fear. Ilaria seethed at being made the target of such a publicised depravity and the enjoyment it offered the foul beast and his followers. Yet despite the loathing Ilaria felt for Onorato, she and any who hadn't laughed, felt just as deeply ashamed for her suffering counterpart next to him.

I glanced about nervously and saw our giant glaring. I expected him to erupt at any moment, to rush the stairs and eradicate Montecchi like a rodent! I was certain I would help him! The only person who displayed no modicum of passion, was the man those poisoned barbs, even that last, were so clearly aimed at.

Unhappily for the gazing wolf, Armand showed no whit of heat or emotion at all and replied calmly.

'Sadly for yourself Montecchi, my wife's not a chattel to trade.'

Ilaria lowered her chin, drawing her shoulders down and back in an effort to match his composure. She wanted all the Montecchi to know they faced two formidable Capulets.

'And despite ...' Armand continued 'this rather embarrassing show of passion over a simple negotiation, if you ever do have a *genuine* mind to sell, then for the sake of doing business calmly, I'm willing to overlook it.'

All the while, Armand glanced casually at each of the wolf's henchman, making sure they felt included as he put their warlord's behaviour on public display.

Armand's voice lifted. 'Moreover ... I'm my willing to offer you *six* times the income value.'

Every pair of eyes, including Onorato's, blinked in wonder at the incredible sum and the affable tone of Armand's reply. Suddenly the hint of a smile creased the corners of Esmeralda's lips. It seemed she was heartened to hear someone, anyone, have the temerity to stand up to the vaunting of her very dangerous husband.

'I'd need to have it independently appraised.' he ran on. 'Yet that can be done on Monday by some merchant you trust in Verona. What say you Montecchi?'

By the look on Onorato's face, he could not believe it. And confound my own ears, I couldn't believe it. Armand still appeared to be making a genuine attempt to negotiate a purchase!

'You misunderstand me Capulet. It's not for sale to *you*!' spat the incensed monster. His eyes bulged at Armand's ability to remain calm in the face of his intense goading.

'Oh. Of course.' Armand glanced at Ilaria. 'Angel I'm very sorry' he said causing her brows to lift in genuine surprise 'but it seems a purchase is now *out* of the question.'

She frowned in confusion at the incredulous remark. Then despite her fear, felt the need to resist the want to smile. I wanted to laugh my guts out of my insides and cry at the same time! Cupid's Balls! How could he remain so calm in the face of such bald derision? Armand stared at the glowering wolf, blue eyes blazed into black.

'But bold condottiere' he said for all to hear 'if you have no stomach to *sell* this estate, perhaps you have the stomach to *wager* it.'

Suddenly I understood. I didn't approve at all yet understood. Like a hunter luring a prize with a tasty trail of bait, Armand had drawn the beast to the front of his hole, to show his face before all. Then he dangled such a juicy morsel of bait at the beast, he felt sure the bragging lout couldn't resist it. Nor, in front of his men, would his ego allow him to back down from that particular style of challenge.

Every eye rested on Onorato. He was gloating evilly. He counted his skill as a warrior to be limitless. But he counted the fortune he amassed to be limitless too. A man of such vast wealth as the primo don of Montecchi felt sure of one thing. No matter what amount Onorato may risk in a wager, unless his rival was a prince of the blood with limitless riches to lose, even if Onorato lost, at the very worst he was sure he could survive the cost of it.

What he may not survive, was the damage to his dark reputation if he failed to accept a publicly offered wager. At that moment, I was sure the Black Wolf of Verona wanted nothing more than to gut Armand from end to end for the sheer thrill of how it would destroy Ilaria to watch him do it. But the vanity of his reputation was calling to him.

'A wager?' he growled 'What *stakes* do you propose?'

'Upon *your* side ...' Armand replied 'this pretty estate of course. You know it's a trinket Ilaria desires, along with the service of any who wish to stay on and help us to run it.'

Onorato pouted in thought. 'What do *you* stake in return?'

Before he could reply, Ilaria pressed his hand.

'Armand please. Let us –'

'Just a moment angel.' His eyes met her calmly. 'Let's give him a chance to consider the terms.' He looked up to Onorato. 'I have a holding in Carentan. A very *large* holding.'

'No Armand!' she spat. 'I can't allow it!'

Onorato grinned to see them at odds. 'Yes boy. Better heed your little bitch. Let her speak for you.'

Armand's expression remained unaffected.

'Judging by Esmeralda's description of this estate, my holding in France is *double* the size. I carry a copy of the deed in our wagon.'

Ilaria gripped his arm.

'Please Armand. Please let us go and be done.'

'Just one more moment angel.' His eyes lifted again. 'It contains an obligation of martial service to hold it. If you win however, I'd be willing to insure you against that charge.'

'Ha!' he spat derisively. 'I wouldn't give you the satisfaction to suggest you could fight on my behalf.'

'As you wish. But that should *suffice* for the stakes upon my side. Any sober judge would say they're more than fair. Indeed, by the value of my estate, they stand heavily weighted in your favour.'

'Say you so?'

'I do. But that *wouldn't* cause me grief in this case.'

'I'm glad to hear it.'

'And so Montecchi...' Armand scanned the faces of Onorato's henchman 'all that remains to be known ... is whether you simply *brag* about the size of your balls to any lackey who'll listen, or whether you *really* have the balls to risk so much.' His voice rose as he taunted.

Esmeralda, still held in Onorato's crushing embrace, pressed her lips hard. Drawing a long breath through her nostrils, she filled her chest then turned to stare at the vile beast she called her husband. This young stranger had dared to challenge him and had spiced the bait by spitting his words back at him. Somehow to me, she suddenly seemed more youthful.

Silence hung in the balance. I felt fit to burst.

Then for the second time, Onorato not only laughed, he burst out of control, cackling with unbridled relish. Armand was counting on a suspicion, feeling sure his rival was addicted to more than just the roll of a dice. Finally the cackling subsided.

'Weighted to *my* side you say? Well Capulet, you may be satisfied.

But if you recall this estate has great *sentimental* value.'

'You did say so.'

'To balance the ledger I want more security.' His eyes glanced. 'Give me your giant as well?'

'Well Montecchi –' Armand began.

'And ...' interrupted the wolf 'all the goods in your train along with the service of all your followers.'

I may not know soldiering, but I understood gambling. Clearly Onorato hoped to use the size of his reservoir of wealth, to out-stake Armand and force him to back down. He valued the image of forcing a rival to cower or submit more than any wealth that he risked.

Ilaria glanced nervously, scanning our people's faces. We had seen what kind of treatment Maxine could expect at the mercy of the prima dominatrix. Now we had witnessed the wolf's ranting too. Every one of us understood our futures might be lost in a single moment, and to what manner of new master and mistress we may be lost to.

Ilaria clutched Armand's arm, green eyes lit with foreboding.

'Armand you *can't* do this. We *must* not do this thing.'

'Angel I know it's frightening.' He whispered. 'But please stay calm. This is now a matter of honour for me. And no matter the outcome, remember we'll still have each other.'

'Armand, what are you saying?'

'I'm simply saying the estate, the baggage are just possessions. I'll never fear the loss of such things while we remain together.'

'Yes of course. I agree but –'

'Don't fear for Maxine. I won't let him take her. But as for our men? Well ... they must work for someone. And perhaps it's better for them to serve the winner than the loser.'

'Armand you can't mean that. Tell me you don't.'

'Don't fret my love, please don't fret. Heaven is watching us.'

Before he could hear another objection Armand stepped apart and shouted for all to hear.

'Montecchi I will wager the stake you ask. Including those in my service with the exception of my mount and Ilaria's woman. He's a tool of my trade, she's contracted to Ilaria personally, *not* to myself.'

Onorato pouted and scanned, resting his eyes on Maxine.

'That's a pity. She's tasty too. I was looking forward to the quality of *her* service'

'You shut your filthy mouth!' I screamed. 'You fucking swine!'

The hot words had leapt from my lips before I knew what came over me. My mace was out in my hand, waving without restraint to threaten the vile beast.

'Oh, ho!' he taunted. 'Even the fucking minstrel has more spine than the master! I like your pluck skinny man. But when you're mine you'll be whipped to an inch of your life for that little outburst!'

'Enough *words* Onorato,' snapped Armand. 'Your men are watching their *great* man of *action*. Yes or no, will you take this gambit?'

'I may.'

'As you know, time is now of the essence for us. And now it's clear to all, that mine is the larger stake to risk, despite your attempt to keep yourself safe by outbidding me. One would think primo Don, that using your wealth to force an honest challenger to back down without a fight, would cut a poor image.'

The wolfish eyes narrowed. 'Be careful what you say Capulet.'

'The time for caution is past Montecchi. If you really have the stomach to risk a *fair* wager, now that mine's the larger stake, you must also agree I have the right to claim the role of *bank* and set the *terms* for our contest. Or does fear prompt you now to deny that too?'

My pulse was racing and Armand's words were racing too, as if he relished the challenge more intensely than Onorato himself.

'*Terms!*' spat the Wolf. 'Which would be?'

'Simplicity itself.' he said reassuringly. 'Six cast of your die to test their veracity.'

'You fear them to be *weighted?*' He pouted mockingly.

'I'll take no offence if they prove *unbalanced*. Nor will you.'

Onorato smiled. With each passing moment now his mood seemed to be lightening.

'In such a case...' Armand ran on 'we'll simply use some method other than dice to ensure we gain a *fair* result. Agreed?'

As I look back now I realise that was a critical moment.

Ilaria, daughter of merchants, once explained to me that if a buyer hopes to purchase something a seller is loath to part with, a clever negotiator creates the mood to sell, by drawing the seller into a flurry of small agreements. This, I now realise, was the first of them.

'Hmm.' Onorato hesitated.

He appeared so unsure I began to feel certain he wouldn't rise to more bait. Then the touch of Esmeralda's hand distracted him, drawing him to see the look of confidence on her smiling face. He couldn't resist that extra goad from her.

'Agreed!' Onorato cried with a laugh.

He launched another smothering kiss on Esmeralda. I couldn't tell if she urged him in the hope he would win or lose. If they lost the villa, her wish to live in the citadel again would occur sooner than expected. I guessed that she also held onto another hope. If the handsome young man she had flirted with won the wager, he would be more inclined to return to Verona each summer.

What's more I felt certain that for Esmeralda, any man who was so unintimidated by her vicious husband was a very rare find. With a husband like Onorato, if she did hope to take a new lover, only a man like that could spark any real interest in her.

Perhaps none of that mattered to her of course. It's possible, for the sake of pure vanity, Esmeralda wanted to be seen to support her husband's reputation and hoped he would win. At that moment however, I sensed it was more likely she wanted to be present, when the beast who treated her so coarsely in front of whoever he pleased, was finally beaten by a better man.

Armand continued. 'We shall have *six* throws to test the die. If satisfied, thereafter we'll risk the entire stake in just *three* throws.'

'Why three, not one?' grumbled the wolf.

'An odd number ensures no challenge can made on the result and... shall make for greater sport. Agreed?'

Onorato hesistated again.

'Bravo!' cried Esmeralda kissing his cheek impulsively.

'Agreed.' cried the now grinning wolf.

'Past Ten is child's play of course. The set has *three* die, each numbered to *six*. All are thrown together. All that concerns us is if the final tally sits *above* ten or *below*.'

'Of course.' Onorato agreed.

'Below ten wins for the *bank*, myself. Above ten wins for the *gambler*, yourself. Ten is a *passe* and must be thrown again.'

'You know the game.'

'Now, because the highest tally possible in a single cast is *eighteen*, the odds for each cast favour the bank ever so slightly.'

'They do!' cried Onorato.

'In this case however, I'm risking the larger stake and claim the right to play as the Bank. And so Montecchi... if we stand in agreement thus far, we need only agree on one final thing.'

'Thus far? We're agreed.' He grinned. 'What's the last?'

'Most importantly ...' Armand lifted his voice as he began to turn. 'all standing here as witnesses under Heaven must understand that once our match is *done* – in two throws or three, whichever it takes – the winner will take all with no hinderance or debate from the loser.'

'Yes!' snapped Onorato greedily.

'And perhaps most importantly, with *no* recourse to offer *either* side a chance to throw *again!*'

'I like it!' Onorato howled. 'Yes we're agreed!'

Though the beast continued to grin, I saw hesitant looks rise on the faces of his men to hear Armand invoke the watch of Heaven against their responsibility to act as true witnesses.

'Done!' cried Armand.

To my surprise, in spite of Armand venturing such a grave risk, and despite my own knees knocking in fear, his tone suggested a carnival-like thrill of entertainment.

'By God Capulet! You've more stomach than I expected!'

Armand swept into a smiling bow at the double-edged compliment. 'Thank you for saying so Montecchi. Now! As we all know the Bank does not cast the die. However –'

'However *what?*' snapped Onorato suspiciously.

'To heighten the drama prima Don, and our enjoyment, instead of having you cast them *all* –' his hands swept to Ilaria and Esmeralda. '– let's have our lovely wives cast the first and second!'

'Then if a third's needed I can throw the last.' cried Onorato.

'Precisely!' Cried Armand with a broad smile.

In answer and to seal it, eyes ablaze, Onorato leapt down the stairs and offered his grip to his rival.

Armand insisted a scribbler be fetched to note the rules and for Onorato and himself to nominate seconds, other than wives, to witness the document. The grim major-domo did the clerical service. As he began to scribble in haste, Armand drew Ilaria to him. He reminded her where the deed for the Carentan estate was kept and urged her to retrieve it.

I was standing by when he did so. Her hands were shaking as he clasped them. Then lowering to a whisper, insisting he had not time to explain, he asked Ilaria to direct Liberati to unhitch Victoire, draw him quietly to the front of the train, and hold him ready.

I wondered at the purpose, of course. Then he leaned more secretively and requested something more. Ilaria knit her brows in confusion as she listened furtively, yet offered no debate. Suddenly, she latched onto Maxine and rushed away to gather the deed. Yes! I followed, to help if I could and hopefully learn more.

In the rear of the wagon, Ilaria found the deed quickly. Her hands were still shaking. Then in a dire moment, we looked at each other. I held her hands to calm her nerves. Impulsively Maxine stretched out her arms and held us all.

'I don't want that vile beast to see me *shaking.*' Ilaria muttered.

'I don't want him to *whip* me to an inch of my life.' I groaned.

'Imbecile!' cried Maxine. 'I don't want to *lose* you to them!'

By the time we returned, of all the absurdities, Onorato had donned a fanciful coat for the occasion. It's garish colouring of lime silk damask was edged with hefty gold brocade that seemed to mimic his own volatility. He had also demanded refreshments to toast the contest. Agitated servers were scurrying helter-skelter, terrified of displeasing him to even the tiniest degree.

I stole a glance at Esmeralda. Despite her statuesque form and effort to be stoic, her demeanour betrayed hints of concern. I felt sure it was more for the safety of her guests than the outcome of the game.

And though she hung at Onorato's side, appearing to be his obedient support, we now understood how much she lived at the brutal tyrant's mercy. Then to my surprise, while the beast was distracted with the scribbling, Esmeralda caught Ilaria's eye and approached us.

'Ilaria please know, I'm truly sorry it's come to this. When he's in this frame of mind he's quite uncontrollable. Dear no matter *what* happens, you must be *strong*.'

'Yes Esmeralda. Thank you, I'll try.'

As their eyes met, all pretence was swept away and the prima Donna spoke darkly. 'And Ilaria. If the worst unfolds ...'

Esmeralda's eyes had lowered. Ilaria glanced downward as something wrapped in soft hide was slipped into her hand.

'*Careful!*' came the hot whisper. 'It's *razor* sharp.'

Beneath the folds lay a finely crafted and deadly stiletto, the first I'd ever seen. Its pommel and grip were fashioned to appear like the ornate handle of a large hair pin. Etched in bold capitals along the cross-guard was one word – MONTECCHI.

Etched along its blade was their fearful motto:

Morte ai nostril nemici – Death to our enemies.

'That point will pierce the hide of a *bear*. The cross-guard's short to fit in a tight sleeve. Most prefer the back of their coiffure –'

'Esmeralda I ...'

'Pray Heaven you don't need it.' she hissed through her teeth.

Esmeralda smiled and nodded, giving the impression they were engaged in less grim chatter. Ilaria's mind raced like a deer attempting to escape a howling pack of wolves.

'Ilaria look at me. If you *do* need it then *don't* hesitate.'

'But surely he wouldn't ...'

'You're in Italy now prima donna. Do you *understand?*'

'I think I do.'

'Grip it *firmly*. Plunge it as *fast* and as *hard* as you can, as many *times* as you can.'

Esmeralda patted her hand, nodding as if they were still sharing trivial banter, then embraced her gently. She turned on her heel, taking her time to sashay back and share a cup with her ranting husband. Watching her go, I couldn't believe what had just transpired.

Cupid's Balls! How had an impromptu visitation come to this?

Onorato drained his share, then smothered Esmeralda with a gasping kiss. It seemed the thrill of great risk was his aphrodisiac. Had the dire exchange between Esmeralda and Ilaria occurred on any other day, in the presence of anyone else, I believe Ilaria would have considered the gesture a girlish prank. Yet on that day, in the presence of the Black Wolf of Verona, it was nothing of the kind.

While Onorato remained distracted with his wife, Ilaria glanced about furtively. Then keeping her eyes on them, she faced her palms to her to conceal the dagger, drew her hands above her head and pretended to adjust her headpiece. Cautiously, she lowered the point and felt the lithe weapon slide firmly into place.

Try as she might to calm her thoughts, Ilaria's breath was heaving out of control. She asked Maxine to fetch a scarf to conceal her anxiety. A few moments later, the gauze veil draw around her shoulders like a wrap of soft armour. It helped her regain some poise. So did the knowledge that now, thanks to her rival, she was armed against an unthinkable threat. Faced with such a volatile predicament, Ilaria felt as ready as she could be.

A round marble table was hefted over from under the ancient sycamore and placed in the open space between the base of the entry stair and the curve of the turning circuit where our train stood waiting. The dented pewter pot, lid and three die were placed upon it. By now Caspar, Liberati, Boccolo and a quaking Fabrizio watched on with a grim understanding that their own futures hung in the balance.

All stood with bated breath, awaiting an outcome that may drastically change the path of their lives. For once in my life I could say nothing. My mouth was shut, my throat was dry. My eyes glanced about, flitting like a dragonfly. Only Caspar was remarkable for his expression of indifference that seemed to mimic Armand's. It made me wonder at it.

All at once, I recalled that only he, Fabrizio and I had ever seen Armand's deportment in any kind of situation similar to this. Despite that fact, Fabrizio looked beside himself with fear. But to see our giant stand so resolutely, made me remember that fateful day in Carentan. I looked at Armand. He was standing calmly, just as he had back then.

Incredibly as he waited he took the time to bask in the warmth of the afternoon sun! Montecchi stalked toward him to make himself the centre of our attention. He drew a vial of wine from a server's tray and presented it personally to his rival.

'Here's to your success Capulet.' his tone was philosophical. He drained his cup without a breath. 'And before it's too late let me just say, *Guelph* or not, I'm beginning to like you.'

Armand smiled, raised and drank. Yet I noticed the compliment wasn't reciprocated. The grim major-domo quietly drew the exquisite glass vials away.

'Your attention!' announced Armand. 'Our wager is set and so it's time to begin! Now you will all be witnesses to our match. No matter the outcome, it will be final, for we stand in full agreement on the terms. Yes?' His hand swept toward Onorato.

'We do.' he said soberly.

'Moreover ...' Armand drew a parchment from the table. 'our terms have been notarised in duplicate by Don Montecchi's clerk.' Armand held his parchment aloft. 'As you can see here, I hold my own copy. Maxine. To *me*!'

Not expecting to be summoned, my sweetheart was standing by Ilaria's side. She blinked in confusion then scurried forward. Drawing away from the Wolf, Armand met her between the table and the edge of our gathering. As they came together he stared resolutely.

'Cat listen closely.' he began calmly.

'Yes Master.' She frowned in confusion.

'Remember the day you asked to drive the wagon?'

'I do.'

'Remember what I said about Ilaria's safety?'

Her eyes leapt wide. 'Oh mercy.'

'That moment's upon us. For her safety do exactly as I say.'

'Yes.'

'You must not *hesitate* or *deviate*.'

'No Master I won't.' she whispered and gulped.

'Take my copy.' He handed it to her cupping her hands. 'I *know* you can ride Cat.'

'Yes I can.'

'And if need requires, ride much *less* like a lady and *more* like a bat out of hell.'

'Yes, yes, yes.'

Her mouth was dry, but her bright eyes blazed with intent.

'Liberati's holding Victoire.'

'Dear Heaven!'

'Stay calm brave girl. Let's show them what you can do.'

'I will.'

'As soon as I turn, walk calmly to Ilaria. After you reach her side, wait a few moments then slip quietly *behind* her.'

'Yes.'

'Hold 'til I *distract* them all. Then walk calmly to the far side of our train and up to the fore.'

'I understand.'

'Stop for none, not even Ilaria or any threat you may hear.'

'Yes, yes.'

'When you reach Victoire mount calmly and quickly. On my saddle is a pouch with a sling. Put the *deed* in it. Put it on.'

'Yes Master.'

'Then wheel and heel and ride *straight* down that *fucking* hill as fast as you can.'

'Oh mercy yes!'

'No matter what happens brave girl, don't halt or look back.'

'I won't.'

A throaty bellow rose behind them. ' Enough canoodling with

your wench Capulet! Let's begin!'

'My apologies!' he cried. 'Just one moment longer and we *certainly* shall.'

'Vile! Lecherous –'

'Forget him Max. The gate below will be shut.'

'Yes.'

'But Victoire knows what to do when he's run at a gate.'

'I see.'

'He won't stop for a threatening guard. You'll have surprise. All I need you to do is *keep your seat* as he leaps that gate.'

'And then?'

'Wheel hard left.'

'Left.'

'And ride like the Devil onto Hazelwood.'

'Never fear. I can do it.'

'You must.'

'Yes Master.'

'No Cat. You're a warrior now. You say "*yes Chevalier.*" '

Her eyes filled with fire. 'Yes Chevalier. Yes I will. But ... surely they'll give chase!'

'With that head start and a light load, not even Pegasus could catch Victoire. In the pouch is a bell. When you're running free and clear ring it loud. Give the deed to Aurelie. Explain our predicament.'

'I have it all.' she said resolutely.

'Then all's well. Have no fear Cat. Heaven's watching you.'

'Yes Chevalier.'

Armand smiled, turned and drew toward the table, raising his hands to draw attention. 'Please listen closely! I'll briefly note the rules once more and we'll begin! In this match, I'm appointed as the Bank!'

He stretched out his words as he spoke. Though I glanced at Maxine as she left Armand's side, I confess even my attention was drawn back to him completely.

'Therefore I'll act as compere and will *not* cast the die myself.'

The sound of a horse braying and hoofs wheeling, broke our concentration! Every eye turned. I stared in confusion at the sight of my sweetheart aboard the giant stallion. Suddenly he leapt and launched into a gallop to disappear in an instant beyond the crest.

'Capulet!' spat the Wolf 'What's the meaning of *that*!'

'All's well and remains correct!' Armand cried. 'My mount and my wife's servant are *not* included in our stake for this match. That was clearly agreed. Yes?'

'It was.' Onorato frowned sourly.

'And so without offering any offence, Maxine's free to leave on my mount to deliver *my* copy of our terms to my sister. That's merely done for safe keeping. And to let Aurelie know, one way or another, that Ilaria and I shall be along soon.'

Onorato's scowl deepened. If Maxine wasn't stopped, he'd have to accept that come what may, he'd have no chance of hiding the truth of our unexpected arrival here. If he intended, as I feared, that Ilaria would not leave regardless of the outcome, then letting that message slip through, would make that foul scheme more dangerous to attempt. Suddenly the sound of another beast stirring drew our attention. A henchmen had mounted and raced away in pursuit.

'What's the meaning of that Montecchi?' Armand called.

'Just a precaution Capulet ... for her safety.'

'How so?' hissed Ilaria.

'If she came off that beast at speed between here and Hazel-wood, without assistance she may not live to deliver anything.'

My blood ran cold at the veiled threat. If his henchman caught up with Maxine, she may not return alive.

'That's very thoughtful.' said Armand masking his concern. 'Now then ... let's continue.'

When I saw Maxine gallop away, I was glad my sweetheart was escaping this fiasco. Now I feared her doing so. I was also not yet convinced that even if Maxine prevailed, the threat of the Cortelannis knowing would stop this venal man from attempting to get his way.

'Now!' cried Armand to draw our attention. 'Madonna Montec-chi and Madame Capulet will throw three times each, to *test* the die.'

He picked them up, parading in a circuit. 'Being satisfied –'

A disturbance sounded at the base of the hill. A shout came to *Halt*. The guardians sounded distressed that a visitor sought to exit without warning. We could see nothing of course, but Maxine recounted it later. Victoire did sail over the barrier, yes. But as he landed, he shunted sharply. With the stirrups still set for Armand, Maxine lacked for firm footing. She swung from the saddle, tumbled across his neck and thumped into the ground.

When the startled guardians lurched towards her, Victoire barred the way as brave Maxine stumbled to her feet. Though dazed and bleeding from the scalp, she scrambled as fast as she could. Then in a wily trick of horseplay, she lifted a foot to the offside stirrup without hauling over, and smacked the flat of her hand to his rump!

The mythical beast burst away as Maxine, hidden from view for a moment, then shunted back into her seat. Charging on she left the dumbstruck guards in her wake as Montecchi's henchman, barely a heartbeat behind, leapt the gate, wheeled and galloped in pursuit!

'Being satisfied the dice are sound!' Armand ran on 'we'll announce the stake is set! At that moment –'

Ka-Clang! Ka-Clang! Ka-Clang!

Armand halted as the sound of a bell rang out, receding along the road. Ilaria and I tried to make sense of it. When we saw the smile it brought to his face however, we guessed at its meaning. Esmeralda's eyes tilted to Heaven as the wolf stared darkly at Ilaria.

I thanked Heaven my sweetheart was safe.
I knew the rest of us were very far from it.

Chapter 16 the Fate of us all

The wolf glared. There was little doubt what the sound of the bell receding along the road meant. Armand swept his hand in an arc as he drew us on with intent.

'At that moment when the stakes are set our match will begin!'

Ilaria glanced at Esmeralda and back again.

'But Armand.' said Ilaria. 'I'm not familiar with this game. If I must participate ...'

'Yes angel of course. In brief, for the sake of this match, Capulet will host as the *Bank*, Montecchi will play as the *Gambler*. Both sides stand to win or lose by the result, usually in one throw. However today, our agreement gives the Gambler three casts if needed.'

'I see.'

'Yet fate may decide the winner in just two throws if the first and second both sit above or below ten.'

'Ah. But remind me once more, which is for which?'

'Below ten wins for the Bank – Capulet. Above ten wins for the Gambler – Montecchi. Ten wins for *neither* however and so –'

'Must be thrown again.' she interjected. 'Now I understand.'

'Quite simple.' He spun with a smile to face Esmeralda. 'And so Donna Montecchi if you please, let's test the dice!'

The prima donna stepped in to receive the set from Armand. She tipped the dice from the pot into her open palm to display them. With the other hand she held the cup upside-down to show it was indeed empty. I could tell that despite her earlier criticism of the game, this wasn't the first time she had participated.

Esmeralda caught Armand's eye and trickled the dice back in slowly, pressing the wooden lid on. She clasped the tumbler with a single hand, fingertips gripped on the edge of the lid. It was simply a test, but anticipation had gripped us all by the throat. Esmeralda closed her eyes for a moment to gather her poise, then opened to look at Onorato standing impassively. She lifted the pot, rattled, tipped and smacked it hard on the table, holding fast against the lid.

Her fingers unlocked to leave it behind as she drew up the pot.

Every eye darted down to know the result.

'Nine!' cried Armand excitedly.

Esmeralda lowered the cup back down then lifted it, lid and all, to offer to her rival. Ilaria's brows lifted. Eyes fixed on Esmeralda, she strode in to accept the offering. The prima donna and premiere dame seemed to agree that, despite the turmoil they were cast into, until a result was known they'd make a defiant show of enjoyment.

Perhaps for Ilaria, the hope that Maxine was now safely away made that easier to do.

She lifted, rattled and threw in her turn.

'Three!' Armand cried with a grin and wink of encouragement.

Before the match I knew little of that game. Yet from my years working in Paris, I understood much about the tricks of gambling thieves. I knew die could be weighted *for* or *against* the chance of a given total. Scoundrels pierced them through the dots to fill with mercury and coax advantage in the way one die may settled as it rolled.

Two casts in a row had fallen *below* ten. If a third such followed, we'd suspect the set may be weighted to favour the Bank. That was most often the case. They could also be weighted *light* or *heavy* to favour shorter or longer periods of play. A more clever thief would have two sets, of course. They'd appear identical but be weighted differently. At some point in the game, by sleight of hand, one set of dice could be switched for the other, generally after much drink was consumed.

I knew Armand's want for the wives to throw the tests and the first two of the match, had a purpose. It offered some insurance against the possibility of a switch occurring before it could have much bearing on the result. What's more, when the Wolf hadn't flinched at Armand's insistence to act as Bank, I assumed he concluded if the die *were* weighted, they must be weighted for a *long* game not a *short* one. That meant that in a short run of throws, any weighting would have less effect.

Esmeralda cast again.

'Eleven!'

The next revealed *fifteen*.

The final test fell to *five*.

The results proved that for a short run of throws, it was possible to tally *above* or *below* ten. Now Armand knew that in a winner-takes-all match of just three attempts, even if the dice were tampered, the odds for this match would be even enough. Yes, that was some relief for me. But I understood one sincere thing about Armand, which I think you know by now. He didn't believe so much in luck as that if his cause was worthy, Heaven would protect him.

For myself at that moment however, despite that great faith of his, I knew if Armand lost I'd become a lackey of the Montecchi! And after hearing that ranting beast promise to whip me to an inch of my life, now I was beside myself with fear.

'Very well friends.' Armand cried 'I am satisfied! Now I declare that our match may begin!'

He sought to control our attention as much as possible, particularly Onorato's. His bold blue eyes met Esmeraldas.

'Now ... the beautiful Donna Montecchi will cast the first.

A boisterous cheer rose from Onorato and his lackeys around us. With a curtsy at the compliment and another to her supporters, Esmeralda took up the instruments again. She seemed relieved to be throwing the first, knowing her result wouldn't decide it all. I felt sure Armand had considered that too.

The Portuguese aristocrat in Esmeralda took hold. She tipped the three dice into her palm and held them with a smile on her upturned hand. Then she lifted the tumbler and in a trickling cascade, spilt them in, one at a time. Her free hand retrieved the lid. Then as if offering a toast, she held the tumbler aloft, tilted it slightly and snapped the lid on. Lowering a hand to hold lid and tumbler as one, Esmeralda revolved in a pirouette to face her grinning husband and blew him a kiss over her free palm.

Suddenly she rattled the tumbler to dramatic effect, spun into a flashing pirouette and slammed the upturned cup onto the board!

Cupid's Balls! It was theatrical in the extreme. Perhaps she had decided if the sport became more entertaining, there was a better chance that her grim husband would endure any result.

But this throw was real! And the cup was not yet lifted!

Every one of us inhaled!

Up it rose to reveal the result.

A frantic moment of calculation followed and then ...

'Fourteen!' Armand shouted. 'The first cast is won by the bold House of Montecchi!'

He thrust a decisive finger at Onorato, who howled with elation. Incredibly, despite that throw favouring the wolf, Armand's announcement encouraged celebration. Montecchi raised a triumphant arm, reaching out to haul Esmeralda in by the waist. He crushed her against him, smacking his hands on her ass and kissing her hard for playing her part so perfectly.

Indeed Esmeralda's effort couldn't have drawn a better result. No matter what came now, the dangerous beast could not hold her responsible for a losing result. And remarkably, at least for a moment, as a great portion of her fear seemed to vanish with that risk, her passion for the beast seemed to flare. Wrapping an arm about Onorato's waist she grinned and drank from his cup. Then she launched her mouth onto his in a smothering, smouldering kiss.

For an instant it was clear how vivacious the volatile pair must have once seemed together.

'The lovely Dame Capulet will now cast the second!'

Ilaria took up the instruments. Armand's blue eyes beamed with assurance. Anyone could be forgiven for thinking he played for sport rather than the risk of his fortune. Following the example of her rival, Ilaria smiled, drew off her shawl and threw it to me. The raucous men of Montecchi bellowed their approval to see her revealed again.

As Ilaria clasped the tumbler in both hands, utter quiet descended. She drew it up to her chest. Then to our surprise, she knelt to pray. Esmeralda pressed her lips together. For a moment Ilaria pleaded with all her heart to Heaven, not to win, but for the strength to bear the outcome no matter what it may be. Her eyes snapped open. She stood and turned to face the grinning wolf. All her fear seemed to have vanished as once again, bright green eyes blazed into black. The beast was mesmerised.

In mimic of Esmeralda, Ilaria held the tumbler and lid aloft in one hand. She blew a kiss to Armand over her fingertips, then spun and lifted high to cast her lot. The cup slammed down. She lifted the pewter veil up high to reveal the result.

'Eight!' came the cry. 'The second cast is won by Capulet!'

Ilaria heaved a sigh of relief. Her heart was racing. The heave of her chest betrayed her excitement yet now she didn't care at all. But for the rest, a lurching sense of danger and exhilaration was rattling our minds, crushing us all in its mighty embrace.

'The tally's drawn!' cried Armand thrusting his hands high. 'Montecchi has one! Capulet has one!' He turned a sharp circuit on his heel. 'Now Montecchi will –'

'NOT CAST the deciding throw!' howled the wolf.

Armand lifted his brows expectantly. 'No Montecchi? What then? Halt and call a *draw*? Are you content with a *stalemate*?'

'Tell me Capulet' he declared loudly 'if this were a duel, then by the laws of chivalry I would stand as the *challenged* party. Yes?'

Armand pushed his pout to one side and tilted his eyes to Heaven. 'I confess, that if this were a duel, that *would* be correct.'

I felt ill at ease hearing that lout want to haggle a hazy point. Was he so intoxicated by the thrill he lingered to draw the drama out? Did he hope to gain advantage by delay or use it to mask deception?

'And so as the *challenged* party' Onorato ran on 'I would set the rules rather than you, the time, the place, the style of contest?'

'Yes. In a duel that would be the form of it. But this is *sport*. And we've already agreed to our terms before these witnesses and under Heaven. Are you asking me to *forgive* the terms you swore?'

Their eyes were locked in a volatile embrace of gamesmanship. Ilaria glared at the beast. Even Esmeralda turned to challenge him. Onorato narrowed his eyes, scanning about.

'Not at all Capulet. I'm a cavaliere and a condottiere.'

'Yes you are.'

'That means I'm a man of *honour*. I've given you my word and I declare that it's my *bond*.'

'I'm glad to hear you say so.'

'Are you? he spat with heat. 'Then I say to you all ...' He snatched up his parchment holding it aloft. 'my word of honour once given in a deed is sacrosanct!' His eyes were spilling with ire at any suggestion it could be otherwise. 'However ... before we're done here I do crave a *small* indulgence of Chevalier Capulet.'

Armand smiled and glanced to Ilaria and back again.

'What's your wish Cavaliere Montecchi?'

'A frivolous adjustment.'

Ilaria caught Armand's eye silently suggesting he mustn't agree.

'What manner of adjustment?' Armand asked.

'As I stand challenged in my own house, I simply ask we play the final throw by *my* rules.'

'Which would be?'

'That *you* cast the final turn Chevalier, not me.'

The beast made that request with a blank expression. I confess it sounded benign yet Ilaria appeared very uncertain. Armand considered it for an instant, then smiled and announced his response.

'It's a trifle. And ... it shall make for better sport! I agree.'

Ilaria's teeth bit into her lip. She watched Armand collect the dice. He turned to his rival, squarely lifting his palm to show all three.

'Come Onorato' he cried. 'Let's play the final round!'

'And just one thing more.' The wolf smiled.

Armand's brow arched in question.

'For this final cast ... Montecchi shall play the *Bank*.'

Armand titled his head in thought. 'Hmm.' He narrowed his eyes. 'Interesting.'

'It's a small indulgence. Meaningless really. What say you Chevalier?' He scanned around his men. 'Will you walk?'

I frowned in understanding. With that request the scoundrel

had revealed he knew the dice were weighted for the Bank. Though the risk of a loss for Onorato would still be significant, this change would weigh the odds of the last throw to be a trifle more in his favour.

My mind ran back to his boast in the villa, that in a contest he would leave nothing to chance if he could help it. And even that final phrase he spoke, *will you walk*, was offered to his rival in the common language of the duel, an invitation to *walk onto the field of honour* together and defend their reputations. To Caspar, Liberati, Boccolo and every Montecchi henchman watching, it was not a personal request, it was a public challenge to Armand's courage.

It seemed the Black Wolf felt he had learned something of his rival. He felt sure such a challenge, couched in chivalric terms, publicly or privately, would not be evaded. He was right to think so. As our world hung in silence, every nerve twitched while we awaited the reply.

The premiere Sieur of Capulet faced the primo Signore of Montecchi. Their eyes held each other. Armand lifted his chin and gazed into the sky. Caspar, Fabrizio and I had all seen him do so before when he faced the English alone in the field at Carentan. He scanned for a moment then came back to his rival, blue eyes blazing into black.

'Very well Montecchi.' Armand said quietly. 'Let's walk.'

'Have at you Capulet.' Onorato growled with a grin.

His hand extended to seal their agreement. Armand took it.

'We stand tied!' Armand cried. 'Yet not for long as I will cast the final throw. Montecchi's now the *Bank*. Capulet's the *Gambler*.'

'Agreed!'

'Donna Esmeralda. Dame Ilaria. Will you do us all the honour of counting the final cast together?'

They looked at each other then came to the edge of the table.

Esmeralda reached. Ilaria took her hand.

'Ladies please remember that I'm no longer the Bank. A tally *below* ten wins for Montecchi. A tally *above* ten is a win for Capulet.'

'Yes.' said Ilaria.

'We understand.' said Esmeralda.

'Donna Montecchi. If I roll ten precisely it will fall to you to instruct me to cast again, until we have a result.'

'Very well.' whispered Esmeralda.

Armand reached for the tumbler. He gathered the dice and spilled them in, each falling in a teasing cascade. He placed the lid on and rattled the cage. Then without pause or looking down at all he turned the tumbler, snapped it down and drew it away. The hint of a smile never left his lips as the wolf's black eyes leapt with expectation.

'Ten! Ten!' shouted Ilaria and Esmeralda.

A gasp erupted from our assembly. Despite any hope to remain calm as judges, Ilaria and Esmeralda hugged in excitement. I screamed like a child and wet my hose to boot! Bite my bare ass, yes I did! None but Fabrizio noticed. He shot me a withering glance of disbelief.

The Wolf licked his broad lips expectantly, then bellowed his anger at the lack of result. Armand stood impassively, waiting for the next attempt. A hush descended as he regathered up the dice. He dropped them into the cup again with no hint of emotion.

Rattle! Turn! SNAP! went the tumbler.

Again he refused to flinch as Onorato's eyes shot to the board.

'Ten! Ten!' cried the judges!

A louder gasp erupted.

Nods and chattering and fidgeting rippled about. I couldn't wet myself a second time, but the result of that throw shook Ilaria. Her hand pressed her heart. Her head became light, knees threatening to buckle. Esmeralda gripped her forearm.

'Throw again Chevalier.' Esmeralda directed.

Onorato's brows pinched in anticipation. Still Armand showed no reaction. Again he gathered the die and his ritual repeated.

Rattle! Turn! SNAP! went the tumbler!

'Ten! Ten!' was the incredible shout.

Now *both* judges held hands on their hearts, embracing like giddy young girls. I screamed in a tantrum of frustration. Surely this result was unprecedented! I guessed from the look on the beast he had never endured such a knife-edged result against a stake of such fearful proportions. His eyes were bulging. His mind was boiling.

I now felt certain Onorato cared nothing for the stake. He desperately wanted to best this French fop. In front of his own men, a Cavaliere must not be beaten by a Chevalier! Montecchi must not be beaten by Capulet!

The screaming Eagle must not bend to the quiet Lily!

Suddenly his piping hot frustration boiled over. 'God's Blood!' he screamed. 'Give me that *fucking* thing! I'll roll the last!'

Esmeralda snapped her hands to her side, rolling her eyes in frustration. It was not the first time she'd watched his temper spill in a public display. But as the frothing Onorato reached for the tumbler, Armand's hand shot out to block his paw.

'I'm more than happy to agree Montecchi. However ...'

'What? What? WHAT?' he blasted.

'Shall you remain the Bank? Or are you now –'

'Yes! YES! I'm the bank! I'm still the *fucking bank!*'

'Onorato!' snapped Esmeralda. 'Calm yourself!'

'Shut your mouth woman!' he spat with blood in his eyes. 'I'll not be commanded in my own home! I will finish this!'

'And I'll *allow* it!' cried Armand. 'Montecchi will now throw the last and continue as the Bank. Judges pay close attention! *Under* ten for Montecchi. *Over* Ten for Capulet!'

'Shut UP!' he bellowed. 'Give me that *fucking* tumbler!'

Onorato snatched the pewter trinket. He plucked up each die and snapped the lid shut then rattled with all his might, bellowing the war cry of a desperate gambler.

'UNDER ten you FUCKERS!'

His massive paw smashed the cup so hard it dented with a crumpling crunch! A broad grin lit his face with expectation. He lifted the cover. But for all his bluster he couldn't bring himself to look!

He lurched back, waiting to hear the result as a frantic moment of calculation followed! I feared I *would* wet myself again! Esmeralda and Ilaria glanced feverishly over the dice. They conferred in a whisper. Armand's expression remained unaltered. Esmeralda's eyes lifted. Her voice rang out.

'The outcome is decided!' she cried. 'Twelve!' She reached for a hand and lifted it. 'The victor is Chevalier Capulet!' Esmeralda turned and embraced him warmly. 'Congratulations Armand.' She turned to Ilaria. 'Oh congratulations Ilaria.' she said embracing her. 'The estate is now yours. I hope you both enjoy it for many years to come.' She turned to her husband who was staring and blinking. 'Onorato. I know you want to congratulate the Capulets?'

While all in our ensemble were slapping each other's backs with smiles, I stole into the wagon and fumbled to replace my hose. I peeped for a moment and saw the staring beast could still not believe it. By all the saints who pray and look down on us from Heaven, not only had he lost a staggering wager in front of his men and these tourists, he had also lost all control.

I reappeared and made toward them. Onorato seemed to be mellowing. After all, he had given his word. And as he had bluntly announced, that was his bond. Moreover our clever chevalier had ensured that our strumpet of a maid, my sweetheart, rode free in time to carry the evidence of the agreement beyond the wolf's reach. The veteran warlord had been handed a rare lesson. Yes, we all sighed with relief and smiled.

As we did so, though we didn't yet understand it, the Black Wolf of Verona was vowing to himself that he would put this embarrassing loss to rights, and do it quickly. At that moment however he had little choice but to present himself graciously in defeat. Indeed, it surprised me to see how well he managed it. Onorato straightened, smiled philosophically and extended his hand.

'Well played, Capulet. I confess I underestimated you.'

Though I desperately wanted to scream my lingering disgust at the beast, not wishing to push my luck, I hung at a safe distance.

'Fortune favoured me today.' said Armand.

'It favours the bold. By the Devil you're that if nothing else.'

Onorato seemed to be more calmly pleasant than we had known him so far. It made me wonder if such a man was more dangerous when he appeared to be more at ease.

'Either way' he added 'today you've managed to profit at my cost. Congratulations. Very few can boast of it. Very, very few.'

'I appreciate your grace in defeat. To yourself and Esmeralda I offer my condolence on your loss. And despite the events that led us to it, please understand, I harbour no ill feelings. And ... I have no wish to *hasten* your departure from here.'

Esmeralda glanced at Onorato. It was clear after the treatment they had received she hadn't expected such generosity from either Capulet. I think she hoped it might affect her husband for the better.

'This has been your home for many years and that of your *famille* for many more. Remain for the summer if you wish. Reap a final harvest. Keep the result to offset this loss.'

Esmeralda stared in wonder but Onorato narrowed his eyes. Perversely somehow, Armand's show of generosity appeared to be rankling the beast as much as his loss to him.

'Armand. Ilaria' said Esmeralda. 'That's very generous yet –'

'Esmeralda not at all.' Armand interrupted. 'Before we return to Lyon I'll ask the Cortelannis to take possession on our behalf until we return ...' He glanced at Ilaria. 'perhaps next summer?'

Ilaria stared coldly at Onorato. 'Perhaps my heart.' she said blankly. 'Yet nothing's ever certain 'til it's done.'

'No.' muttered Onorato. 'Fate's a fickle mistress. I confess it'll be hard for our *famiglia* to see this estate pass to a Guelph.'

Armand knitted his brows to hear him say so.

'In truth Onorato, before today we'd never considered the division between those factions to amount to more than *forgotten history*.' Ilaria squeezed his hand. 'I'm sorry you feel so deeply on that score. Perhaps from today, we can leave such differences behind us.'

I smiled as I listened. Before our tour started, Ilaria had told me she hoped in time to teach her warrior husband to play the perfect host and the diplomat. She guessed he would warm to it eventually. Now he was surprising her how ably he could play both roles already.

'Yes I agree.' Ilaria said stiffly. 'Don't you Esmeralda?'

Esmeralda pressed her lips in a polite smile but withheld further comment. I guessed she feared Onorato's opinion on such issues were too emphatic to challenge. If the beast agreed to any of that wisdom, he didn't say so. And until he did, I felt sure his prima donna would continue to hold her tongue.

'And now' said Armand 'I know Ilaria is anxious to depart.'

'Respectfully' said Onorato 'I would advise it.'

'Of course. Yet if I may Onorato, before we go I feel obliged to say one last thing.'

'That's your risk to take.'

'I want you to understand, we came here with nothing but peaceful intentions. Certainly with no intention to give offense.'

'I'll accept that.'

'Thank you. For myself however, as a chevalier, as I'm sure it is for you Onorato, this outcome is now a matter of honour.'

'Yes. I agree that it is.'

'And so unfortunately, decorum demands the wagered loss you suffered here today, cannot be forgiven.'

'I agree. Don't *risk* a thing if you can't afford to *lose* a thing.'

Onorato's tone was conciliatory but becoming more strained.

'Precisely.' said Armand. 'Perhaps in time somehow –'

'Armand.' Esmeralda cut in. 'You're *too* magnanimous. Please take your leave of us now and go in peace.'

Clearly she felt it was better to say no more. The prima donna knew her husband's limits. Though he still remained civil, instinct urged her to send us on our way. Armand smiled politely and nodded.

'Caspar!' he called.

Our impassive giant lumbered in. He halted and bowed.

'Chevalier.' said the deep rumbling voice.

Montecchi considered him quietly. I felt sure he'd like nothing better than to test his skill against our monolithic warrior. Caspar looked young of course. I could tell the wolf was sizing him up. But he had already underestimated one rival today.

'We depart at once. Fabrizio will drive for Maxine –'

'I can drive for Maxine.' Ilaria said confidently.

The Montecchis widened their eyes in surprise. Esmeralda and

Ilaria exchanged a glance of respect. Armand squeezed Ilaria's hand.

'Yes angel you certainly can. Very well. Unhitch Dilettante for me. Boccolo will lead. You and I shall follow with Liberati. Allez.'

'Yes Chevalier.'

The giant stalked away and began to bark orders.

'He respects you.' said the Wolf. 'I can see it in his eyes.'

'The feeling's mutual. And now good people. Fare you well.'

No, Ilaria wasn't unhappy to take her leave. Yet despite it all, she felt she'd made a friend in Esmeralda. And so she reached for her hand to draw the prima Donna aside to offer an intimate farewell.

'I have a token of yours to return.' Ilaria reached for her hair.

'Keep it Ilaria. Unless I'm mistaken, you'll attract more reasons to have something like it to hand.'

'Mercy I hope not. And I hope you understand Esmeralda, for my part I did nothing consciously...'

'It's not your fault. But mark me pretty prima donna. *Having* that weapon to use and knowing *how* to use it are not the same thing.'

'Yes.'

'A woman like yourself must learn to use it. Then when the time comes ...?' The look in her eyes spoke for the rest. 'You remind me of myself as a newlywed.'

'I'll take it as a compliment.'

'You have a brave husband. Few would risk against Onorato as he did. But Armand can't be with you every hour of every day. Even with a husband as feared as mine, I haven't been safe in his absence.'

Ilaria's brows lifted.

'Oh. I wouldn't have thought so.'

'But it's true. Be vigilant Ilaria. The life ahead of you isn't as safe as the life you've left behind.' She glanced at Onorato who was watching them with interest. 'Go now and quickly.'

When our company rode through the gate at the base of Sycamore Hill, the sun was hanging low. The guardians seem perplexed as we passed. News had reached them of the match and its result. Perhaps both now feared they may be wanting for employment.

It had been a day of unrivalled events.
Yet the day was not done.

Chapter 17 Vale of the Hazelwood

Armand still thought of her as little Aurelie. Yet his far-flung sister was now a mother of three and respected prima donna of the esteemed House of Cortellani. We heard that among Verona's elite she was also considered an *exotic* beauty. You may recall that just one month before Ilaria was born, the Capulets waited to know if the Marchand's would have a boy or a girl. A girl would be promised to Armand. A boy would be promised to Aurelie. Ilaria's birth meant Aurelie was then free to be promised to another.

And so, she was betrothed to Sabatino, primo son of Alfonse Cortellani, a close war companion of their father. Before *any* of them were born, that Italian cavaliere had been a twenty-one-year-old seeker of fortune when he met Armand's father Olivier. Alfonse had ventured into southern France seeking military service. He arrived in Lyon just after Jeanne D'Arc convinced the French Prince Charles and Princess Marie to summon a host and break the siege at Orléans.

It was the first engagement Chevalier Capulet and Cavaliere Cortellani served in together. Soon the newly raised force ventured northwest to join the French host. For a short time before, they were told to *wait*. As you can imagine, when young martial men are told to wait for even a short time, they grow impatient. And so while waiting for the levy of forces to conclude, sporting matches were arranged for those hot-blooded young men who struggled to cool their heels.

That was how Alphonse and Olivier met: as rivals in competition. Fate saw them pitted against each other in all manner of contests. Each managed to best the other until both agreed, a little begrudgingly, to declare a draw. At the close of competition they also agreed to drink and eat together. One day later the Duke de Bourbon issued departure orders. And so on the eve of their going, the fiery duet drank themselves into a riotous stupor ... for a start.

Then laughing and lurching, they entered a dubious quarter of Lyon and scandalously celebrated by sampling the distractions at an infamous carnal house. Yes, yes I know. One was already betrothed! And yes it sounds more like a chapter from my own nefarious past. Had they met in the poor outskirts of Paris? No, they still wouldn't have met me for I wasn't yet born.

However, after that adventurous and somewhat sullied start, the warlike pair became inseparable in the company of a third. Yes, a newly minted Chevalier named Michele de Toulon! God help our own forces for the sake of keeping that trio in good order. They served shoulder to shoulder at the infamous Siege of Orléans under the command of Olivier's father and uncle, themselves commanded by the Maid herself.

In the bitter fighting that followed, the young Italian's exploits earned him a reward from our Duke, a territorial stake located near Valence. Like Olivier, however, Alfonse was the heir to his faction. That meant familial responsibility of course. And so after hostilities ceased, the loyal friends parted.

Yet before taking their leave, with the approval of Dame Margot, who liked the young Italian greatly, they made a pact to unite their families at a future time. In time as you know it came to pass that the eldest daughter of Capulet wed the eldest son of Cortellani. By the time they wed, Aurelie had met Sabatino but once. In the year before their marriage, on the day after her birthday, he arrived all the way from Verona to court her for two short weeks under strict supervision.

Thirteen years older than Aurelie, Sabatino was none the less a charming, respectful cavaliere with a calm demeanour. And despite the years between them, she was constantly remarked to appear more mature than her years and he was slim with boyish good looks. And so from the start, taken all together, they seemed rather closer in age.

One year later, Aurelie's father-in-law-to-be failed to arrive at the wedding. Sadly, while halted in Bergamo upon the journey from Verona, her father's dearest friend had died. Sabatino arrived thereafter with four brothers in support but no sisters or parents. His anguished mother had returned with her grief-stricken daughters to bury their father.

When Sabatino Angelo Pietro Cortellani stood in the cathedral awaiting his betrothed, Aurelie Lisette Maria de Capulet, he was no longer a primo son but a primo don. And so when Armand's little sister departed Lyon to begin a new life so far away, her four new brothers already hailed her as their new prima donna.

Now, after our remarkable encounter with Aurelie's passionate neighbours, I was about to meet that mythical woman for myself. The sycamores had fallen behind us. Yes, we were greatly relieved to be free from the jaws of *Sycamore Hell*. But we dreaded to hear Montecchi hoofbeats rising behind us. I wouldn't feel safe until we entered the Cortellani estate.

For the sake of departing as hastily as we could, Armand rode bareback between Caspar and Liberati at our rear. Stout Boccolo led us forward. In Maxine's absence, Ilaria drove the carriage wagon, I drove the second and Fabio the last. Oh yes I know, I swore not to call him Fabio. Yet sooner or later ... well you know what I mean.

I scanned the late afternoon sky from my perch as I reflected upon our harrowing ordeal. Already the sun was threatening to press its tired weight on the hinterland. Slowly the puffs and wisps and quietude drew my mind in. In my reverie I heard a bell toll upon a hillside. It was like those we'd heard at Sycamore Hill, a coded alert to warn of an approach.

Armand cantered past to consult with Boccolo. I guessed we had all but reached our destination. Soon I would see their far-flung estate and the guarded gates of a sanctuary would appear. Perhaps a keeper in the image of Saint Peter himself would assess the newcomers? It made me smile to think how reverently he'd bow to Ilaria and let her pass, then take one look at me and tell me to save my time and go straight to Hell!

Oh you know I couldn't help having such thoughts. Somehow it calmed me to think of him scowling and reprimanding me. I hoped that by the sound of the bells, Maxine knew we were arriving. No doubt she'd be sick with concern, wondering if the Capulets would arrive alone or still be in our company. Within a few minutes of the first bell's toll, followed by a relay of three more, we rounded a wide curve and arrived at the ostentatious entry portal.

Oh sweet friends I tell you, by the miraculous grace of God, by every Saint who prays and every sweet Angel that sings in Heaven, what a welcome relief it was to see. And though the avenue beyond the entry was long, unlike the steep climb at Sycamore Hill, this rose very gently. From where we halted at the imposing gate I could already see the majestic household rising at a distance. Such was its splendour, I felt sure any visitor would feel compelled to consider the correctness of their appearance before venturing on. I certainly did so.

Yet the stout guardians passed us through without incident.

The broad avenue was lined with hazel trees of course, that reached up to join over our heads. Though they appeared to be planted for decor, hazels were already bursting from every limb. I guessed in a month, the nuts would begin to fall and could imagine the feast that these and the orchards beyond would offer.

The manicured egress led us on, evoking a sense of being drawn magically through. Yes, it was somewhat like the lure of the sycamores before. But the effect of this path felt more enchanting. And it prompted me to recall Ilaria's instructions before my last entrance upon the mule. Now, even though I drove a team, the way was so easy, the turnings so gentle, that I risked lowering the rein to let them have their head.

Yes, I began to play to announce our coming. But then after just a few moments, we were in a sanctuary and my team followed the wagon ahead so sedately, that I grew bolder. Hefting my lute to my back, I leapt off the board and scurried ahead to climb up with Ilaria!

'Marcel! Who's driving behind us?'

'Tais-toi little bitch and mind the path.'

'Ooh you scoundrel! I allowed that once in your wicked lifetime. Never again.'

'Yes Madame.'

'But I'm glad you're here to play us in.'

'Something festive?'

'After the fiasco we endured, something restive.'

'Your wish is my command.'

Moments later, we hailed the sight of an immense structure looming ahead with a vast array of meticulous gardens.

The cultivated landscape ran out from its walls in every direction with strolling grounds immediately before the imposing entry plaza. The grand edifice was seated on a gentle rise, resplendent in a different way from the ancient austerity of Sycamore Hill. For the sake of ensuring his bride felt more at home when she arrived, Sabatino adapted the front of their villa in the style of a chateau.

He also added a new wing, hoping the result would entwine their cultures in a harmonious blend. At a glance it did so magnificently. Yet despite its lyrical name and glamorous appearance, once glance revealed his powerful *famiglia* had also designed Hazelwood to keep danger out. Like Sycamore Hill, it too was a stronghold. Yet it was good to feel that protection envelope our train as its weary occupants drew to a standstill.

A reception entourage stood in wait on the wide entry concourse. Foremost of all on the grey marble treads, prima donna Cortellani cut an elegant figure upon the arm of her husband. And sweet mercy I tell you, the woman who stood before us was striking. Most striking of all was how much her features were a match with Armand, it was mesmerising. Cupid's Balls! I can't think why I hadn't expected it. The appearance of their entourage was striking too, yet in such a different way from the stark images that greeted us when we met the prima donna of Montecchi.

Aurelie stood resplendent in a flowing gown of gold and grey damask that draped a full body length behind her. Where it drew up from the ground, it gathered in luscious folds under a high waisted band of black silk brocade. Above that the damask lifted to either side, like a many-folded fountain of fabric to form a plunging neck. It framed a low square cut bust we'd found so many Italian women seemed to favour.

The neckline revealed a silken pearl chemise below. From her chest the damask splashed into wide, puffed shoulders that gathered then decadently puffed again. Generous slashes through the outer arms revealed more silk beneath. Summer is the season for silk, and nothing sets its value apart more than the contrast of rich brocade.

To crown it all, the prima donna's head was swathed in a heart shaped escoffion of grey silk damask, draped with sails of pearl gauze to match the colour beneath. These tapered to the waist, entwining her dark brown tresses, which fell beyond her knees. At the end, they were tied in a startling punctuation with decadent cloth of gold. She turned to whisper to her children behind her, revealing a plunging backline that mirrored the front, both meeting at the hips to mimic the falling trail of gauze.

The dramatic effect of it all, ensured the composition drew attention from every possible view. At her neck was a silken band bordered with velvet. It matched the gloss of her lips and was studded above and below with delicately cut pearls. Finally where the sleeves emerged from the final puff, they ran on in a flow of golden silk from elbow to wrist. This too was studded with pearls, but these were shaped to diminish in size as they met the cuff.

If the prima donna of Montecchi was the high priestess of Sycamore Hill, then the prima donna of Cortellani was the enchantress of Hazelwood. And behind the enchantress, peeping over her shoulder, was our heroine Maxine. She appeared more than greatly relieved to see us all. In a moment we'd hear how the prima donna had planned to wear something *less* astonishing. But when Maxine arrived unexpectedly, telling her story of our encounter, she also provided a more detailed description of her brother's new bride.

Maxine touted Ilaria as the heiress to an haute couture empire who now designed her own couture. And so Aurelie suddenly decided to wear something far more exhilarating. Gauging by Ilaria's reaction to our first image of Aurelie, the impact was worth the fuss. For after Armand leapt from the unsaddled gelding to drew around the wagon and assist Ilaria down, she seemed mesmerised.

As she gazed, Ilaria reached out her hand. Then her eyes leapt, and a smile lit her face when Armand gripped her waist instead and lifted her high. Aurelie rolled her eyes as he did so, sharing a smiling glance with the handsome Sabatino. Ilaria was hovering and turning and descending slowly, floating like an angel, as her doting husband spun on his heel with a mischievous smile.

He lowered her to the ground and offered his arm. After the grizzle and frenzy of the Montecchis at Sycamore Hill, it felt as if we had entered a mythological kingdom of grace, poise and blissful peace. I glanced and shared a smile with Maxine, losing myself in the comfort of her welcoming eyes.

Then on the prima donna's face a single, gorgeous, questioning brow began to arch. 'After four years apart we expected to meet my exalted brother and his lovely wife!' Aurelie began in mock reprimand.

'Aurelie let me *explain*.' He lifted a hand to stay her.

She drew forward with her husband stern with displeasure.

'Instead we've met a magnificent stallion we *believe* belongs to him. Or darling ...' She turned to Sabatino. 'was it the King of *France?*'

'Mia cara I believe' Sabatino said drily 'the King of France used to have one just like it.'

Ilaria's smile was widening.

'Aurelie –' Armand protested again.

'We also met a close server whom we *believe* belongs to *her!*' Her eyes met Ilaria who pouted in mock contrition. 'Yet the server in question was covered in dust with a lively *bruise* upon her forehead.'

'Oh no!' Ilaria cried.

'Oh yes, strange woman that I've yet to meet! And I fear she's *broken* a rib besides!'

'Cat did you *fall?*' asked Armand soberly.

'Yes Chevalier!' she cried with a ridiculous grin.

'Did she *fall!*' spat Aurelie. 'Why you tardy lout! She certainly *did* fall! Though she looks far too happy about it!'

'Yes she does.' said Armand with a smile. 'Well done Cat.'

'Well done? What would be well to do is to explain why she was ordered to come *clanging* a bell and *leaping* at my gate –'

'Our gate mia cara.' Sabatino said patiently.

'Yes darling *our* gate, galloping like a wild bandit into the House of Cortellani bearing satchels and erratic tales of –'

'Oh Lee Lee tais-toi and just give me a moment to explain.'

The servers ranged upon the stairs gasped in shock and lifted hands to their mouths.

'You disrespectful brute! No one tells me to shut up in my own house! And if they do we say *stai zitto* not *tais-toi*!'

As Sabatino reached Ilaria's side she leaned in secretively.

'Dear Heaven is this typical?' she whispered.

He repressed a smile. 'Perhaps we'll know in a week or two.'

'Aurelie!' Armand bulged his eyes. 'Introduce your husband to my wife so they can chatter as I hug the life out of my little sister.'

'Oh! Introduce my *husband*? My husband who, until our bell alerted us to your arrival, was preparing to storm our neighbour's estate with a dozen men-at-arms!'

'Sabatino!' Armand pleaded. 'Is she *this* difficult with you?'

'No. Much worse. Since our first child she's become *very* bossy. But I love her.'

'Of course you do.' Aurelie looked incredulous.

Sabatino stepped closer to greet them with a warm smile. 'I welcome you both to *Valle del Nocciolo*. Armand!' his arms extended. 'It's good to see you again.'

The two men embraced heartily.

'Ah you're so tall and strong. You were still a squire when we met so briefly.' He turned to Ilaria. 'This of course is your lovely –'

'Wife Sab, yes.' Aurelie interjected. 'But let me be first darling. Oh Ilaria welcome!' They hugged and kissed and patted and smiled. 'For so many years before I married, we saw each other in flits, but never really met.'

'No.' said Ilaria. 'I'm so sorry.'

'Tush darling, that's not your fault it's mine. By the time I was old enough to wed, I should have taken more notice of the girl we all knew was to be his bride.'

'Oh no, not at all.'

'Yes I should have paid more attention. What was I thinking?'

'Perhaps of your own match.'

'Perhaps. Yet by the time I departed you had only just become a demoiselle in waiting.'

'Yes.'

'But Heavens Ilaria look at you! Now you're a beautiful woman and a premiere dame.'

'Thank you so much. Oh, thank you both. We've come a long way and it's so good to finally be here.'

'You're welcome. Oh, you're welcome.' Aurelie hugged Ilaria tightly again. 'Now darling greet my husband while I deal with ... AHHH!' Aurelie squealed.

True to his threat, no longer able to wait, and with no respect for haute couture Armand swept Aurelie from the ground and crushed her to him. He swirled and enmeshed himself in her train, smothering her cheeks with kisses. Her servers giggled and glanced at the sight of their stern prima donna being treated like a little sister.

'Oh Aurelie!' said Armand, laughing like a boy. 'You're just the same as you ever were!'

She threw a sideward glance at Ilaria.

'No I am not! I'm far more mature. *Far* more glamorous. And *much* less shy of bullies like you.'

'By thunder you are!' He grinned. 'You're all those things.'

'Now big brother ... *Chevalier* Capulet! Put me down gently.'

'No!' he cried.

The servers giggled again, hiding smiles behind hands, leaning and whispering to each other.

'Heavens Ilaria he hasn't changed at all! We'll have to tame him properly together. Now lummox, put me down! I want to introduce your lovely wife to our beautiful children.'

Seeing Armand and Aurelie so close together, the resemblance was even more striking. The large blue eyes, perfect noses, full lips and thick dark hair of both Capulets appeared nearly identical. Aurelie was the second child of seven, yet the only surviving daughter of two.

She was not as tall as Armand's six feet, though taller than Ilaria and nearly as tall as her husband. Perhaps because she grew among five muscular boys, her voice shared the deep tone of her brothers. It made her sound alluring in a very different way to Ilaria's soft, high tones that I was growing so used to.

And seeing both women together with their husbands for the first time, if Ilaria appeared to be the epitome of French grace, then despite her roots Aurelie appeared to be the epitome of Italian glamour. Indeed she exuded it in her manner, speech and movement without the slightest effort – unless she was being swirled in her big brother's arms. For that fleeting moment, the protesting manner of a little French girl had betrayed her completely.

The instantly fond quartet were charming together. For myself, having grown up in the poor outskirts of Paris, it made me wonder what it must have been like to grow in such a family. In that moment I confess, I felt as if all their lives were charmed. Moreover, the charming and grounded Sabatino seemed the perfect foil for Aurelie's vivacious energy.

I judged him to be a little more than thirty years, closer in age to Esmeralda Montecchi. It made me wonder how friendly the Cortelannis were with their neighbours. Sabatino's features bore the hallmarks of his Italian origin. His hair was black, his brows heavy, yet plucked to shape as so many dons we had seen had a penchant to do. His open brown eyes were kind and expressive, with a thoughtful, considerate look to them.

And he wore a pointed beard and moustache that he kept neatly trimmed. He was slender in build like myself, yet more muscular. Perhaps that's the difference between warriors and musicians. To match his wife's elegant couture, Sabatino was also dressed immaculately. Though his choices for contrast and colour were more sedate.

Above he wore a many folded houppelande of brown and amber silk damask with velvet edges. Its deep square neck revealed the ruffling billows and round tied neck of his fine linen shirt. To frame it below, the linen hem fell slightly below the outer garment. At mid-thigh height, a pair of silken hose wrapped his legs, mulberry to one side, cream to the other. Finally, on his feet were a shining pair of short-toed crackows that completed the image of him.

Sabatino turned and brought their children forward one at a time to greet their uncle and aunt. Of their three – Angelique, Vincenzo and Pietro – their daughter was eldest, while the youngest was still held at his wet nurse's teat. All were met fondly and fussed over but soon dismissed. It allowed the couples to engage more intimately in the balmy summer air while hovering domestics held at the ready, engaged in hushed banter.

Unlike our experience with Onorato an hour before, Sabatino treated us all, and I confess, anybody I ever saw him encounter, with civility, sincerity and care. Though it leaps ahead in our story to say so, to me he has always seemed the model of an elite gentleman. And like most Italian Cavalieres, Sabatino had a love of horses, horsemanship and racing in the saddle. A topic he and Armand became engrossed in as Aurelie and Ilaria began to chatter away together.

Our wagons were moved to allow the men to unload what was needed. I lingered near my sweetheart as they did so while Maxine held close to Ilaria. After being scolded and assaulted by Donna Montecchi, I understood her reluctance to stray and her want to watch every moment like a hawk. The couples drifted back together. Once they did so, it didn't take long for the tale of events at Sycamore Hill to unfold in earnest.

I knew better than to attempt to sing or prattle for the moment. Yes, I was already eager to impress these cultured newcomers, but would save my effort for later. I watched Maxine as she hovered near Ilaria but I scowled at the sight of the bruise from her fall. However it was impossible not to be drawn to the conversation of our betters. I cradled my lute as I listened, fingertips drifting over its strings.

Armand and Ilaria, yet mostly Ilaria, recounted the drama of it all. Aurelie and Sabatino became more and more stone-faced as they listened. When they heard the outcome of the dire game that had ended it all, a great silence fell. By their reactions, the Cortelannis were not nearly as surprised as one may have expected. Aurelie stared blankly at Armand.

'Only my big brother could enter the northern hills as *my* expected guest, stop just two miles from my home, then arrive two hours late to announce he's now my neighbour!'

'It was Ilaria's inspiration to call on them. I would have arrived sooner but empty-handed.'

'I don't feel inspired. Despite the outcome I wish we'd never gone up that hill.'

Aurelie frowned and pouted.

'It's more than just an outcome darling.' she said soberly. 'Sycamore Hill's a smaller holding, but also the envy of all in Verona.'

'What an extraordinary turn of events.' said Sabatino. 'You couldn't have known it of course, but Onorato's more than just a formidable man in these parts.'

'It didn't take us long to gather that.' Armand conceded.

'He's not someone whose anger many would choose to ignite.'

'Now we've met him, I'd agree.' Armand glanced at Ilaria. 'Yet he did seem to take the loss with rather good grace.'

'Good grace?' said Aurelie. 'Onorato Montecchi?' She stared in disbelief. 'If he did so it's the first example *we've* heard tell of it.'

The Cortelannis exchanged a knowing glance.

'It's true.' said Sabatino. 'Onorato's not known for losing *anything* with good grace.'

Armand wore a sceptical frown. 'Hmm. I felt, by the end, he seemed quite philosophic.'

'Philosophic?' spat Aurelie. 'The Black Wolf of Verona?'

Ilaria's brows lifted.

'Is that what they call him? Ugh! I'm not surprised.'

'I like Esmay of course.' Aurelie added. 'It's hard not to feel for her tethered to that brute.'

'Yes.' said Ilaria. 'I felt we had a connection too. Though she began to flirt outrageously with –'

'Oh tush darling.' Aurelie interrupted. 'Bored pastoral prima donnas merely flirt for entertainment.'

'I can attest to that.' groaned Sabatino.

'Oh be quiet Sab. I'm not bored. And you're lucky to have me.'

'Yes mia cara. And?'

'And be still. You know I love you. But mercy, with a husband like Onorato? I'd be desperate enough to flirt with *any* man but would only feel safe enough to flirt with a *tree*.'

'Or a *priest*?' said Ilaria.

'Yes clever girl.' Aurelie narrowed her eyes and took her arm. 'Whenever the wolf's away she flirts with our new Friar by the river.'

'Oh she mentioned him.'

Aurelie leaned to Ilaria like a fond friend.

'Darling I know Esmay is a handful. But she was a great support to me when I first arrived. Recently however, for fear of proximity to him, many have begun to avoid her.'

'Most recently *ourselves*.' Sabatino frowned.

'Oh?' said Ilaria. 'She suggested you were all quite close.'

'We have been for years 'til the start of this spring. Oh Sab, you tell them the story. It makes my blood boil.'

My ears pricked, interested to know any gossip about the notorious couple. Particularly how they may have fallen out with such dear friends who lived so closely.

'Schechter is the livestock agent in Verona. We know him well. He was preparing to offer the finest display of horse flesh I've seen outside Venice. He knows my passion for horses and invited me to an early showing of one in particular. An extraordinary Spanish stallion.'

'Sab agreed to bid on it.' said Aurelie. 'So did Onorato.'

Our eyes lit to imagine how the wolf would covet such a thing.

'The bidding began vigorously.' Sabatino ran on. 'But before it could end, Onorato received an urgent summons to attend the Podestà at the Square of the Lords.'

Aurelie gripped Ilaria's arm.

'Oh darling you won't believe what happened next!'

Sabatino held his breath for an instant and pressed his lips. 'Would you like to tell the tale mia cara?'

'No darling you're doing so well.' She rubbed his arm playfully.

'Thank you. Well ... Onorato was in a huff that he had to exit the auction. He left his elderly bean counter to bid in his place.'

'While he was gone' Aurelie interjected 'Sab won the bidding!'

Ilaria narrowed her eyes and glanced at Armand. 'I'm sure the brute we met would have little patience for that?'

'I knew he wouldn't be happy.' Aurelie added.

'In Onorato's absence ...' Sabatino continued 'the bidding rose sharply and his doddering man fell into confusion. Then doubting his limit, failed to counterbid me in time.'

'I see.' said Armand thoughtfully.

'The final price was a small fortune. But I felt it was fair for such an extraordinary beast.'

'It must rankle him to see you ride it.' Ilaria smiled thinly.

'Sab never got the chance to ride it.' Aurelie said darkly. 'After the sale he went along to the holding stall. But just after he left us, Onorato returned expecting to claim it for himself.

'Oh no.' said Ilaria.

'Oh yes darling. When the lout heard he'd lost it of course, he flew into a vicious temper.'

'We've already seen that side of him.' said Armand.

'Most of Verona's elite society has seen that side of him. Oh, he threw a violent tantrum. And after the brute dressed the old man down before us all, he belted him viciously and stormed out like a petulant child! It was insufferable.'

'I can just imagine it.' Ilaria shuddered again. 'Ugh! He made my skin crawl with disgust.'

'What that fuss occurred ...' said Sabatino quietly 'I was in the stable and saw none of it. Yet even at that distance, I heard most of it.'

'Now for the *worst* of it. Tell them darling.'

'Soon thereafter I heard him again. He entered the stable.'

'Onorato confronted you?' asked Armand soberly.

'Before making payment I went in to check the beast again, to ensure it was sound.'

'Of course.' said Ilaria, tense with anticipation.

'When Onorato appeared at the door, he was attended by two followers, both well-armed. He wasted no words of course.'

'I can imagine that.' hissed Ilaria.

'He offered to double my bid to purchase it.'

'I'm sure that was hard to refuse.' said Armand.

Sabatino stared grimly. 'It *was* my friend. I *did* refuse. Despite being alone I denied him politely, tried to make light of it but then –'

'He insisted you reconsider your answer?'

Aurelie's eyes widened in anger.

'The cretin ordered his men to draw!' she spat with venom.

'It's true. It suddenly occurred to me that, when he arrived, I heard him send the ostler away. At the time when he did so –'

'You couldn't have appreciated the *purpose* of it.' said Armand.

'No. Not so subtly, I began to realise that if I refused again ...'

'Yes. Now I've met him Sabatino, I'm sure you wouldn't have left the stable alive.'

'It was a hefty price. He had the gold to hand. And so I *took* it.'

Sabatino held his eyes squarely. Aurelie reached for Armand.

'Sabatino's not a coward.' she said hotly. 'He carries the scars from many campaigns of brave service. The last in a company commanded by that –'

'Of course. I'd never doubt it.' He looked at Sabatino. 'Our father said your father was the bravest man he ever met. I know his premiere son was styled in his image.'

'That's much too kind of you to say.'

'Not at all.'

Aurelie flung her arms impulsively about Armand's neck and kissed him. 'Oh you lout. Ilaria, he's already made me cry.'

'Not before time.' Armand hugged her. 'But sincerely Sabatino, now we've seen Onorato's antics in person, I feel there's no doubt that you did the right thing.'

'Thank you. But you understand the point of our story is –'

Aurelie cut in. 'That was his reaction to the loss of a *horse*.'

'It was.' Sabatino added. 'So if either of you may be hoping...'

Before he could complete his warning, a bell on the hill of their foremost vineyard rang out. Four pairs of eyes turned to see.

An amber glow painted the horizon.

The sun was all but set. Yet someone was approaching.

We all walked forward together.

After that first warning bell two separate chimes sounded.

Upon the avenue in the failing light, a pair of riders, well-mounted by their vague appearance, came on with intent.

Chapter 18 an End to the Day

Two muscular coursers halted against the draw of their reins. Aboard one sat the wolf's brother Aldobrando. Even from the far distance, Sabatino recognised the second son of Montecchi and informed the Capulets while the silent duet came on. Now halted and afoot, a pair of calf-height boots of finest leather wrapped at the heel by elegant silver spurs, jingled and marched towards us.

The warning bells had also drawn Caspar from the stable where he had been assessing the state of our beasts. He stalked out noise-lessly to investigate. From my vantage at the rear and to the side, I saw him closing with interest. He halted to hang back a little, drifting behind a column that framed the forward portion of the entry plaza. I'm sure at such times our warrior giant felt the hair rise on the back of his neck, just as mine began to do. Yet he showed no sign of it to any within eyeshot.

Sabatino led the elite quartet forward.

Aurelie followed to Armand's left, Ilaria to his right. Before any parley could join or begin, Liberati and Boccolo emerged too with Fabrizio following in their wake, all moving just as noiselessly as Caspar. Both veterans had rearmed and stood to either side of Maxine, herself now directed by Ilaria to hold back. Fabrizio held at my side. He was wide-eyed, realising as we all did by then, this visita-tion look unfriendly.

'This is the brother Esmeralda spoke of?' whispered Ilaria.

Aurelie nodded her confirmation as Ilaria considered him. We all recognised his follower from the wolf's pack, the elder guardsman from the gate. We would learn soon enough: he wasn't only Ono-rato's sergeant-at-arms, but his blood cousin too. Now the grim vet-eran stood in support to Aldobrando and carried an *object* of interest.

'You weren't expecting them at this hour?' asked Armand.

'Not at all.' replied Aurelie.

'Esmeralda said his wife just delivered a son.' whispered Ilaria

'Donatella. Yes, I saw him a few days ago. Romeo, sweet child.'

'Romeo *Amicus*.' said Armand glancing at Ilaria.

'Amicus for *friendly*.' she echoed his earlier comment.

'Yes angel.' His eyes rested on the object. 'Though I suspect this visit from his doting father may not be friendly.'

Aldobrando halted. His eyes swept the Capulets for an instant, then held on the Cortelannis.

'Sabatino. Aurelie. My apologies for this unexpected intrusion at such a late hour.'

'Nonsense Brando.' Sabatino said affably. 'You're well met here at any hour.'

The two appeared to be on civil terms. Aurelie smiled pleasantly as she stepped forward and extended her hands, receiving a polite embrace and his kisses.

'Brando. I hope Donatella's well and little Romeo's healthy.'

'She is. He is. Thank you Aurelie.'

'Yes man ...' added Sabatino 'you must be proud. Congratulations on the birth of your son.'

'I do confess, I am very proud. On behalf of Donna and myself, I thank you both kindly.'

'Now my friend, what brings you to us at such a late hour?'

'I hope to be brief.'

'Not at all man, take your time.'

Aldobrando's glance swept the Capulets.

'I've been urgently apprised of events which transpired today at Sycamore Hill.' He glanced again. 'I assume you've been informed of what's occurred. Or at least by now ... you have a *version* of it.'

'We've heard the tale of it.' said Sabatino.

'I'm told those events involve your new guests.'

'Not guests Brando, *famiglia*. My *brother* and *sister*-in-law.'

'I see.' He knit his brows. It seemed the fullness of that detail took this particular Montecchi by surprise.

'Allow me to present them to you darling.' said Aurelie.

'Of course.' Aldobrando pressed a polite smile.

'Cavaliere Aldobrando da Montecchi, this is Chevalier Armand de Capulet and his wife Madame Ilaria de Capulet.'

Aldobrando bowed, kissing Ilaria's offered hand as she smiled thinly and curtsied with restraint.

'Armand and Ilaria are the premiere sieur and dame of the *martial* House of Capulet in Lyon.'

I had never heard anyone describe Capulet as a martial house, yet it wasn't untrue. I felt sure that description served a purpose.

'Are they?' Brando's eyes narrowed betraying further surprise.

'Yes they are darling. And they've come all this way on their marriage tour to visit us.'

'Newlywed? I see. Then my congratulations to you both.'

My own heartbeat was rising. I knew little of mighty *familles* or *famiglia* but was learning quickly. It seemed Aurelie hoped her offering would temper Brando's approach to the matter.

Sabatino glanced at Armand.

'Brando and I served together last season in our never ending spat with Milan. Under his brother's command no less.'

'I see.' said Armand.

'Armand's recently returned from the war in Normandy against the English. He fought at that battle in Formigny that we've been hearing so much about.'

Brando held for a moment. Every new factum appeared to surprise him. He mentioned a *version* of events. I felt he was beginning to question the version he had heard. After spending a moment in thought he turned his attention to Armand and Ilaria.

'Chevalier. Madame. Truly I wish we were meeting under happier circumstances.'

'That's gracious of you to say Cavaliere.'

'Thank you. Alas however ...' He glanced at Ilaria. 'I've not come as the bearer of glad tidings.'

Ilaria's expression grew dark. Aldobrando stepped in to face Armand. Behind his shoulder, his man ushered in support. But their movement drew Caspar from the shadows and by all that's Holy, the image of our giant advancing gave that duet significant cause to hold.

Suddenly they were confronted by the sight of Caspar behind

Armand's shoulder, towering like a foreboding spectre. Brando and his grizzled sergeant couldn't help but stare.

Cupid's Balls! I wanted to kiss the giant ninny!

'By your reaction Don Montecchi I presume my reliable squire is now at my back? The sight of myself alone would not normally instil so much caution.' Armand turned his head. 'Yes, there he is. We met on the field in Normandy.'

'Indeed. We've heard tell of your fight against the English.'

'Caspar fought bravely in Carentan.' Armand said quietly.

'I imagine he did.' said Brando.

'Upon the *other* side.'

Aldobrando's eyes opened wide. His follower frowned in confusion. It was the first time I'd heard Armand willingly reveal that information. Yet by the result I understood why.

'He fought ...?' Brando sputtered. 'Well that means that *you* ...'

All at once it seemed every notion the second son brought with him through the Hazelwood gates must be questioned. If the man before him had defeated the monster towering behind him? What mischief from Pandora's box was he about to release for the sake of his rash brother's misadventure and familial pride?

'I implore you to pay him no mind.' Armand continued. 'If memory serves, you were about to offer me *less* than glad tidings.'

Ilaria came to his side, reaching a hand to lace their fingers.

'Madame Capulet, you may wish to step back.'

'I'm where I belong Don Montecchi. Now say what you will.'

'Very well.' he said calmly. Yet her insistence to remain had rattled the grim herald. 'Chevalier Capulet. I'm sent to you on an errand of Honour.'

'I understand.' Armand replied calmly.

'On behalf of my brother Onorato –' He glanced at Ilaria again. 'Chevalier, may I suggest you and I repair to a more private place to discuss this matter alone?'

Ilaria squeezed Armand's hand. They shared a knowing look.

'I appreciate your offer to do so Cavaliere. And I already suspect that, unlike your loud brother, you're a man who invites decorum and respects protocol.'

'I like to think I am.'

'However, given the grim nature of the mistreatment Ilaria received so recently at your brother's hands, I believe there's little you have to say that she doesn't deserve to hear.'

I felt certain Brando was judging by the look in the Capulets eyes, what he was now hearing spoke more to the truth of the matter.

'I see.' said Brando creasing his brows with concern.

'And given what I understand of Don Cortellani's recent experience with Onorato ...'

Brando glanced at Sabatino with even greater surprise.

'I believe ...' Armand ran on 'it may also benefit me to have himself and my sister remain to bear witness to whatever you have to say. I can't speak for *their* want to know of course. They may wish –'

Aurelie interrupted. 'To hear plainly darling what *new* mischief your unruly sibling is getting up to!'

'Really Aurelie' Brando replied 'perhaps you could refrain...'

'Don't you ride through our gate uninvited at this hour and chastise me Aldobrando Montecchi!' she spat with purpose. 'Armand and Ilaria are our *famiglia*! Any issue you come to solicit that impugns their honour, comfort or safety, is now and will forevermore, be *our* business too.' She stroked Sabatino's arm. 'Don't you agree darling?'

'Of course mia cara. Eloquently put.'

They held together impassively.

Armand pushed his lower lip into his upper and returned his attention to Aldobrando.

'Well Cavaliere it seems clear where everybody stands. And so what say you on behalf of your brother? His man bears me a gift?'

'I regret to say he does.'

Brando turned to take a steel gauntlet from his silent follower.

'Chevalier Capulet. This is our primo don's gage of honour.'

'Onorato has large hands at least.' said Armand calmly.

My own eyes leapt wide. Cupid's Balls! I had to cover my mouth to save from spurting a laugh at that retort. Despite her anxiety,

Ilaria's eyes widened too. She squeezed his hand to repress her reaction. Yet Brando ran on as grimly as death itself.

'Upon his behalf Chevalier I offer you this *incentive*.'

With no further ado he lifted the gauntlet and launched. CRACK! The blow struck hard and made Armand flinch as Ilaria gasped in shock. She'd expected venomous words not volatile actions.

Sabatino and Aurelie hadn't moved. Nor had Caspar as Brando tossed the token down at Armand's feet.

I had flinched too and now I held my breath in anticipation of the sequel, expecting a hefty thump in reply from Armand! But before he could think to do it, a delicate hand lifted at his side, spread, launched and smacked the shocked cavaliere hard upon his cheek!

Montecchi looked aghast, glaring in protest at the ill behaviour. But Ilaria's green eyes were wild with anger, glaring venomously at the man she'd met just moments before.

'I accept you're upset Madame.' He snapped in embarrassment. 'So I shall ignore –'

'*Upset!*' she hissed. 'That was to your despicable brother from me. You come to us and strike my husband as if *you* have just cause? After the treatment we experienced at the hands of that *vile* beast! Are all Montecchi men such *dogs* of indiscretion!'

'Angel please, let's give him a chance to deliver *all* his message.'

'I will Chevalier. Here's the rest. Onorato calls you a liar, a cheat and moreover a cad for the mistreatment of his wife.'

'The mistreatment of *his* wife?'

'Ilaria please –'

'Mistreating his wife' Brando ran on 'before witnesses Madame. Moreover for the use of deceptive means to claim victory in what should have been a *fair* game of chance. The result of which dispossessed our primo don and faction of our familial estate.'

'*Deceptive* means!' Ilaria burst with contempt. 'What manner of deception is being practiced here by you *foul* liar?'

'I can swear to you myself Madame, that upon close inspection the set of dice used in the game were found to be weighted.'

'*Were* they indeed?' snapped Ilaria.

'Yes they were.'

'Yet an important factum to note Don Montecchi is that they *belonged* to your despicable brother!'

This time Brando looked far less surprised.

Ilaria ran on. 'I'm sure Esmeralda herself will confirm –'

'Our prima donna ...' he interrupted 'has assigned her signature in witness to all I contend here.'

'No! No she wouldn't *dare* ... Oh ... oh I see. That venal brute has forced Esmeralda to –'

'Angel' Armand interrupted softly 'it's *no* matter.'

'Armand how can you say such lies are no matter?'

'That's why he was instructed to strike *before* offering this inventive account.'

Aurelie drew forward reaching for Ilaria's shoulder. 'Darling these absurd accusations are merely for show. Done for assurance.'

'He knows we have witnesses of our own angel, who will swear just as emphatically that *none* of it's true.'

'I'll swear to it!' cried Maxine.

'So will I!' called Fabrizio.

'And I! said Caspar.

'And me!'

Cried Liberati and Boccolo almost as one.

'And I'll bare my ass at all Montecchi liars before I'll ever –'

'*Marcel!*' Armand shouted. 'The next person to speak out of turn will earn my grave displeasure. My apologies Signore. Now angel please, let the gentleman finish.'

Though we fell quiet, I felt if he had any doubt before, Brando now understood his brother's claims were a gross deception. And to be fair I must confess, the man appeared to have little stomach for his task. Yet he was the younger brother to a primo don who wasn't just a totem, but one of northern Italy's most feared mercenary warlords. Long before that day Aldobrando had learnt, when the Black Wolf of Verona became set upon a course, nothing could sway him from it.

Ilaria fell silent too. Brando looked blankly at Armand.

'Thank you. Chevalier Capulet it's my sworn duty to declare to you that Cavaliere Onorato da Montecchi challenges you to defend these claims on pain of death.'

It took a instant for his meaning to settle. Ilaria's eyes leapt.

'NO!' she screamed, boiling with fury. 'That is *outrageous*!'

Aldobrando stared blankly. 'Or Madame if your husband prefers to avoid a conflict, he may do so by offering my brother immediate and *satisfactory* reparation. What say you Chevalier?'

Armand frowned quizzically. 'Which would be *what* precisely?'

'Dismiss your claim to Sycamore Hill and sign your irrevocable acknowledgement of his right to its possession. I had a document drawn for you, ready to sign, seal and witness.'

'That was done hastily.' Armand replied glibly. 'May I see it?'

For all the heat that had burst from Ilaria when she heard the challenge issued, when Armand requested to see the deed, she looked greatly relieved. Despite the hurt of such false accusations, it was clear she felt nothing was worth the risk of his life against the value of any prize won in a game of chance.

The sergeant drew the deed from a satchel slung across his chest and offered it mutely. Armand studied it for a moment.

'Hmm. Look angel. No *apology* required. No *admission*. Just sign over possession and ... all's forgiven. Magnanimous.'

In the moment that followed, Armand appeared to be at odds over how to choose. But his quietly sarcastic tone made me wonder. Indeed, since Carentan I had observed that our stoic master seemed at his most decisive when offering the impression he was indecisive.

Brando and his man took that bait however, holding their breaths and betraying their desperate hope to be quit of it all. I observed Armand observing their reactions.

'And so Chevalier?' said Brando.

Ilaria cut in.

'Why he'll forego the claim of course. No one should risk –'

'Angel' said Armand turning to take her hands. 'I'm sorry to interrupt you.'

'Armand no, what are doing?'

'Caspar.' Armand said quietly.

'Chevalier.' The giant stepped forward.

'I seem to have misplaced my glove.'

Ilaria's brows knit. 'Armand?' Her face blanched. '*No!*'

Caspar drew off his massive steel gauntlet. 'I have one to spare.'

Montecchi and his sergeant exchanged a nervous glance.

'Armand' Ilaria gripped his arm, whispering feverishly. 'Please my heart, please this makes no sense. To risk so much and for what? Aurelie. Sabatino. Help me –'

Sabatino's arm wound gently around her. 'Ilaria. You must give your husband a moment to do his duty.'

'His duty is to *me*.'

Armand took her hands. 'Angel please don't fret. I know Heaven is watching.'

'Don't you *dare* say that to me again! *Armand* I *forbid* this!'

But Aurelie's arm had reached for her too and held Ilaria firmly. The prima donna looked gravely into her brother's eyes. Armand drew up to the unwelcome duet.

'Cavaliere.' He displayed the gauntlet. 'It's larger than my own. But the magnitude of your brother's capacity for deception, appears to defy all measurement.'

Despite his warning before, I broke into a cackle of laughter! To hear such a reply at such a time! Every eye turned to stare at me.

'*Marcel!*' hissed Maxine hotly. She smacked my shoulder.

'Armand' Ilaria pleaded 'please my heart. Please don't do it.'

Aurelie firmed her grip. 'Once he's been struck before witnesses darling, the damage can't be undone.'

Ilaria stared with disbelief. She scanned Aurelie's face. She looked at Sabatino.

'What are you saying? But of *course* it can.'

'No darling it can't. Even if you sign over the estate he'd be compelled to challenge the scoundrel or be labelled a coward forever.'

Sabatino added. 'And Ilaria, if Armand becomes the *challenger* it will put him at a disadvantage. This is the best way. The only way.'

Ilaria's eyes were full of foreboding, her mind filled with the image of that dangerous beast we met on Sycamore Hill. For the sake of sheer vanity he wanted to kill her husband. Instinct screamed at her to protest. But with the Cortelannis' voices added to the rest Ilaria felt trapped. Sabatino sensed his impact might make a final difference.

'Armand? If you're *going* to do what I *think* you're going to do.' He glanced at Aurelie. 'I'd like to offer my service as your Second.'

Armand turned to his sister. The blue eyes of one Capulet blazed into the other. She knew for the sake of his safety; Sabatino's help may mean the difference between life and death. Moreover for Armand, as a stranger challenged in a strange environment, it would put the issue beyond question that this quarrel was a matter for the Cortelannis too. If local law became involved in any sequel, that would have a great impact.

'I'd be honoured to have your company.' said Armand.

'Then I'm at your service brother.' Sabatino turned to face the Montecchis. Armand leaned to Sabatino.

'At least Onorato's offered me a *deed* for this transaction. Your affair at the auction left you without so much as a *bill of sale*.'

'It's true.' Sabatino stared the Montecchi duet. 'That's the true nature of the man.'

'Perhaps this opportunity can *remedy* that.' Armand met Brando's impatient stare. 'And so Cavaliere it seems I have an answer.'

Armand lifted the parchment and tore it in half and again and again and then let the pieces fall like snowflakes upon the gauntlet lying at his feet. Finally he smiled and crouched to take up Onorato's gage and look Aldobrando squarely in the eye.

'Don Montecchi. As a Chevalier of the noble French order of the Golden Fleece, I accept Onorato's gage of honour. I tender mine in proxy for him to hold as *my* keepsake.'

Despite his right to strike Brando with the massive steel gauntlet, it was given peacefully.

'Of course.' Brando bowed to receive the grim token.

'Moreover Don Montecchi, by the laws of chivalry I declare myself to be the *challenged* party in this affair. Agreed?'

Aldobrando glanced at the sergeant. There was great advantage in that status. Yet nothing either man could say would dispute it.

'Agreed Chevalier.'

'As such, I claim my right to choose the *location*, *timing* and *nature* of our combat. You agree they're mine by right to choose?'

'I suspect the rules of the duel are much the same in France as in Italy. We accept you have the right to choose. Name your terms.'

'As for time I'll meet Onorato half an hour after sunrise.'

'As you will Chevalier. What *month* and *day* do you prefer?'

Armand knitted his brows as if perplexed.

'Why ... in the *morning* of course.'

'In the ...?' sputtered Brando in confusion. '*Tomorrow* morning?' His man was blinking in surprise. 'You're quite *certain* –'

'Cavaliere I'm certain of very little in this world with the exception of two things. I know that I love my wife beyond all measure. And I know beyond all *doubt* that half an hour after sunrise tomorrow, whether your brother shows or not, I'll be waiting to meet him.'

'I see.' Brando tried to say it soberly yet he was clearly shaken.

'Furthermore, Onorato claims the estate in question is at stake here and *nothing* more. I agree to that in *principal* however ...'

'However?' Brando tilted his eyes to Heaven and sighed as if little more could surprise him now.

'As I'm the challenged party and he seeks a fight to the death.'

'He does.'

'Then I seek to add *more* collateral upon *his* side.'

Brando frowned. 'That's an unusual request.'

'Yes. But I think you'll agree the extra is a mere *trifle*.'

Montecchi pouted in thought. 'What is this trifling thing?

'Onorato *extorted* the sale of a stallion from my sister after it was won fairly at auction.'

Aldobrando's brows shot up. He glanced at the sergeant, whose guilty look seemed to suggest that version was the truth of it.

'That incident suggests a *pattern* in his wretched behaviour, which any court of judgement would be interested to consider.'

'Yes and so?'

'And so I consider that act to be an injury to my blood kin and cannot allow it to stand.'

'Your blood kin?' Brando raised his brows. 'I was told that my brother purchased the beast from Sabatino, your brother-in-law?'

'He did.' snapped Sabatino with a smile. 'But I purchased it as a gift for Aurelie' he lied 'Armand's blood sister.'

'That's true!' Aurelie lied with a convincing pout to punctuate.

'Even if it was purchased to boil for soap ...' said Armand quietly 'I insist that it be included.'

'A *horse?*' Brando pleaded, nodding in disbelief.

'It must be brought to the designated place. And though that matter is important to me, as your own reaction suggests it's enough of a trifle for you, as Onorato's proxy, to consent to it.'

Brando scanned the company before him. He lifted his eyes to Heaven again. Somehow the disarming request seemed to have calmed his demeanour.

'Given you've been challenged to the death Chevalier, it *is* a trifle. I agree to the addition of this *disputed* horse. Moreover I ask nothing in return as *surety* against it.'

'I appreciate that gesture.' said Armand.

Brando turned to the sergeant-at-arms.

'The stake now includes the disputed beast. You have my word Chevalier it shall be brought to the location where, as they say, *the victor shall harvest the fame and spoils.*'

'Finally I'll reveal my choice of *location* and dictate the *rules.*'

'As you will.'

Armand glanced at Ilaria .

'I understand there's an ancient arena within the citadel.'

'There is.'

'That shall be our place.'

'It's somewhat public. At sunrise however ...? As you wish.'

'Each principal shall have a second and third but no more.'

'Agreed.'

'There'll be no armour for combatants. No upper body covering of any kind or coverings to the feet.'

'Noted.'

'We'll strip outside the arena *before* making entry. Agreed?'

'Agreed. Declare your choice of *weapons* and we're done.'

'I require just one. A poignard.'

The Montecchi duet exchanged a glance of surprise.

'Just a dagger? Nothing more?'

'Precisely. Caspar may I have your poignard.'

The giant drew his sharp steel dagger and handed it over.

'This is the like of what I shall bear. Take it is as a guide. I'll bring three more as near to identical as I can. Tell Onorato to attend with that and two similar weapons.'

'Of course.' said Brando handing it to his man.

'Principals, seconds and thirds ...' Armand ran on 'will arm from the shared arsenal.' He glanced at Aurelie. 'However, unless foul play deems it otherwise, *only* the principals will engage.'

'Agreed. If Sabatino is to be your second –'

'I am.' he said bluntly.

Brando looked at Aurelie. 'Then Aurelie, as Onorato's second I want it to be clear, that unless foul play necessitates me to, I have no wish to engage a friend in anger over this matter.'

'Thank you for that Brando.' she replied. 'I won't forget it.'

Brando hung in thought for a moment.

'Chevalier if I may say so ... you seem rather well versed in the rules of the duel?'

'Do I?' Armand replied innocently.

Blue eyes stared calmy into eyes the same shade of black as his brother. I could tell he was attempting to gauge as much about this rival as he could, anything his impatient brother may have overlooked. Though it was clear the Black Wolf was the brawn of the Montecchi, I began to wonder if Aldobrando was far more than just his shadow.

Armand had one more point to raise. 'Now before I conclude, I do crave an indulgence?'

'Another trifle?'

'A point of order which I'd like to discuss *privately*. If we can agree the bulk of our business is done, then our bystanders have the *critical* details, I'd like to send them in.'

'By all means Chevalier.' He scanned about and rested on Ilaria. 'So far this is the most *public* challenge I've ever attended.'

With that agreement, any who would not be present at the combat were dismissed and trailed inside to await a final summary. Yes, that was meant to include Aurelie and Ilaria. No, Ilaria would not agree to leave, and so Armand drew her aside for a moment.

'I'm staying here with you.'

'Angel there's nothing I'm about to say to him I won't tell you as soon I rejoin you.'

'And so there's no reason for me to withdraw.'

'No *obvious* reason. But if I have a moment alone with Montecchi, I think I can gain an important concession. It may tie Onorato's hands against foul play.'

'Oh you know that scheming beast will try anything –'

'I know. And I hope to avoid the worst of it.'

'What's worse than killing for mere vanity. Oh Armand I wish that I'd never –'

'Don't say it my love. This is Onorato's doing not ours. Sooner or later we would have crossed paths with someone like him. In future we'll be more cautious. But for now, please go in and keep everyone's spirits up. I'll follow in a moment to share the rest with you.'

Ironically, a festive banquet of welcome was laid within. Ilaria and Aurelie entered together, both glancing back before they disappeared. I could tell any appetite Ilaria had was shattered by foreboding. For myself, instead of entering with the rest, I idled behind Caspar.

Hovering quietly, I hoped that if I was noticed they wouldn't force me to withdraw. If they did so I planned to protest that as a teller of tales, *posterity* required my presence. Brando saw me hovering and did question my presence. Perhaps after that threat to *bare my ass* he wondered if I had stayed to do it!

Armand seemed minded to send me away but then relented.

'He's a bit addle-headed Signore.' he said. 'Pay him no mind.'

Brando glanced again, then dismissed my presence as quickly as his brother had done. I never thought I'd be grateful to hear Armand describe me as an imbecile!

'Cavaliere, would you allow your man to stand-off for a moment with my squire?'

'To what end?' Brando asked cautiously.

'As a stranger to Verona I'd like to discuss an item in *private*. But I need the assistance of a native like Sabatino to guide me. I sense you both respect each other. I hope, it's not *too* much to ask.'

Brando considered for a moment then conceded and sent his man to stand at a short distance with Caspar. The pair looked odd together as Armand and Sabatino remained with Montecchi.

'Despite the formality, may I call you Aldobrando?'

'Despite the formality, Brando will suffice.'

'Please call me Armand if you wish to. Brando I assume you agree that we'll require the services of a reliable *marshal*.'

'Yes Armand, I agree.'

'As our referee, he must meet us outside the arena with enough independent support to challenge either party. He must also be allowed to confiscate all weapons before we enter.'

'Also agreed.'

'Hopefully Brando, a formidable man will come to mind. Some-one yourself and Sabatino agree would not favour *either* side.'

Both men considered for a moment.

Sabatino's eyes lit with inspiration.

'There's a man in the western Borgo at *The Dragon*. I'm sure Brando knows him.'

'Hartvigson?'

Sabatino nodded and glanced at Armand.

'Your man's not the only giant in Verona. Gunter's a beast.'

'Most call him the *Viking*.' said Brando.

Armand knit his brows. 'The man sounds promising.'

'He looks fallen from grace' Sabatino added 'but is an ordained knight. He runs a tavern and bordello with his mistress and famously hates *everyone*.'

'I agree.' said Brando. 'He fought for Verona against Milan as an independent. He's *feared* by all. I doubt even Onorato would attempt to take Hartvigson singlehanded.'

'And he's served privately as a marshal before. We have time to arrange it. I can send someone straight away. Brando?'

'I can think of no other who'd be *truly* impartial. Agreed.'

'To be safe' Armand added 'he's like to need a score of men.'

'Then he'll need a sizeable retainer.' Brando replied.

'I'm happy to stand for that cost.' offered Sabatino.

Aldobrando frowned in protest. '*Both* parties can assure him the *winning* side will make good on his cost?'

'Agreed.' said Armand. 'He must be allowed time to inspect the arena before we enter. And finally we should agree, that no horses other than his own may enter the field.'

'All *reasonable* precautions Armand. But now the sun has set and so I must ask ... are we at an end?'

'All but one final request.'

Brando knit his brows, scanning from one man to the other.

'I must say, I'm not sure why my man couldn't overhear any of what we've discussed?'

'Not so far. Yet my last request requires his absence because I know he's Onorato's man.'

'I'm Onorato's *brother*.'

'Yes Brando but unlike your follower, I accept Sabatino's judgement that you're a man of honour.'

'Very well. Let's hear the last.'

Armand looked at him candidly.

'In the name of fair play I'd like your word on something.'

'In the name of fair play, if it sits with my conscience, I'll oblige. What is it you want?'

'You know Onorato's nature. I'll say no more than that. But given I'm a stranger in a place where he has *great* means to draw on

...'
...

'Yes?'

'I'd like your word to keep the marshal's identity a close secret, just between ourselves, until we meet again at sunrise.'

'You fear Onorato will attempt to persuade him to favour our side? Or perhaps lay an ambush against his force before he arrives?'

'I didn't want to say so much directly Brando. But yes.'

Suddenly I understood the importance of this favour. If the wolf could manage to bribe or coerce this man before dawn, he would. If not, he may lay an ambush to keep his party from showing for our protection, then ambush ourselves in turn when we arrived.

'Armand I'm sorry to admit' Brando whispered 'that you already seem to know my brother too well.' He glanced at Sabatino. 'In the name of fairness to all, I swear on my life to keep this secret between just ourselves until we meet at sunrise.'

Brando offered his hand to seal the pact.

'I'm greatly in your debt.' said Armand.

'No, I'm still in your debt. You're owed a blow in return.'

'I refrained for the sake of asking this favour.'

'But I hit you hard.'

'I recall it. Though Ilaria did my duty for me. '

'I recall it. Please tell her, I'm glad Donatella can't hit like that.'

Three smiles warmed their parley. Against my want, I found myself not hating him.

'Now I must go. We'll meet again too soon.'

Moments later, the Montecchi were gone in the gathering darkness. Sabatino led Armand inside, discussing whether Brando could be trusted to keep his word. He felt he could, but also felt that precaution wouldn't be needed if the Viking agreed to be their marshal. It made me wonder just what manner of man he must be.

All too soon, we would see for ourselves.

Inside, Aurelie and Ilaria sat in solemn conference, holding delicate beakers brimming with strong wine. The elite quartet discussed the extraordinary cascade of events. From their discussion, Ilaria began to accept that once Armand was struck by Brando, there was really no way to alter the course of what had followed.

The extra conditions were discussed quietly, including Brando's agreement to keep the marshal's identity a secret. At least with that concession, any surprise Onorato may hope to spring and turn the odds in his favour, should have been thwarted.

Sabatino queried the decision to meet Onorato so quickly. Yet Armand insisted the shock of that timing would keep him off balance. All agreed the beast wouldn't have expected to need to fight so soon. Armand also reasoned that the longer he waited, the more Onorato would seek to gain knowledge of his strengths and weaknesses, or use his local influence to gain advantage in other ways.

'No.' He drained his cup. 'My best play is to act immediately.'

Finally, a promise was made to put off more talk until the matter was concluded. A deep pall of quiet enveloped us. I plucked my lute gently. The notes seemed to echo the sombre mood that had descended. I glanced at Ilaria. She now seemed determined to wear a brave face. It caused me to recall the night before Armand rode to war. They were unwed on the eve of his departure, and so couldn't spend the night making love together. Instead they remained on the balcony of Chateau de Capulet, holding each other until the sun rose.

As this night may be the last evening they spent together, Ilaria decided not to waste it in more talk and tears. The fire in the dining hall began to wither. Most were still lounging, dulled by wine and worn by the events. Ilaria stood quietly and took her leave with Maxine in her wake. Perhaps ten minutes later, having shared a final vial with Aurelie and Sabatino, Armand took his leave too.

Yet just before he retired Sabatino's messenger returned.

'Gunter's agreed?' asked Aurelie.

'Yes he's confirmed.' Sabatino sighed with relief.

The marshal would arrive before sunrise with a dozen retainers. At the suggestion of the man himself, who it seemed was no stranger to such matters, a surgeon and a holy scribe – who could offer last rites and notate the facts for the record – were added to his list of absolute requirements.

'With Gunter in charge, we don't need to fear interference.'

'He sounds formidable?' said Armand quietly.

'You'll understand when you meet him. Now man I'm sure none of us will sleep well tonight. So go and make love to your wife.'

I offered to play for them as had become their habit when retiring. This time he suggested I refrain.

Hearing him say so made me uneasy.

I saw him up to their door, knowing Maxine's chamber was again next to theirs. Hovering at the threshold, I peeked in. Against the cool of the evening air, Maxine had ensured they had a warming fire. She knew they'd spend what was left of the night above the bedclothes. Finally, to lure their senses, she had filled the chamber with aromatic incense.

By the time I entered the adjoining chamber, Maxine was waiting for me. Now we were lovers this may become a luxury we could enjoy more frequently. As I joined her in the dark we whispered our greetings yet agreed not to become intimate ourselves until we knew the Capulets were occupied or sleeping. It seemed Maxine's effort to set an enticing mood hadn't been wasted however. Almost immediately after I entered Maxine' chamber, they began to make love so passionately and completely, it was hours before the sound abated.

On that night of all nights, perhaps any ambience I might have added would have made no difference. I felt sure they would have made love on the sand of a scorching desert if needed. When love feels so threatened, the urgent need to express its depth means the mind and body seem to know no limits.

I was still used to intimacy being a casual pleasure. Yet by the Capulet's example, I was beginning to learn it could be a sacred vow instead. A pledge to offer someone for a lifetime.

Sweet friends I ask you sincerely, while time is there for the taking to spend together, until that time is done, why would any not use it to express their love for each other as passionately as they can? For every next day, as each walks out the door to go about their lives, who knows what misfortune fate may have in store for them.

Finally, we heard nothing but the sound of crickets stirring.

I confess that all through that night, Maxine and I were too distracted to do more than hold each other. She fell asleep in my arms. Less than an hour after she did so, I heard muted sounds of stirring beyond the wall in the Capulet's chamber. It was still dark and quiet.

I knew the time had come.

Our Story Continues:

Book 3: Justice

Book 4: Ambition

Book 5: Retribution

Book 6: Folly

9 781763 837973